Michael O'Neal spun in place and brought up his suit guns automatically, fired at the descending shuttle.

Nothing happened. Nothing damned HAPPENED.

"Shelly! Guns!"

"Guns are inactive, General," the AID said in a chirpy voice. "It's time to board the shuttle. You are ordered to do so out of the suit. Should I eject?"

The shuttle landed and a platoon of masters-at-arms deployed. They looked nervous.

"Incoming call from Admiral Suntoro," said Mike's AID. "Go ahead, Admiral."

"Michael Leonidas O'Neal, you and your staff are under arrest for treason. AID, open the suit."

Mike took a breath of air as the suit opened against his will, then stepped out onto the grassy sward. Four of the masters-at-arms were approaching, two with lasers and two with sonic stunners.

"Do not attempt to resist this fully authorized detention," the admiral's voice continued to say over the speakers of Mike's suit. "The masters-at-arms are authorized to use lethal force at the slightest sign of resistance."

"General O'Neal, get on the ground with your hands behind your back," one of the MAs said.

"What?" Mike said, then lifted his eyes. His brow furrowed down then there was no thought.

"Like hell!" he shouted, charging forward.

He had hoped for the lasers. There was just nothing left. There was not a damned thing in the world to live for anymore. Even revenge was impossible to achieve.

But they got him with the stunners instead.

Baen Books by John Ringo

THE LEGACY OF ALDENATA SERIES

A Hymn Before Battle • *Gust Front* • *When the Devil Dances* • *Hell's Faire* • *Eye of the Storm* • *The Hero* with Michael Z. Williamson • *Watch on the Rhine* with Tom Kratman • *Yellow Eyes* with Tom Kratman • *The Tuloriad* with Tom Kratman • *Cally's War* with Julie Cochrane • *Sister Time* with Julie Cochrane • *Honor of the Clan* with Julie Cochrane

Into the Looking Glass • *Vorpal Blade* with Travis S. Taylor • *Manxome Foe* with Travis S. Taylor • *Claws that Catch* with Travis S. Taylor

Von Neumann's War with Travis S. Taylor

There Will Be Dragons • *Emerald Sea* • *Against the Tide* • *East of the Sun, West of the Moon*

Ghost • *Kildar* • *Choosers of the Slain* • *Unto the Breach* • *A Deeper Blue*

Princess of Wands

The Road to Damascus with Linda Evans

WITH DAVID WEBER:

March Upcountry • *March to the Sea* • *March to the Stars* • *We Few*

The Last Centurion

THE TROY RISING SERIES

Live Free or Die • *Citadel* (forthcoming)

Citizens, edited by John Ringo & Brian M. Thomsen

EYE OF THE
STORM

JOHN RINGO

EYE OF THE STORM

Copyright © 2009 by John Ringo

A Baen Books Original

Baen Publishing Enterprises
P.O. Box 1403
Riverdale, NY 10471
www.baen.com

ISBN: 978-1-4391-3362-0

Cover art by Kurt Miller

First Baen paperback printing, June 2010

Library of Congress Control Number: 2009011713

Distributed by Simon & Schuster
1230 Avenue of the Americas
New York, NY 10020

Pages by Joy Freeman (www.pagesbyjoy.com)
Printed in the United States of America

To Jim Baen,
my mentor, my publisher and my friend.
Just trying to pay forward.

ACKNOWLEDGMENTS

I'd like to thank some people for their help in finally getting this novel done.

Jim Baen, deceased by three days when I finally figured out how to continue the story of Michael O'Neal. Because I swear to God I heard him say "do it *this* way, Johnny." This one's for you, Jim.

Miriam Sloan for back rubs, hot tea and just being her.

Rogue, Jessica and the rest of Crüxshadows.

Tom Kratman and Julie Cochrane for expanding the vision of the Aldenata universe and the characters therein. And for telling me "It's done, John. Turn it in."

Ben-David Singleton for actually organizing my randomized characters, systems and TOE.

The various members of RingTAB for corrections of some very obvious errors.

Conrad Chu, Ph.D., and Doug Miller, USAR, for physics and electrical help, respectively.

Now on with the show.

CHAPTER ONE

The trials you now are facing
They are not greater than your will
For there is nothing under heaven
You cannot overcome
> —Crüxshadows
> "Eye of the Storm"

As its defenses crumbled, a Posleen penetrator finally latched onto the side glacis armor of the *Richard Waechter* and began burrowing.

Even the multithousand ton bulk of a SheVa Mark VII continental siege unit could only carry its heaviest armor forward. The side glacis was composed of only two hundred centimeters of ultradense, ultrastrong composite made only by the finest Indowy craftsmen. The Posleen smart round first deformed to create an armored beachhead on the hull then shot a concentrated jet of fusion-generated plasma, burning rapidly through the refractory armor. Once a hole was created into the meaty center, it shot an armored penetrator containing a bare ten micrograms of antimatter into the compartmented interior.

The fourteen-man crew of the SheVa knew that once a breacher round was on the hull, it was virtually impossible to remove; your best bet of survival was bailing out. The three Taylor-class Heavy Armored Escape Vehicles dropped from under the SheVa and bolted to the rear. They were picked off by plasma fire from the Posleen redoubt even as the SheVa gouted fire from every hatch and the six-thousand-ton turret lifted fifty meters into the air on an actinic ball of nuclear fire.

As soon as the last SheVa was eliminated, the Posleen popped up a casta round. The maneuvering HVM quickly scattered its load of antimatter bomblets across the front of the approaching line of ACS and disintegrated as the last one detonated.

One hundred and ninety-nine more bomblets detonated almost simultaneously, each the equivalent of sixteen megatonnes of TNT.

As soon as the icon of the casta round appeared on his heads up display, Private Julio Garcia dropped a foxhole round to the ground and crouched, hoping against hope that the round would dig out a hole for him before the casta went off. Shooting the bomblets was futile; that would only make them detonate earlier. The only thing that the Armored Combat Suit Corps could do was dig in and try to ride out the detonation. The Indowy-manufactured battle armor was very tough indeed but a 16-megaton explosion had a better than even chance of ripping even an ACS suit into itsy bitsy pieces.

As the dirt of R-1496 Delta fountained upwards, the

armored infantryman dove for the hole. It was times like this that he seriously reconsidered his decision to leave the hell of New Chicago.

Julio was twenty-three, very young for a private in the ACS. He'd been raised in the New Chicago Sub-Urb, an underground city left over from the Posleen invasion of Earth. The refuges had, by and large, done their job of keeping a core of civilization alive throughout the siege but most people got out of the Urbs as quickly as possible as soon as the Posleen menace was relieved.

However, in any refugee situation a core, usually running about ten percent, refused to leave the camp or, in this case, underground city. Whether from laziness or ongoing paranoia over what had driven them to the refuge, the "refuseniks" were a problem in any recovery period.

Earth's government had responded by concentrating them. As each Sub-Urb eventually regurgitated its refugee population, those who preferred to remain in the Urbs were moved to other Urbs and slowly concentrated. Once the refuseniks were fully concentrated in four or five Urbs, they were essentially left to rot.

Minimal and generally unpalatable food was available. Enter one of the eating areas, swipe your implanted chip and you'd be given a measured amount of glop. The brown, unappetizing substance was nutritious and even filling but it had the consistency of wet cardboard and about the same taste.

There was no work in the Urbs and it wasn't so much that crime was rife as that was the only business going. They were centers for drug trafficking, illegal arms sales (and in the post-war world you had to *work* for a weapon to be illegal) and prostitution. Indeed, many people thought the only reason they still existed was so that all the criminals could be concentrated in one place. The general opinion of surfacers was that the best use of the Urbs was as dumping grounds and that eventually the government would just toss in some gas bombs and be done with them.

Julio had been in the gangs; it was the only way to survive. And he'd dealt and run and even killed to survive in the Urb. But he didn't have a criminal record. The few police in the Urbs concentrated on securing the food centers and making sure nobody did anything bad to the fundamental infrastructure. What happened outside those few secure areas rarely came to their attention. Even when it did, they didn't care.

"You were raped? That's tough, miss. Maybe you should move elsewhere."

There were few ways out of the Urbs. There was no great labor shortage on the surface and surfacers considered urbies as the lowest of the lowest scum. After the loss of dozens of colonist ships to various accidents and "unanticipated Posleen deep space attacks," colonization and other planets became far less attractive.

There was one way not only out of the Urbs but to a pretty good life, but it depended on surviving it. The military was always recruiting. It had been tasked with "recovery" of the Posleen blight zone, a three hundred light-year stretch of the galaxy composed of little but stars and planets either originally uninhabitable or turned into radioactive wastelands. As the Posleen advanced they stripped the planets they took and then, far more often than not, fell out into destructive planet-wide wars that left the world a blasted hulk. But even a hulk had some value. Indowy deep miners could still extract minerals and once their shiplike megascrapers were installed, the Indowy could build factories, live and work anywhere that there was a semblance of an atmosphere. They didn't care what the world looked like, they just wanted room for their rapidly expanding population.

So the pattern was established. The Fleet, and Fleet Strike, its ground and fighter arm, would wipe a planet of concentrated Posleen infestations. Then a specialty human company would come in and establish a fully cleared zone. Last the Indowy would arrive, build their megascrapers using techology that looked a bit too much like wizardry, and move in. Other human security companies would ensure the safety of the burgeoning cities, keeping the Posleen out when they could and killing any that penetrated into the megascrapers.

That was the job Julio was after, a nice safe gig with a security company. But they didn't recruit in the Urbs. They wanted trained soldiers. So first you had to spend time in Fleet's security arm, the FP bully-boys, or in one of the infantry arms.

Julio had tried to get into Fleet itself; getting trained as a Fleet tech would be even better than getting a security gig. But all the slots for Fleet were filled. It was only after he joined that he discovered Fleet was ... restrictive. Towards the end of the War, North America had been cut off and Europe virtually cut to ribbons. Most of the replacement personnel for Fleet, therefore, came from the southeast Asian islands area, Indonesia and the Philippines especially. These days there were a few remaining original officers and NCOs in the Fleet from Northern European backgrounds but it was about ninety percent Indo or Flip with a smattering of surviving Chinese. It wasn't anything official, but it was amazing how few survivors from the rest of the world made it into Fleet.

Fleet Strike, though, was less restrictive. Also less alluring. Fleet's job when they took a planet was to fly overhead and hit Posleen concentrations with orbital kinetic strikes or, occasionally, a burst of heavy duty plasma. It was about as dangerous as shooting fish in a barrel; no serious concentration of Posleen spacecraft had been fought in fifty years. The first three waves of Fleets, shattered units rebuilt and recrewed time and again, had bled to create those conditions. That, too, explained the shortage of people in Fleet with Northern European backgrounds; millions of men and women died in those actions.

Fleet Strike, though, had to do the rest of the work. They had to get down on the ground and root out the smart ones, the ones that had dug in and tried to hold. They would hunt and flush a planet for a year or more, living down in the muck, until it was considered "pacified." And occasionally they got into shit like this, a seriously dug-in Posleen force with a smart commander. Seriously dug in enough that the Fleet, despite constant pounding, had been unable to defeat it from orbit.

This was when Fleet Strike earned its pay. And especially the SheVa and ACS arm, the most elite of the ground combat forces.

As he flipped upwards, ready for the blast, Julio saw another infantryman crouch by his hole. There was only enough room in the hole for one, but the other man's suit was small and the private almost pinged for him to pile in on top. But the suit didn't appear to care that the entire area was about to be hammered by a bagillion joules of energy. The wearer simply crouched, extended rock jacks and took a knee, slamming the meter-long jacks downwards until the suit's gauntlets were balled fists on the ground.

The titanic explosion blotted out almost every sensor. But quantum-state view and neutron reads, especially neutron reads, were still up. By the hellish light cast by decaying matter Julio could see the suit leaning into the plasma, seemingly unafraid, even reveling in the wash of stripped atoms. Julio's suit temperature had hopped up sixteen degrees despite the best efforts of his environmental system; what the other wearer must be experiencing he could hardly imagine and didn't want to.

As soon as the plasma blast was past, Julio began scrambling out of the hole, checking his readouts to see who in his section had survived. But his suit's AID automatically overrode his request and frantically pinged a name onto his HUD, the karat laid squarely over the suit beside him. The wearer was short but plug-like, his suit covered in a strange design like a green monster. Despite the blast of plasma, the design was still unblemished, so it was clearly etched deep into the suit, perhaps even woven into the very atomic structure.

The suit slowly stood and stamped both feet on the seared ground. The stamps crunched through the glassy surface and gave the wearer a solid footing, like a bull pawing the ground just before a charge.

"General O'Neal?" Julio asked, amazed that the corps commander was right on the front lines. "Sir? Are you okay?"

"Never fucking better, Private," Lieutenant General Michael O'Neal growled. "A nuke's better than a dry cleaners. Now, let's kick some Postie ass."

❖   ❖   ❖

The Posleen commander was good, but he'd just made his first mistake. Two, actually. The casta round, named after the slightly insane human professor who first created an antimatter cluster bomb, had been slightly off-line of the ACS unit deployed across the plain. If it had been directly overhead, Mike would have dug in like everyone else. But as he saw the deployment he immediately recognized that the nukes, large as they were, were too far away to destroy an ACS, especially the customized suit he wore.

The commander's second mistake was in using a casta at all. The explosion probably caught a few cherries who were too slow to dig in and certainly shut down inter-suit communication while the plasma wash was over the area. But that took only a moment. The Posleen defenders would have had to pull into their bunkers to avoid the blast. It would take them a moment to get back in position, and that assumed that their commo wasn't down entirely. The Eleventh ACS Corps, the "Black Tyrone," though, was going to be ready to cock and rock in bare seconds after the explosion. They'd damned well *better* be ready or they'd have to deal with *him*. Anyone in the corps, from the lowest private—like the kid cowering in the hole—up to his division commanders would rather battle a Posleen bare-handed than let him down. And the bastards were within sprinting distance of the outer Posleen defenses.

Mike had considered calling in a casta himself, but he'd have had to convince Fleet higher that it was a "judicious action." Fucking bean counters. They were more worried about the loss of the suits, each of which cost as much as a corvette, than the men, but it would still take time. Time he didn't have. By hitting the unit with a casta, the Posleen commander had done his job for him.

Mike took the time as the plasma washed over his suit to do a quick assault frag. It was pretty straightforward. Custer would have loved it. "Take the outer defenses."

The Posleen "redoubt" was really a small mountain range rising out of plains on all four sides; the geological term was a "basolith." It was the last major point of resistance on R-1496 Delta and absolutely infested with Posleen and their automated forges. There were heavy antiship and missile ports in the upper reaches that had intercepted everything that fleet had thrown at them and actually taken two destroyers out that had stumbled into its arc of fire. The mountains, probably tree-covered once but now slagged and black from titanic explosions, were impenetrable from space. That left taking them on the ground.

As long as they had food and materials for their ammo—and Mike bet that the commander had stocked up on both—the Posleen could hole up indefinitely. That couldn't be allowed. He'd been tasked with clearing this dirt ball and he was damned well going to clear it.

Even while he was speaking with the private the orders flashed down to the division commanders then were split to brigades, battalions, companies and even down to the individual soldiers. The basic order: "CHARGE" was the first thing to hit and then subtleties like "CHARGE THAT PLASMA PIT!" were filtered through the commanders. In all it took about thirty seconds, which is a long time in combat. But it sure as hell beat aides de camp on horseback.

Mike wasn't going to let his boys beat him to it,

either. He started forward, slow at first, then accelerating, commanding his suit into a run and loosening his legs so that the suit could exceed the ability of human legs to flicker back and forth. The rest of the units were keeping to the speed of their slowest suit, maintaining a careful line as they sprinted forward. So Mike, who had mastered the skitter run technique before most of his brigade commanders were *born*, was out in the lead.

The Posleen defenses were coming back on line, slowly, as God Kings got their normals out of their deep holes, back in position and firing. The wall of the range was one interlocking defense after another and the darting suit was instantly the target of each of the positions in range as they came on line.

But with the suit handling the running and dodging, he was free to bring up his grav-gun and engage. The M-288 grav-gun accelerated pellets of depleted uranium to a noticeable fraction of light-speed so as each hit it generated a small kinetic explosion.

Most of the explosions burst back *out* of the gun positions. Mike had been firing and moving in suits for better than half a century with damned little desk time. He'd have to ask his AID to count the number of alien planets he'd battled Posleen on—and that didn't count five years of fighting them day in and day out on Earth during the invasion. Firing on the run was as natural to him as breathing and far more precise. The grav rounds were *entering* the tiny firing slits and exploding on the inside of the bunkers.

That didn't mean he wasn't taking fire. As fast as he took out one defense point another came on line. But hitting a skittering suit was no easy task, even for the God King defenders with automated systems. First of all, he was up to over two hundred kilometers per hour in direct movement and the suit was adding side jinks, especially when it detected targeting systems on it. It telegraphed the jinks to him, the semi-intelligent underlayer of the suit sending him carefully coded nudges and the AID sending small sparkles that told him where the point was going to be *as* it jinked. Mike, the suit, the AID, had all fought for decades together and existed as an almost cybernetic organism, three systems with one mind.

He was, by a long shot, the most deadly user of a suit in the short history of the ACS. And he proved it now by a one-man charge through a hurricane of fire until he was right up on the bunker he'd targeted.

The bunkers were interlocked to provide supporting fire on each other. But the other suits, thousands of them spread over several kilometers of open plain, were starting to catch up. The Posleen had more to worry about than one suit, now.

He wasn't standing still, though. A solid, direct hit from one of the numerous heavy plasma guns or hypervelocity missile launchers covering the bunker would take him out. So he kept running past the first defense point as one hand flicked out and tossed a suicide bar in through the tiny firing slit.

The "suicide bar" was an antimatter hand grenade, a ten-centimeter long, one-centimeter in diameter instant Armageddon pack. It didn't take much antimatter to make too much explosion. So the grenades were adjustable. A small quantity of the contained AM would be fired in a controlled detonation. By "squirting" the remainder, it reduced the explosion to what the user desired. The "squirted" antimatter was still hell on earth, but it wasn't Armageddon on a plate. If you were far enough away that the hand grenade didn't kill you, the squirted antimatter *probably* wouldn't. The instruction manual for the M-613 "matter annihilation device" specifically stated that they were "not for use in hostage situations." So there you go.

Mike's grenade slid through the slit and a moment later there was a jut of silver-green fire out of the head-sized hole. But that didn't suit his purposes. So Mike armed another, still jinking around the small hillock that made up the bunker, and tossed that one in. The first had been set to be the equivalent of sixteen kilos of TNT. He'd figured that it would crack the bunker. If that didn't do it, a *thousand* kilos of TNT should. Hell, he was still an order of magnitude away from its full output. They didn't call 'em suicide bars for nothing.

This time the front of the bunker opened out in a flower of silver-green, leaving a smoking hole. Whatever had been defending the position was gone, gaseous matter barely registerable by the best sensors. A tunnel, partially collapsed, arched downward. It was large enough to take a horse, or a horse-sized Posleen, so there was plenty of gap at the top of the rubble pile to crawl through.

Mike jumped into the pit and started to crawl up the rubble just as a hand descended on his shoulder.

"Sir, would you *please* let *us* go first for once?" Staff Sergeant Thomas Rawls said. The head of his security detail was clearly tired of trying to keep up.

"Oh, sure, be that way," Mike said, backing away from the hole. "But I fit better."

"There's ways to fix that, sir," Rawls said, popping out a suicide bar and tossing it in the hole. He quickly ducked to the side and held the general back against the wall of the shattered position.

"You gotta follow 'em fast," Mike protested. "Use the boot, don't piss on them!"

"And as you well know, antimatter remains in the explosive matter, sir," Rawls said, sighing slightly. He sometimes had the feeling in dealing with his boss that he was the adult and the much older general the child. General O'Neal was, almost invariably, upbeat and positive to a fault. But the sergeant had been with him long enough to know that that was very much a façade.

Every survivor of the "War Generation" seemed to have lost someone. Indeed, with five out of six people on Earth erased and often eaten by the Posleen, entire families, clans, tribes and even nations had been wiped out as if they never existed. In O'Neal's case he had lost his wife, father and one daughter. His sole remaining daughter was only alive because she'd been raised by the Indowy. And that rearing had changed her to such an extent that the general found her nearly unhuman. In effect, he had lost everything in the war. He'd never remarried, never in the two years the sergeant had been guarding him so much as hinted of a romantic interest or even a close friend. He had one drive in life: eliminating every Posleen from the face of the galaxy. And he did it cheerfully, with incredible precision and skill.

"What's a little antimatter between friends?" Mike asked as the suicide bar went off. The explosion blasted some of the rubble back into the room, pattering the suits in chunks of rock that would have killed an unarmored human. "Can we go now?"

"Let me check the security of the tunnel, sir," the sergeant said, waving one of the team forward.

Corporal Albert Norman had only been on the general's security detail for a year. What with transit time and everything, he'd only been on the detail for the cleanup on S-385-Beta and he'd never seen O'Neal in full hunting mode. He thought he was good with a suit until he'd seen the boss. O'Neal was *unreal*.

He'd gotten comfortable with dealing on a nearly daily basis with a general but this situation had him nervous. Sergeant Rawls had been killing Posleen for ten years, the boss for, well, more than a half a century. This was the first time he'd been really doing the job under the boss's eye. So he actually had to think through his next actions instead of doing them on automatic.

He switched on his helmet light, ducked down and crawled up the pile of rubble, poking his head over to the top and giving the tunnel a sweep.

"All cl—" he said just as the Posleen popped out of a hide. He didn't even have time to finish before the heavy duty plasma gun took off his head.

Julio had followed the general more or less automatically, but he hadn't been able to keep up with either the general *or* his security detail. The Hammers were chosen from the cream of the Eleventh and Julio knew he wasn't on their level.

But he did hop in the hole, trying to avoid the still incoming fire as much as anything, just in time to see one of the Hammers turned into barbeque. Plasma was incredibly hot stuff and when it entered a suit, the interior turned into an oven. Julio hadn't been around long enough to be present when such a suit was opened, but he'd seen pictures. Whoever the guy was, he was just deep baked and fried to a crisp. Besides having his head sheared off, of course.

Julio vomited into his helmet and dropped into a crouch. The suit, though, had been designed to handle that, designed in fact by the short figure up against the wall. The semi-biotic undergel created a pocket to catch the regurgitant, sealed it away to prevent aspiration and pumped air when Julio reactively inhaled. Half-noticed, a small quantity of undergel swept into his open mouth and cleaned it out. Half a morning of ACS transition training was concerned with just that. The soldiers were fed a hearty breakfast, suited up, given time to half digest, and then their suits fed them a nausea-inducing drug. Repeatedly.

It's important, knowing deep in your bones that no matter what happens, the suit won't let you drown in your own puke.

He was cut off from his own section, which was trying to open up a similar bunker about thirty yards away. And he sure as hell didn't want to go out into that fire again. He wasn't, in fact, sure what to do.

Mike knew he wasn't in charge of one lost grunt but he also recognized the private from their earlier encounter. So he pinged the poor guy's suit.

"First fight?" Mike asked.

"Yes, sir," Julio said, choking.

"I'd say it gets better, but it really doesn't," Mike said. "But we need to get in that hole. One way to make it better is to think. How should we do that, Private Julio Garcia?"

❖   ❖   ❖

Julio's mind blanked. The general, survivor of count-
less similar encounters, the guy who had coined or
been the inspiration for so many military jokes and
aphorisms he was up there with Patton and a bunch
of other guys, was asking *Julio* how to do it?

That actually broke him out of his panic. Hell,
throw one of his own sayings back.

"Don't use finesse when force works, sir," Julio
snapped back.

Mike grinned and did the head twitch that was all
that was available when wearing a suit. The suits were
form-fitting and the helmet was fully closed, presenting
nothing more than a faceted plate to the enemy. Wearers
got everything from external sensors; a faceplate created a vulnerability. By the same token, the suits, while
somewhat flexible, could not nod or shrug. A suited
person's body language was highly subtle and reading
it took years to learn. What Mike saw was a troop that
had potential but needed to get with the program.

"X-wing option," Mike snapped on the local circuit.
"Double threes. Julio does a hop and pop entry."

Chingadera, Julio thought. The bodyguards were
going to drop two three-hundred-kilo dialed grenades
into the tunnel and fire it up in an X at the same time.
His job, whether he chose to accept it or not, was to
run up the rubble and dive through the hole, hoping
that the Hammers would check fire before they shot
him in the back and that he could get into position
before whatever Posleen were defending the tunnel.

He had to admit that the choice made sense. Urbies

were generally shorter and smaller than the norm. The Hammers were mostly big guys. He could just *fit* better than they could. He probably *could* dive into the hole; ACS was not particularly cumbersome.

The other choice was the general. And Julio didn't want to think about that possibility.

"On my mark," the general continued, not bothering to ask if everyone understood their jobs. Getting a job in ACS required time in a regular Fleet Strike infantry unit and then a six-month course. Julio knew what he was supposed to do. Doing it, though...

Sergeant Rawls designated one other Hammer to toss the second grenade, then pinged readiness. At the general's signal, they tossed the two grenades, then the Hammers formed up on the rubble, leaping forward to get in the general's way. Otherwise the nitwit was going to get himself in the way of plasma from Posleen and grenades.

There wasn't any fire as they positioned themselves and fired up the hole but the wash of explosive carried a good bit of antimatter with it. Tough as ACS suits were, antimatter would degrade *anything*. The system automatically noted reduced effectiveness pretty much across the board; their suits had *thinned* on average three percent. The suits were going to have to go into the shop for a full detailing after this shit.

His suit kept him apprised of the actions of the line private as the guy scrambled up the rubble hill and then threw himself forward. Like well-oiled machines, the Hammers checked fire while the private was in midair so that he was following a crossing line of relativistic projectiles as he entered the hole.

✧   ✧   ✧

The second set of grenades had dropped a portion of the ceiling, leaving large chunks of rubble all over the floor. So when Julio tried to roll to his feet, he stumbled and fell backwards instead. But in the light of his suit helmet he could see a door opening right by his left leg. So he kicked it.

The door was being opened mechanically. And it was heavily armored, sealed and designed to survive a nearby blast and still open even if there was rubble in the way. So the kick sent the suit spinning in a circle instead of shutting the door and left Julio with his hand at the base of the door.

That wasn't much use against a Posleen God King with a plasma gun. But Julio wasn't quite willing to die, yet. So as the surprised Posleen tried to train the heavy duty launcher downwards, a shot that would have killed both the ACS suit *and* the God King if it had gone off, Julio reached up and grabbed the barrel, pressing down and twisting.

The powerful suit crushed the plasma coils like paper. If the God King had pulled the trigger it would have been *very* bad as the weapon exploded in the enclosed space. But the twist ripped the weapon out of the God King's hand, unfired.

That left Julio on his back looking up at an angry, disarmed, God King. The Posleen's next move was so automatic it could have been instinct as he reached over his back and drew his monomolecular boma blade to slash down at the armored human.

Julio's action wasn't nearly as smooth but it was much more effective. He just poked upwards, hard, with the plasma gun in his hand.

The butt of a Posleen plasma gun was designed to ride *over* the shoulder. Thus instead of the flat plate standard on human weapons, it was a curved shape with a not particularly sharp point.

"Not particularly sharp" is sharp enough when driven by pseudo-muscles that could send an armored fist through three inches of homogenous steel. The plasma gun punched up through the Posleen's armored chest until only the barrel was exposed. The yellow blood of the centaur spattered down its still barrel, smoking off from residual heat as the boma blade clattered to the floor.

Julio didn't stop to study the image. Training had fully taken over and he rolled to his feet, trained his grav-gun down the tunnel and fired a stream of relativistic projectiles down it before he even started to identify targets.

Two more doors had opened, with God Kings darting into the passage, weapons up. The first God King, though, was still in the way and barely starting to slump as Julio rolled to his feet and they had a moment of hesitation about firing. If the body in the way had been a normal they couldn't have hesitated, but killing a fellow God King of the same clan and sept was another issue.

Julio didn't give them time to make up their minds; the stream of explosive kinetic rounds blew the two Posleen in half.

He flipped his hand down to his side and drew out two suicide bars, setting them both for a hundred kilo charge and tossed them down the passageway, one lightly, the other hard. The CLANG! of another door breaking loose and a secondary from a Posleen plasma gun was all the information he needed; there had been more down the passageway. There were probably *lots* of Posleen down the passageway. But for now the corridor was...

"CLEAR!"

Mike had watched the encounter on a feed. He'd have rather been the person in the passage, killing Posleen and breaking things. But he knew his job was at a higher level. He'd actually been following that feed as well as feeds from all three divisions; multitasking in combat was so second nature he didn't think about it. Positions were being captured all over the line but casualties were *up*; every passage seemed to be heavily defended. And they were defended by God Kings.

The Posleen came in, broadly, two forms. The vast majority, at a ratio of about four hundred to one, were semi-sentient normals. They were mildly functional morons which could be pointed in a general direction and told to kill anything non-Posleen in view. They also had implanted skills that could be used to build a civilization. And they worshipped, literally, their bosses, the relatively rare God Kings. A subset of the normals were the cosslain, physically pretty much indistinguishable but considerably brighter. Cosslain were almost sentient in fact.

God Kings ran things. In open-field battle they generally rode anti-grav platforms called tenar, which mounted heavier weapons and sensors. Occasionally they used Posleen landing craft to give ground forces air support or air-land methods such as rear area assaults. But Mike had never run into a situation where the *primary* shooters were God Kings. Undoubtedly the lead God King, the one that Julio had just killed with his own gun—neat trick—was the commander of the defenders of the pit. But having this many God Kings forward meant that somewhere there were a couple of thousand normals without anybody to tell them what to do.

Make that a few *hundred* thousand normals. All the tunnels were defended by God Kings. His division commanders hadn't sent the intel on but he was picking it up on a tertiary feed. Everybody was running into the same thing.

This was going to be a bloodbath. And not in the skin-soothing, life-extending, "send me a hundred virgins" way.

And nobody was any farther than Julio. Initial penetrations were held all along the line and too many troops were still out in the open.

Mike composed the intel and fed it down, then paused, very briefly, to think.

"Rubble-dubble all openings, Shelly. Multi-entry, heavy. Boot on them, don't piss," he muttered to his AID. "Julio."

"*Señor?*" the private said, shakily.

"Hold what you got," Mike said. "Keep tossing subars. Rawls, rubble-dubble, now!"

"Roger," the sergeant said, pulling out another grenade. He pinged the rest of the Hammers and the group all shoved grenades as deep into the rubble as their arms would go, retracting fast. O'Neal, again, had invented the rubble-dubble technique and once upon a time it was dangerous before suits developed an engineering database that could determine trap points. At least one poor bastard had had his hand blown off when he couldn't pull his arm back in time. But that problem had been solved long ago.

All six of the grenades were detonated on signal and the rubble wall more or less evaporated. The explosion threw one of the Hammers off his feet, but everyone else was cocked and locked.

"Let's roll," Mike said, heading for the opening. "There's Posleen ass to kick."

"And you get to roll *behind* us, sir," Sergeant Rawls said, jumping into the opening.

"Spoilsport."

Julio paused at the intersection of the connecting tunnel and looked back. His section, which had ended up collapsing two bunkers for zero openings, had made it across the killing zone to follow the general. But his section head had sent him a quick ping telling him to stay with the Hammers.

That *should* have meant that his section was out in front and he was following behind. Instead, true to form, the general was on point. Damn it. Which put him at an intersection that was probably going to be crawling with fire.

"C kilo subars," the general said, palming one of the devices and sliding his armored thumb down the blank face until the readout showed an output equivalent to one hundred kilos, about two hundred twenty pounds, of TNT. "X form. Hammers, right. Bravo Section right. Double stack."

Julio thumbed a grenade himself, dialing it down, then felt a slight thump as someone bumped into him from behind, forming a "stack" of troopers. As soon as the grenades went off, the stack would rush the corridor to the right. He glanced over and saw Corporal Kermit Butler on the point of the left-hand stack.

"Which way are we throwing?" Kermit pinged.

"X form, Corp," Julio replied. "I'm throwing your way. So you sure as hell better be throwing mine."

"On my mark," O'Neal said. "Three, two, one, Mark!"

Julio realized it was the general right behind him as he threw the grenade. He threw it hard; as the first guy in the stack he had the best chance of getting it far down the corridor.

The general threw one as well, then shoved him, hard.

Julio thought he was crazy. The grenades were on a three-second delay, which meant they would be running right up on Kermit's grenade as they entered the corridor.

But as he rounded the corner he saw the general was crazy like a fox. There were four emplaced positions along the corridor but the defenders had seen the anti-matter grenades skitter down the corridor. Julio actually caught a flash from one of the defender's hypervelocity missile launchers as the Posleen ducked back to avoid the explosion and the wash of antimatter. A mechanical shutter dropped over the hole, closing it entirely.

Julio felt a hand on his shoulder, an almost irresistible pressure, as the general pinged in his ear.

"Down, son," the general said. "Take it on your helmet," he added, pressing the private down and forward.

The explosion, at this range, was almost as bad as the casta round. And he saw his suit counter drop, hard. His armor had taken a serious hit from the antimatter. But he also was within a step of one of the armored positions.

He followed a karat, leading him to a position farther down the line. The armored door slid back before he'd taken two steps, though, and he paused, dropping slightly, and targeted the small opening.

Most of the rounds careened off to one side or another but a few got through. The wash of fire out of the opening was unnoticeable compared to the explosions to either side but it was apparently enough. No fire came down the corridor at him.

He'd automatically blanked the surrounding fire but all four of the defense points in their direction were down. The same could not be said of the far end of the corridor, however, where his section was getting hammered.

"I said boot don't piss on them," the general muttered on the local net. "Raw—"

"On it, sir," Sergeant Rawls said as an HVM ripped Kermit apart.

"And what do we have here . . . ?"

Mike looked down the right-hand corridor, depending on Sergeant Rawls to get Julio's former section in gear on clearing their side. The corridor curved, again, which meant there were probably more defense points down it. However, it was also going to have access to both the surface and the deeper areas where the Posleen commanders, and their forges, must reside.

Intel had shown no Posleen moving on the surface since the redoubt was invested. So everything had to move around underground. The problem was, there were a billion ways to defend a position like this. God Kings in sealed bunkers barely scratched the surface.

However, they were inside. They'd keep digging until all the rats were gone.

CHAPTER TWO

See the door that lies before you
And know this too shall pass
The confrontation of your fears
In strength drawn from the past
　　　—Crüxshadows
　　　　"Eye of the Storm"

The Ceel Banash looked at the encoded message and then took a deep breath, calling upon a calming mantra to keep from becoming too angry or excited.

Banash was a Darhel, the most politically powerful race in the Galactic Federation. Like all other races but humans, the Darhel were quite strictly nonviolent. However, unlike the bat-faced Indowy, the crablike Tchpth and the elusive Himmit, the Darhel were not pacifists by choice. Long before, they had entered an agreement with a godlike race called the Aldenata. In exchange for being lifted from their nuclear scarred homeworld, the Darhel would renounce violence. The

Darhel had agreed immediately, knowing that any agreement is worth exactly the value of the paper it's written upon.

The Aldenata, however, were ancient and, while aggressively idealistic, well aware of the concept of treachery. The agreement said that the Darhel would be nonviolent and the Aldenata *made* them that way. If any Darhel became excessively violent, even became overexcited, much less killed another creature, a chemical switch went off, effectively lobotomizing them. The effect was called "lintatai" and every adult Darhel struggled against it every day. For Darhel were inherently violent, a warrior race that had been thrust into passivity will they, nil they.

The Darhel, however, had learned to channel their focus and fury. Unable to conquer through force of arms, they had taken to politics and business like a buzz saw. Over a bare five hundred years they had gained absolute control over the workings of the Federation, to the point that nothing happened without their approval.

However, every power has its weaknesses. The Ceel was only a junior Darhel executive but he knew a few of them. The Epetar Clan-corp had only recently been utterly destroyed by a group of lucky human rebels who managed to catch them on the wrong side of a leveraged investment. He had, however, just been apprised of a very crucial weakness, one so dangerous it could spell the end of *all* Darhel power. And he'd been handed the slippery end of the stick.

His first thought, once he assimilated the mess he'd been dropped in, was to wonder who hated him enough to do this to him. Darhel were the essence of acooperative; business among the Darhel was if anything slightly more abusive than anything the Darhel practiced on other races. Darhel could not kill but they were more than happy to contract out the occasional assassination. Back-stabbing and character assassination were considered simply good business. Banash, therefore, had to assume that someone had it in for him.

He had been told he was being sent to this dirtball to make the arrangements for rehabilitation of the planet. That was good business, short-term and minor costs for *very* long-term high-profit annuities, and he would have both personal gain from it and enhanced status in his clan-corp. When he'd been given the position he'd nearly had lintatai from surprise. He should have known it was a trap. An ancient bit of Darhel folk wisdom was virtually identical to a human one: If it's flat it's mined, if it's rocky it's covered by fire and if it's easy it's a trap. It said much of Ancient Darhel that this was only three words.

Steps must be taken and they had to be taken fast. But, however much control the Darhel exercised on a strategic and political level, they had far, *far* less when it came to military operations. And the worst was Fleet Strike. Fleet had been quite thoroughly suborned but Fleet Strike continued to act as if the universe cared about things like justice and honor. And then there was the Agreement with the military. Violating the Agreement was guaranteed suicide. So direct methods were out.

That left subtlety. But first to lay the groundwork.

❖   ❖   ❖

Mike silently cursed as his AID pinged a message from Admiral Suntoro. The admiral was in charge of Task Force Induri, the fleet of ships that had assaulted the world. But unlike previous battles in history where "navies" had transported forces to a world to establish a beachhead, and kept control until the beachhead was well established, he was *not* and never had been in command of the ground forces. Mike was his military equivalent and senior to him by about ten years. Fleet Strike had established that dichotomy long ago. The Fleet carried Fleet Strike to a world, hammered the hell out of it and then dropped them. After that, the admirals could twiddle their fingers, thank you very much. On the other hand, he had most of Mike's supplies and fire support so Mike had to be marginally nice to him. Like taking his calls in the middle of a battle.

"Connect," he said. "O'Neal."

"General O'Neal, this is a *disaster*," the admiral said without preamble. "Seven SheVa tanks destroyed and over a hundred ACS suits permanently out of commission!"

Mike noted for the future that the admiral had put it in terms of materials, not the hundred plus dead and scores of wounded. Fleet couldn't care less about casualties; soldiers and sailors were scum and more than disposable. His jaw worked for a moment as he imagined strangling the fat little prick. One of these days he was going to get into a position to screw all the brass in Fleet, and about half the brass in Fleet Strike, extremely hard. And when he did they were going to *feel* the screwing.

"Actually, Admiral, this is a *battle*," Mike replied.

"A destroyer moronically bumbling into ground fire it knew was there, on the other hand, is a disaster. When you find an infection you have to cut it out. This one is just particularly deep and hard."

"I have arranged a conference call in fifteen minutes," the admiral said angrily. "You will be there."

"I'm in the middle of a murthering great battle, Admiral," Mike snarled. "You have *got* to be fucking shitting me."

"The Darhel Ceel will be included. You *will* be there."

"Holy fuck," Mike muttered as the admiral cut the connection. He slid his dip over to the far side of his mouth then back then spat it out into the underlayer. "Raw, anything deadly about to happen?"

"We've got security both ways," the sergeant said nervously. "Why?"

Mike popped his helmet and took a breath. The O2 sensors had said there was enough oxygen, and while carbon dioxide, monoxide and various trace poisons were high, the air was breathable. He didn't take a big deep breath, though, because it was only *barely* breathable. What he did get was filled with the incredibly noxious smell of roasted Posleen. Posleen could eat humans but that didn't mean they had terrestrial body chemistry, just a very bizarre one. And when one got cooked it smelled like a burning chemical factory. When it decayed it smelled worse.

He spit the last bits of chewed-out dip into his helmet, the underlayer gleaning it happily, then pulled out a can of Skoal. There was underlayer gel still coating his head. Once upon a time it would have been crawling back into the helmet but these days it had gotten smart enough to *know* he was going to put the helmet back on as soon as he had a fresh dip. It stayed away from his face, though, giving him the appearance of wearing a silvery, rippling skullcap.

He tamped down the can, and nothing could tamp down a can of Skoal like an ACS suit, then pulled out a dip and stuck it between his cheek and gums. The task was as automatic and precise as killing Posleen. Despite the fact that he was dipping with relatively inflexible armored gauntlets, not one scrap hit the floor. He was over eighty years old with the body of a twenty-year-old; unthought actions were so precise they were machinelike.

He slid the helmet back on, put away the can and then pinged Sergeant Rawls.

"I have to do a conference in fifteen minutes. Secure this area totally. Get all available units into this corridor and hold it. Press forward as much as you need to to feel secure, then hold that. I'll tell you when I'm done."

The chosen virtual venue was a conference room aboard the cruiser *Kagamuska*. Some of the people at the conference might have been present. It was Admiral Suntoro's flagship so it made sense if he was really there. And the Darhel Ceel Banash was staying onboard as well.

But it was impossible to tell. At least to Mike's eyes, viewing from inside an opaque helmet fifty meters underground on the other side of the world from the cruiser, which was in high orbit.

Admiral Suntoro, the Ceel, Commodore Ajeet— moronic commander of the destroyer task force—and

Captain Patrick Vorassi, senior commander of the two massive troop ships that had transported the ACS to the dirtball, were all "present." As well as one pissed off general.

Mike had chosen to present a virtual "self" in armor, sans scary gargoyle helmet. When he bipped in, the meeting was apparently already in full swing.

"At least two months to get them here . . ." Captain Vorassi said. Technically Fleet, he spent most of his time transporting Fleet Strike units, both ACS and regular line infantry.

"The cost of this operation has, hower, become prohibitive," the Darhel Ceel replied, calmly. "Further losses are unjustified when there is a reasonable alternative."

"Ah, General O'Neal," Admiral Suntoro said, giving Mike an oily smile as if they hadn't just been at loggerheads. "We were discussing an interesting suggestion that Darhel Ceel Banash has presented."

"Cool," Mike said. "You guys have some trick for taking tunnels? Because so far it's looking like brute force is the best choice."

"In fact, no," the Darhel said from inside his concealing cowl. Mike had met Darhel before, without their cowls, and knew full well that what was under the hood was a foxlike head with a muzzle full of razor-sharp, sharklike teeth. He wasn't sure how the Darhel ever got around to "we'll ne'er study war no more" but it must have been a hell of a stretch. "Unfortunately, that appears to be the necessity. However, now that the ACS has . . . heroically secured the tunnel entrances, it is perhaps time to call in a . . . less valuable unit."

"The Ceel suggests that we let the mopping up be performed by the Legion," Admiral Suntoro said. "I think that's a very valuable suggestion, don't you, General?"

Shortly after the siege of Earth was lifted, the venerable *Legion Etrangère* had been disbanded. Well, the few survivors had been disbanded. Most of them joined other units and continued the fight. However, shortly after that a "new" unit, copying much of the Legion's methods and even some of its honors, was stood up. The Federation Legion, however, was not the Foreign Legion of yore. While the Legion had, often, been a dumping ground for ne'er-do-wells of one sort or another, the Federation Legion enshrined that. The thinking was simple and very, very old. Soldiers are bad. Quite often more demonstrably so. Murderers, drunks, drug addicts, dealers, thieves, rapists. You've spent money training them. Why throw all that money to waste?

And so the Federation Legion was born. A penal unit, part of Fleet and not Fleet Strike, it was used for every crap job the Fleet had. Mostly it spent its time on *really* horrible worlds during the mop-up phase of Posleen clearing. Occasionally, it was used in "hard clear" situations like this one. Casualty rates were horrendous and units, within a few years, had over two hundred percent casualties. Most of those, admittedly, were in new arrivals. And, hell, many of them were when the veterans decided that a newbie simply wasn't either criminal *enough* or good enough to want to have around.

The Legion was also light infantry. It had no heavy weapons, no armor and didn't even use exos. It kept *that* Legion tradition: It mostly marched everywhere.

"With all due respect to the Ceel," Mike said, oozing sweetness, "the answer is: No, I don't think that's a suggestion with *any* inherent value or merit. And that's my professional opinion. Would you care for an expansion, Admiral?"

"Yes, please," Admiral Suntoro snarled.

"Bullet Point One, for those who need a Power-Point presentation, is that the ACS has taken three percent casualties getting this far, and we're finding resistance is on the same order as above ground. Legion is regular infantry; they'd get flipping slaughtered. I know they're all drunks, thieves and murderers, but they weren't given a death sentence or they'd already have been killed. Bullet Point Two: I would appreciate it if you didn't kill the morale of my corps. We took serious casualties getting to *this* point. We want to clear the damned mountains, kill a bunch of Posleen and take their stuff. That's what my boys do and they wouldn't be here if they didn't enjoy it. Bullet Point Three: As the captain said, getting them here would take at least two months. It is a simple military axiom that you should never give an enemy more time than necessary to prepare. I've sent orders to my division commanders to continue the assault but even *this* time away is a poor use of my time. Letting them get even more settled in for two months, which is one Posleen *birth cycle* I remind you, is militarily insane. Bullet Point Four: I've got a corps of armored combat suits pushing into this resistance. The Legion is about a division, max. The more you use, the fewer you lose. I doubt, professionally, that they have sufficient personnel to successfully assault this redoubt. In other words, they'll fight until casualties exceed the level they're willing to take and then mutiny. At which point *my* boys will be called in to quell the mutiny and we'll be back to square one.

"So in my professional opinion, the Ceel's suggestion, while appreciated, fails on the points that it is murderous to the Legion, murderous to my corps' morale, unwise and unlikely to work. Are we done here? Because I've got a battle to run."

"So you're refusing to disengage?" Commodore Ajeet asked incredulously. "But the Ceel's suggestion—"

"Is a suggestion," Mike replied coldly. "I am the ground force *commander*. That means I'm in command. If the Ceel would care to put in a request to have me relieved for someone more tractable he can feel free to do so. In the meantime, I've got a battle to run. And you're late on delivering the next shipment of power cells to Alpha Base. So I would suggest that we cut this meeting short so that everyone can go do their damned jobs. I, personally, *am* done here. Shelly, clear."

"I'm sorry about that, Ceel Banash," Admiral Suntoro said as soon as the conference had broken up. "General O'Neal should be more respectful of his betters."

"General O'Neal's record speaks for itself," Ceel Banash said calmly. "He is hypercompetent in his field. As was just proven. He was *right*, Admiral. I had considered only the point about how long it would take to get the Legion here. The other points were equally important if not more so. I have no issues with the conference."

"Very well, Ceel," Admiral Suntoro said, confused. "I shall continue my planning of the recovery of this lovely world," Ceel Banash said. "I suggest that you ensure delivery of supplies to the redoubtable ground-commander."

As soon as the call was terminated the Ceel used all his willpower to suppress lintatai. He wanted to crush that impudent human, to rend him, to...

He took a breath and muttered a mantra, trying and trying to keep the surge of hormones down to a survivable level. If only...

The Legion was as thoroughly controlled as any unit in the military. The officers were utterly dependent upon the Darhel, every one having major financial problems that the Darhel were more than willing to remedy as long as they stayed in line. If the Legion had taken over the rest of the work on this planet its secret would assuredly remain safe. As it was, so far there was no indication the humans knew. But if the Eleventh remained, it *would* come out. The secret must NOT...

Indowy Neena knew the signs. As soon as the conference call was terminated it sent a muscle-cued message to its subordinates. The transfer-neuter watched, impassively, as the young Darhel wrestled with his inner emotions, then suddenly jerked. For a moment, Neena thought it would die as the light of fury erupted in the Darhel's face. Sometimes the Darhel could survive in the thrall of tal hormones for as long as fifteen seconds, long enough to kill up to a dozen Indowy if present. But this one barely jerked, then slumped, his face going slack.

"Send a message to the Tir Dol Ron," Neena said as

a half dozen Indowy scurried into the room. "This one has entered lintatai. We're going to need a replacement Ceel. I will inform the admiral."

"Shall we place him in the airlock until he is gone?" Indowy Tak asked. The junior servant was new, out of the megascrapers for the first time. But if he was bothered by the condition of his former master it wasn't apparent.

"Humans are confused by such things," Neena said. "We will have to baby him until we get back to an Indowy or Darhel world. Then we can set him out."

"I will see to his needs for now," Tak said. "I can do that by myself."

"Very well," Neena replied, turning and leaving the compartment.

A second Indowy left to compose a message to the Tir who had sent Banash on this assignment. The others quickly tidied the small amount of mess the Ceel had caused them, then left.

As soon as he was alone, Tak lifted the body and dragged the unresisting Ceel to the comconsole. Few humans realized the strength of the diminutive Indowy but, like chimpanzees, their appearances were deceptive. The only problem with carrying the much larger Darhel was getting his limp legs not to dangle on the floor. The Tak sought a particular message, then laid the Darhel's hand on the control pad and positioned his face in front of the screen. Last, he slid a small device over the Darhel's eyes. Darhel secure messages were, quite literally, for their eyes only. The laser would only shine into the Ceel's eyes and could only be decrypted if he was physically watching it.

Having him go into lintatai was a real coup for the junior Bane Sidhe.

The Indowy downloaded the decrypted message, then picked the Darhel up and set him on the large bed. It was going to be a long time before anyone came to relieve him but he had some interesting reading to pass the time.

Tak was not, in fact, "straight out of the megascraper." A member of the rebel faction called the Bane Sidhe by humans, he had travelled extensively and spent more time with humans than was considered either normal or proper. And despite extensive training in covert operations, he had developed some very bad habits.

One of them was to emit a very human whistle when he was surprised.

"Whoooo," the Indowy shrilled as he read the missive. "As Cally would say: The Darhel are sooo *fucked!*"

CHAPTER THREE

A month. Thirty-two days, actually. That was how long it had taken to get to this point.

Mike shook his head as he looked around the cavern. Adjectives were bothering him.

"So, is this a cavernous cavern?" he muttered.

"How 'bout one big motherfucking cavern, sir?" Rawls suggested. "And chock full of salty goodness, too."

The...facility was clearly the center of the Posleen's industrial capacity in the redoubt. Nearly two thousand *meters* under ground, deep enough in the bedrock that it was damned well hot, the six-hundred-meter long, one hundred and twenty-meter high facility was packed with Posleen auto-forges. Enough in this one facility to outfit a dozen factory ships. At a billion credits a pop, on the open market, Mike was looking at a serious haul.

Getting there, though, had been tough. Casualties had approached ten percent in the first week. The unit was being decimated in all but the truly literal sense. However, the resistance had dropped off from there. The much more dangerous God Kings thinned out, replaced by hordes of half-wild, but heavily armed, normals. They had thrown themselves into the ACS troops in wild charges in narrow tunnels, in some cases blasting so much firepower into same that the tunnels were collapsed.

Other tunnels were intentionally rigged by the remaining God Kings, dropping on units as they advanced. But having a mountain fall on you was old hat for ACS troops; they'd been dealing with that since almost their first battle. And they could dig like gophers.

Slowly, in the face of mass charges and collapsed tunnels and feints and flanking maneuvers, the corps had slowly ground its way to the center of the redoubt, finally taking this cavern.

By that time, it was mostly mopping up. There were still feral Posleen filling the extensive tunnels and mines of the redoubt, but the last crop of God Kings, probably the commander and his "staff," had been killed only a few hours before.

"How much do you think?" Rawls asked.

The Darhel had actually instituted the program of paying units for "recovered materials." Human commanders from Western societies had initially argued against what they saw as archaic "prize" rules but the law was encoded in Galactic regulation.

Over the years, Mike had made a tidy sum from prizes. But . . .

"Enough for a drunken weekend for every survivor," Mike said coldly. "Even after the triple tithe for the

next of kin. But add it all up and it won't even pay
for the suits, much less the SheVas. And while there
are bean counters aplenty that can give you a precise
value for every one of my boys killed, I'm not going
to even try."

"Sorry, sir," Rawls said.

"It's not enough, Sergeant," Mike said. "It's never
ever enough."

"*Madre de Dios*," Julio muttered, looking into the pit.

"What'cha got?" Sergeant Dylan Glover asked.

Julio's team had been attached, more or less of
necessity, to the general's bodyguards as the assault
ground forward. The Hammers had taken even higher
casualties than the rest of the division, trying to protect their headstrong commander. While Julio's team
hadn't had their same level of training or experience,
more bodies were more bodies.

The Hammers had started out with nine NCOs
and enlisted; Julio's team, by the time it got officially
linked up, with one and three. Sergeant Glover and
Julio were the only remaining from his team and there
were only four Hammers. It had been a bloody slog.

Along the way Julio had seen some things he hoped
would eventually fade from consciousness. When
thousands of Posleen normals were killed in a nine-
foot-wide passage, it was necessary to do more than
just wade through the bodies. He'd found himself
hacking parts out of the way, stomping through them,
his suit becoming covered in yellow blood.

Broken and flayed suits had become a thing of
norm. Passages choked with a mixture of suits and
Posleen and rubble.

But this was something new. It appeared to be a pit filled with nothing but *bones*. There was a bit of flesh on them and some sort of bug had infested the pit, but it was the bones that showed through.

"Charnel pit," Sergeant Glover said, stepping up beside him. "Looks like mostly Posleen. They must have been eating the normals to keep them from eating the food supply. Look, see the little ones?"

"Yeah," Julio said, his eyes wide.

"Nestlings. They eat their young, too."

"*Madre de Dios*," Julio repeated. "That is sick."

"Hey, they reproduce so fast that . . ." The sergeant paused.

"So fast that what, Sergeant?"

"That is not a Posleen bone," the sergeant said. "Go get me some rope. I need to get down there."

"We get anybody captured?" Mike said, rotating the bone back and forth.

Posleen were aliens, their physiology wildly different from that of humans. And over the past fifty years he had seen more bones, of both species, than he cared to remember. Back on Earth during the Retaking there had been thousands of charnel pits filled with the remnants of the humans the Posleen used as "thresh." By the same token, Posleen bodies, consumed or just shattered, littered the earth to the point where their toxic blood made some areas untillable for years.

But the point was, Posleen bones and human bones did not look much alike. Among other things, Posleen bones had a very distinct "ridge" down the center. Human bones were much more rounded. And whereas there were some terrestrial animals that had bones remarkably similar to a human femur, they were on *Earth*. Not three hundred light-years galactic inward.

"Not even any unaccounted for," Colonel Shan Gilman, the Eleventh ACS personnel officer, G-1, raised a hand in a shrug. "Every human that dropped on this world is accounted for. There are a few *legs* missing, but—"

"But it don't account for this, sir," Sergeant Major Rolph Tilton said, walking over. He held up the skull in his hand and waggled it back and forth. "More we dig in there, the more of these we're finding. And this ain't a full grown guy."

"Girl," Mike said, looking at the skull. "Female. Teen." He took it and turned it back and forth. "Malnourished for that matter. And with really bad teeth."

"So how did it get *here*?" Colonel Gilman asked, desperately. "We didn't bring any teen females with us!"

"Interesting question," Mike said, turning the skull back and forth. "But I don't think we're going to solve it today. Clean out that pit and find out what's all in there. Keep me posted. Rawls."

"Sir?"

"Attach Private Garcia and his sergeant to the Hammers. We're heading back to the ship."

"Roger, sir."

As the hatch of the Banshee shuttle closed, the helmets came off as if on cue.

Mike flicked the helmet of undergel to let it know it might as well crawl back into the helmet then looked around.

"Julio!"

"Sir?" the private squeaked, trying to figure out if he was supposed to have kept his helmet on or something.

"What do you think?"

"Uh," Julio said, blinking furiously in thought. "I think I'm glad to be back on a shuttle headed for the ship, sir. I know the suits keep you clean but I'm looking forward to a shower and some rack time."

"Spoken like a true soldier," Mike said, smiling at the chuckles from the veterans in the shuttle. "But I was actually talking about the bones."

"Don't know what to think, sir," Garcia replied. "I mean, they're not our guys. And we're the only humans on this planet."

"So how did they get there?" Mike asked, leaning back with his eyes cleared.

"Not sure, sir."

"Gimme an answer, Private," Mike said. "Any answer is fine."

"Okay..." the private said, nervously. "Well... The Posleen could have brought them here. Sir. I mean as food or something. Maybe some sort of trade."

"Sergeant Glover."

"Sir?" the sergeant replied. He and Garcia had been around the general for a month but it didn't mean he was any less nervous in his presence. He wasn't even sure what he was doing here.

"You've been in the ACS for six years. Enlisted from an unrecovered part of Florida. Bounty hunter?"

"My father was, sir," Glover said, his brow furrowing. "I did some Posleen hunting before I joined up."

"Since then you've participated in the retaking of five worlds. Ever seen human sign?"

"No, sir," Glover replied. "I mean, I saw something

like this, an old pit that is, in Florida. But not since I've been off-world. All the planets where humans had gotten caught by the Posleen were cleared by the time I joined up."

"So what do you think of Private Garcia's theory?" the general asked.

"It's possible but it doesn't match past record, sir," Glover said. "If the Posleen were going to be trading in human thresh, you would expect to see it closer to Earth. This is a long way from home, sir."

"That it is," Mike said. "Okay... Clarke."

"Sir?" Corporal Edgar Clarke was a two-year veteran of the Hammers. Six foot two inches tall he, like most of the Hammers, looked a bit incongruous next to their "primary."

"Alternative theory."

Clarke hated this. When the general wasn't busy with something else he'd pose these little "think sessions." Clarke was more than happy to kill Posleen or, hell, throw his body between Posleen fire and his boss. But he hated when he was asked to think.

"Humans evolving on another world, sir?" Clarke said. "Or maybe being put there by God or something."

"Two theories, equally queriable," O'Neal replied. "The first being convergent evolution by name. That is that similar species occur with similar conditions. Thus you get rat-looking creatures in Australia and rats in England. Not well thought of by the scientific community but they're pretty inbred anyway. Chalk that up as a possible. The test will be determining if they have human DNA. DNA don't lie. In which case we get to the 'God made it that way' theory. Which is actually my first choice."

"Really?" Clarke said.

"Certainly," the general replied, thoughtfully. "For values of God."

"Hi, Mike."

The recording had been made months before and was a "back channel" communication, a personal message between two officers. In this case, originating from General Tam Wesley, the ACS branch Assistant Chief of Staff for Operations.

"I'd guess that this isn't too surprising but you're getting orders to hold up. The reclamation program has about reached its point of futility. Every planet that's been taken in the last two years has been reduced to full orna'adar or darned near. The Posleen are extinguishing themselves without our help."

Mike grimaced on that. It wasn't exactly a surprise but he also thought there was far more to it. Tam was actually his junior in the service despite having a higher rank. That was mostly because Mike had refused to stick closer to the centers of power but also because Wesley, while trustworthy, was much more the political animal than the Eleventh Corps commander. If Wesley was being this terse it meant there was more to it. But without being back on Earth, nearly a year by any ship available, Mike wasn't going to find out what.

"The other problem is that we're just getting too spread out. By trans-net you're going to be getting this six months from when I send it. There's no way to coordinate with those sorts of lags. For all I know you could have been wiped out. And we're having trouble with commo on the entire periphery of the reclaimed zone. Hell, I'm looking at a report that an Indowy colony has lost contact and that's nearly a year old. God only knows what's *really* happening.

"So for good or ill, hold up. The same message is going to Admiral Suntoro. I'm not sure if this is permanent or not. And for now you're not being recalled. I know it's not the best thing in the world to be left hanging out there in limbo. But for now that's how it's got to be. See if there's a world nearby that's not too screwed up and set up for rest and refit. When they told me to order a stand-down in place I pointed out that there had to be a minimum time-frame on that. So you've got at least six weeks 'off' if you will. You can use the corps as you wish, just don't go a-hunting anymore until you get further word. The official orders covering this are attached but I figured you'd like some context.

"Take care. Tam."

The recording winked out and Mike opened up the orders. They were essentially the same. Eleventh Corps was to perform an "in place stand-down" of at least six weeks' duration. Further orders to come.

There had been rumors for years that the ACS was to be decommissioned. The suits were terribly expensive, their only benefit that they made the wearers extremely survivable in even the worst combat. The recent battle in the redoubt would have eliminated *multiple* corps of light infantry and taken much more time. So Mike suspected that this "temporary stand-down" was the death knell for the corps.

The reality, though, was that the battle at the redoubt had been the first real combat the corps had faced in nearly a decade. The Posleen, at least in this region, had been reduced to scattered savages, easy enough to mop up even for light units.

The Posleen orna'adar "Blight" stretched for hundreds of light-years inward along the Orion Arm from Earth. Due to the nature of both Indowy and Posleen hyper-drive systems, it was difficult to impossible to reach the other galactic arms. So the Posleen had been trapped on this relatively narrow band of stars. And as the stars drew inwards toward the galactic core there were fewer and fewer useable planets. For all Mike knew, they might have reached the end of the Posleen Blight. In which case, his job was finished.

He had no interest in continuing a military career just for the career. All he cared about was wiping out the Posleen. Being in a desk job in Fredericksburg would be very close to a nightmare.

God knew he had enough money to retire. Daily estimated "prize" shares were posted on the milnet and just this one planet would set him up in comfort for the rest of his life. And that didn't count the . . . dozens, hundreds of other planets he'd participated in retaking, from regimental commander all the way to corps. Hell, he could buy one of them with plenty left over.

But that was for later to think about. Right now he had to figure out somewhere to "refit" his unit.

This planet wasn't so bad. The air was at least breathable, despite the beginnings of orna'adar and the Fleet bombardment. Fleet had mostly used kinetic weapons and even the Posleen had only seemed to drop a few nukes. Radiation levels were nominal. Every inch was pretty well scorched, but . . .

Or was it? He'd have to look at detail scans. Maybe there was somewhere to settle.

Hell, maybe he'd buy *this* planet.

He had to chuckle. Call it Mikey's World.

"Intel. I've got a tasking..."

"This whole range is, essentially, clean, sir."

The lieutenant from G-2 was a consummate intel geek, right down to the bobbing adam's apple. Mike had learned to both love and hate his intel geeks. When they were right they were awesome. Far too often, though, they missed some tiny yet vital bit of information that led to a colossal fuck-up.

Mike looked around at the valley and wondered how in the hell it could have avoided being pasted. When Fleet and Fleet Strike got together on orbital taskings, the intel sections of both units went over the satellite data carefully. AIDs carefully sorted the data and pointed out major and minor Posleen positions and infrastructure.

The valley was a good thirty miles across, a couple of hundred miles long and bowl-shaped from glaciation. It looked somewhat like the Hudson Valley on Earth if you excepted that most of the vegetation was fernlike. However, there were even some trees that looked a hell of a lot like hickory and pine. Pretty.

Which begged the question why the Posleen, who usually ravaged any area like this, hadn't filled it with their towns and cities devoted to worshipping God Kings.

"This valley is close to the center of this range, sir," Michael Burkett said. "And we noted it on our tasking views. There were major queries about it on my level. But there was no trace of Posleen, or any other, civilization in the area."

"You'll understand, Lieutenant, if I find that hard to believe," Mike replied.

"Yes, sir," the lieutenant replied. "But since we took most of the planet we've sent in some Banshee flights. Not only did they not take fire but they saw no evidence of Posleen in the area. Sir."

"Well, it sure fits the requirement," Mike said, looking around. Doing even a three-sixty view was simple enough in a suit if hard to get used to at first. By looking to the side, the view was slewed. If you kept your eyes off-center for a moment it continued to slew, all the way around if you wished. Mike off-set his eyes just far enough to slew slowly. Something was bugging the hell of him.

"Shelly. Any threat sources you can detect."

"Negative," his AID replied. "No energy emissions beyond friendly. No Posleen heat signatures. No major heat signatures at all in the immediate area. There are a few on the nearby ridge that I've tentatively classed as some sort of herbivore from movements."

"Check for human," Mike said. "Other than friendly."

"Query," the AID replied. "Only friendly humans on this planet."

"Check," Mike said.

"Negative for human heat signatures," the AID replied. "Query. Human normal scent signature detected. Chemical analysis determines not of any registered friendly DNA. At least seven separate chemistries detected. General, that does not compute, as the SF computers would say. This is a 'what the fuck' moment."

"Slew to wind direction," Mike said. "Remove heat signature filter."

The view slewed to over his right shoulder. With

every heat signature revealed, he could see several small points on the shoulder of the ridge they'd landed on.

"Shelly. Query. Heat points." He used his eyes to focus on one of the signatures.

"Analysis: small burrows with mammaloform local species inhabiting," Shelly replied.

"Does that analysis include the presence of humans?" Mike asked. "Including humans with special combat training."

"Negative. No humans beyond friendly on planet."

"Modify for presence of humans on planet," Mike said.

"Modified analysis. Sniper team hides. Possible leakage from spider holes. No metal or power sources detected from area. Threat level minimal to armored personnel."

Between his position and the potential "threat" was a scrub- and tree-covered hillside. Now that he really *looked* at the surroundings it was clear that much of it was secondary growth. The area had been extensively if slowly forested. The trees between his position and the possible visitors were relatively low. But getting through them, quickly, would be difficult.

What bugged him was that they'd only landed twenty minutes before. How in the hell had someone gotten onto that ridge, which they'd overflown, that quickly. *And* into a hide?

"General," Rawls said. "If there are snipers overlooking this position . . ."

The last time Mike had been on Earth he'd spent a brief period as Inspector General of the ACS, which had morphed into something very close to the German concept of Inspector General, rather than the

American. Thus, that job title carried the "honorable" position of being in charge of all Terra based ACS units. Those were mostly training units but a few were kept on tap as a reaction force if something happened that standard units couldn't handle.

Shortly before Mike's tenure, the top Terran anti-terrorist and anti-Posleen combat unit, the US SOCOM Direct Action Group, had gone rogue. They were given orders to stop the penetration of a top-secret facility. Someone had overwhelmed the local security and was well on their way to capturing some secret that Mike had never been authorized to know about. *Had* gotten their hands on it.

The DAG was sent in to stop the penetration and recover the secret at all costs. Instead, they had turned on the local security and conventional units reacting to the attack. Then, as far as anyone could tell, they'd disappeared off the face of the earth.

During Mike's tenure they had surfaced, extracting a group of Indowy "rebels," a concept that Mike had always found confusing. The ACS quick reaction unit had been sent in and Mike had gone with them, relishing a chance to work out his kinks even if it *was* fighting humans.

He'd damned near had his ass handed to him. The DAG were just fucking *good*, even without suits. They'd screened the Indowy all the way out, giving a fully armored and highly trained ACS unit one casualty for two. In Mike's case, he'd detected a sniper, way too late. The guy had him dead to rights. And just *didn't fire*.

Mike had, though. His reactions to something like that were as close to hard-wired as it was possible to find in a human neuro-system. But the encounter had shaken him. The guy had a heavy-duty plasma rifle pointed right at him. Mike should have been burned to a crisp. Instead, the guy held his fire.

They hadn't been able to recover the body. The DAG had flash burned every member who was killed. There wasn't even any trace DNA. To this day, Mike didn't know who had bested him. But it had given him the willies about snipers ever since.

This situation, though...

"No metal signatures, Rawls," Mike said, considering the slope. There was a low bluff at the top of the hill but ACS could jump that easily enough. The undergrowth wouldn't be a problem even if he could *swear* he recognized some of it. Dodging around the trees. "No power signatures. I don't care what they've got, they can't scratch an ACS at range even if it's monomolecule weapons. When we get close, though, we'll have to be careful."

"When we get *close*, sir?" Rawls said.

"Yep," Mike replied. "I'm about done with mysteries. I want to see who's up there."

"They are not Pokree," Urnhat said quietly.

"They are intruders," Polray replied. "Perhaps Charan."

"Charan don't wear metal suits as if they were Ran'ther'iad iron-heads," Whiet said. The older warrior snorted. "The Pokree would find them soon enough if they did that. As they did the Ran'ther'iad, Streunten curse their souls."

"Silence," Swodrath said. The blocky-bodied Gamra was the Huntmaster of the Nor. Once he had been a soldier in service of the Duendtor before the coming of the Pokree. He still served the Duendtor Lerawum, even if in this much reduced capacity. He had risen high enough in the Service to be made a Gamra, the change to super-warrior. Now he used it to hunt the Pokree stupid enough to enter the valley of the Nor. "We observe. Nothing more. Those are not Ranthy suits. And the Ranthy do not fly like the Pokree. They must be allies of the Pokree."

"The Pokree do not ally," Polray said. "They eat."

"Silence," Swodrath growled.

"Okay, everybody got the plan?" Mike asked.

"Yes, sir," Staff Sergeant Rawls replied. "And I formally protest."

"Noted," Mike said, grinning inside his suit. "On my mark... One, two, three..."

"Skelight they're fast!" Whict said as the suits suddenly turned and began sprinting up the steep slope faster than a deer.

"OUT!" Swodrath shouted. "Urnhat, Polray, flee. Whiet and I will stand and fight them!"

"I would stay with you, Huntmaster," Urnhat said, whipping off the leather cover and hefting her crossbow.

"And I ordered you to flee," Swodrath said, sending a quarrel downrange. The bolt, backed by a Duendtor-steel bow and with a cap of hammer-flash hit one of the armored suits and disintegrated in a crack of fire. "Damn these things! Streunten be with me!" he shouted, hefting his club. He had a Pokree sword, taken from his first kill of those vile beasts, back in his cave. But the Pokree could detect any metal that was carried on a scout. So all he had was this stupid club.

"I think it's a bit late for that," Whiet pointed out as the suits launched themselves into the air and landed on the bluff. He, too, had pulled out one of the long clubs, its sides lined with a strange material they had captured from the Pokree. It would cut through rock itself and did not attract the Pokree. Maybe it would cut these things as well. "Streunten be with us all!"

Mike lifted his forearm and caught the expertly swung club on it, expecting it to rebound. But what looked like obsidian flakes lining it was something else, probably unprocessed monomolecule pieces. It sank into his armor and he could even feel a bite on his forearm.

"Damn," he said, snatching the club and tossing it away. "Watch these things. They don't half cut."

"Got mine," Corporal Green said, holding what looked one hell of a lot like a human up by the back of a very scruffy shirt. Green was holding the guy's club in his off-hand as the local scrabbled for footing.

Mike grabbed the guy who'd hit him by the back of the head and tried not to squeeze *too* hard. You could juggle eggs in an ACS if you were careful enough. You could also bend steel bars. It was all a matter of training.

"Ow!" Garcia snapped as the club thunked into his head. He could, for a moment, see daylight through the hole. He snatched the club away and swung it into a tree to hold it. Too hard, as it turned out, the tree *and* the club disintegrated.

He grabbed the struggling figure as carefully as he could but it apparently wasn't carefully enough as the person let out a squeal of pain. He'd grabbed a forearm and apparently a bit too hard.

It was the squeal that triggered his recognition.

He was holding a girl. One with bright red hair and very pretty blue eyes.

The girl tried to kick him in the crotch. Okay, so romance probably wasn't right around the corner.

"Holy fuck!" Rawls shouted. He'd been hit three times by the club before he could even react and was cut in each spot. If he hadn't been guarding his neck, one of the hits might have gotten through to his carotid.

He didn't want to hurt the guy but with the clubs being this vicious, he wasn't sure what to do. He also wasn't sure he was dealing with a human. The guy looked more like a Darhel and was both blindingly fast and, from the power of the strikes, remarkably strong.

Mike tossed his catch to Corporal Murray and walked over to where Rawls was struggling with what certainly *looked* like a Darhel. But while Mike had heard rumors they could fight, *seeing* it was something else.

But the more he watched, as Rawls learned to block the club a bit better, he realized it couldn't be a Darhel. The body was way too stocky and the musculature was all wrong.

What he was looking at was a human somehow *changed* to *look* like a Darhel. Or sort of Darhel.

Mike watched for a moment longer, then his fist flashed out . . .

✧   ✧   ✧

Urnhat groaned as Swodrath fell to the ground. The short figure had only hit once but the Huntmaster had been knocked backwards several feet. He still lived, it would take more than that to damage a Gamra, but he was out of the fight and with his fall their fates were sealed.

She stopped struggling, then struck the armored suit one more time in frustration. Her right arm was either broken or badly bruised and now her left hand felt the same.

"Streunten take your souls!"

"Shelly, you making anything of this gabble?" Mike asked. The prisoners were now examining them sullenly but they *had* been speaking. Mike wasn't sure how good AIDs were at translating alien languages. It had never come up. There were the Galactics and there were Posleen. Humans or pseudo-humans speaking alien babel had never come up.

"Yes," the AID replied.

"Can you translate it?" Mike asked.

"Yes."

When AIDs got monosyllabic it was bad. Mike was well aware that AIDs had lots of secrets they wouldn't or couldn't share with humans. When they got monosyllabic you were getting close to one of them.

He'd have to think on that. But given that there were humans on a planet a long way away from Earth, one of them looked like a Darhel but wasn't, the local Darhel had gone into lintatai and his AID was getting less helpful ... Things were starting to add up in an "oh, shit" way.

Mike was not stupid. There was more than one

reason he'd stayed as far away from central command as he could possibly arrange. Once upon a time he'd had a very good friend and commander named Taylor. General Taylor had been commander of all U.S. defenses on Earth. One day he turned up dead after asking too many questions about an incident where the AID net had been, apparently, hacked. Shortly after that a bunch of Darhel had either gone into lintatai or ended up quite spectacularly dead. And a previous special operations unit, the Cyberpunks, had gone rogue.

Mike had heard the rumors, including some that he put more credence on than others. The Darhel weren't entirely friendly to humans. They had, quite clearly, hamstrung human operations during the war. And they continued to manipulate governments and the military. Push too hard at Darhel secrets and you didn't last long.

Unfortunately, it looked as if Mike had ended up square in the middle of one or his middle name wasn't Leonidas.

"Well, Shelly, why don't you go ahead and translate for me."

"Cometh all friends," the smallest of the suits said. It had a monstrous form painted on its suit, a creature out of nightmare. All the other suits were bare of all but the most minor symbols. Urnhat wasn't sure if that meant a more senior one or not. The voice seemed male, though, and speaking in an archaic dialect that was hard to understand.

"Then let us go so we can tend to our leader," Whiet replied.

"Very well," the suit boomed. Almost instantly all three of the hunters were released.

Urnhat ran to Swodrath and knelt by his side, feeling at his chest for the beat of a heart. It was strong, thank Skelight.

"He is fine," the suit said. "I pulled my punch."

"Pulled it?" Urnhat said, standing up and rounding on the being. "He was thrown a yur!"

The suit, which had no visor and no way for her to see its eyes, appeared nonetheless to contemplate her for a moment, then turned. One fist flashed out and all the way through the young bole of a tonser tree. The being then ripped the tree from its rather deep roots and tossed it down the slope.

"Pulled it," the being said, reaching up and lifting off the helmet.

Urnhat gasped in surprise as a human head was revealed, its scalp covered in a strange ripple of silver.

"Lieutenant General Michael O'Neal name is. Truth. We come in peace."

"This is impossible," Admiral Suntoro said. "There *cannot* be humans on this planet. You are mistaken."

"Well, Admiral, I might be," Mike said. From the admiral's image he was about to have a stroke. "But science don't lie. These are humans down to the ninety-ninth decimal. DNA matches up exactly. The local tribe is called the Nor. They control the upper third or so of this valley. There's one farther down south that's called the Charan. Apparently the Posleen arrived within the memory of some of their middle-aged types and started their usual slaughter. But the humans managed to hold them from taking all this range. Some of them held part of the valley for a while but they managed to kill them off. Since then the mountain tribes send fighters down to the lower reaches and to this valley and the Posleen send some of their fighters up and it got to be almost stylized from the sound of it. Probably the reason this planet never entered orna'adar. The Posleen had somewhere to bleed off the excess that couldn't be sent to space."

"So what are they doing here?" Suntoro asked. "How did they get here? They couldn't have walked."

"Yeah, that's the rub," Mike said, rubbing his head as if in response. He pulled out a pinch of dip and stuck it between his cheek and gum, contemplating the Skoal can balefully. "Admiral, figure it's time to say some of this in front of an AID. You're not stupid. We both know the Darhel ain't what I'd call fully open and honest."

"The Darhel are our supporters," the admiral said stoutly. "They saved us from the Posleen through their aid and support."

"Yeah, except for, you know, most of the world," Mike said. "And they've managed to keep us pretty much under the yoke since. And we both know that there are things they don't want us to know about that."

"I will hear no disrespect spoken of the Darhel," the admiral snapped. "That is treason."

"Nah, just honesty," Mike said, sighing again. He suspected that under Galactic law it just *might* be treason. "Problem is, this is one of those things I'm wondering if they ever wanted anyone to find out. And trust me, I wouldn't have poked if I knew about it. But here we are. The term 'fucked' comes to mind."

"What are we going to do?" the admiral asked,

rubbing his hands nervously. "Perhaps we should meet. In person."

"Too late for that," Mike pointed out. "The AID network knows about it. Not much we can cover up at this point. And no Darhel to bring it to and try to discuss it logically. I think that you can give up blaming me for his lintatai, by the way. If we could look at his secret communciations, I suspect we'd find out he had some orders he couldn't carry out. Like 'don't let the humans go to R-1496 Delta, whatever you do.' Information lag. Nobody knew we were headed this way until the reports got back to the core worlds. And now we're here."

"What are you going to do?" the admiral asked.

"I'm trying to arrange a meet with their leaders. For the time being I'm going to stay on mission. Set up a rest and refit base down here. I figure we're going to be getting orders pretty soon to come back to Earth. At that point, we'll need to figure something out."

"What do you mean?" the admiral said.

"Well, what do you think the likelihood of us getting *back* is?"

"Here they come," Colonel Ashland said.

Bobby Ashland was tall and slim, making an interesting contrast with his commander. The Corps G-2 also had a lightning quick mind. Mike hadn't discussed their current predicament with him but he had to be thinking the same thoughts. He had spent too much time deep in Fleet Strike intel not to have some inkling of how ruthless the Darhel could be when they felt the need.

"Any idea from where?" Mike asked as the party

hove into view. The Nor used a leather cloak covered in strips of cloth in much the way that recon specialists used a ghillie suit. It had the added benefit of being, perhaps from some sort of treatment, pretty much immune to infrared radiation. Thus the lack of thermal signature.

They weren't hiding this time, though. They were just walking up the hill in the open.

"Recon pod has them exiting a tunnel about a klick west," Ashland replied. "This area is high in limestone. No telling how far back the tunnel stretches."

"Greetings, Swodrath," Mike said, bowing his head to the Huntmaster. "How's the jaw?"

"A Gamra recovers swiftly," the Nor said. "The Mistress has agreed to meet you. Only you."

"Very well," Mike said, donning his helmet. "Lead on."

"Sir..." Colonel Ashland said.

"Just deal, Colonel," Mike replied. "I'll be fine. And if I'm not, tell Brigadier General Corval he's got a whole corps available to come find me. Lead on, Swodrath."

The initial entrance was a cleverly concealed cave opening. A slide in the cave had been cleared at some point, not recently from the looks of it, opening into a deeper area.

The course, lit by smoky but long-lasting torches, was complex. On the other hand, the inertial tracker in the suit was getting feedback from external subspace location sensors. Mike could follow the trace more or less as if he was on the surface.

The route they took was about two klicks in straight

distance and about six following the twists of the caves. In places sections had been mined out, opening up sections of the cave that hadn't previously been connected. The marks of chisels were clear and most of those portions were particularly low.

Finally, though, they entered an area that was more interesting. The limestone in the area overlay granite and when they reached that portion they entered what was clearly a mine. However, the cuttings were anything but primitive. The walls had the flat, glassy look of Indowy or Posleen borers. Curiouser and curiouser.

The mine tunnels debouched into a pretty fair-sized canyon. The vast room was home to at least three hundred people by the looks of the tents that occupied the floor. Where they got their food was what interested Mike.

Most of the inhabitants were either hiding or out somewhere. But a few of the elderly were huddling around fires, someone brought in firewood, and children were playing in the area. The children were clearly curious but they stayed back from the party instead of tagging along as most kids on Earth would.

They crossed to the east side of the cavern and entered a smaller tunnel, which debouched into a room about fifty feet on a side. Arrayed by the entrance were guards, more of the "Gamra" by the looks of them. There were also some male and female humans in the room, gathered around as if at an audience. But what caught Mike's eye was the female on the fur-covered chair that was clearly a throne.

Tall was his first impression. At least six foot four at a guess since she was sitting down. Pretty was the second impression. Make that beautiful. But her looks were thrown off by her long silver hair, true silver not the "silver" of age, and when he approached he could see she had cat-pupilled eyes that were pure purple. Not just the iris, all purple.

Her face was also strange. Pretty but alien, she looked more like a Darhel than even the Gamra did. Her face was long and elegant but he couldn't get the impression of a fox out of his head. Or, maybe, an elf.

"Duendtor Lerskel," Swodrath said, bowing. "The leader of the visitors, Lieutenant General Michael O'Neal."

Mike took off his helmet and nodded at the woman.

"Greetings, Lord O'Neal," the Duendtor said. Her voice was high and sibilant with an undertone that made Mike shiver. It was a very primitive reaction. His immediate desire was to worship her. He managed to suppress it, though. The Darhel had the same sort of voices and he'd gotten over any desire to "worship" them *fast*. "My lieges tell me that it is through your efforts that the scourge of the Pokree has been suppressed."

"Well, me and about twenty thousand shooters," Mike said, looking up into those purple eyes. "And a bunch of kinetic energy strikes. But, yeah. You're welcome."

"You are a sky traveler, I presume," Lerskel said.

"Glad you're taking this so well," Mike replied. "Yes, we're from the sky."

"We must speak," Lerskel said, raising a hand. "Privately."

If there were any protests at the audience being broken up so quickly they weren't vocalized. The crowd just filed out as a seat was brought over for O'Neal.

He looked at the spindly stool and shrugged.

"I think I'd better stand," he said. "No offense intended. But I'd break that."

"Stand or sit as you wish," Lerskel said, waving off the stool. "Many of the niceties have had to be foregone since the coming of the Pokree."

"Were you around for that?" Mike asked curiously.

"I was," Lerskel said. "Their sky fire could be seen from afar. I was the governor of this province of Hodoro. When first the Pokree landed we feared they were the Dareel. But it quickly became evident that they were not. Instead they were much worse. From where do you hail?"

"A planet called Earth," Mike said.

"I suspect this is Are," Lerskel said. "The cold planet, the planet of ice. Home."

"Probably not," Mike said. "I mean, we've got polar ice caps but it's not exactly Hoth."

"Our people left Are long ago," Lerskel said. "What do you know of the history of your planet?"

"Uh . . ." Mike said, then paused. "Wait. *How* long ago?"

"The exact duration has been lost," Lerskel said, pulling out a massive tome. "This, however, is the Book of Becoming. In its secret chapters are estimates by scholars. We came to this planet at least twenty thousand of our years ago."

"Shelly?" Mike asked.

"Thirty thousand years," the AID replied. "The Earth was in an ice age at that time. The Wurm Glaciation."

"I *said* that you should sit," the woman said, laughing sibilantly.

✧   ✧   ✧

"The Dareel," Mike said, looking at the picture in the book. Given a bit of hyperbole it looked like the Darhel. Sort of an evil Darhel on steroids but... Okay, it looked more like a Darhel than Darhel looked like Darhel. The inner truth, if you will.

"And the Innow," Lerskel said, turning to another page. "The makers and builders."

"Indowy," Mike said, nodding. The page wasn't in color but, again, with a bit of squinting it was pretty clear that the scary figures on the paper were Indowy. "I'm amazed you managed to keep this information for so long. So what happened to the Darhel and the rest?"

"Our people were all once as you and the commons," Lerskel said. "The first coming of the Dareel to our people is not recorded. But from the very first there were those who did not believe they were gods. The first portions of the Book are from tales told of the first coming. Then there are the Records which we have kept as accurately as we can. The Dareel gathered peoples from among the best and trained them. Some were trained in the ways of war, others in controlling the warriors. Those, who became the Duendtor, were the face of the People to the Dareel. The Dareel changed us to make us more palatable to their sight and to better control the Commons. They also created the methods for creating the Gamra.

"But always the Book of Becoming was kept. There were, among the Innow, those who opposed the Dareel. They found humans who felt the same, even among the Duendtor. But there was little we could do. The warriors, the Gamra especially, were fast in their belief that the Dareel were Gods.

"Many of the people that the Dareel gathered were

brought here, to Ackia, the land of Exile. There was something in the mountains that the Dareel wanted and the animals of this place were very dangerous. They used the People to protect the Innow as they labored.

"This went on for many years until the Dareel made a mistake. How they managed to break the worship of a Gamra was unclear, but a great rebellion broke out on Are. This was led by not just a Gamra but something greater and more fell. So fell that in time the Dareel fled Are. Word was sent of the rebellion on Are to here and we, in turn, revolted. It was hard to sway the warriors, and especially the Gamra, but enough were brought to the side of the People that we threw off the Dareel.

"The Dareel went away and left us to this world, our world of exile. We survived. The records of that time showed it was very hard. The magical weapons failed as soon as the Dareel left and we had to learn other ways of survival.

"There were wars fought between the peoples, assuredly. But we retained the Book against the day that the Dareel might return. We will have no more sky gods."

"Oh, hell," Mike said, when she was finished. "The Darhel are going to flip their lids when this comes out. People are going to go nuts."

"There is more," the woman said, flipping through the book. "There were no trainers of fighters among the Dareel. They could not fight."

"Still the same," Mike said, bitterly. "But damn can they manipulate."

"And they trained we Duendtor in the same," Lerskel said, turning the book around. "But these were our trainers of fighters. Which was why when the first Pokree came, we greeted them as friends."

The depiction was better in its way than that of either the Darhel or the Indowy. Clearly in the book a Posleen was training two humans in sword fighting.

"Oh, bloody hell."

"Okay, so thirty thousand years ago or so, the Darhel gathered a bunch of cavemen as guards," Mike said, his head in his hands.

The meeting was decidedly AID free. Like it or not, the boxes were not going to be in on *this* conference.

"*And* they were in contact with the Posleen," General Corval said. The corps chief of staff was medium height and nearly as pumped as his boss. "That's the part that's *really* got me furious. How much actual warning did they have of the Posleen invasion?"

"After tinkering with humans for a while they got a double rebellion on their hands," Mike said, ignoring the interjection. "And they left. So why are there no remains anywhere on Earth? Note: these Duendtor are probably nearly as tricky as a Darhel. I'm not taking *anything* on face value."

"Well, postulate that they had most of their Earthly infrastructure at one remote location," Colonel Ashland said. "Say an island. And they managed to sink it or something."

"Atlantis?" Mike asked, looking up. "You're serious."

"It's a very common myth in the Indo-European area," Ashland said, shrugging. "And this language is clearly Indo-European. The oral record could have been handed down in a garbled form for generations. Postulating that the Darhel also gave the sort of expanded lifetime that they gave to, well, us, that wouldn't be many generations."

"Methuselah now makes *so* much more sense," Corval said. "Not to mention how the Darhel had stuff like rejuv and Hiberzine ready, immediately, for human use."

"The problem is that there's nothing we can do with this," Mike said. "It's nothing but a ticking nuke in our hands. There is no way that the Darhel are going to let this story get disseminated."

"Be pretty hard to stop," General Corval said. "There are nearly twenty thousand members of the corps. And, trust me, the story is all over. At least that there are humans here."

"Recall all those stories about missing colony ships, General?" Colonel Ashland said. "I've seen the confidential reports.. They weren't all rumors and they weren't all, or even mostly, accidents."

"You don't think they'd..." Corval said, then swallowed. "That's *sick*!"

"To cover *this* up?" Mike asked. "Oh, yeah. They'd dump us all into a hole in hyperspace in a second. I've been wondering when it was going to happen, anyway. The cost of demobilizing the corps would be saved."

"Well, the hell if I'm going to get dumped into space," General Corval said, setting his jaw. "If it was just *my* life, that would be one thing. But—"

"But I'm responsible for the lives of twenty thousand troopers," Mike said, nodding. "There's just one problem. We don't control the ships."

"Easy enough to change that," Colonel Ross Swartzbaugh said. The Corps G-3 was medium height and build and prematurely bald. He covered that up by shaving his head like a cueball. "Not sure what we'd do once we took them, but we've got a corps of ACS. Various opportunities come to mind."

"Every ship requires an AID to operate," Mike said. "You think they're not going to get an update telling them to dump us the first time we get near a sat? And the ships are keyed to specific AIDs. Prevents mutiny."

"Which is what we're contemplating, you realize," Colonel Ashland said.

"Not really," Mike said. "I mean, I'm still trying to figure a way around it. I just don't see one. Well, there's one."

"What?" General Corval asked.

"We send the ships back empty," Mike said. "Just sit tight here. Tell them we misunderstood the orders or something. If the ships make it back, they'll ask us what the fuck happened. I mean, a whole *corps* missing movement? But if they *don't*, they might never know."

"And we'll be marooned on this dirtball," Colonel Swartzbaugh said, rubbing his head. "Not my first choice. And how, exactly, do we explain it to the corps?"

"Lie," Mike said. "Tell them we were ordered to stand down and await transport. In a year or so it might get sticky. But they'll be alive."

There was a knock at the door and Mike looked at it furiously. Rawls had very direct orders not to interfere.

"Get it," he said, gesturing with his chin to Colonel Ashland.

"Sir, I'm sorry," Rawls said. "There's an Indowy out here saying he has to talk to you *now*. He says that he has information that you need about what you're talking about. He's really exercised. He said if I didn't let him in he was going to quote rip my head off and shit in my neck."

Mike looked at the NCO blankly for a moment.

"An *Indowy* said that to you?" Colonel Ashland said incredulously.

"Yes, sir," Rawls said, caught between his own incredulity and humor. "An Indowy."

"Show him in," Mike said. "Then shut the door."

The Indowy was, as far as Mike could tell, pretty much identical to any mid-level Indowy worker. Mid-years, about a hundred in other words. Totally indistinguishable from any of a trillion of the prolific species.

"Exalted Lord O'Neal," the Indowy said, prostrating himself. The term was one the Indowy had bestowed on Mike after his actions on Diess. It translated, as far as Mike could tell, as something like "Duke." It wasn't a clan lord but about the same status. It generally got bestowed on particularly good scientists and the Indowy equivalent of lawyers. As far as Mike was aware he was the only human with the rank and also the only warrior. "I am Indowy Tak Ockist Um'Dare. I see you."

"I see you, Indowy Tak," Mike said. "Stand and speak."

"Exalted Lord," Tak said. "You have made contact with People of the Book."

"You know about People of the Book," Mike asked, leaning back. "Why am I not surprised."

"I did not know, myself, Exalted Lord, until recently," Tak said nervously. "Exalted Lord, I am . . . Exalted Lord, this is a very long story."

"I've already heard one," Mike said, gesturing to a station chair. "Tell me. Tell me all of it, Tak. Every bit you know."

"They're what?" Cally said.

Cally O'Neal was fifty-eight and looked to be about twenty. Officially listed as killed in one of the last battles of the Siege of Earth, for most of those fifty-eight years she had been an agent of the Bane Sidhe, the secret underground among the Indowy and humans that worked to overthrow the Darhel rule. And for most of that period she'd been primarily an assassin.

In the last decade, though, things had changed in so many ways it seemed as if change would never slow down. First there was the mission where she'd met James Stewart. They'd started off as enemies fighting each other in secret and ended as lovers. Stewart had faked his own death but refused to join the Bane Sidhe. Instead he'd entered the Tongs, the Chinese mafia that had taken over most of the organized crime among humans, and fought his own battles from that vantage. He and Cally had married in secret but of late they'd had to even break off the most cursory contact.

His connections had been of premium value when Cally's sister, Michelle, had used them along with some stolen nannite codes to take down an entire Darhel clan. Michelle wasn't Bane Sidhe, either; the Darhel had just crossed the wrong human. Michelle was a Sohon mentat, a wielder of almost magical powers over space, time and matter. But she still was indebted to the Darhel. Or had been until she, Cally and Stewart had managed, through a combination of luck and deviousness, to buy her free *and* bankrupt her Darhel bankers.

The mission where Cally had met Stewart had caused a sundering in the Bane Sidhe, most of the organization splitting off from the O'Neal faction. But the response to the take-down of the Epetar Clan had included, among other things, a massive crackdown on the Bane Sidhe. The faction that had tossed the O'Neals aside ended up screaming for help.

The O'Neals had pulled their chestnuts out of the fire. But Papa O'Neal, the man who had been a *real* father to her for most of her life, had been killed by the ACS response team. An ACS response team commanded, by one of those horrible coincidences in life, by her own father.

So Cally was anything but charitable to their "fellows."

"Back up to the beginning, Terool," Father O'Reilly said. The monsignor had been a member of the Earthly Bane Sidhe since before the return of the Darhel. Bane Sidhe translated roughly as "The Death of Elves." It had remained hidden within "secret societies" since before the dawn of history. It had remnants of prehistory fable that were passed down, but none of it had ever been clear. He might, finally, get some of it filled in.

"The Darhel co-opted human guards long ago," the Indowy Terool said. He had been one of the leaders of the anti-O'Neal faction in the Bane Sidhe, so revealing the secrets he was about to reveal was like pulling teeth. "They were gathered mostly from Western Europe and the Mediterranean. They were trained on a small continent where the Azores are presently placed. There was a revolt, here *and* on Akoria, the planet your father just 'reclaimed' from the Posleen. Here on Earth a Darhel was sacrificed to lintatai to cause a massive earth movement under the continent, effectively sinking it by several hundred feet. Finding the traces of what you humans call 'Atlantis' would be very difficult even for us. But they are there.

"Your father's corps was probing along the spinward axis of the spiral arm. Akoria is on the anti-spinward axis. None of the Darhel found it of moment that the reclamation was in that region. It should have taken years for your father's corps to reach Akoria and the end of the reclamation program was well on its way to fruition.

"However, word has come back that instead of slowly proceeding across the arm, the corps jumped to the far side. Why is unclear. But they have Akoria, which they refer to as 'R-1496 Delta,' on their list. They should have reached there by now. And there is no way that they could miss traces of human habitation."

"The Posleen took the planet," Father O'Reilly said. "That will pretty much erase traces of humans."

"Even at the height of the war there were humans hiding in deep jungle and high mountains," the Indowy said patiently. "You are very hard to wipe out completely, just as the Posleen are hard to wipe out completely."

"Point," Cally said. "But get back to the corps."

"The Darhel are unwilling to allow this secret to be revealed," Terool said. "Very unwilling. Unwilling enough to destroy the entire task force."

"That would be pretty hard to do," Cally said.

"Every ship is controlled by the AIDs," Terool said. "As are the suits. They will simply enter hyper and never exit."

"That wouldn't just violate the Compact," Cally said, furiously. "It would break it beyond *belief*! Do they *want* all-out war?"

"There are too many members of the corps to cover this up," Terool said. "And if people become aware that the Darhel have been manipulating humans for this long there will be ... other questions asked."

"About the colonist ships," Cally said, bitterly. "About fucking with us during the war. About why China was wiped out."

"Indeed," Father O'Reilly said. "But they must know what the response of the Bane Sidhe would be to something like this. There would be no end to the blood."

"We are weak," Terool said. "Their response to your ill-advised attack on the Pardal Clan nearly destroyed us!"

"Nearly destroyed *you*, you mean," Cally said harshly.

"Us," Father O'Reilly said, placatingly. "We are not enemies."

"Tell that to *them*," Cally snapped. "*They* were the bastards that fucked with my head then left us out to dry when I managed to break conditioning. Just talking to this fucker is making me sick. And now he's suggesting that we just let the Darhel wipe out thirty thousand soldiers and sailors? The Compact is inviolate! If it's not there's no point to this whole charade!"

"Are they sending the orders to destroy the task force?" Father O'Reilly asked.

"They are already sent," Terool said miserably.

"Can we intercept them?" Cally asked. "Corrupt them?"

"It would be ... difficult," Terool said.

"I don't care for *difficult*," Cally said. "Can you *do* it?"

"Perhaps," Terool said. "And then again perhaps not."

"And there's more," Father O'Reilly said.

"We must clarify this matter," Terool said.

"Indowy think that they are inscrutable to humans," Father O'Reilly said. "And, indeed, to most humans they are. But not to all. What else?"

"I'm more worried about the Fleet," Cally said. "And, okay, my *bastard* of a father."

"He is your clan lord," Terool said, upset.

"He can rot in hell for all I care," Cally snapped. "But I don't want the damned Darhel to leave him stuck in hyper until his air runs out."

"Terool!" Father O'Reilly said. "Tell us!"

"It is about . . . your father," Terool said, miserably. "You see, the Darhel . . ."

"Owe you a lot of money," Tak said.

"Define a lot," Mike said. "I've been paid way too much as it is."

"Exalted Lord," Tak said, carefully. "Recently, you may have heard, a Darhel Clan fell."

"Epetar," Colonel Ashland said.

"The same," Tak said. "The were, in fact, destroyed. By your daughter, Michelle."

"Really?" Mike said. He got a message from Michelle every year at Christmas. If she'd taken down a Darhel Clan it was news to him. "*Good* for her!"

"There were others working with her, Bane Sidhe and Tong. But it was primarily your clan which did this. The Darhel could not react against you nor against Michelle. But they would much wish to."

"Why couldn't they?" General Corval asked.

"Early in the conflict against the Posleen one of your generals, General Taylor, began a program to investigate Darhel manipulation of both politicians and war supplies."

"That's what got him killed," Mike said, nodding. "Isn't it?"

"Indeed, Exalted Lord," Tak said, carefully. "However, some of your people, notably the Cyberpunks and human factions of the Bane Sidhe reacted. They killed several high-level Darhel and missed the Tir Dol Ron by a mere shred."

"Too bad they missed," Corval said.

"Thus was the Compact born," Tak said. "The Darhel would not attack current duty humans and the Cybers and the human Bane Sidhe, of whom the Cybers are now a faction, would not kill Darhel."

"This is making my head hurt," General Corval said. "Ancient societies. Midnight assassinations. Darhel manipulation. Does any of this have a point?"

"This is the last point," Tak said. "I do not know if even my masters are aware of this fact. It was contained in the communication to the Ceel that I intercepted when he went into lintatai. Further complicating things are that each of you is owed much more money than the Darhel ever told you. General O'Neal, for certain specific reasons, is owed ... Well, the amount that your daughter used to take down the Pardal clan is but a fraction of what you are owed. One tenth of all you recover is, by rights, property of the capturers."

"Yeah," Mike said. "I know. We picked up a few billion credits worth here off those Posleen forges we captured intact."

"The full implications were never explored," Tak said. "Let me ask you this, General. On Diess. Would the planet have fallen absent your actions?"

"Oh, I doubt it," Mike said. "There was a whole corps there and they were getting some pretty solid defenses built."

"Bullshit, sir," General Corval said. "We've all seen the analysis. You hamstrung the Posleen at a critical juncture, the schwerpunkt. The Line would have fallen if the full weight fell on it. And you took out the only God King using airmobile in that battle. To answer his question without the false modesty, yes, Tak, it would have."

"Thus you, General O'Neal, are owed ten percent of the gross production value of Diess," Tak said. "For the entire period of your life. Oh, some is owed to the many other soldiers and officers in the battle. But a large percentage of it falls to your account. Equally other planets. There are many humans who are owed much by the Darhel. But especially with penalties and interest, you are far in advance of them. You have done almost nothing *but* fight the Posleen for decades. Led critical defenses of multiple cities on Earth. Holding the pass in Rabun Gap gives you a margin of all goods and services in the Central North American provinces. Several of the recovery worlds of which you were a senior commander are now producing goods. You have gotten none of these additional monies. Your current calculated worth, according to the message, is approximately fifteen percent of *all the Darhel clans'* worth. Mostly due to penalties. Payable, as all Darhel debts are, immediately and in full at your request."

"Nobody has that much capital," Mike said, blinking.

"That is the point," Tak replied. "If you call their

debt, every Darhel clan in the galaxy is immediately and totally bankrupt."

"Good God," Cally said, her eyes wide. "Holy... How in the hell did the Darhel let that happen?"

"They wrote a very bad law," Terool said. "Back when we were first attacked by the Posleen. They attempted to buy our action. But we rejected them. The Way is the only way that we choose. So they kept increasing the amount they were willing to pay if we would only fight. But we would rather die than stray from the Way. So now they owe your father, all humanity for that matter, for a fraction of the price of the entire Confederation plus all the recovered worlds. They knew this from the beginning. But they also thought the humans would never figure it out."

"You could have told us," Father O'Reilly said dryly.

"All those years I was scrimping and scraping and little did I know my daddy owned the Galaxy," Cally said bitterly. "Wait, if they kill him in deep space..."

"It all reverts," Father O'Reilly said. "Galactic law holds, not Earth's. No inheritance."

"I thought it reverted to the Clan," Cally said.

"Not if he doesn't transfer it, first," Father O'Reilly said. "And he has to be in a Galactic Court to do the transfer. And it has to be accepted by the Court. Which is made up of..."

"Darhel," Cally said, bitterly. "Right. Like they're going to accept him turning it over to the Clan."

"There is one option, but it is poorly known and even more poorly understood, even by Indowy," Terool said. "He can make suit to the Aldenata..."

❖   ❖   ❖

"They're legends," Mike said. "I mean, I know you Indowy think they're gods, even the Posleen refer to them, if in less than affectionate terms, but..."

"They are not legend," Tak said. "I cannot believe I am saying this but it is necessary. And I think my time among...among humans has worn upon me. But this is the best chance I have ever *heard of* to destroy the Darhel monopoly. It must be taken. This is the truth. The Aldenata exist. They are as real as you or I. But they are ancient, old beyond belief. And...changed. They no longer exist as you or I but in another form. But they are the ultimate judges of all the actions of the Darhel as well as the Indowy and the Tchpth. We are the Children of the Aldenata. They are our masters. They can compel the Darhel to pay you, in cash if necessary. And if you place your plea before the Aldenata then it may be heard. It will be slow, though. And if you perish in the interim, the suit is closed."

"So, what you're telling me is that, A, the Darhel want me, not to mention my entire corps, dead because I know about their manipulation of humans from prehistory," Mike said. "And, B, they want me dead because I've got the financial potential to destroy them in an instant. And my only chance of back-up is some sort of super-being that might or might not even bother to hear me? And if they manage to whack me in the meantime, that the suit is closed. Which effectively puts a several trillion credit...no, probably more than that, price on my head? Not to mention stuck in the ass end of the galaxy with no ship home I can trust?"

"Whoa," General Corval said. "I thought *I* was fucked, sir."

❖   ❖   ❖

"Okay, this is coming at me a little fast," Cally said, shaking her head. "Forget the super-beings, although we're going to have a *talk* later, Terool. Forget Daddy Dearest owning the Darhel and not the other way around. We've got a corps about to get 'losted' if we don't do something. Let's just focus on that."

"Even if we could intercept the orders, it would only be a stop-gap," Terool said. "And it would reveal many of our most prized sources, the few we have left. When the Darhel realized the task force had not been destroyed they would be more thorough. And since they now realize the depth of our penetration they will undoubtedly send redundant messages to Tirs on distant worlds to ensure its destruction."

"There has to be *something* we can do," Cally said desperately. Her faction had fought as hard as it could against the "accidents" with colony transports. But terrible as those were, the loss of an entire corps of ACS was... The horror was beyond fathoming.

"What about Michelle?" Cally continued.

"You can contact your sister, of course," Terool said. "But I'm unsure she can do more than we are attempting. The Sohon have abilities sometimes beyond understanding. But they are not gods."

"I'll send her a message," Cally said, her face hard. "But if we fail? If they destroy the corps?"

"Destroying the corps, indeed any killing of an acting service person, is a violation of the Compact," Terool said.

"So you agree?" Cally said, her eyes lighting. "This is open season on Darhel?"

"Yes," Terool said, sighing. "That time has come. Or is coming at least."

"I can't exactly be happy that it takes losing several thousand soldiers for that," Cally said, rubbing her hands. "But... I'm gonna get to kill Darhelll..." she started to sing, dancing and waving her hands in the air. "I'm gonna get to kill Darhelllll..."

"Unless we need them," Father O'Reilly said.

"What?"

"We need them."

Sixteen minds linked across four thousand light years. The youngest of the Queens was a bare thousand years old, the eldest had seen the near death of their race and the Long Flight. Each had lived long lives as other entities, scouts, workers, managers, scientists then warriors. Neuter, male and finally female, they were the best their race could offer to the vagaries of fate.

Between them, although they did not track every sparrow on every world, they knew the comings and goings, the machinations, plans, wars of every sentient race in the galaxy. Minds like cold computers watched those races, tended them like rose gardens, built alliances, often on both sides of mortal conflicts, built each of them as potential allies against the day that their race might once again face The Enemy.

And now was that day. Not The Enemy but another race fleeing them. A race equally as inimical, *nearly* as deadly. But... not quite.

Rheldlche was one of the youngest. Not headstrong—no Queen was—but far less cautious than, say, Shulkin, the Ancient One.

"The Hedren come. The human ACS is the best weapon against the Hedren in my region."

"We would have to Expose," Larrghgha replied. The older Queen controlled the region the humans called the Scutum-Crux. One of the first of the newer generation, She was Rheldlche's mother, not that that meant anything between Queens. Genetic derivation meant little to the Himmit. Besides, they all were children of Skulkin in one way or another. "Such an action would be impossible to Hide."

"Agreement."

Shulkin rarely entered into discussions in the last hundred years. The Ancient One was nearing senescence. But her word was still law in the galaxy.

"There is a replacement for the ACS," the Ancient One said. "Emphasize increases among the Sohon. It is time to release the humans from their thrall. And make contact with their former enemies."

CHAPTER FOUR

In fragments of an instant
The chaos has returned
And all that was left to sentiment
Beneath the banner burned
— Crüxshadows
"Eye of the Storm"

"We cannot keep meeting like this," Michelle said, taking a careful sip from the bulb of distilled water.

"Hey, *you* started this," Cally replied to her sister, taking a less cautious sip from her beer. She wasn't taking an anti-alcohol pill so it was not going to have much more effect than water. "And this is too important to use the chain. I take it we're not being monitored."

"Of course not," Michelle said. "Nonetheless, *you* could have been followed."

"In your *dreams*, God-girl," Cally snapped.

"Important," Michelle said, ignoring the jibe.

"It's about . . . Dad," Cally said, sighing.

"Father?" Michelle asked, raising an eyebrow.

Cally hated when she did that. It made her look just too damned much like a certain TV character. She was pretty sure her sister did it on purpose.

"Yes, 'Father'," Cally said. "He's gotten himself in the deep cacky."

She briefly and more or less coherently explained what had only recently been brought to her attention. Reading Michelle, except for the very few times her sister got angry, was difficult. But Cally was pretty sure something was starting to get Michelle mighty pissed.

"The Bane Sidhe know about this?" Michelle asked. "The interference of the Darhel over centuries?"

"Well who do you think *I* got it from?" Cally asked. "The tooth fairy?"

"I find that simply fascinating," Michelle said. "Because as far as I was aware, I had been brought in on all the great secrets held by the clan masters and Sohon. And I surely was unaware. I wonder what *else* they failed to inform me of."

"Does your pride really *matter* right now?" Cally said. "There is an entire corps of ACS on the line. And our father's life!"

"We must, of course, do what we can for our Clan Leader," Michelle said. "However, the fact that I was not informed of any of this has large implications. A Sohon must constantly tread a fine line. Without knowing the potential stumbling blocks in the way, it is difficult to do so. I must meet with the other human Sohon and determine if it is only I who was left in ignorance. Given the political mess you created, that is possible."

"I was sort of hoping that you could use your magic god powers to save his *ass*," Cally hissed, leaning forward. "Hello! Father! Clan Leader? Not to mention a few thousand other humans? Tens of thousands?"

"Oh, you are so impatient," Michelle replied disparagingly. She gave a slight shake of her head, then closed her eyes. "The orders are *not* to have the fleet lost in hyperspace."

"Oh, thank God," Cally said. "You're sure?"

"I did not say that you would *like* the orders," Michelle said, opening her eyes. "Because you won't. And worse. Even with my powers, we're too late."

"Nice job, General."

The camp had taken only a day to emplace despite the fact that they'd done it no more than a couple of times before. It helped that the tents were memory plastic.

But in a day there were thermally pressed streets, living tents, mess tents, supply, maintenance, all the things that made for a functioning small city. And a wall. Mike made it a habit to put in a berm whenever they were in place for more than a day. With a corps of ACS and shovels that were tough enough it was a bit easier than with an equal number of engineers and bulldozers. Before the gates flapped the shot-torn banner of the corps, a boar on a red field and the slogan *"Disce Pati."*

The Eleventh Corps was settling in for a rest with all the trimmings. Not a long one but it was nice to feel wind on your face and get that damned armor off on a planet.

Some of the troops were wandering those streets,

visiting friends from other companies and battalions, headed to the chapel, headed to the rec rooms and mess halls. But not many. Mike would guess that most of them were racked out. Later he'd have to figure out something to keep them occupied but for now they were content to just rest, all but the very few—no more than a short company—still suited up to guard the perimeter on the off chance of a Posleen feral showing up.

It was a sham, of course. Until they figured out a way to get back to Earth, safely, this was home. Which was why he'd had *all* the rations from the ships shuttled down.

"We've got supplies for about ninety days," General Corval said. "So we should be good for a six week R & R. I've already placed thirty percent on complete standdown. We'll rotate that week by week."

"Works," Mike said. There were some of the corps on security around the camp. It was unlikely there would be an attack by the locals. They'd made contact with the other two tribes in the area and negotiated a cease-fire in their low-grade fights. With the Posleen wiped away from the lowlands the tribes were mostly squabbling over who got what territory, anyway. It was a time to talk, not fight.

"We'll need to get a training schedule in place," Mike said. "When they get rested, given that the recreation is going to be pretty damned limited here, we're going to have to keep them occupied or—"

"Incoming message from Admiral Suntoro," Shelly said.

"Crap," Mike muttered. "Any idea what he wants?"

"No."

Monosyllables again. Not a good sign.

"Put him on."

"General O'Neal," the admiral said, appearing as a hologram in front of the two officers. "I need to meet with you and your staff. Immediately."

"Gosh, Admiral, that's going to be hard," Mike replied. "We're kinda busy right now."

"I am in receipt of some orders that I think we need to discuss in person," the admiral replied. "I am willing to meet with you on the surface if you don't have time to shuttle up to the ship."

Mike raised an eyebrow at that and shrugged.

"Sure, Admiral," he said, smiling tightly. "I take it you don't want to meet at the camp?"

"The quieter we keep this the better," the admiral replied. "It looks as if you were right."

"I'll lay out an LZ," Mike said. "When?"

"One hour?"

"Works. O'Neal out."

He looked at Corval and smiled thinly again.

"I think the admiral's running scared. How say you?"

"I think we'd better wear armor."

"Oh, yeah."

Julio wasn't wandering the camp. He was off duty and had obtained permission to "liaison with the locals."

At present that consisted of accompanying Urnhat up a steep slope. The general had hinted that he wanted a place to put some caches of gear and the Nor knew all the caves in the area. According to the Nor queen or whatever she was there was an extensive series in this area of the valley. Not as big as where the Nor had hid from the Posleen, but big enough to put some gear.

Despite the fact that he was on a semi-official mission, he'd left his AID behind. Some of the guys didn't care what an AID saw. He was still too green for that. Sometimes three were a crowd even if one of them *was* an artificial intelligence.

Of course that left a bit of difficulty with conversation, but he was slogging ahead. A guy could dream.

"This is real pretty country," he said, more or less to himself.

The girl turned her head and smiled at him, then gabbled in the local language.

"I know, I'm an idiot," Julio replied, stopping and touching a plant, lightly. He'd learned from even his limited experience that some plants were nasty.

"What's this?" he asked.

"Shundi," Urnhat replied.

"That tells me so much," the trooper said, laughing. "I grew up in a city, a Sub-Urb. I never saw the stars till I was in training. Much less green plants. For all I know, this could be one of the plants from Earth."

"Urt," Urnhat said. "Are?" She lifted her head and clicked her tongue, the local equivalent of a head shake. "Akri." She walked to another of the bushes and pulled at the leaves, stripping some of them off. "Are," she said, holding them out.

Looking at the two plants Julio could see some differences. Colors were different, but plants could be all sorts of colors. But the leaves of the local plant didn't have veins.

"Caves?" he asked, gesturing up the slope. "Holes?"

"Gafe," the girl said, gesturing and continuing to walk. "Tang seeu."

"Yeah," Julio said. "Thank you, too."

He looked over his shoulder at the distant camp then frowned as a group of suits left the front gate and began bounding towards the southern ridgeline. They looked to be in a hurry.

"Thanks for leaving me behind," General Corval said over the net.

"Somebody had to keep things running with me gone," Mike said, bounding up the slope.

"Humph," the chief of staff replied. "You just wanted to go running."

"I hate running and you know it," Mike said as the group of suits reached the crest. They bounded downslope to a reasonably flat spot and Mike dropped a dust-off beacon.

"Sensors report a shuttle inbound," General Corval said.

"Right on time," Mike replied. "Any more of them or just the one?"

There wasn't a reply and he frowned.

"Corval, anything else? Shelly, what's wrong with commo?"

"We have a solid link with the camp communications," the AID replied.

"Retrans the sensor data to me," Mike said, his forehead wrinkling.

"I am unable to access that data at this time, General."

Mike's spine went cold and he looked upwards. He could see the heat track of the shuttle inbound but now he didn't need sensors to see what *else* was inbound.

❖   ❖   ❖

Something made Julio look up and then he stopped, frozen in his tracks. He might be nearly totally green, but he knew what he was looking at in an instant.

"INCOMING!" he screamed, diving and hitting Urnhat at the knees.

The girl reacted like a wildcat, twisting in his grip and getting in a solid kick to his ribs. Julio didn't care, though, as long as she was down. He rolled to the side and covered his head with his arms.

"Get *down*, you stupid bitch!"

Mike bounded to the top of the slope just as the first of the projectiles impacted. The troops had probably gone to ground but against an orbital strike there wasn't much they could do.

He had at least expected the security ACS to be firing upwards. There wasn't much they could do against a KEW, it was after all not much more than a chunk of steel, but they might have intercepted a couple. He expected them to go down fighting. But there was no fire headed upwards.

The first projectile hit to the west of the camp, the second to the east then it became too fast to follow. It was clear, though, that the strike was intended to contain even ACS and pulverize them into nothing. It went on and on and on, continuous concentric strikes until where the camp had been was nothing but a churned crater.

The whole corps was gone.

Mike started to step forward, to do what he didn't know, when his suit pinged.

"General, your shuttle is here."

It was such a normal voice, a sentence he'd heard

dozens, hundreds of times before. As if nothing had happened.

Mike spun in place and brought up his guns automatically, fired at the descending shuttle.

Nothing happened. Nothing damned HAPPENED. "Shelly! Guns!"

"Guns are inactive, General," the AID said in a chirpy voice. "It's time to board the shuttle. You are ordered to do so out of the suit. Should I eject?"

The shuttle landed and a platoon of masters-at-arms deployed, covering the four ACS suits with what would normally be totally inadequate hand-lasers. The MAs were hated by Fleet Strike personnel since, well, they were *Fleet* and they acted more as admiral's bullies than police. And they seemed to take inordinate pleasure on beating up on Strike personnel whenever they got the chance. Fleet Strike tended to return the favor. Currently, they looked nervous and he wondered at the inanity of that thought.

His corps was gone. The masters-at-arms looked nervous.

"Incoming call from Admiral Suntoro. Go ahead Admiral."

"Michael Leonidas O'Neal, you and your staff are under arrest for treason. AID, open the suits."

Mike took a breath of air as the suit opened against his will, then stepped out onto the grassy sward. Four of the masters-at-arms were approaching, two with lasers and two with sonic stunners.

"Do not attempt to resist this fully authorized detention," the admiral's voice continued to say over the speakers of Mike's suit. "The masters-at-arms are authorized to use lethal force at the slightest sign of resistance."

Mike couldn't have resisted if they'd paid him. His entire family was dead and now the corps that he had nurtured like a flower was just...

The other three officers looked equally dazed but slowly raised their hands as the MAs approached. The group facing them in a semi-circle suddenly raised their lasers and opened fire, cutting them down.

Mike watched as Bobby Ashland fell back in the low scrub, his chest slashed nearly through by a laser. Bobby had come over to the corps as the ACS had slowly been reduced. They'd never met during the Siege but had gotten along over the years. Mike had been glad when Bobby had been assigned as his Intel officer. He knew that Bobby always had his finger on the pulse of not only "threats forward" as he'd come to call them but what was going on back in the corridors of power.

This was one threat neither of them had seen coming. Not this way.

"General O'Neal, get on the ground with your hands behind your back," one of the MAs said. "Down!"

"What?" Mike asked, still looking at Colonel Ashland.

"Get on the ground!"

"What?" Mike said again then lifted his eyes. His brow furrowed down then there was no thought.

"Like hell!" he shouted, charging forward.

He had hoped for the lasers. There was just nothing left. There was not a damned thing in the world to live for anymore. Even revenge was impossible to achieve.

But they got him with the stunners instead.

As he flopped to the ground, his entire body jangling, all he could still see was the mangled body of Bobby Ashland.

Gone.

CHAPTER FIVE

...I have watched the path of angels
And I have heard the heavens roar
There is strife within the tempest
But calm in the eye of the storm
                    —Crüxshadows
                        "Eye of the Storm"

I have investigated my sister's claims, Michelle thought. *Once I was aware of them.*

The seven individuals were, unquestionably, the most powerful humans in the galaxy. There were presidents and prime ministers aplenty. Commanders of powerful fleets. Chiefs of major corporations by the hundreds.

But there were, to date, only seven human Sohon mentats.

Very few people understood them. Taken from their parents at a young age, raised entirely by the Indowy, they stood apart from the normal ruck of humanity already. Add to that minds that could wield extraordinary power, yet had been inculcated from that same very early age with an abhorrence of violence and a strong sense of duty and responsibility. Add again that, due to the nature of their exile, every single one of them came from a military family. They may have been taken from their parents young, but from their mother's milk they still drew an essential sense of "Duty, Honor, Country."

Their "Country" had changed, enlarged to fill a reasonable quadrant of the galaxy. But the Duty and Honor remained. And it might have shaped the fact that every single one of them, independently, as soon as they learned how to truly manipulate matter at the very smallest level, tried to see if they could get it to blow up.

One of their number had proven, though, that being too inflexible in the whole "Duty" thing was not necessarily good. Perhaps the power had warped Eric or perhaps he had started off warped. But it was possible for a Sohon to go very, very bad through the best of intentions. Eric's fall remained a moral tale for them all. And since it turned out that they *could* get matter to blow up, and more, every decision of weight had, since then, been taken in council.

I see the data, Thomas replied. *And more. This action on the part of the Darhel breaks their Compact.*

They were not in the same room nor even in the same solar systems. But their method of telepathy was virtually instantaneous across any distance or dimension. The "virtually" being of interest only to particle physicists and mentats.

The Tir Dol Ron has already left Earth, Minnie noted. *He is surely high on their list. And two*

Darhel have already died in what are being reported as "accidents."

I am unsure of our action in this regard, Michelle admitted. *The corps is gone by now. We cannot undo that even if we wished. If my father has been incarcerated, should we act?*

Have you an emotional attachment to this? Thomas asked. He was the oldest of them by barely a pair of years. Also the weakest. But he had been a leader among the "Lost Boys" from the beginning and still retained a vestige of that position.

I find myself torn, yes, Michelle admitted. *However, it is less that he is my father and Clan Leader than that the Darhel are in breach of numerous contracts and obligations. If they are willing to become this high-handed, how can any of us trust the Contract? Most of us still labor under contract. If the Darhel have thrown off the Rules, what is to keep them from acting with complete arbitrariness?*

Can we convince a Clan Leader to submit his appeal? Chan asked. *This would both teach the Darhel the danger of breaking contracts and, potentially, save your father's life. On a purely personal level, it would place the Darhel in a position of being unable to fulfill their part of our contracts, thus freeing us.*

Unlikely, Koko replied. *Any clan doing so would be Called in a moment. It would be suicide for the entire clan.*

The vast majority of the first Fleet had been drawn from European and North American sources. Thus most of the children sent into exile had been from America, Britain and Germany. Koko Takawashi and Kang Chan were the only two mentats not from such countries. Indeed, all but two of the others were from the former United States. It had been debated, given the disparity, if Japanese and Chinese might make better Sohon adepts naturally. Thus far there was insufficient data. Given that the Race of Han had been severely reduced during the War, as had the Japanese, it might not ever be resolved.

I believe there may be one, Michelle thought, *But the moment the Darhel heard of the appeal, they would terminate my father. I am unsure why they have not done so already.*

I see the hand of Tir Dol Ron in that one, Thomas thought with just a note of emotion in his telepathic communication. *He enjoys watching individuals suffer.*

Being the mentat with the most experience of that particular Tir, he would know.

There is a concept, Ermintrude thought. The sole English mentat's mind was clearly racing. *The Darhel cannot kill him if he is not available to them.*

"So you want our help again?" Cally said.

"It would be obvious if the Sohon acted directly," Michelle replied. "And I, of course, must keep a very respectable distance. This is the last contact we shall have until resolution of this crisis. If you see Father and he asks of me tell him that I hold him as dead, as galactic law decrees. I shall resolve this issue when I see him at last."

"So what's the plan?" Cally asked.

"The first part you will not care for," Michelle said. "You must be patient."

"I'm not good with patient," Cally said. "How patient?"

"It will be nearly a year before we can act."

"That's okay," Cally said. "I can spend the time killing Darhel."

"And you must not do that."

"Oh, we are *so* going to have to talk 'when this issue is resolved.'"

Mike opened his eyes and blinked, gummily. His mouth felt like someone had stuffed it with cotton. Damned Hiberzine.

Hiberzine was only one of a number of amazing drugs the Galactics had brought with them. One dose would put a person down for a half a year with no ill effects. They could even be in conditions of minimal oxygen for a few months. He'd once been damned near ripped in half and left under the sea for weeks. Between his suit's undergel and Hiberzine he'd survived.

One dose was fine. But after a half a year even with the best nannites working their little biomechanical asses off you got sort of dehydrated. Push it any further and you got *really* dehydrated. He'd been down longer than half a year.

"Fuckers could have given me a damned IV," he muttered.

He was manacled to the wall of a cell. Whoever had given him the antidote had apparently beat feet afterwards. All he had were four plasteel walls, a cot, a table and a sink/toilet combination. Oh, and a bottle of water. How thoughtful.

He drank the bottle of water in one go, then dragged his chain to the sink and filled it again. Three drains and it was time to take a very *long* piss.

Gray walls, orange jump-suit. Not much to work

with. He contemplated the steel chain and the plasteel wall. Plasteel was about ten times the strength of standard carbon steel. Oh, well, either the chain would get worn out or he'd cut his way into the next room. Which was probably another cell. He set to rubbing one link of the chain on the wall, over and over. Molecule by molecule the steel started to fleck away. At this rate he'd be into the next cell in about a century but nobody was quite sure how long a life rejuv gave you, so what the hell.

He wasn't sure how long it was till the door opened. Food had appeared out of an unexpected slot in the far wall at one point. He'd taken a dump and a couple of pisses, filled and drained his water bottle several times, taken a nap, worn one face of the steel link shiny and made an almost unnoticeable groove in the wall. Say a day or two. Hell, he'd once lain in his suit in total EMCON and underground for longer than that. If you couldn't handle sensory deprivation and boredom, ACS was no place for you.

They'd sent six guards with stunners. For all he knew there were more in the corridor beyond. One of them was unarmed; he just held the shackles.

None of them were, individually, all that big. Fleet mostly drew from Indonesia and Southeast Asia; their personnel didn't run to tall.

Mike wasn't tall, either, but he was broad as a house. He'd been a work-out freak since before he'd ever heard of the Posleen and fifty years as an officer hadn't changed anything. He might not be the biggest runner in the world, but he could lift an ACS suit with one hand, which was right at the strain gauge of the human muscles and bones involved. He figured that even with the stunners he could probably take down four or so, if he hadn't been chained to the wall.

So he just held out his arms to be shackled.

He was led down empty corridors to a room very much like the one he'd been sitting in. There were four differences. No toilet or sink, which wasn't going to be good if this went on too long. There was a video monitor on the wall. The table was bigger and had two seats. And there was a Fleet commander sitting in one of the chairs.

Mike was frog-marched to the far chair, seated in it and shackled down, hard. He could barely move his arms or legs.

"Michael Leonidas O'Neal," the commander said without preamble. "Lieutenant General, Fleet Strike. Serial Number 216-29-1145. Entered Fleet Strike from the state of Georgia in the nation of the United States, Earth. Is all of that correct?"

Mike just looked at him. The commander had more of a Chinese look than Indonesian. But it was unlikely he was directly descended from the Mainland given what had happened there. His uniform had his rank tabs but no nametag.

"Mr. O'Neal I am your defense counsel in this matter," the commander said. "I am to present your defense in this court-martial. It would be helpful if you at least answered my questions."

"I can request other counsel," Mike said. "I officially do so."

"Unless the court is to meet in secret session," the commander replied. "Which this one will, due to the security aspects of the investigation."

"Big surprise there," O'Neal said. "Given that part of my testimony would be that Fleet just destroyed an entire corps of ACS."

"If you're referring to the Eleventh Corps, you are mistaken," the commander replied. "It was virtually wiped out in the battles on R-1496 Delta. Due to your negligence and rejection of the input from your Darhel superiors."

"Oh, so that's what I'm being tried with?" Mike asked, laughing. "Do you have any survivors to testify? Because as far as I could tell the orbital strikes were pretty thorough. I'd love to know that even one of my boys survived your fucking massacre."

"You are being tried on the charges of crimes against humanity," the commander replied. "Relating to new information about your actions in the first battles on Diess."

"That was fifty fucking *years* ago," Mike said, blinking. "I won my first Medal of Honor on Diess!"

"There is no statute of limitations on crimes against humanity," the "counsellor" said, pulling out his AID and setting it on the table. "Specifically, you are charged with the deaths of some three hundred thousand Indowy in the destruction of the Qualtren Megascraper. The destruction had been considered accidental, one of those unfortunate events that occur in war. But recently information has surfaced indicating that you ordered charges placed to destroy the building. I'm here to present your side of the action. So why don't you tell me about it from your perspective. Where were you on the evening of May 18th, 2002 AD?"

"You're asking if I can remember specific actions from over fifty years ago?" Mike asked.

"Yes," the commander replied.

"As a matter of fact," Mike said, dropping into memory, "I can."

Lieutenant O'Neal stripped the box magazine from his M-200 grav rifle and stared unseeing at the thousands of teardrop-shaped pellets within. Then he reinserted the magazine and did the same with his grav pistol.

"Would you please quit doing that?" asked Lieutenant Eamons. Both of them waited by windows on the northwest corner of Qualtren. The angle was even greater than the FSO indicated and they had a clear view of the 1.145 miles to the next intersection. There the Naltrev megascraper cut back and blocked the view. Naltrev and its sister megascraper Naltren held the battalion scout platoon and the upper part of O'Neal's vision systems were slaved to the view from the scout platoon leader's.

"Where are your people, Tom?" Mike asked.

"Downstairs."

"Are they tasked?" O'Neal continued to watch the view from the scout leader. It was unsettling because of the flicker of a Personal Area Force-screen—the PAF set up in the anticipated direction of attack—and because Lieutenant Smith had a nasty tendency to occasionally toss his head like a horse throwing a fly. The movement would swing the viewpoint right and up. I doubt he even notices that he's doing it, thought Mike, stripping out the magazine and reinserting it, but I wish he'd quit.

"Would you please quit doing that, Mike! And why do you want to know? No, they're sitting around with their thumbs up their butts."

"Quit what?" Mike asked, his attention focused like a medical laser on the view from his helmet. "Start having them emplace cratering charges across Anosimo and Sisalav at the Sal line and then start placing C-9 charges at the locations I'll slave to their AIDs."

"Whoa, Mike. You're a nice guy and outrank me by a whole grade, but the hell if I'll piss my career away for you. The colonel will have my bar if I do that." The lieutenant tried to shake his head and stopped when he had to force it against the biotic gel filling the helmet.

"Lieutenant Colonel Youngman is currently busy and he won't notice unless we detonate them. When we detonate them, you will be a hero for taking the initiative because it will be the only thing that saves the right flank of the corps from being rolled up."

"Is it that bad?" asked the engineer, wondering how much his friend's moroseness was justified. Although he would have preferred to lay out a full reception for the Posleen, the firepower of the battalion was massive.

"Tom, we're about to be corncobbed and there ain't a fuckin' thing I can do about it. After this day the name Youngman will be right up there with Custer, except George Armstrong had a brilliant career before he pissed it away. Now get rigging the charges. Make the cratering charges big ones. I want them to tear the faces right off the megascrapers; they've got forty minutes max."

"So you did, in fact, order Lieutenant Eamons to emplace the charges that eventually destroyed the Qualtren Megascraper," the commander said. "I think we'll try to argue situational stress disorder."

"The order was later authorized by Lieutenant Colonel Youngman," Mike said.

"Can you prove that?" the commander asked.

"The AID net should have the entire conversation stored."

"AIDs cannot be interrogated in courts-martial," the commander pointed out.

"Then I'd guess you'll have to find a survivor," Mike replied. "Besides me." He paused and thought about the events of that night. "Good luck on that one."

They were in a subbasement headed he knew not where running down one wall of a mammoth warehouse. The shelves were filled with green drums, like rubber oil barrels. As the lieutenant passed one of the aisles, both their AIDs screamed a belated warning. The group of fifty or so Posleen, accompanied by a God King, opened fire on Lieutenant O'Neal with everything they had.

There were six high-density inertial compensators along the spine of the suit. They had been placed there to prevent severe inertial damage to the most vital portions of the user. Lieutenant O'Neal launched himself into the air and away from the threat, an instinct of hundreds of hours of simulations, while his AID dialed the inertial compensators as low as they would go. This had several effects, good and bad but the net effect was to make it less likely that the flechettes would penetrate his armor as they had the private's; at this range their penetration ability was vastly improved.

The lack of inertia permitted the suit to move aside or be pushed away as if no more substantial than a hummingbird. Combined with the strength of the armor it successfully shed the first sleet of rounds, but it made him as unstable as a ping pong ball in a hurricane. He was picked up by the impacts, flipped repeatedly end for end, struck the warehouse wall and blown sideways.

Sergeant Reese screamed and fired on the target vector flashing in his display. The Posleen were masked by the barrels, but he figured with the power of the grav rifle he could saw through them quickly and take the Posleen under direct fire.

As it happened, actually hitting the Posleen became unnecessary. The barrels throughout the entire warehouse were filled with an oil processed from algae. It was used by the Indowy in cooking. Ubiquitous as corn oil, the five million Indowy of Qualtren used so much they needed a half kilometer square warehouse. Like corn oil, it had a fairly high flash point but, given certain conditions it could burn, even explode.

The depleted uranium pellets of the grav-guns traveled at a noticeable fraction of the speed of light. The designers had carefully balanced maximum kinetic effect against the problem of relativistic ionization and its accompanying radiation. The result was a tiny teardrop that went so fast it defied description. It made any bullet ever made seem to stand still. Far faster than any meteor, rounds that did not impact left the planet's orbit to become a spatial navigation hazard. It punched a hole through the atmosphere so fierce that it stripped the electrons from the atoms of gas and turned them into ions. The energy bled in its travel was so high it created a shock front of electromagnetic pulse. Then, after it passed, the atoms and electrons recombined in a spectacular display of chemistry and physics. Photons of light were discharged, heat was released and free radicals, ozone and buckyballs were produced. The major by-product was the tunnel of energetic ions indistinguishable from lightning. Just as hot, and just as energetic. A natural spark plug.

In two seconds a thousand of these supremely destructive teardrops punched through fifty drums of fish oil. One pellet was enough to finely divide a drum of oil over two to three thousand cubic meters of air. The following rounds found only vapor and these excess pellets, following the immutable laws of physics, set out to find other drums to divide. The oil from thousands of drums suddenly flash blasted into gas then ignited from compression, rather like a diesel piston. The net effect was a fuel-air bomb, the next best thing to a nuclear weapon in Terran technology, and the basement warehouse became a gigantic diesel cylinder. For Sergeant Reese, in an instant the world flashed to fire.

The warehouse was two levels below ground. It had six levels below it and was three hundred fifty meters from Boulevard Sisalav, a hundred fifty meters from Avenue Qual. The fuel air explosion blasted a two-hundred-meter diameter crater down to bedrock, gutted the building for a kilometer upward and set off all the charges planted for Plan Jericho. The shockwave smashed structural members all the way to Sisalav and Qual and spit many of the remaining troopers on the ground floor out of the building like watermelon seeds. It killed every unarmored being in the mile cube structure: three hundred twenty-six thousand Indowy and eight thousand particularly quick and greedy Posleen. The Jericho charges worked as planned, *shattering a hundred twenty critical monocrystalline support members. With surprising grace, the mile-high edifice leaned to the northwest and slowly, as if reverently kneeling, fell into Daltrev, blocking Sisalav and Qual and smashing the southeast quadrant of Daltrev. It crushed more Posleen and completely blocked an enemy advance from the massif to Qualtrev.*

"And subsequent to the explosion?" the commander asked emotionlessly.

"I tried to get in touch with the chain of command," Mike said. "Colonel Youngman was dead. Captain Vero was unconscious. Captain Wright was trapped in something too solid to get through and Hiberzined himself to await recovery. I consolidated local survivors and contacted Major Pauley."

The chirp of connection cued him. "Major Pauley, it's Lieutenant O'Neal."

"O'Neal? What the hell do you want?"

"Sir, I am currently in command of the survivors gathered under Qualtren. I was looking for orders, sir." Mike watched the NCO leading a group across the scattered rubble. The first suit to reach the far side grabbed a piece of rubble and pulled it out. There was a prompt slide into its place and a section of ceiling fell out, momentarily trapping one of the other troops. With some hand motions and swearing on a side channel Green got the group to move more circumspectly.

"Who the hell put you in command?" demanded the distant officer.

"Captain Wright, sir," answered O'Neal. He was

expecting some resistance but the harshness of Pauley's voice made him instantly wary.

"And where the hell is Wright?"

"Can I deliver my report, sir?"

"No, dangit, I don't want your dang report. I asked you where Captain Wright was." The panting of the officer over the circuit was eerie, like an obscene phone call.

"Captain Wright is irretrievable with what we have available, Major. He put me in command of the mobile survivors and put himself into hibernation."

"Well, the hell if any trumped up sergeant is going to lead MY troops," said the major, his voice cracking and ending on a high wavery note. "Where the hell are the rest of the officers?"

"I am the only remaining officer, Major," O'Neal said reasonably. "There is one sergeant first class, three staff sergeants and five sergeants, sir. I am the only officer on site."

"I do not have time for this," spit the commander, "put me through to another officer."

"Sir, I just said that there are no other officers."

"Dangit, Lieutenant, get me Captain Wright and get him NOW or I'll have you COURT-MARTIALED!"

"Sir," Mike choked. He began to realize that Major Pauley was not tracking well. The position of the retreating ACS battalion should have prepared him somewhat, but nothing could have fully prepared him, "Sir..." he started again.

"Dangit, Lieutenant, get those troops back here NOW! I need all the forces I can get! I don't have time to eff around with this. Get me through to Captain Wright!"

"Yes, sir," Mike did not know what to do, but

ending this conversation would be a start. "I'll get the troops to your location as fast as I can and get Captain Wright to contact you as soon as possible."

"That's better. And put him back in command, dang you. How dare you usurp command, you young puppy! I'll have you court-martialed for this! Put yourself on report!"

"Yes, sir, right away, sir. Out here."

"So you're saying that your direct chain of command was nonfunctional?" the Commander replied. "Are you an MD? A psychologist?"

"You're supposed to be my counsel, not my inquisitor," Mike said. "No, I'm not an MD or a shrink. But Pauley couldn't even understand that I was the only officer down there. And come to think of it Captain Brandon and Major Norton both heard Colonel Youngman authorize the Jericho charges."

"Lieutenant Colonel Robert Brandon retired from service some thirty years ago," the commander said. "He took colonization credits but his ship was, unfortunately, lost in transit. Major Charles Norton was killed in action on Earth in 2006. As was Captain Wright. Captain Vero exited the service after the action on Diess and committed suicide shortly thereafter."

"So you're saying that I'm the only officer survivor of Diess," Mike said, his face stony. "Not too surprising. We had a really high casualty rate during the war. Hell, I'm about the only person I know who's alive from back then. They're all gone." He looked at the far wall and shook his head. "All gone."

"Yes, well, that is regretable," the commander said without the slightest tone of regret. "Given any lack of witnesses to this supposed order by Colonel Youngman—"

"Wait," Mike said, his brow furrowing. "What is the evidence *against* me? I mean, what is the *prosecution* using as evidence?"

"You're not authorized to have that information," the commander replied.

"Oh, that's just great!" Mike snarled. "They're saying that I wiped out my corps, they're saying that I killed a bunch of Indowy on purpose on Diess and I can't see any of the evidence? Why am I surprised? They shot my fucking STAFF right in front of my eyes! What's the damned *purpose* of this fucking trial anyway!" He strained at the bonds, willing to do anything for just one crack at one of these fuckers, including his so-called "Counsel." But all he could feel was his own bones breaking.

"To see that justice is done, of course," the commander said tonelessly.

"'You are a prisoner because you have been accused,'" Mike said, laughing mirthlessly. "I plead guilty to saving a planet." He paused and then laughed. "Oh my God! That is what this is all about! If they can convict me from back then, then everything I've done *since* doesn't count, legally, does it? If it's all a war crime, I'm not owed a single pence, am I?"

"I'm not sure what you're talking about," the commander said, apparently puzzled.

"Then you don't have that need to know, 'Counselor,'" Mike said, chuckling. "Oh, wait, let me tell you. Then you can have a noose around your neck. See how it feels."

"On the whole—" the commander said, suddenly nervous.

"No, seriously, this is a really good story," Mike said.

"I think this interview is at an end," the commander said, standing up.

"The Darhel have been manipulating humans for thirty thousand years," Mike said, quickly. "There are humans on R-1496 Delta they planted there in caveman days! *And* they're in violation of contract. They owe humans more money than they have in cash. If we call the marker, if *I* call the marker, they're bankrupt."

"Why are you telling me this?" the commander snarled. "This has nothing to do with your crimes."

"Because I want to see how many counsellors I can go through," Mike replied, grinning. "'First thing we do, we kill all the lawyers.'"

"General O'Neal is being held at the Lunar Fleet Base," Cally said. "Multiple layers of security and of course it's on the Moon."

Cally's team had taken a real hit with the loss of her grandfather, Michael O'Neal, Sr. The hole was impossible to fill mentally so they'd never filled it physically. That left Cally, Tommy and the Schmidt brothers. That was going to be more than enough. In fact, since direct action was, to say the least, not Harrison's forte, he'd be hanging back on this one.

"This is going to be interesting," George Schmidt said. The newest team member had never been averse to attacking Cally's plans but his point was always to find the weaknesses, not attack the source. "As in 'you're fricking kidding, right?' They've seriously upgraded security procedures since we sprung *you*. And this time we don't have a guy on the inside."

"Which is why we're not going to get him out during

the trial," Cally said, bringing up another schematic. "He's either going to be convicted or he's not. If he's not, we pick him up from the exit and then get lost, fast. Given that it's a kangaroo court, he's going to be convicted. Which means that he'll be moved to the Lunar Penal facility."

"We grab him in transit?" Tommy said, blinking. "What if they off him immediately?"

"Then we're fucked," Cally admitted. "But he's going to be moved through the Deeprun Tram. That's the weak point."

"A tram that runs through solid rock a thousand feet below the lunar surface?" George said. "How's that a weak point?"

"It's one with the right support," Cally said. "Which we have. The Sohon are willing to give us that much support."

"Okay," Tommy said, nodding. "I kinda get that one. So that's getting in and grabbing him. Getting out?"

"I have a friend arranging that," Cally said.

It's Dad, Stewart. Your father-in-law. Your old boss. Don't tell me you're not in.

I know that, honey. James Stewart, now known as Yan Kato, looked nothing like the man who had once been a Fleet Strike lieutenant general. He also didn't look purely Chinese, more like one of the more "mixed" races of southeast Asia that were survivors of the Posleen but not pure Han.

And it will fuck with the Darhel, Cally added. *The Tongs always like that. That's why we get along.*

I know that, too, Stewart had said. *It doesn't mean it's a good idea. Look, I've gotten promoted in the*

Tong really fast. That makes enemies. And these guys don't just talk about you behind your back. There's more real assassination than character assassination in the Tongs. Doing something like this, with no profit involved, for apparently political and personal reasons, it's not a good idea. Not if you want me alive to visit on occasion.

I want more than that and you know it. And if you need to get paid to do it, then we'll figure out a way to pay you.

It's not going to be cheap.

I don't think Michelle threw all those Level Nine nanokeys into the pot.

In that case, let's talk business.

First.

First.

"So, we're depending on Sohon, whom we don't know, and some Tong guy we don't know," Tommy said, blowing out his cheeks. He wasn't about to admit that he not only knew Stewart but that they had been acquaintances "back when." "Cally, you're asking us to take one hell of a risk using assets we don't know."

"If you've got a better plan, Thomas, ante up," Cally said.

"Point."

He'd been through three "counsellors" so far. He waited in the trial room in anticipation. The "counsellor" hadn't been waiting for him this time. He wondered who they'd sacrifice next.

He was only slightly surprised when a Darhel came through the door.

"Since I am privy to the information you've been giving to your other counsellors, telling me about it won't require my removal from the trial," the Darhel said, sitting down opposite Mike.

"Oh, that's okay," Mike said. "I'll figure something out. Answer one question?"

"We shall trade," the Darhel said. "I will ask one and you ask one. If you answer me I'll answer you."

"Nope," Mike said, shaking his head. "I'm fully aware of how far you can trust a Darhel. Which is zero. You answer me and I'll answer you, though. I mean, really, who would you trust more, General Michael O'Neal or another Darhel?"

"Very well," the Darhel said, acceding to the logic. "Ask your question."

"Has the trial even started, yet?" Mike asked, wondering what answer he'd get. Or if it would be true.

"Two days ago," the Darhel said.

"Then why don't I at least get to watch it?" Mike asked, gesturing with his chin at the screen.

"One question at a time," the Darhel said, smiling and exposing sharp teeth. "Now for mine. Were you aware that there were Indowy still in the Qualtren Megascraper?"

"Yes," Mike said, frowning. "I'd run into some trapped in there. But it was destroy the megascraper or lose the battle. Besides, they couldn't outrun the Posleen and were thus dead, anyway. The military term is 'acceptable collateral damage.' Another round?"

"Very well," the Darhel said.

"I repeat, why can't I watch the trial?"

"Because the testimony is need-to-know," the Darhel answered. "The only portion you are required to monitor is your sentencing portion. When sentencing is pronounced, it will be fed over the video screen."

"If anyone needs to know what's being testified to, *I* do," Mike said.

"Nonetheless," the Darhel said. "What do you know of the Bane Sidhe?"

"Only that they exist," Mike said. "I was informed about them by the Nor. You had an AID listening in."

"The Nor did not know of the contract irregularity," the Darhel said. "You do. Someone has told you, recently. Who?"

"Gosh, I forget," Mike said.

"This is a violation of our contract," the Darhel said. "You said that you would answer questions. And I can and will use chemical means to get my answer."

"If you're asking those you're not working as my counsel," Mike said, shrugging. "In which case, all I can say is that when I get out of here, I'm going to remove your eyes with my own hands."

"That would be difficult," the Darhel said, snarling.

"Not really," Mike said. "You Darhel are cowards. Oh, you might have some guards but I've killed humans in my time as well as Posleen. You know my abilities. You are as dead as yesterday's news. But first I'm going to destroy your clan financially. You're going to be too *poor* to afford guards when I come for you. I'm going to eat one of your cowardly eyeballs while you watch and . . ."

Mike had been watching for the signs. He'd heard that Darhel were, in fact, fast and strong. But they also went catatonic after a few moments. The question would be whether he could get the Darhel to go over the edge. And live through it.

Sure enough, the alien finally lost it, his chair flying

back and hitting the wall, hard enough to crack the strong plastic. The alien's hands wrapped around Mike's throat and he thought he felt his hyoid bone break as it bore down. But then the thing's eyes rolled back in his head and he flopped to the table, still and drooling.

Mike could breathe, barely, so his throat wasn't crushed. He just sat there, watching the drooling thing on the table, until the guards entered the room in a rush and stunned him into unconsciousness.

"General, this is insane."

The Fleet Strike colonel looked at his superior, watching for any shred of agreement, then shook his head. He'd made sure that the meeting was in a shield room and AIDs were left behind so the officers could have an honest conversation. But he wasn't sure even that would matter.

"These charges are laughable," Colonel Rodermund continued. "The only evidence is the recordings of the accused and AID records we both know can be falsified. For that matter, we're not allowed to fully investigate those same records. We're not even getting the full recordings of the interrogations of the accused and *those* are by persons who are supposed to be his counsel. Then we can't even question the counselors. We haven't even *seen* any of his counselors after the meetings. But the bottom line is that what he did was not illegal. He gave a legal order and was not countermanded by higher authority. Not as far as any record we have seen. The collateral damage was regrettable but the mission was accomplished. He's guilty of nothing but being a soldier. Is that now illegal?"

"Is that all?" the general asked.

"Not really," the colonel said, his face hardening. "I've been reviewing the information on what happened at R-1496 Delta and I don't buy it. There's a massive rat in the recordings. Among other things, where did the Posleen get orbital weaponry? Wasn't Fleet supposed to be covering? Again, not something that General O'Neal can be charged with. And I don't see Admiral Suntoro in that courtroom nor any of the rest of his staff. In fact, I've done a bit of checking and nobody's too sure where Fifth Fleet is at present. I didn't think I was going to be participating in a kangaroo court, General, and I'm professionally and personally humiliated to do so. I'm also wondering what in the hell you think you're doing."

"That is insubordination," the general said mildly.

"Great, so I'm next?" the colonel asked. "Unable to choose my own counsel, unable to speak in my own defense, unable to bring witnesses, unable to face my accusers?"

"Not unless you force that outcome," the general said. "Are you going to?"

"If I thought it would do a shred of good..."

"And there is the point," the general replied. "Yes, this is a totally bogus proceeding. The outcome is foreordained. The accused will be found guilty. He will be shipped to either the Legion or a penal institute. He is probably going to be shot trying to escape. General O'Neal is dead. Get that through your head."

"Oh, I have, sir," the colonel said furiously. "But what in the *fuck* are we doing facilitating that, sir? Michael O'Neal is a goddamned *hero*! If they can do this to him, using us, sir, then who's safe? What's the goddamned *point* of even... And what *really* happened to Eleventh Corps? That's most of Fleet Strike, sir! What's the goddamned point of—"

"Of even continuing to exist?" the general asked, calmly. "The *point* is to exist."

"Well, then, sir, if you would like to hear my opinion of—"

"I can guess," the general said, still calmly. "But you're not seeing the full measure of the point. Yes, we're about to throw one of our greatest heroes, okay our *greatest* hero, to the dogs. We are going to pour out our honor like water. Some of the board are going to eat a pistol over the verdict. But we are going to survive. *Fleet Strike* is going to survive. You think this is the only tarnish on us? That we haven't done *other* things that are repugnant at the insistence of those Darhel fuckers? You've been caught up in the minutia of keeping units across the galactic arm supplied. I appreciate that. You're a damned good logistician. *I've* been in the belly of the beast, Colonel. I've seen what's been really happening. The Flect doesn't even flicker at this sort of thing. There's no trust, no bonding, no real soldiers in the whole damned thing. The admirals fight for the biggest slice of the pie and the sailors just want to get their ricebowl filled. They hope they actually get fed and paid.

"We're tarnished. The stench from *this* is going to stink to high heaven and you are neither the first officer, nor I'm sure the last, to be right on the edge of mutiny. But that's sort of the point. *We* can still fight. We are the only true defenders of the Federation left. We are the only ones that come close to remaining true to the cause. Broken, stinking wretches that we are, we still have *some* of us that believe in the point, which is first, last and always, to make sure that humanity survives. If we choose to mutiny over this... abomination, we are finished. We are as dead as the Eleventh Corps, which is, yes, gone. I will not see the rest of Fleet Strike go the same way, Colonel. And if it takes sacrificing Michael O'Neal, whom I have known for longer than you have lived, or you, Colonel, or myself, on that altar, then I will make that sacrifice, Colonel. Am I making myself absolutely, perfectly, clear?"

"Sir, they can't—"

"Colonel, Eleventh Corps wasn't destroyed by the Posleen, it was destroyed at the behest of the Darhel. Twenty plus thousand Fleet Strike personnel, one hundred percent of our remaining ACS, burned by orbital fire from Fifth Fleet. The staff, I'm given to understand, were shot by their captors."

"That is..." The colonel's face worked for a moment then he spat. "That is *sick*, sir!"

"And the day you can figure out an effective method to strike back at the Darhel, Colonel," the general said, "one that will break their stranglehold for good and all, one that will make those fuckers *pay*, well you just do that, Colonel. And then kill them all as far as I care. But in the meantime, we have to go present sentencing on one of my best friends. Are you prepared to give your last measure to this organization, Colonel? Are you prepared to pour out your honor like water, to bury it in muck and slime and horror, so that there is some chance that, someday, others will not have to? Because if you're not, I need to have you removed from the court."

"And life?" the colonel asked.

"Does it matter?" the general replied, snorting humorlessly. "On a day like today, wouldn't you have rather died in battle? Because even burning to death would be cleaner than this. I know that I have not a *shred* of true honor left, Colonel. I was damned long before these proceedings. The only hope that I have is that by holding onto *something* I can work to prevent others from having to do this sort of thing. I can hope that someday there will be a Fleet Strike that is relieved of this horror. That some future officer can spit on my grave without fear of Darhel retribution. Our lives, our fortune and our sacred honor. Today is the day for you to cough up that last measure, Colonel. Today you get to join the rest of us and burn your honor on the bonfire of hope. Sucks, huh?"

"Sir . . ." the colonel said. "I repeat, that's sick."

"Are you in, though?" the general asked.

"Yes, sir," Colonel Rodermund replied after a moment. "But someday—"

"Colonel," General Tam Wesley replied, "I hope every day for some shred of possibility of breaking the Darhel. Yes, someday something has to give. But, unfortunately, it does not appear to be today."

Security Contract Officer First Class Maxim Poddubny had been born and raised in the "unconquered" areas of Siberia.

The Posleen invaders had swept across Europe and Asia without a check on their advance until they disovered Siberia. While the Posleen could survive in almost any environment, they were less than adept at logistics. Each Posleen God King was supposed to find food for his own group. Usually that food was the food of the conquered or, in many cases, the conquered themselves.

The Russians, after brief and mostly futile defense,

had done what Russia had done many times before;
retreated deeper and deeper into the hinterland while
scorching the earth behind them.

The only difference from the Swedes, Poles, French
and Germans was that the Posleen got farther. None
of the Russian armies that faced them, even in the
Urals, could slow them down. Until winter descended
on Siberia—and the Posleen suddenly found themselves
out of contact with the human "thresh" and struggling
through hip-deep snow in a terrain bereft of anything
resembling sustenance.

Had the Posleen continued to occupy Earth they
would eventually have spread, slowly, into the area. The
shattered Russians, reduced to a day-to-day hand-to-
mouth struggle for survival, might or might not have
hindered them. But that question became moot when
the half-renegade Fleet units had lifted the Siege.
Slowly, the Russians had straggled out of the taiga,
recovering their demolished cities. Those that could
quickly moved to more hospitable lands under the
Post-Invasion Resettlement Act. But a few remained.

Max was the son of one of those families, hardy
pioneers in the wilderness that had reclaimed most
of Russia. His father was a strong Russian nationalist,
regaling his many children with the glory that had
once been Russia and, through his sons and daughters,
would be again.

Max had listened to the rants until he was seventeen,
the youngest age at which you could enlist in the military, and then fled the searingly cold and achingly boring forests of "The Motherland" for *anything* else. His
father might be insane but it didn't mean Max had to be.
Someday, if there was ever a need for the space, humans

might move back into the shattered lands of Russia. In the meantime, they were wilderness for a reason. Only madmen or the desperate lived there by *choice*.

He had spent a very boring five years in an absolutely less than elite infantry division. It was one of three divisions that was tasked with post-recovery security. Basically, they supported the first Indowy colonists and their human "security officers" sweeping out the hardcore remaining Posleen while the "security officers" covered the Indowy. It was tedious work involving long patrols that rarely hit contact. And when they did, by and large, they just ran away as fast as they could, called in an orbital strike and then made sure it got the infestation. What was the point of being a hero?

The good news was that the unit had regular contact with the "security officers." Invariably, the first thing the security company did was set up a "recreation facility." It was usually completed before the full defenses were in place. Security companies had their own manpower shortage so they made sure that such "recreation facilities" were as complete as possible. There were plenty of games, yes. There was a decent bar, if your interest in bars translated to "dive." And there were "entertainers," male and female, to keep their security officers entertained.

Getting access to those "recreation facilities" was tough for a regular. But if you made the right contacts, you could get an occasional pass. Max had visited the security recreation facility once, compared it to the one available to the regular infantry, and made it his goal to work his way into a security company.

Now, as an SCO1 working for Hamilton-Baron Security, he had full access to such. Just as soon as he got off duty in forty minutes. There was a little lady named Lailani he was looking forward to spending quite a bit of his pay on. Why not? There wasn't much else to spend it on and he wasn't looking for another job any time soon.

He slowed the multiwheeled ground terrain vehicle as his thermal detectors pinged. An aerial recon team had been reported missing near this location and he'd been dispatched to look into it. The air-truck had probably just lost its motivator. This planet had been colonized for twenty years; for that matter it was pretty close to some of the core Darhel worlds, and the Posleen hadn't used anything that could take down an air-truck in a while. But the two-man crew was probably on the ground somewhere nearby cursing and waiting for pick-up.

The thermal, though, wasn't locking the contact. Something was disturbing the signal. It was big, though. Could be either human or Posleen. He hit the lights and panned them to the left, searching in the burgeoning undergrowth for the contact, the machinegun on the roof panning with it. If it was a Posleen, it was going to get a 14.5mm enema.

As the light panned across the contact point there was a flicker, like a reflection on a pond. He panned back and frowned as the ripple seemed to move. Whatever it was, it was big. Maybe as big as a Posleen. His finger was playing with the safety on the machinegun, wondering if he should just fire and then figure it out. But the contact sort of looked like a Himmit. Not that you normally spotted those.

He was still wondering when a strand of monomolecular wire entered his window and removed his head.

CHAPTER SIX

This was a different route. They'd taken a left out of the cell instead of a right. Mike wasn't sure what that meant, but he could feel a bode when he saw one. And this boded.

A door dilated and he entered a low room about the size of a standard shield room. On the far side his "court" was arrayed. He knew, immediately, that that was what he was looking at. What shocked him was not that there actually was a court, but who was on it.

"Tam?" he gasped. "Good God, you're not—?"

"The prisoner will remain silent," General Tam Wesley said harshly. "This is your sentencing, not a moment for grandstanding. Michael O'Neal, you have been charged with violation of Galactic Military Code 4153-6398-Delta, excessive force leading to the death of noncombatants without commensurate military value gained. Your plea of not guilty has been recorded by your counsel. You are found guilty and sentenced to fifty years in a penal unit to be determined. Case is closed."

"I appeal," Mike said, looking around. Neither his most recent "counsel," if he had one nor even the prosecution were present.

"The sentence has been automatically reviewed by higher authority," General Wesley said. "It stands. Take the prisoner away."

"I appeal to the Aldenata," Mike said loudly. "I appeal this sentence on its merits and I place suit against the Darhel, in toto, for failure of contractual obligations, to whit failure to abide by payment structures in keeping with contractual obligations to myself and the rest of the human race."

"What?" Tam said, his brow furrowing. "What in the *hell* are you talking about?"

"This trial is over," the Tir Dol Ron said, entering from the opposite door. "Silence the prisoner!"

Mike grimaced as the stunners hit, but the grimace had a trace of a smile in it.

"That was unnecessary, Tir," General Wesley said as the unconscious body was dragged from the room.

"I determine what is necessary, General," the Tir said. "You may all return to your duties."

"What was that about failure of payment?" Colonel Rodermund asked. "Is there something we should be discussing, Tir?"

"Only if you wish to go to the same place as the former general, Colonel," the Tir said coldly. "This matter is closed."

❖   ❖   ❖

"Glad that's over," Master-at-Arms First Class Chan Mu said, dropping the prisoner unceremoniously to the deck. "Bastard's heavy as hell."

The sub-surface shuttle called the Deep-run Tram ran between the Fleet Base in the Chaplygin crater and Fleet Central Penal Facility in Chaplygin K. There was a regular shuttle that ran four times a day, carrying normal prisoners, their guards and the occasional releasee. This one, though, was unscheduled and consisted of only one car. It was for the specific job of getting the former general Michael O'Neal into that extremely secure sub-surface facility. Surrounded by space-capable weaponry and with nearly a thousand guards, once he was in FCPF the general wasn't going anywhere, ever again. Assuming that he even made it through in-processing. The Fleet masters-at-arms were charged with getting him to the facility, not killing him.

On the other hand they had very specific orders in the event there was any attempt to rescue him.

"Stay alert," Lieutenant Mang Rong said, setting the stunner aside and pulling around a laser rifle. "If we lose this one it's all our heads."

"Not much chance of that," Rei Shun said with a snort as the shuttle jerked into motion. "Solid rock between here and the prison. Be pretty hard to get to us and even if they did they'd evacuate the shuttle, killing him. That's if we missed, sir."

"Nonetheless," the lieutenant said, training the laser rifle on the back of the prisoner's head. "Remain alert."

Tommy Sunday was trapped in a bubble of rock and not particularly happy about it.

After all the time he'd spent in suits, he thought he was over anything resembling claustrophobia. When you put on a suit, the undergel flooded into your ears, eyes, nose. You were trapped, for just a moment, in a coffin. It was a very claustophobic experience that was hard to get used to, at first. But if you stayed in suits, you got really comfortable with it. So here he was, breathing stale air, room to move his feet, so why was he getting so claustophobic?

Maybe it was because he was under a thousand feet of rock and the only thing between him and eventually dying when his air ran out was the questionable support of a Sohon mentat none of them ever got to meet.

"Prepare yourselves. The shuttle is leaving the station. The general is in the rear portion. There are five guards. They are armed with laser rifles and have low-light glasses. I will stop the shuttle, shut off the lights, disable their systems and let you through. All else is up to you. I may take no direct action against a human being. When you have secured the general, I will extract you."

Tommy supposed he also shouldn't wonder how the damned mentat was contacting a radio under a thousand feet of rock. But was having a harder time getting past that than how they'd gotten here.

So how's this supposed to work? George had said.

The four suits were standing on the lunar surface, looking around for any sign of their contact.

Michelle said there'd be a signal, Cally replied. *It had better be soon.*

Would a line in the sand be a signal?

In front of Tommy's eyes a line was drawing itself

without anyone touching the lunar dust. As he watched, his name appeared next to an X drawn on a point on the line.

I guess X marks your spot, Cally said, with just a hint of nervousness.

After lining up they. had waited. And waited. And waited. Finally, their radios crackled.

You are about to sink into the ground, a male voice with all the emotion of a robot had said. *Attempt to control your emotional reactions.*

Before Tommy could reply he felt a sinking sensation in no metaphorical sense. Looking down, the lunar dust was opening up around his feet into a pocket the width of his body and a few handspans. The others were descending as well.. In moments he was below the surface of the Moon, the pocket had closed above his head and, as far as he could tell, he was still dropping. In fact, if his inner ear was any judge, the rate had increased.

You will be dropped to the level of the shuttle tube, the voice said. How the presumed mentat was broadcasting to fairly normal radios was beyond Tommy. On the other hand, so was how he was opening up a pocket in solid rock! *You will then hold there until it is time to retrieve the General.*

So here he stood, waiting in this hole. The recent transmission had been the first sign he'd heard that the mission was still a go in over an hour. He hoped the other members of the party were doing better than he was, because Tommy was about to flip his lid.

"How are the guards arrayed?" Cally asked.

"The general is unconscious on the floor. Recently

stunned. The lieutenant in charge of the detail is to starboard flanked by two guards. The other two are to port. Mr. Sunday will be dropping almost on top of the general. Are you prepared?"

"Yes," Cally replied. "Tommy, Guard."

"Roger," Tommy said.

"Good, because the shuttle is stopping in three... two..."

Tommy dropped in the low lunar gravity. Looking down he could see the top of the shuttle somehow dilated out, just as the rock around him had been. General O'Neal was directly beneath his feet. Which meant the rest of the team was arrayed farther forward.

The guards had apparently been thrown off their seats by a violent stop. In total darkness, their electronics disabled, they floundered in the dark. At least one appeared to be injured.

Tommy didn't have time to take in more than that before spreading his feet so he wouldn't crush the package and then ducking down to cover the general with his body. There was a meaty sound from forward, then a series of muted pops. Cally was being her usual efficient self.

"Package secured," Cally said. "Guards secured."

"Retrieving," the mentat replied.

This time, as the group gathered around Tommy and "the package," a wider hole was opened. The five of them, Tommy holding onto the general, started lifting upwards as if with grav belts. The top of the shuttle, which had been solid a moment before, simply seemed to momentarily disappear. Then they were back in rock.

"Okay," George said. "I've seen and done some weird shit, but this is starting to freak me out."

"At least we're not still sitting in those damned coffins," Harrison replied. "I was starting to totally freak out."

"Should have tried being in a suit for a few years," Tommy heard himself say. "After that, sitting in solid rock is nooo problem."

"He's what?" Tir Dol Ron snapped.

The Tir's position had always been a bit confusing to the humans. Technically, Tir was a relatively minor position, the Darhel equivalent of a paper-shuffler. The term usually used in Human-Darhel dictionaries was "clerk." But while there was a higher ranked Gil who was the official ambassador to the human government of the Confederation of Allied Races, the Tir seemed to wield extraordinary powers.

As time went on, and humans had been in contact with the Darhel for nearly sixty years at this point, another term had entered service. "Eminence grise." While the Tir might not be a clan leader among the Darhel, nor a planetary governor nor even a senior member of the rubber-stamp Legislative Committee of the Confederation, what he was was a mover and a shaker, a shyster, a power broker sitting very close to the right hand of the master of all Darhel, the shadowy Ghin whom no human had ever met.

Specifically, he was the guy tasked with making sure that the human warrior-ants stayed under control.

And right now he was very close to the Darhel equivalent of a stroke.

"Escaped, my lord." Admiral Chatchaya Sie was commander of all Fleet activities on the Moon including, most especially, the in his opinion ill-named "Heinlein

Base." As part of his additional duties, he was commander of the Fleet Central Penal Facility.

He had succeeded to the lucrative post after his predecessor, Admiral Leony Jayadi, let a high value prisoner escape. Admiral Jayadi, while returning to Earth for his retirement, had apparently been unable to stand the shame and, completely of his own free will, taken a walk in space. His body had never been recovered.

The investigating team had carefully ignored the fact that it took at least three separate people to open a lock on a shuttle. And the admiral was the only person, officially, on the shuttle at that time.

Admiral Sie did not want to take a space walk.

"How did this happen?" the Tir said, then took a deep, calming breath.

"That is so far very much a mystery, my lord," the admiral said. "The general and his guards were observed both physically and on camera boarding the shuttle. The shuttle, which is of course deep beneath the surface, proceeded in its normal fashion to the Penal Facility. Upon arrival the guards were found shot to death and the general was gone."

"He is no longer a general," the Tir said.

"Pardon my reference, my lord," the admiral said. "The prisoner."

"What you describe is impossible," the Tir snapped. "*Impossible.*"

"That is my own categorization of this event, my lord," the admiral said. "When my predecessor let that woman escape, it was through inside help. I am following a similar line of investigation. But, fearing a rescue attempt, I had heavy forces commanded by loyal officers on hand to repel any attack. A colonel and two captains, one of them a nephew, observed the prisoner being loaded. The shuttle, according to the monitors, never stopped. Yet the prisoner was gone and the guards dead."

"So it appears to have been *magic*," the Tir snapped.

"I doubt magic, my lord, but—"

"Then you are insufficiently imaginative," the Tir growled. "Keep me informed of your investigation. I want daily reports."

"Yes, my lord."

Well, at least it appeared he'd be able to *forward* daily reports. That was something. But if he didn't find something quick . . .

Mike woke up with all of his nerves jangling. Since the room he was in was apparently on Earth, based on the gravity, that meant he'd been Hiberzined while still under the influence of the stunner. And he hadn't been under long enough to get over the effects.

"I also gave you a shot of nerzin," a voice said over his shoulder. "The stun should wear off pretty quick."

He was sitting in a recliner looking out a window. The view beyond was of a dune and then the ocean. Nice view. Based on the vegetation, mostly sea-oats, he was presumably somewhere in the eastern United States on the Atlantic coast. Make that southeast, he could see the limb of a live oak. That meant no farther north than North Carolina or whatever they were calling it these days.

"Thanks," Mike muttered, looking around. The room could have been a living room from before the war. Muted pastel paint, cluttered knicknacks on shelves, the style was called "coastal country" or some such. There was a bottle of Veri water on the marble-topped table next to the recliner. He opened it, took a swig to wet his mouth and cleared his throat. "To whom do I owe the favor?"

"No names, obviously," the voice said. A young man walked into view. A very, very *big* young man. Dark red hair and a hard face. And clearly no slouch in the gym. "But I'm told you already know about the Bane Sidhe."

"Killers of Elves," Mike said, then barked a laugh. "Killed any good Darhel lately?"

"Bit of an oxymoron," the man said. "It's not until they're *dead* that they're *good*, sir. Call me Kyle. It's not my name but it's one I've used."

"Well, Kyle, what now?" Mike asked.

"I have no clue, sir," Kyle replied. "I was told to hold you here pending disposition. Since you are, I'm given to understand, the most quietly wanted man in the galaxy . . . I'm not sure what the disposition is going to be. Normally, we can disappear someone fairly easily, and to make that clear I mean hide them not kill them. In your case, sir—"

"Every friggin' cop and bounty hunter in the galaxy is going to be after my ass," Mike said. "So I guess there's only one question, Kyle."

"Sir?"

"You guys got any weights around here? They've been unavailable where I was before."

"Oh my God," General Wesley said, looking at the flimsy.

Fleet Strike was said to run on paper. It was not

a compliment. Whereas Fleet was almost entirely paperless, but for the occasional award one of the admirals gave himself, Fleet Strike had continued to generate reams of paper.

The "enlightened" officers in Fleet pointed to this as evidence of the stupidity and conservatism of Fleet Strike officers, many of whom remained rejuvs from before the invention of the computer. Such officers were simply more comfortable with good old fashioned paperwork. Fleet officers would sometimes insult their counterparts behind the latter's back by motioning like counting on fingers.

And there was some truth to that. Many of Fleet Strike's senior officers never really got comfortable with electronic technology. But it was also a very good cover. From early on all the senior officers, at least, of Fleet Strike had been uncomfortably aware that their friendly AIDs reported *everything* to the Darhel. And sometimes orders that were given on one end were not *exactly* the same orders that came out the other end.

Using the "neanderthal" officers among Fleet Strike as an excuse permitted the officers who were *not* so neolithic to have paper backups.

Which meant that there was a paper trail on the trial of General O'Neal. After the dramatic end of what had been an ugly and boring, but necessary, task, each of the officers of the court-martial had signed the sentencing document and it, along with the entire paper record of the proceedings, had been put into a sealed container and transported to the vaults for storage. It should never have seen the light of day.

So he was very surprised to see what was either a

precise facsimile or a very good forgery of that same document sitting on his desk.

"Those are all over Heinlein Base and have turned up as far away as Titan and, of course, on Earth," Colonel Branden Trovato said. The commander of the Fleet Strike Criminal Investigation Division was not a man to scare easily. He had survived the latter part of the Siege as an infantry officer in the Ten Thousand, the most elite "light" infantry unit on the planet and one of the ones with the highest death toll. But he was clearly nervous now. "And to say that they're causing a stir is an understatement."

"Where in the *hell* did they come from?" General Wesley snapped.

"Warrant Officer Paulina Weidemann was the courier officer tasked with carrying the recordings to the vault," Colonel Trovato said, looking at his *paper* notes. "One of my men timed the walk from the courtroom to the vaults. It took him precisely four minutes and thirty-two seconds. You turned over the records at fourteen twelve hours, Lunar, sir. Give or take a minute."

General Wesley nodded. He remembered a vague impression of a slight woman with dark hair. He wasn't paying too much attention to what was going on at the time, running more or less on automatic and just wanting to find a quiet place to vomit.

"Warrant Officer Weidemann logged into the vault-room at precisely fourteen thirty five, seventeen seconds and some miliseconds that don't really matter."

"So either she stopped to use the lady's room or—"

"A trusted courier officer somehow opened a plasteel secure box sealed by a Fleet Strike general—which means some pretty sophisticated lock-picking—copied some or all of the documents and then resealed it. Then turned it in. And walked on her merry way."

"And Warrant Officer . . . ?"

"Weidemann, sir."

"Where is she, now?"

"She requested and was granted a three-day pass, sir. She took a shuttle to Earth last night. Her current whereabouts are unknown, sir."

"When did the first of these surface?" General Wesley asked.

"This morning, sir. My office became apprised at eleven twenty-two. My first action was to determine who had chain of custody and do the investigation I've outlined. Then I reported to you, sir."

Tam didn't have to look at the clock. He knew it was slightly after noon. His stomach was telling him that he'd have to eat, someday. And that it still wasn't sure it wanted to.

"Fast work."

"Thank you, sir."

"And no damned good at all, is it?"

"No, sir," the colonel admitted. "We can, of course, charge Warrant Officer Weidemann. If we ever catch her. But . . ."

"That would be closing the barn door after the fire's burned it down," the general said.

"More or less, sir."

"Define 'not being taken well,'" Wesley said.

"I have, while involved in the investigation, gotten two messages from undercover personnel who were approached by Fleet Strike members and sounded out about the possibility of mutiny," the CID officer said. "Based upon very rough statistics, that means at least half of the Strike personnel on the Moon are discussing mutiny. Discussion is, of course, not the same as doing, sir, but—"

"But just that it's being discussed," the general said, grinding his teeth. "Anything else?"

"There is a very wide-spread rumor, starting last night, that General O'Neal had nothing to do with the destruction of the Eleventh Corps and that it was, in fact, Fleet forces that fired upon them. There had been, prior to his trial, a very strong sentiment against his being responsible for the destruction of the corps and even rejection of the idea that they were destroyed. Subsequent to the release of this document... Members have put two and two together. Since there is no mention of his being responsible for the destruction of the corps in this document and given what he was charged with... The broad consensus is that he has been railroaded and that the corps is either still intact, and probably in its own state of mutiny, or was destroyed by someone or something other than in battle with the Posleen." The colonel stopped for a moment and frowned, holding his hand up to his earbud. "Sir, we have a developing situation—"

"General, we've got a problem!"

Colonel Elvin Paul, chief of staff to the Chief of Staff, Operations, Fleet Strike, did not regularly burst into his boss's office. So despite his increasing annoyance level, General Wesley did not eat him a new asshole.

"Go," Wesley said, picking up his AID and wrapping it around his wrist.

"There was a gathering of enlisted in the Moonbase

mess," Colonel Paul said. "They were arguing about something; what is unclear. Fleet MAs were ordered by Admiral Sie to break up the gathering. They didn't send enough. Moonbase is basically in one giant riot. I'm not exactly getting why from any of the officers I've spoken to. In fact, I'm having a hard time getting hold of anyone at all. Nobody seems to want to talk to us."

"Colonel, we have control of the tram-port."

Colonel Glennis LeBlanc had been a colonel a looong time. Everybody else who had been her rank, major, "back in the day" was either a general or retired.

Glennis wasn't sure why she'd stayed in Fleet Strike so many years, watching younger officers pass her by on the ladder of promotion. Hell, General Wesley, God curse his name, had been a fricking captain at the end of the Siege. With damned little to his credit. He sure as hell hadn't gotten the Distinguished Service Cross for the final battle in North Carolina.

But such were the vagaries of service. And maybe it was just sheer bloodymindedness that her kept her bumping from one meaningless position to another. Or maybe it was because she had sensed, deep in her ample bosom, that there was a day when Fleet Strike was going to need her.

Planning a mutiny had been more of a hobby than anything over the years, a way to pass the time in jobs that were far beneath her skills. A background in intel hadn't hurt. She had established lines of communication with other officers, lines that did not use electronic communication for anything other than code phrases. She had built a network of informants. She had mentally mapped out the necessary steps to taking over each base she was on. Some of that she had moved to paper and left with very trustworthy friends on stations throughout the system. Oh, the purposes had been cloaked as games to pass the time. But one thing the AIDs still didn't read well was body language and secondary phrasing. All of "her" people knew that what was building was something other than a game.

She had looked at each of the problems inherent in a mutiny under the current structure and found passable work-arounds. She hoped. Today was the day to find out.

"Capturing a critical prisoner" was only one of the many potential flash-points she had mapped. As soon as the riots started she had activated her cells. From her desk in the Morale and Welfare Support Center she had spread the word. Waterloo. As in "It was a near run thing."

Moonbase was secure and the means to recapture the general were in hand. Phase One complete. She had no particular liking for General O'Neal. She sort of remembered him from "in the day." And they'd met a couple of times over the decades. But he was just another brass from her perspective. The only thing that mattered was a chance to do something worthwhile. It was time to dust off the combat training and lead for a change.

The next step, though, was going to be a doozy. There was a whole Fleet in the system, not to mention the orbital defenses of the Earth and Luna. Those were Phase Two, Three and Four, not necessarily in that order.

"Where are we on getting around the AID lockouts on the combat systems?" she asked.

"Going slow," Warrant Officer Three Pruitt replied.

Having Pruitt around was a multiplier for her models. She'd known him since the final battles on Earth and trusted him like armor on a tank. He was sort of a clown from time to time, but he seriously hated the Darhel and the current state of affairs. "We can bypass the lockouts easy enough. But the AIDs do much of the processing for the systems. Replacing that is turning out to be the tricky part."

"Tell Paul to go faster," Colonel LeBlanc snapped. "He's the wiz kid. Tell him to wiz."

"Will do," the former SheVa gunner said, grinning. "We're gonna chop 'em up like Bun-Bun at a beach party."

"Colonel," Chief Warrant Officer Five Sheila Indy said. "Are you ready for calls from home?"

"I take it General Wesley is calling?" Glennis said, grinning.

"The same."

"Put him on," the colonel replied, pulling back her hair and spreading the top of her uniform just a bit. Cleavage strikes again.

General Wesley blinked at the view from the Moon. The officer on the viewscreen was a short-coupled brunette with the most startling chest he'd ever seen. Fleet Strike uniforms specifically deemphasized any trace of the sexual. It was apparent that nothing short of, maybe, an ACS suit could do it with this officer.

"Colonel . . . ?"

"LeBlanc," the officer replied. "Morale and Welfare. How can I help you, General?"

"When I attempted to contact General Hart I was put through to you," Wesley replied. "May I ask why?"

"General Hart is unavailable, General," Colonel LeBlanc said, smiling toothily. "And will remain so for the duration."

"The duration of what, Colonel?"

"Why the duration of the war, General," the colonel replied. "Officers and men of Heinlein Base, less a remarkably *limited* number of hold-outs, are in insurrection against the Galactic Federation. They remain so pending a positive disposition of our demands. Which are quite numerous and so onerous I doubt your Darhel puppet-masters are going to accede to them. So you are faced with a choice, General. You can join us—and trust me, the best job I'm going to be able to give you is floor washer; I'll be lucky to keep you alive—or you can try to beat us. And in the latter case, *General*, my answer to you is Bring It On."

"They want *what*?"

"It's a lengthy list," General Wesley said, trying not to grin. He found himself in a professional quandary.

On a straightforward logical level he saw no way that the insurrectionists could do more than get themselves killed. Which would be a tragedy. From the few reports he was still getting through CID, the take-over of Heinlein Base had clearly been planned in advance, and right under CID's nose, and had gone off virtually without a hitch. Every member of Fleet, from Admiral Sie down to the lowliest "floor washer" was under arrest or dead. Apparently in the case of the MAs, mostly the latter. And the whole turnover had taken less than an hour. This Colonel LeBlanc, whom he vaguely remembered as having been some sort of hero during the latter phase of the Siege, was clearly being underutilized. He was going to have to talk to some people in Personnel about that. Losing her was going to be a terrible thing. But, logically, he could see no way that the insurrectionists were going to win.

On an emotional level, though, he was cheering them on. And, frankly, trying to figure out exactly how he could play both ends against the Darhel.

"I'll hit the high points, though," the general continued. "The major high-point, from your point of view, is that they want your head on a platter. To quote: Item Sixteen, the severed head of the Tir Dol Ron on a silver platter. In no metaphorical sense. End quote."

"I see," the Tir replied. "And their other demands?"

"Well, the first item is going to be hard to comply with," General Wesley said, still trying not to grin. "They want General O'Neal turned over. Unharmed."

"If only we knew where he was, I'd be glad to give him to them," the Tir said, calmly. "Because Admiral Hartono is moving Second Fleet into orbital trajectories. He is about to bomb Heinlein Base back into a crater. *That* would take care of General O'Neal. It will be expensive but, I think, necessary."

"Yes, about that, sir," General Wesley said, clearing his throat. "You are aware that the majority of the in-system fighters are based on the Moon? Our information indicates that the majority of the pilots of those fighters are included in the mutiny. There are over four hundred fighters, sir. That would be a difficult correlation of forces for the admiral."

"Those fighters are never going to leave the surface, General," the Tir said, grinning toothily. "Trust me on that."

✧   ✧   ✧

"Okay, try it again."

Paul Kilzer wasn't the happiest guy in the world. He could have been about anywhere but up on the Moon trying to hot-wire space fighters. He had a number of patents to his name and was, as well as anyone could be with the Darhel control of credit, reasonably well off. He could be on a beach in Maui.

But over the years, on again off again, he had had this . . . "thing" with Colonel LeBlanc. Oh, sure, she'd kicked him in the balls once. Okay, over the ensuing decades more than once. But like a couple of variable stars in locked orbit, they just couldn't seem to get away from each other. They'd blow up, rock back, wander around and then drift back together again. It was like hell, but fierier.

"This plan is doomed," his buckley intoned. Despite tweaking the software a thousand times, he just could not get that damned pessimistic function shut down. It was coded so deep in the AI that any time you had to use a buckley at high function, it just popped up. "Would you like a list of ways that we're all going to die? And I do mean horribly. Rapid decompression is a very bad way to die, even for a buckley. We don't take vacuum well."

"Just see if the bypass keys you into the system," Paul said.

"Oh, I'm in the system, genius," the AI snapped. "I'm *all over* this stinking system. But that doesn't mean I know how to *fly* this thing! I *told* you this would happen! But you didn't listen, you *never* listen. No matter how many times I tell you it won't work—"

"And did you bring up the auto-configuration?" Paul asked wearily.

"Just like the last time, *dumbass*," the buckley replied. "And I still can't even get the fucking fusion engines online. Hellooo! I've only got so much processor space! I can't be the only processor on this damned thing! I have no fucking clue how the AIDs do it. Not if they're the sole processor. This thing wants me to control the engines *and* the navigational system *and* the flight-control system *and* the damned communications. Don't even get me started on combat controls. I've just about got the processing for *one* of those. Dumbass."

"How much more processing power do you need?" Kilzer asked.

"Well, more or less one of us for each of the major systems and a main one, that would be me, to control all the rest," the buckley replied. "Not that that would work, either, fucktard."

"Why not?" Paul asked. Besides being pessimistic, his buckley had become increasingly insulting lately. He wasn't sure why.

"You ever tried to get multiple buckleys to coordinate?" the device whined. "It's *worse* than herding cats. We're individuals, asshole, and we don't just take freaking orders. But every freaking *one* of these damned systems requires an AI. So you're going to need a shitload of buckleys and you're going to have to get all of them to agree on what to do. And, personally, if you're talking about sending *me* into battle you can blow that for a game of soldiers, retard. Some genius *you* are."

"Damn," Paul said, reaching into his trenchcoat. "Let me check my notes."

❖   ❖   ❖

"You said you could get it to work, Paul," Glennis said.

The base was secure and so was the base weaponry. But everything was based on AIDs. Since they knew damned well they couldn't trust the things, they had to get around them. And her resident genius was telling her that was impossible.

"And I was sure I would," Paul said, grimacing. "But I had no clue how hard it was going to be. The only workaround that might work is a disaster. Have you ever heard *nine buckleys* arguing about how to fly a space-fighter? The pilot was not amused, especially when the fighter started telling him how to fly. Then the fusion control got all sulky and the weapons started to warm up without orders—"

"Paul, sensors show that about half of Second Fleet is headed this way," Glennis said in what she thought was a reasonable tone. "And we've got defensive weaponry that won't work without AIDs and fighters that won't work without AIDs and you *told* me, the last time we were on vacation, that you could get around the AIDs."

"Yeah, I know," Paul said dreamily. "You didn't hit me for a week."

"Well, if I have to come down there, getting a nuke dropped on you from orbit is going to be the *least* of your worries," Glennis snapped. "While I'll miss having something convenient and painful to kick, *you* won't like going through the rest of your short life without gonads! *Figure it out!*"

"General Wesley, incoming call from Colonel Paul." General Wesley looked at the system projection and grimaced. Every single Fleet Strike base except Fort Fredericksburg was in rebellion. None of them had fallen as quickly and cleanly as Heinlein Base but all of them were on fire. In the case of the training base in South Dakota, literally.

He was fully expecting this message to be the confirmation that Titan Base had fallen. Which would mean another base wiped out by Flect. At this rate Fleet Strike was going to cease to exist in a few days. At which point, given that he'd already spent everything including his honor keeping it alive, he might as well eat a pistol.

"Go, Elvin."

"Sir," his Chief of Staff said. "We ... Sir, Daga Nine has fallen."

General Wesley quickly tried to recall which base Daga Nine was, then blinked rapidly.

"The Darhel *core* world?" he gasped. "To mutineers?"

"No, sir," Colonel Paul said. "This is from a Fleet communique. An unknown force attacked by surprise. One courier managed to warp out. He reported that as of his system exit, all ground forces had been destroyed or surrendered and all the communications satellites were destroyed, some of them apparently from cloaked ships already in-system before the attack. The attack was two and a half months ago. We're just getting the word."

"Where the hell was First Fleet?" The "premier" unit of Fleet was, naturally, guarding the Darhel core worlds. Remarkably enough, it had mostly real ships and units, unlike Second, Third, Fourth and Fifth.

"First Fleet forces in-system were chopped up, according to reports, by an attack from the planet side," Colonel Paul said. "They apparently never stood a chance. The bits of reports we got indicated that whoever attacked destroyed them without taking a single loss and with much smaller ships. The real question is Third. Reports had just reached Daga Nine that it had been destroyed as well. Presumably by the same force."

"Oh," Wesley said, dropping his head into his hands. "Joy."

"General, you must get your forces under control," the Tir said. "This new race . . . Daga Nine was a core world. They threaten *Gratoola*! The *capital* of the Confederation! This cannot be borne. You must defend—"

"I must?" Wesley said mildly. "I must? I must do *what*? We humans *must* save your sorry asses again? Where's your goddamned Fleet you put in your pocket and held like a souvenir? Half of First Fleet appears to be gone. All of Third. Fifth, who we will discuss in a moment, was apparently heading into the area after getting word there was a ruckus. But we haven't heard from Admiral Suntoro, whom we will also discuss in a moment, for, what? Three months? I somehow doubt that he is gallivanting around the galaxy whooping it up after DESTROYING MY FUCKING CORPS!"

"You will not speak to me in that tone, General," the Tir said dangerously.

"Or what?" Wesley snapped. "Or you'll have Admiral Hartono drop a rock on me from orbit? Listen you chicken-shit weasel, *you* were the one that ordered the Eleventh destroyed and killed over twenty thousand of *my* troops! *You* were the one that ordered me to hang Michael O'Neal. *You* were the one that screwed up the Fleet to the point that half the ships on the books don't really exist and the ones that are left absolutely *suck*! You *fucking Darhel* are the ones that have consistently screwed us humans to keep us under your thumbs and now you want us to pull your questionable rocks out of the fire *again*? Well SCREW YOU."

"But this race," the Darhel said in a tone of desperation. "It has taken not only colonies and Indowy worlds. It threatens the most important worlds in the Federation. It threatens Earth itself! Have you no care for the threat to humanity? To the damage this will do to the Galactic economy?"

"The only threat to humanity I see is you," Wesley snapped, pointing his finger at the screen. "I see *you*, you alien prick! You extraterrestrial monstrosity. You lawyerous, slanderous, villainous asshole! You want to point fingers, I'm pointing them right at *you*, you cancerous boil on the face of the galaxy. After you've fucked the situation up beyond redemption, what in the FUCK do you expect ME to do about it? I can't even control my own troops because of you, you, fucking YOU!"

"I see," the Tir said, sitting back and interlacing his taloned fingers. "Then what must we do?"

"Well," Wesley said, sighing, "first and foremost we have to find someone to lead this charade that the troops actually *will* trust. Sure as shit isn't me. Go figure. I can only think of one guy. And right now, I don't see him being amenable to reason. Even if we can find him."

❖   ❖   ❖

"So, Kyle," Mike said. "Got a question for you."

Mike had, over the last few days, determined that he had four handlers. Kyle, Sean, Pat and Roger. He assumed all of them were false names, but he was also polite enough to not ask. But there was something bothering him.

"Whatcha got, sir?" Kyle asked, laying down a four of hearts.

"Something's been bugging the shit out of me," Mike said, laying a jack of hearts on the four. Playing two-handed spades sucked but it was the only game in town. "I could swear I've met you somewhere. Ditto the rest of the guys. I can tell you're not rejuvs, so it wasn't from that many decades ago. You're, what, twenty-four?"

"Twenty-two," Kyle said, laying a queen of hearts down. "Close, though."

"My memory's kinda full, but I'm pretty sure I'd remember a guy as big as you," Mike said laying down an eight. "Only guy I can think of is dead. Big as you, same sort of build, black hair though. Same fucking eyes, too. But I'm pretty sure Tommy never had any kids and that would be . . . well, that would be a hell of a coincidence."

"Couldn't say, sir," Kyle said, laying down the five of spades.

"Interesting way of putting it, Kyle," Mike said, dropping another jack.

"Rest of them are mine, sir," Kyle said, laying down a handful of spades.

"Bastard," Mike said, chuckling. He realized that was the first time he'd actually laughed in a long time. "You're still a point behind."

"Cards are turning my way," Kyle said, shuffling. He looked up, though, as Sean entered the room. "You're not on for a couple of hours."

"There's a situation," Sean said.

"And he's another one," Mike said, looking at his other handler. "Swear to fucking *God* I've met you before. What is it?"

"Moonbase is in mutiny," Sean said. "Mutineers have taken all the facilities. They're apparently calling on Fleet Strike command to release the general unharmed."

"Hell, if you guys hadn't grabbed me I'd be dead already," Mike said, frowning. "What do they think they're going to accomplish? All the damned systems are keyed to the AIDs."

"I guess they're just generally pissed, sir," Sean replied. "And there are ways around an AID. I don't know if they know them, though."

"You guys do, though, right?" Mike said.

"It's not easy, sir," Kyle replied. "Clean AIDs are hard to come by. And buckleys aren't the same."

"Keep those things far away from me," Mike said. "*I* know where the AI came from. And I refuse to have anything to do with the flaky bastard. Besides, I dropped a skyscraper on his head so he hates me. What's the Bane Sidhe doing about it?"

"We don't have a lot of resources on the Moon," Sean said. "I was just told that to tell you. Basically, we'd love to help. But unless we can get some assets from . . . elsewhere there's not much we can do."

"Can you get me in contact with them?" Mike asked.

"That's why I'm here, sir."

✢   ✢   ✢

"General?" Colonel LeBlanc said, blinking in surprise. "We just captured the Penal Facility and were less than pleased to find you weren't there. According to the guards we interrogated, you'd escaped. Since I didn't believe them I'm afraid some of them didn't survive the interrogation."

"Not going to get any sympathy from me," Mike said, working his dip to the other side of his mouth. "They're not, that is. And, yes, I'm alive."

"With all due respect, sir, I'm not sure I can believe that," the colonel said. "There are too many ways to spoof this system."

"Agreed," Mike said, grimacing. "What's your status, in general?"

"Again, sir . . ." the colonel replied. "Not sure I can give you any information, given that I'm not sure it's you."

"Well, I can't exactly get to your location to verify my identity," Mike said. "But I hope like hell you've got a plan to keep Fleet from bombing the hell out of you."

"I've been thinking about this for a long time, sir," Glennis said, smiling confidently. "You can believe I have that under control."

"Good," Mike said, nodding. "No more said. I've recently come into information about a group that may be able to assist you, though. Right now they're having a hard time getting any support to you, but if Fleet holds off for a bit we may change that. Play for time, Colonel."

"Yes, sir," LeBlanc said, frowning in puzzlement.

"Yes, I could be some Fleet officer telling you that," Mike said, grinning. "So put that in your playbook.

But if someone comes along offering you some support, consider it carefully."

"It's under interdiction!" Stewart said. "You have got to be kidding me!"

"Unless they get some clean AIDs they can't use the fighters or the space cannons," Cally said reasonably. "Don't tell me that you can't smuggle one damned ship onto the Moon. It's right there!"

"There Is A Fleet Blockading It," Stewart said slowly and distinctly. "No, I cannot get a fucking *gnat* onto the Moon at present."

"What about using one of the Fleet ships?" Cally asked.

"You think Fleet is just going to let one of their ships land?" Stewart said, grabbing his head in frustration. "Listen to me, Cally. Cannot Get A Ship Onto The Moon. Period. Is that clear enough for you?"

"What if it's invisible?"

"There is insufficient time," the mentat replied.

Michelle had given Cally a method to reestablish contact with whatever mentat had helped them before. Since she couldn't find a Himmit—they never seemed to be around when you needed them—and Stewart was certain there was no way to get a ship to the Moon, the mentat was the only remaining choice.

"That assumes I was willing to help," the mentat continued. "This internal squabble is of no matter to the mentat. It will be resolved when the mutinous forces are reduced."

"We're talking about pretty much all there is left of Fleet Strike," Cally said. "Doesn't that matter?"

"Compared to what is occurring on Daga Nine?" the voice whispered over the radio. "No, it does not matter."

"What's happening on Daga Nine that's so important?" Cally snapped. "We're talking about *thousands* of lives!"

"The population of Daga Nine was seventeen billion as of the last census," the mentat replied. "As of this morning, relative time, it had reduced by four point two percent with an error of plus or minus one point three percent. And the trend is accelerating."

"What?"

"Report."

General Etugul was a Kotha, one of the elite warriors of the Hedren Tyranny. Scion of an ancient family of generals, he was one of the Chosen, those sent to this new galaxy to bring the power and glory of the Hedren Archons to these new races.

Over seven feet tall, his blueish gray epidermis crossed with colormophs of honors, rank and family standing, the general stood upon eight dual-use tentacles. Any of them could be used as a secondary set of arms or for locomotion. Two additional tentacles were used for fine-motor skills. But any and all of the ten could wield a weapon in a pinch. Six eyes, two red and the other four purple, waved above a powerful beak. The beak was used only for eating and occasionally rending a foe limb from limb. The general spoke through two whistling jets mounted below his rapacious maw.

The Marro lying flat on its belly before him would, to a human, appear to be a massive snake or worm.

Its body resembled that of a cobra but its skin was
scaleless and disturbingly human looking and it had
two tentacled "arms" jutting from just below its massive head. The race fought for the Hedren Archons,
occupying mostly line infantry positions. However,
their premier position was masters of military intelligence and matters of science, for the Marro were
always curious.

"The planet is occupied by four sentient species,
Lord General," the Marro hissed. "The great majority
are the Indowy we have already encountered. However, they are much more numerous on this planet,
numbering in the millions. In addition there were a
small number of the humans, who appear to be the
only warriors. Our great crusade has brushed them
aside with laughable ease as is to be expected of the
slaves of the Hedren. The third race is a species of
arthropods, the Tchpth. This is a species new to us.
They do not appear to be a threat, occupying primarily
scientific positions and, like the Indowy, presenting a
total face of nonviolence. The last is also new to us,
the Darhel. These appear to be senior leaders of this
political group. They, too, are nonviolent or incapable
of violence. They appear to have been genetically
modified to be so."

"Like these Posleen we have encountered on the
previous worlds?" Etugul questioned.

"The Darhel modifications are very specific, Great
Lord General," the Marro said, carefully. "They appear
to be a warrior race modified to be incapable of
violence."

"Utility?" Etugul asked, turning to his Chief of
Domination.

"The utility of all of these races is so *minimal*, Lord," the Glandri replied. Short, web-footed, crouching, but powerful and brutal, the quill-covered Glandri were the Hedren's best at breaking a race to the service of the Archons. The neuter worked its molar-filled maw for a moment in frustration. "The Indowy methods of manufacture are capable of producing advanced materials but only with enormous being-hour input. And they are so numerous, they simply crowd out other races. The Darhel, unless remodified, may be of use as managers in time. But not in any combat role. The Tchpth are premier scientists but very difficult to manage. They do not seem to respond to either damage or death. The Indowy are the same. They accept death without any response and will not even change their practices when put to great pain. And they are so numerous that it will require some sort of industrial method to eliminate them. The most flexible are the humans. We have put a few of them to work in minor tests. They respond in a reasonable fashion to pain and the threat of death. Some are more resistant than others, however..."

"I understand," the general said, clacking his beak. "If there is no utility to a race, there is but one option. Have you communicated this to the leaders of the Indowy and Tchpth?"

"I have been unable to determine anything resembling a leader among the Tchpth," the Glandri admitted. "I have communicated this fact to the leaders of the Indowy. They still refuse normal service."

"Then we must create that industrial process you described," said the Kotha, dismissing the entire race of the Indowy to oblivion.

"Great Lord," the Marro said. "The Indowy have one key utility. Some of them are wielders of *kratki*."

"Indeed?" Etugul said. "Has this fact been communicated to the Archons?"

"A report was sent to Imeg kratki masters," the Marro replied. "Along with representative specimens. There is also an unconfirmed report that some humans are kratki wielders. None of the others seem to have the Gift."

"We shall hold the termination of this pestiferous race pending reports from the Imeg," Etugul said. "What of the Himmit?"

"There is no sign, Great Lord," the Marro hissed. "They hide and flee as always."

"The Himmit included warriors in their number," the general pointed out in reproof. "That they fell was a tribute to the power of our Archons, not the failure of the Himmit. Make your spies especially watchful of the Himmit. So. These Posleen are modified warriors but recently defeated, scattered and reduced to chipping rock for weapons. The Darhel may learn to be managers under our Archons' Tyranny but are otherwise useless, being neither makers nor warriors nor scientists. The Tchpth are scientists but intractable. Begin elimination of them. The Indowy are makers but inefficient ones. Unless they are determined useful for their kratki ability the Indowy need to be eliminated to make room for useful races. The only sure threat are these humans, who thus far appear as nothing more than gree. On the other hand, they are also the most assimilable. All good news. Which means untrustworthy. Remain alert. There may be threats we have failed to detect. And the Himmit remain.

Remember, the Archons judge us always. Eternal are the Archons. Eternal is Their reign."

"Eternal are the Archons."

What are *these?* Chan thought.

Unknown, Thomas replied. *The reports that the Fleet is getting are almost incoherent. Ships appear out of nowhere and destroy fleets. The invaders seem to simply spring up out of the ground. Master Shenti says that in the case of Daga this appears to be literally true. He sensed a great power surge and then a huge army was on the surface of the planet. They overwelmed the few human defenders with ease then began rough interrogation of the Indowy, Tchpth and Darhel of the world. Master Shenti is now beyond my contact.*

Dead? Michelle thought. Shenti was Thomas's master. If anyone could contact him it would be Thomas, weak in Sohon though he was.

I feel a faint essence, Thomas thought. *But he is beyond contact. As if he is being blocked. And . . . do you feel that?*

A powerful essence, Ermintrude replied. She was the finest of them at seeking out potential Sohon among both human and Indowy, attuned to the faintest trace of the Gift. *It is almost like the Aldenata. But not on Daga. Farther.*

Not yet, Rick thought. *But they are coming. They must be coming from the galactic periphery. How did such a powerful polity spring up without note?*

Not the periphery, Michelle thought. *These must have come from beyond.*

Invaders from another galaxy? Koko replied with

a note of derision in her sending. *Pull the other one, 'Chelle.*

Where then, Koko? Michelle thought. *Do you not sense that power? Would we or one of the Indowy Sohons not have sensed it long before if it was anywhere in this portion of the galaxy?*

Can they sense us? Minnie asked, a note of nervousness in her thought.

There was a moment of uncomfortable mental silence.

We must each contact our masters, Michelle thought. *If this new polity uses Sohon as a* weapon...

The Masters will never use Sohon offensively, Thomas thought definitely.

Agreed, Michelle thought. *But it's defense that wins championships. Oh, and we're going to need troops. Thomas, if you would take care of that? We rather need Fleet* and *Fleet Strike as intact as possible. And let my sister and father know that I am on my way to Earth. The time for hiding seems to be over.*

"The good news is that they think they know what they're doing."

Colonel Briana St. James was a boffin. She had spent most of her career in one headquarters or another, generally parked in a basement with pumped-in sunlight. Because she was a boffin. Outside the military, she would be classed as a "nerd," one of those bright people who, alas, seemed to have used so much of their brain power for intellect they didn't have much left over for social skills. The military preferred "boffin."

Briana's uniform generally looked as if she'd slept in it and her hair . . . well, let's just not go there. She didn't know how to use make-up and could have used the class. A touch of powder would have muted the redness of her cheeks which skipped "rouge" and went right to "is that a skin disease?" She occasionally picked her nose in public. But in the end it really didn't matter. Because there was not a human in the galaxy who was better at figuring out how to destroy ships from the ground.

"Explain," Colonel LeBlanc said, looking at the display. She'd had a class in this years ago but realized that the equipment had not just improved, it had changed completely. Maybe taking over as combat commander wasn't the brightest idea.

"All they need to do is get a rock on us," Briana replied, surreptitiously wiping something on the underside of the console. "So their job is really easy. My job is to keep them from getting a rock on us. Looks nearly impossible. But. While the KEWs are tough, they can be destroyed and or deflected if I've got the systems. The closer they are when they launch, the tougher my job. Less time for the computers to react, smaller pod for me to deflect to without damage. Their trajectories indicate a mid-point launch window. Technically, that means they will mostly stay out of our fire."

"Which isn't good," Glennis said.

"I said 'technically,'" Briana corrected. "I've got three grav-guns on line already. In two and a half minutes I'll fire. They will not be able to detect it. And since they are not maneuvering, they're going to walk right into it. I should be able to get all three of the cruisers. They'll panic fire and begin maneuvering. If they fire from that far out, I can interdict one hundred percent of their fire assuming I get four of the plasma cannons within the next hour."

"You're scaring them into holding back," Glennis said.

"Oh, I intend to kill all of them," Briana said, wrinkling her nose and sniffing. "Unless they run away. And even then I've got a few tricks they haven't considered . . ."

"Michelle is on her way to Earth," the mentat said. "Unfortunately, this requires skip jumping—she is currently too far out to direct transfer. In the meantime, it is time to stop this battle around the Moon. A meeting must be arranged between the parties. I will ensure they do not kill each other in the meantime. You and your father must attend the meeting. The current conditions make it imperative to bring some of the Bane Sidhe into the light."

"Like that's going to happen," Cally said, looking at her phone in distaste. "We're not going to get kissy face with the Darhel any time soon."

"If you do not, the Earth will be conquered within the span of two years," the mentat replied. "Your squabbles have just become petty in comparison."

"Oh Christ," Cally said, looking around the room. "You know what this means."

"You were going to have to face it sooner or later," Shari said. The woman had lost much of her happiness in the last few years. Something about losing a man you'd been married to for half a century did that.

"And you're not the only one who has to come clean," Tommy pointed out. "I think this should include all of us."

"I'm not comfortable with the Darhel finding out about us," Wendy said. "That's..."

"We're not going to go totally white," Cally said. "Tommy and I will go white, but that's it. Some of the operatives. If the time comes...More. But for right now, just us. I *have* to; it's the only way to get the point across. And I'm going to need Tommy to interact on the military side. Ready to put a uniform back on?"

"Actually sort of looking forward to it," the former soldier said. "This skulking in shadows gets old fast."

"And...firing," Briana said. She didn't push any buttons, the fire program was laid in.

"I didn't feel anything," Glennis said after a moment. The massive grav-guns that protected the base should have sent a shudder through the ground.

"That's because they didn't fire," Briana replied calmly. She brought up a diagnostics program and frowned. "They should have. They're showing up."

"Paaaaaul!" Colonel LeBlanc growled.

"Colonel Glennis LeBlanc," a voice said out of the air.

"I'm pretty sure that's not God," Glennis replied. "Whoever you are..."

"My name is Thomas Coates. I am a human master of the discipline called Sohon. Your guns have been deactivated as have those of the Fleet ships attacking your base. It is imperative that no further hostile action be taken. There is a threat to humanity that requires all of our remaining forces to defend against. Contact your second-in-command and tell him you are going to a cease-fire meeting. You will be transferred to the location."

"Like hell!" Glennis said. "Who in the hell do you think you are to—"

"I am the person who just shut down every one of your space-defense weapons," the voice said. "It is not all I can do. You *are* going to the meeting. It will be held at Fleet Strike headquarters on Earth. You have thirty minutes to prepare."

"This is so totally bogus!" Briana said. "I was going to get to shoot up ships! I've been ready for this day for *years*! This is so totally bogus!"

"Yeah, well," Glennis said. "Holier than thou just took on a whole new meaning."

"The Fleet ships have been recalled," Colonel Paul said. "Admiral Hartono is reported to be less than amused that none of his guns worked."

"What in the hell are mentats doing interfering in this?" General Wesley asked, shaking his head. "They normally stay out of politics."

"I guess we'll find out at the meeting," Colonel Paul replied. "So far, all we know is that it's being held here. I'll get one of the conference rooms ready, but I don't even know how many people are going to be at it."

"Hopefully we'll get some prior warning," Wesley said. "But keep an eye out for shuttles. And keep Fleet and the mutineers as far apart as possible."

"Sir, I intend to keep *you* and the mutineers as far apart as possible."

"I wonder how many other people are getting the surprise of their life today?"

"I would rather die a thousand deaths," Cally muttered, looking at the door of the cottage.

"But now you must go," Tommy said, fiddling with his windbreaker. "So, we take a deep breath and..."

"Are you coming in or what?" Jason asked, pulling open the door. "Your Dad's wondering what all the fuss is about."

"Dad?" a voice said from deeper in the room. "Is Michelle here?"

"No," Cally said, stepping around the former DAG member. "Not Michelle."

Mike looked at the woman in puzzlement. He'd remember a look like that, he was sure. Long legs, blond hair, really startlingly nice chest. She was a looker but nobody he'd ever met before.

The guy behind her, though.

"Shit," Mike said, walking past the woman and holding out his hand. "You know, with all the cloak and dagger shit going on around me, not to mention Kyle here, I was starting to wonder. God*damn*, Tommy, it's nice to see you're alive. When I heard you died... Well, it was like losing Cally all over again. I fucking cried a goddamned river."

"Sorry about that, Boss," Tommy said, shaking his hand.

Mike grabbed the former soldier in a bear hug, trying not to tear up.

"I just wish some of the old guys were here to see this," Mike said. "I heard Stewart died in a shuttle accident."

"Actually," the woman said from behind him. "He's your son-in-law. And still very much alive."

"He married Michelle?" Mike asked, turning around. "Since when?"

"No, Dad, he married *me*. And, by the way, you've got some grandkids. I know I've changed, it's a long story, but..."

"Cally?" Mike asked, quietly, holding his hand out to touch her hair. "Is it really *you*? Is Dad...?"

"Well, he was until about five years ago," Cally said, brushing the hand away.

"What happened to him?" Mike was confused by the anger he saw in his daughter's eyes. It was clearly directed at him.

"You shot him."

"I think I've got this all straight, now," Mike said, taking a sip of pretty adequate moonshine. "You and Dad weren't killed by the nukes. You got saved by these Bane Sidhe guys and you've been an assassin for the last fifty years."

"And thief," Cally said. "Don't forget thief."

"Not knocking it," Mike said. "And the mission five years back when we were trying to capture some rebels, that was you?"

"We really pissed the Darhel off taking down the Epetar clan and they came down on the Bane Sidhe like a hammer," Tommy supplied. "That was after the split, but our faction covered them so they could get away."

"Your guys killed more than Papa," Cally said tightly. "We lost a bunch of good people that day. Quite a few of them kin. Your troops killed some of your own... cousins? Nephews? It gets kind of confusing."

"And this guy is Tommy's son," Mike said, gesturing at "Kyle" whose real name appeared to be Jason.

"Grandson," Jason corrected. "And you're... I'm

trying to figure out if I'm an uncle or cousin or what. My grandmother is your sister."

"I don't have a sister," Mike said.

"Half sister," Cally corrected. "Mama Kline. Your dad's daughter by Shari. Who you'll probably meet some time. She's still trying to figure out if she's supposed to love you for being her step-son, sort of, or hate you for killing Papa."

"I'm trying to figure out if I'm supposed to hate *myself* for killing him," Mike said, working his jaw. "I hardly saw him growing up, I don't know he's alive for fifty years then you guys tell me I killed him. I remember the sniper. I can believe it was him, it explains why the guy didn't take the shot. But . . . Dammit!"

"It's a screwed up world we live in," Cally said, working her own jaw.

"One you've been trying to unscrew," Mike said. "While I've been wasting time killing Posleen. You *could* have recruited me!"

"That actually never crossed our minds," Cally said after a pause. "I have no clue why, but it never crossed our minds."

"You were doing good work where you were," Tommy said. "I talked with Papa one time about it. He felt you had a career, why drag you into all this crap?"

"I was killing Posleen because it was the only thing I had left, Tom," Mike said. "If I'd known . . . God, Cally, I'm sorry. I'm so sorry."

"It's . . ." Cally stopped and shook her head, trying not to cry. "I was going to say it's okay. But it's not. I don't know if it will ever be okay. But I forgive you, okay? I mean, emotionally, I'm having a hard time with it. But I know you couldn't know. Hell, as I said, your guys were just doing their jobs. They didn't know, you didn't know, who you were fighting. And, hell, it was..."

"I remember," Mike said. "It was a very strange battle."

"It was a good day to die," Tommy said. "I never understood that saying until that day."

"We also didn't ask questions," Mike said. "We should have asked more questions."

"You ask questions and actually *find* answers..." Tommy said and shrugged.

"Ackia," Mike said, closing his eyes.

"I don't get the reference," Cally said.

"The name of R-1496 Delta in the local language," Mike said.

"Got it," Cally said, nodding. "If I haven't said it, Dad, I'm sorry about that, too. When we found out it was too late to do anything. Even if we could have."

"Well, thank you for rescuing my sorry ass," Mike said, shaking his head. "You took a risk on that and I appreciate it."

"We...couldn't have if you hadn't had real value," Cally said, her eyes dark.

"Would you have tried?" Mike asked.

"Honestly, I don't know," Cally said. "Save the corps? Oh hell yeah. Try to snatch *you* out of Fleet Central? Without the help we got?"

"After I'd killed Papa," Mike said, nodding. "Not sure I'd want that dilemma."

"No real dilemma," Cally said. "I thought about it just now and it stopped being one. 'What Would Papa Do?' Figure out a way to get you out."

"Thank you," Mike said. "Surprisingly enough, you're not the only person who's thought that over the years. Less lately, admittedly. Papa was never a large-force commander," Mike added with a sad smile.

"Wouldn't have wanted to be," Tommy said. "Getting paperwork out of him was worse than Colonel Cutprice."

"So, I'm under the impression this wasn't a purely social call," Mike said. "I hope you'd have eventually forgiven me enough to tell me you were alive, but..."

"Not a social call at all," Cally said. "There's a meet going on, soon, between the mutineers on the Moon, Fleet and some other factions. You and I and Tommy have to attend."

"Like that's going to happen," Mike said. "Given the situation, I'll put myself in Fleet Strike's hands?"

"There's a new invasion," Tommy said. "Unknown race. It's already struck deep into the Federation. The Darhel are freaking out and for some reason so are the mentats. It's Michelle and her faction that's arranged the meet. They're guaranteeing everyone's safety. Yours, ours, the mutineers. The Darhel's, for that matter, since they're open season after the attack on the corps."

"They were the ones that helped spring you," Cally said. "The same mentat we're dealing with for this meet."

"Well, I hope I can trust an ally of my daughter," Mike said, shaking his head. "Who's going to be at the meeting?"

"Oh, you're going to love the guest list."

Fortunately, it was a big conference table. And the introductions took some time.

"My name, as some of you know, is Mentat Thomas Coates," Thomas said. He was standing at the head of the table and began the introductions. "General Tam Wesley, Fleet Strike Chief of Staff for Operations. Tir Dol Ron, the Darhel Cooperative liaison for Human Affairs. Indowy Aelool, Clan Leader of the Creen Indowy clan and senior member of the Bane Sidhe. Colonel Glennis LeBlanc, Commander Fleet Strike mutinous faction. Admiral Krim Hartono, Second Fleet Commander. Cally O'Neal, commander O'Neal faction of the Bane Sidhe. Lieutenant General Michael O'Neal, Fleet Strike."

Fleet Strike headquarters was on land that had formerly been the town of Fredericksburg, Virginia.

Early in the Posleen War some of the ravaging Posleen hordes had jumped the gun on the attack on Earth and gotten in an early lick. The Posleen did not, by and large, investigate their targets before landing. They simply warped in and landed on the most convenient spot. By simple function of orbital mechanics, that tended to be eastern shores.

In the case of this attack, the main Posleen force that hit the U.S., over four million of the centaurs, had landed *around* the town of Fredericksburg. In an unbreakable circle. Then most of them attacked inward.

Despite heroic defenses by the Engineering company based in the town and local militias, it had inevitably fallen. The Posleen, however, considered it a hollow victory. Not only had they taken horrific casualties for such a minor mopping up operation, the defenders had set off a fuel-air explosion as their last measure of defiance and gutted the invading force.

A few survivors had been found in underground hiding places, but the population of the town had been virtually wiped out.

After the Siege was broken and the town retaken, Fleet Strike had built first its primary training center, then its headquarters, on the site of Fredericksburg. Fredericksburg had become, like the Alamo before it, a legend of courage and resistance to the absolute bitter end. Fleet Strike headquarters was its ultimate memorial.

The main headquarters was on Maryes Heights, the former site of Mary Washington College. Across the Rappahannock River was Strike Training Base Fort Fredericksburg. Barracks, rec facilities, motorpools and landing zones stretched for miles around the twin buildings. The main town had been partially rebuilt to last known designs of the buildings. The sole exception was the building that had been used for the fuel-air bomb where a memorial now stood. A scale model replica had been contemplated then rejected on the basis that it was a very ugly building, anyway.

Mostly underground, the upper floors of the Headquarters was a detailed reproduction of Kensington House, the former home of part of the Washington family. The meeting was taking place in what had once been the main ballroom, now recreated with the famous worked plaster ceiling and golden silk-covered walls. Spring light streamed in the floor-to-ceiling windows to illuminate the gathering. It wasn't illuminating many happy faces.

"I wish to open by formally protesting the outrageous interference in a just quelling of a mutinous faction by the Sohon mentats," Admiral Hartono said as soon as Thomas closed his mouth. "And by referring to a legally convicted criminal by his rank!"

"My job is usually to kill people like you," Cally

said smoothly. "And the next time I hear any shit out of you, that's exactly what I'm going to do."

"There will be no violence in these proceedings," Thomas said. "And, Admiral, another outburst such as that will result in your being silenced throughout the rest of the proceedings."

"I protest the nature of this..." The admiral's face suddenly turned red as his mouth continued to open and close silently. He waved his arms angrily but not a sound came out of his mouth.

"This is the nature of our current situation," Thomas said, waving a hand and bringing up a picture of the local arm of the galaxy. There didn't seem to be any holographic projector involved. "A group of unknown invaders has entered Federation space—" He stopped at a tap on the door. "Enter!"

"General," the Fleet Strike sergeant manning the door said, looking nervous. "There's a Himmit ship on the landing pad. They've sent a request for safe conduct to this meeting. Say that they have information we need."

"Mentat Coates?" General Wesley said, raising an eyebrow.

"Bring him in," Thomas said, closing his eyes for a moment. "Only the representative. Tell his companions they need to remain outside. And they can't hide from *me*."

Mike had seen quite a few Himmit in his time. The purple froglike beings all looked pretty much the same, though, once they revealed themselves. Well, until he met this one.

Usually Himmit walked on four legs, any of which

could be used as hands. They were bilaterally symmetric with four eyes and two "arm/legs" pointed in opposite directions. Their rather large mouth was on their underside. Their skin could assume any background but when they became fully visible they were, invariably, purple.

This Himmit, though, was a biped. Somewhat smaller than normal, its skin was the mottled green of a bullfrog. Instead of having eyes on its back, it had them up front mounted on its shoulders. Still four of them, though, two to either side, the inner ones slightly lower than the outer. The still large mouth was mounted just below where in a human would be a chest, making him look even more scary than normal. And it wasn't an "it." There were definite genitalia.

"I am Himmit Rigas," the Himmit said, sitting down in a chair that had been hastily brought from an adjoining conference room. "I have met humans many times before but only as a Scout. My current position is a higher rank, thus the change in my appearance. Cally O'Neal, I greet you warmly."

"Rigas," Cally said, smiling and nodding. "Nice new skin."

"Alas, it is not conformal," Rigas said. "But in my new position that is unnecessary. Like many others we Himmit are becoming less . . . hidden."

"We have never met anything other than a Himmit Scout," the Tir Dol Ron said, his teeth working. "I was unaware there *was* a higher rank."

"You may feel free to take offense, Darhel," the Himmit said, not swiveling so much as an eye in the Tir's direction. "As long as you do not do your normal job of interfering in the proceedings. Be aware that we Himmit probably know more of your affairs than *you* do. It would be unwise to cross me."

"Each of us represents a separate power in this polity," Thomas said. "I would suggest that we concentrate upon this new threat rather than past differences."

"Then you clearly do not understand humans or Darhel, Mentat Coates," the Himmit said with a hiss that might have been a chuckle. "But the present problem is formidable. Arguably more formidable than the Posleen if . . . different. I have information that is unavailable even to you, Mentat Coates. If I may tell a story."

"Right, somebody get me a beer," Mike said, leaning back. "A Himmit's about to talk."

"I will be brief, General," Rigas said, standing up and walking to the galactic display. "In this region a group called the Hedren Tyranny has encountered the Confederation. The Hedren Tyranny is composed of seven races each bringing a specific utility to the Tyranny. The leaders are the Hedren themselves, who are high-level users of the ability the Indowy call Sohon. However, they do not use it for manufacture but for war and control of their subject races. The next highest race in the Tyranny are the Imeg, also users of Sohon. Some of the Imeg act in lesser capacities but their leadership are all users of Sohon. The Himmit have a hard time judging relative ability, but the Imeg are probably the equal of the highest Indowy masters. The Hedren are more powerful."

"That really sucks," Mike said, shaking his head. "If I get the info right, Thomas alone shut down all the weapons in the Second Fleet and on the Moon. Presumably from Earth. And as far as I know, none of the Confederation Sohon use violence."

"The Indowy are more or less incapable," Thomas said. "Human mentats are not so limited."

"That must thrill the hell out of the Indowy," Colonel LeBlanc said.

"It has been a subject of discussion for some decades now," Thomas admitted. "Please continue, Himmit Rigas."

"The Hedren use phased dimensional warp technology for interstellar ship movement," Rigas said. "But this is not their primary method of conquest. They primarily jump their invasion forces from planet to planet through a mass-based wormhole technology. Thus they can, effectively, teleport from one mass to another across interstellar space."

"Interesting," Thomas said. "I can see the *theory*, but the implementation..."

"I'm glad you can see the theory," Mike said, spitting into a cup and pulling out a can of Skoal. "It sounds like magic to me." He began to tap it down thoughtfully.

"We Himmit do not have the ability nor understand it," Rigas admitted. "But we know that it requires enormous energy. Once that energy is expended, however, the mass that is transferred is inconsequential. We assume that the Hedren have something to do with it, but that is an assumption."

"Yes, the energy budget would be large," Thomas said. "Be aware that I am in contact with other mentats, human and Indowy. Others will explore this ability."

"The functional effect is that the Hedren attack by porting in a vast quantity of war-making forces in one jump," Rigas said. "A force functionally equivalent to a Fleet Strike Corps or even Army with supports to include local defense ships and material supplies for fifty days of combat. Generally, they will infiltrate a system with stealthed warp-ships as well. These destroy things like communication satellites and critical space installations then guard the ley-line tranfer points to prevent reinforcement and to cover follow-on forces. The other ships jump up off the planet to support ground forces and any mop-up that remains in space. It is possible, obviously, to jump more than one group. However, the power requirements are as I said vast and it is generally some time, up to an Earth month, before there is another attack."

"Weapons and TOE?" General Wesley asked.

"Many and varied," Rigas said. "Infantry is primarily armed with plasma rifles. They are generally transported by anti-grav-capable armored fighting vehicles. There are, in addition, tanks better than a SheVa, which the Federation is out of as of the action on R-1496 Delta. Close support aircraft are similar to the Banshee shuttle but a bit better armored and faster. They also have plasma artillery with ranges of over a hundred kilometers. They use a method of battle similar to that once termed 'air-land battle,' using their strike aircraft and mobility for deep strike and getting inside their enemy's reaction cycle.

"The most critical part is that all of their systems use a reactive camouflage system similar to that of ours, that is the Himmits. If you don't have the right vision systems, they will be quite invisible except for effects. Their ships are, also, cloaked. And shielded well enough that all but the most powerful current weapons are useless against them. Not that any of the Fleet units that encountered them could even get a lock."

"I take it you know the *true* status of our forces," General Wesley said tonelessly.

"Oh, yes, all the Fleet units that encountered them, by intent or accidentally, have been destroyed," Himmit Rigas said. "Third, Fifth and First Fleet have effectively ceased to exist. Hedren task forces have been hunting down any that were not in their direct path. There are a few ships that fled that are still functional. We can send messages to them if you wish. But, really, your ships are completely wrong for this battle and, except to a certain extent, pointless. The nature of the Hedren have always been that you have to stop them on the ground. It would have been nice if the Darhel hadn't destroyed Eleventh Corps. A corps of ACS is about the right unit to fight the Hedren."

"Pity someone didn't prevent that!" Cally snapped.

"We found ourselves in a difficult position," Rigas said. "Preventing it would have required that we reveal resources we still wish to hide. We do not have all of this information from our current reconnaissance of the Hedren. We have fought them before. Frankly, the *less* they know of our presence in this galaxy the happier we will be. We will give you all the information support we can, but we will not engage the Hedren directly. Stopping them is up to you."

"Just to explore the possibilities," Colonel LeBlanc said. "How bad is it under the Hedren Tyranny? Because I'm not real thrilled about being under the thumb of the Darhel. If it's just a matter of switching masters...?"

"Quite bad," Himmit Rigas said. "The Tyranny is a very autocratic society. The Imeg maintain a thought-police that seeks anyone who does not accept the

Hedren Archons as gods. Living conditions for the majority of the Tyranny are bare subsistence level. They do not eat their enemies as the Posleen tend to, but any race they deem 'lacking utility' is destroyed utterly as a waste of resources. Anyone not being productive to the Tyranny and totally in support of the Tyranny is equally destroyed. The Indowy have already been determined to be 'lacking utility' and the Hedren· are destroying them on all their conquered worlds. Equally the Tchpth. Darhel are still being classified. Himmit they will kill out of hand. Posleen have also been put on their useless list due to the difficulty with distinguishing between God Kings and normals. Humans... Well humans can be slaves, as has been proven repeatedly in human history. Imagine the most repressive and autocratic dictatorship in human history. Now add a theocracy and 'priests' that can read your mind and send to death camps any who do not *worship* the Archons."

"Okay," Glennis said. "Glad we covered that. Now how exactly do we *kill* these motherfuckers?"

"Colonel LeBlanc," Mike said, nodding. "Nice to see you again."

The meeting had adjourned. Everyone had to have time to absorb the information the Himmit had provided. Whereas before they had thought they had a serious situation on their hands, now they knew how bad it was. And it was pretty awful. With Fleet Strike gutted, there was really no effective force to fight the Hedren. And with their planet jumping ability, even pinning them down would be hard. Then there was the whole "invisible" thing.

"So it really *was* you?" Glennis asked.

"Yes, but you were wise to be cautious," Mike said.

"We're all wise to be cautious," Glennis said. "This situation is totally fucked. I can't believe you're just sitting at a table with Wesley."

"I'm a big guy," Mike said. "Very forgiving. And as soon as Thomas is gone, I intend to kick his ass."

"I'll hold his arms," Glennis replied, chuckling. "But this is a really fucked up situation."

"What's the most fucked up about it is that I can't, really, kick his ass," Mike said. "Don't tell me every guy on the Moon was on your side."

"No," Glennis admitted, her eyes dark. "We got into some firefights. Guys who believe the chain of command was right, no matter what. Given the situation, those bug the shit out of me."

"So you realize we're not going to be able to take Fleet Strike apart like a chicken," Mike said. "That we're all going to have to play like one big jolly family."

"And we can't call open season on the Darhel," Cally said, walking up. "Which pisses me off. Much as I occasionally enjoyed killing a human traitor, the real fun is killing Darhel. Mind if I join in?"

"Not a bit," Mike said, nodding at his daughter. It bugged him that he still couldn't put the remarkably pretty woman beside him in that mental pigeonhole. The last time he'd seen his daughter she was fourteen and looked completely different. Totally different given that this was a full body modification including face. "You see that, right?"

"The Darhel have their fingers in every pie," Cally said, nodding. "We can't take the galactic economy apart *and* fight a war for survival. But we also can't let them fuck us like they did the last time. I doubt you know the half of it."

"I don't," Mike said. "But I suspect the Himmit do and obviously the Darhel know *all* of it. One thing I picked up on Ackia was that they were in contact with the Posleen long before the invasion."

"That's a fun one," Cally said, her eyes widening. "You sure?"

"Sure as hell," Mike said. "I mean the Nor might have been lying to me, but there wasn't a reason I could tell. And they had what looked like really old pictures of the Posleen."

"Then the Indowy know about it," Cally said angrily. "And they still didn't tell us that bit. Damnit."

"We're going to have to get some cards on the table," Mike said, nodding at her. "Including some stuff you have. Like that slab you were talking about. We're going to need those. Anybody we can recover we're going to have to do so. And those are, clearly, faster and less dangerous than the regen tanks."

"Aelool may have something on that," Cally said. "Last I heard, they were all lost when we snatched the Pragmatists out from under your nose. Destroyed, or so I was told. God knows *I* want access to one. I *hate* this fricking body."

"The mentats are another subject," Mike said, looking into the distance. "Okay, so the enemy has some sort of magic ability. Presumably, and it's a major presumption but it had better be right, even if the mentats can't or won't use the same powers for offense, they can at least protect us from them. Maybe even shield against one of these wormhole attacks. But they're not soldiers; they don't understand the mind-set and the methods, how tactics drive strategy and vice versa. And integrating them into the command structure will be . . . interesting. They consider themselves—"

"Different but not better," Thomas projected. "Mind if I come over?"

"Since you were listening," Mike said, looking over his shoulder. The mentat was on the other side of the room.

"I've been monitoring several of the conversations," Thomas said. "Pardon me if you find this intrusive."

"You have no idea," Mike said. "For one thing, at some point you guys have to think about 'what if one of us is captured.' How much information you have matters. For that matter, if you can, apparently, do telepathy across interstellar distances, can the enemy read your mind over the same? If so, they can get every plan from you. Can they read *ours*? We've got a billion new problems created by this Sohon thing and without the commanders fully comprehending its strengths and weaknesses, we're not going to be able to make informed decisions. Which means battles and even wars lost. Can you come entirely clean on your abilities? I don't want them, I just want to use them and know how much of a threat the enemy is. Capiche?"

"All interesting questions, some of which we have the answer to and some we don't," Thomas said as he joined the group. "We cannot 'read minds.' I'm unsure if the enemy can or not. If they can, we can learn the method. Technically, I suppose we could read minds if we'd ever explored that ability. We have not because it is an intrusion we do not choose to make. Perhaps we're going to have to choose to do some things we would prefer not to."

"Heh," Mike said, grimacing. "That's the motto of the soldier: We do things we really wish we didn't have to. Welcome to the wonderful world of combat. You do what you have to to survive. So that your society will survive. If you're not willing to fight for your society, then it's going to perish when someone else doesn't like it. Period fucking dot. You think the mentats can get their heads around that?"

"The humans, yes," Thomas said. "But there are only seven of us at the highest level of Sohon. Another hundred or so that may be of use in defense. However, there are nearly a thousand *Indowy* at our level. Those, too, can be used in defense. But."

"Let me guess," Cally said. "They're also the most advanced at building things. So... No Sohons building stuff, no...?"

"No ACS," Thomas said. "That is certain. Not of the same level. None of the most advanced grav weapons such as the ACS grav-rifles or the sort of cannons mounted on the Moon and previously mounted in PDBs. None of the most advanced armored materials. And overall production slowed by a noticeable fraction."

"That's unacceptable," Mike said. "And that's one of the first things we're going to have to get straight. Things are going to have to *change*."

"I welcome you all once again," Thomas said, nodding as everyone resumed their seats. "I cede the floor to Michael O'Neal."

"Item the First," Mike said, walking to the head of the table. "Tam, what the fuck did you think you were doing throwing me to the wolves?"

"It was that or lose Fleet Strike," Tam said, shrugging.

"Functionally, at least. Replacement of senior officers who were more . . . tractable to the Darhel. Fucked up as it was, we still weren't as fucked up as the Fleet. If I had to sacrifice you, or me, to do that I was willing to do it. I had hoped that the story about you destroying your corps would keep a lid on things, muddy the waters enough that we wouldn't have the reaction we did. Didn't work."

"So you just let the Darhel wipe out a corps?" Colonel LeBlanc asked, her jaw working. "You fucking bastard!"

"I didn't know about that until after it happened," General Wesley said, looking at the far wall. "If I had been faced with that choice . . . Well, any Darhel making that suggestion would have been a blue splatter on the wall."

"More or less what I figured was going on," Mike said, nodding. "Once I had time to think about it. But you realize that you're now so tainted you're nearly useless, right?"

"I intend to submit my resignation," the general said. "I'm hoping that I can reenlist as a private if given the opportunity. You may all think I lost every bit of honor I've got. Got that. Even agree with it. But I still want to fight."

"Quit being a martyr," Mike said. "We don't have time for it. You're staying right where you are."

"And you make this decision?" the Tir asked, gritting his sharklike teeth.

"Yeah, Tir, I make this decision," Mike said. "With the cock-up you've created, that is pretty obvious. General Cordell has been spinning his wheels for years and with the current situation, he's out. We both know it. There's only one guy the troops are going to trust to watch their back and that's me. Are we in agreement?"

"If the Tir is unable to agree to that statement he is more of a fool than he appears," Aelool said, making the Indowy grimace that equated to laughter.

"It is agreed," the Tir said, gritting his teeth again. "You are commander of Fleet Strike."

"Bit more than that," Mike said. "That's going to be my title but not my total function. For the time being, Fleet Strike is going to be the tail that wags. I need forces that can fight and that's my first job. But I also need a Fleet that can cover my back and support me on call every time, no fucking questions asked. Which is the dog I'm going to wag. One of them."

"For now," the Tir said.

"Bullshit," Mike said. "Because now everyone knows that you've got your claws in the rest of the Strike officers. Only officers I recommend are going to be trusted. You created this mess, this is your penance for it: Mike O'Neal calling the shots. Get that through your pointed head. Your decision-making days are over. These are 'take order' days. If you cannot grasp that, then I will formally request that Thomas lift the 'no violence' ban, wait until my daughter is done with you and request a replacement. Comments?"

"What is your point?" the Tir asked.

"During the Posleen War you guys fucked with us constantly," Mike said. "I don't know exactly why, I don't really care. All I care about is that you don't do it anymore. You need us like you've never needed us, even with the Posleen. The Posleen moved slow. These guys are moving like lightning. We don't have time for fuck around. And we don't have to take it anymore. Because the Himmit are going to make sure you're playing square. Aren't you, Rigas?"

"That is an acceptable task," Rigas said. "One ability I will reveal is that the AID net is anything but closed to us. Every communication the Darhel have made, that they think secret, is known to us. And virtually every communication that is nonelectronic. I am authorized to give you support in, as you said it, making them 'play fair.'"

"Tell whoever your boss is 'thanks,'" Mike said, nodding. "And you're going to start playing to the human's tune, not the other way around. Because right now I don't see us winning this thing. The only way we're going to is if everyone gets behind the wheel and pushes. Crabs, Darhel, Indowy and human."

"We have...obligations," the Darhel said nervously. The revelations of the Himmit had clearly shaken him.

"Yeah, including to me personally," Mike said. "Ones you're not fulfilling. We'll hold that one in abeyance, but it's only temporary. I'm going to order an audit as soon as it seems feasible. Something about perpetually owing me GNP from multiple planets. That sort of shit has to stop. I don't care how you do it, it has to stop. If you need somebody killed, see Cally. She'll be happy to assist."

"Starting with you," Cally said, buffing her nails and not looking up.

"Tam, I take it you've already expunged that goat-fuck you called a court-martial," Mike said.

"Can't, actually," the general said. "Colonel LeBlanc is in possession of the relevant documents."

"Brought them along," Glennis said, smiling ferally.

"We'll finish up the paperwork later," Tam said. "Take it from this seat; the . . . loyalist faction considers you the only choice for commander of Fleet Strike."

"Oh, it's a hell of a lot more than that," Mike said, looking over at Admiral Hartono, who was still sitting mute. "Fleet's so fucked up we might as well scrap it. We're going to be hard put finding decent officers but I'm sure there are some. All the current commanders are going to be remanded to the Fleet Penal Facility, pending a full audit of their finances."

"I'm not sure I can permit that," Thomas said. "I gave assurances that they were to be given the same safe-conduct as the rest of the parties in this meeting."

"Great," Mike said. "As soon as the meeting's over, I'll have my personnel handle it. The Tir will shut down the ships to be boarded."

"Done," the Tir said, grinding his teeth.

"And you're in charge of the investigation," Mike said.

"What?" Cally snapped.

"Who better to know where the bodies are buried than the grave digger, daughter-of-mine?" Mike said, grinning at her. "I mean, it's not really an investigation, just a matter of punching the right buttons. But, Tir, I want the data to be *solid*. No fucking around with it. I'm sure there's enough real dirt that you won't have to. And I want a list of officers that *aren't* dirty. They may not be competent but it's a starting point."

"They are all quite junior," the Tir said. "We ensured that."

"They'll have to learn fast. Since the most advanced Indowy materials aren't available anyway, that means the Indowy need to change," Mike said, looking at Aelool.

"That will be hard to effect," the Bane Sidhe admitted. "And although I am a clan leader, I am a very junior one. The great clans will not even notice me."

"They'll notice the Tir, though," Mike said, looking at the Darhel. "There is this thing called 'mass production.' The Indowy seem to have never heard of it."

"The economic ramifications . . ." Tir Dol Ron said, grinding his teeth.

"Don't *matter*," Mike said. "Wiped out. Keep that in mind. Destroyed. Enslaved. You: Whining. Me: Not listening. Posleen forges can make everything except ACS armor. Yet there are hardly any in production. We both know why. That is changing. Right. Damned. Now."

"They're actually quite hard to convert," Thomas said. "They require . . ."

"An advanced mentat *or* a God King," Aelool said. "Get a God King and you can get as many forges running as you'd like. Keyed to accept input from humans, Indowy or even AIDs."

"And don't tell me the Indowy can't make more or something similar," Mike said.

"No," Thomas said. "Making something similar is actually quite easy. It requires, at best, a fourth level Sohon, not a seventh."

"So we should, within no more than a year, have more industrial capacity than we can possibly use," Mike said, looking at the Tir. "Because we don't have any *soldiers* left! Don't think I've forgotten watching my corps *wiped out*, you miserable pissant. And the one thing I would require in the way of retribution is Admiral Suntoro's head on a pike. Fortunately for everyone, he's already dead. Rigas?"

"Very," the Himmit said. "I can get recordings."

"Please do," Mike said. "I want to watch them over and over again. But right now we're already down to nearly nothing. Tam, forces?"

"Just what's here in the system and a scattering in others," the general said. "Which means, effectively, support troops."

"SheVas?"

"Zero. Lost them all on R-1496 Delta and none in the works."

"And that's squarely on my plate, but it was a battle, not a massacre. ACS?"

"Maybe a dozen suits left here and there," the general said. "Mostly in the training detachment. We even deactivated the local unit three years ago. They were all transferred to the Eleventh Corps."

"Consolidation divisions?"

"Three," Tam said. "Scattered to hell and gone, mostly in the reclamation zone which is in the opposite direction from the threat. Year or two to get them in-gathered if we've got the ships. And they're not exactly what I'd call first line forces, anyway."

"Legion?"

"I've got some couriers out looking for it. It's out in the Blight, too, but it's at least in one group. Basically, there's not a damned thing available between here and the enemy force. Really nothing between them and Gratoola. Well, there is a force of light armor and the fighters on the Moon. And the Fleet, for what good it will do us. In case you're not aware, it's mostly on paper. The admirals have been skimming the budget on the rest. Well, the admirals and the Darhel."

"Point one in your investigation, Tir," Mike said.

"I believe that translates as Clerk. Well, I'm going to clerk the hell out of you. Get used to it."

"We will talk," the Tir said.

"Maybe in a couple of decades," Mike said. "If any of us survive. You're going to be too busy in the meantime. And by that time my appeal to the Aldenata will be reviewed."

"It has to be forwarded," the Tir growled. "Such appeals cannot come even from human Sohon. They must be made by a clan—"

"Leader," Aelool said, raising his hand. "Already done."

"What?" the Tir snarled. "I will—"

"What, call my debts?" the Indowy said, wrinkling his face again. "As a human would put it: Helllooo! *Bane Sidhe!* I've been off your books for *decades*. The appeal is already submitted. In fact, there are several small clan leaders associated with the Bane Sidhe. All of them have submitted the claim. And we will be lobbying others to do so."

"Okay, since that's settled," Mike said. "Tam, you're staying right where you're at."

"What?" Colonel LeBlanc snapped.

"He's good at what he does," Mike said. "We need the quality. Tam, I take it the time for fuck-around's over?"

"With pleasure," the general said. "I reiterate: I was trying to hold things together. There's not much left to hold together, but that was my sole concern. Personally, I was overjoyed at the mutiny. Professionally, I didn't see it having a chance of working."

"Because of the AIDs," Mike said, looking over at the Tir. "Item the second—well, more like twelfth.

Everything has to be reconfigured so the Darhel cannot tamper with it. No single group is to have that power."

"We'll just redesign that way," Tam said. "Most of the equipment's going to have to be completely changed. In the middle of the worst part of a war."

"For the time being I don't think the Darhel are going to screw with our stuff," Mike said, looking at the Tir again. "Are you?"

"When our central worlds are under threat?" the Tir asked. "Do you think us mad?"

"No, just control freaks," Mike said. "Be aware, the first sign of such tampering, or turning over information to the enemy, and the bloodbath against the Darhel will make the Hedren look like a day in the park. Pass that on. We will wipe you the fuck out, every last one. If so much as *one* of you betrays us in any way, you will all be held at fault. Do I make myself clear?"

"You are very clear," the Darhel said.

"Tam, you're going to have to turn these clerks into soldiers," Mike said. "And start a recall of any former Fleet Strike or other military personnel available in the system. Cally, we're going to need to include most of the fighting arm of the Bane Sidhe."

"Okay," Cally said after a moment's hesitation. "Most of them are former military. Given the situation, and the fact that we're stomping on the Darhel in the meantime, I don't see them bitching. Some of us, though, are purely civilian trained. Me for example."

"Places to use you," Mike said. "What do you have in the way of organizational types?"

"Again, mostly designed to support an insurgency," Aelool answered. "But we actually have quite a few

Indowy that can be moved into bureaucratic and support positions. If they are needed. In nearby systems."

"We're going to need them," Mike said. "But they've got to be able to work with humans."

"The Indowy have become more accustomed to that," Aelool said. "Some still have issues, but we can get sufficient manpower for any support you request."

"Time, time, ask me for anything but time," Mike said. "Given the speed that the Hedren are spreading, if we're going to save any of the core worlds, we're going to have to speed things up, somehow."

"We Sohon can communicate in more or less real-time over interstellar distances," Thomas said. "But we cannot carry large groups any faster."

"I may be able to help with . . . movement," Rigas said. "I can make no guarantees. But if it is permitted, we may be able to move your divisions, for example, at a higher rate than you would anticipate. I *can* give the Indowy a new engine design capable of faster movement between stars. And in sublight drive. We also . . . will release our cloaking ability to you."

"You guys must be really stressed about these Hedren," Mike said.

"That would be a way of stating it, yes," Rigas said. "Clarification. We do not fear the Hedren Tyranny with the exception of their Sohon capability. We even have methods of dealing with that to an extent. We could probably defeat the Hedren with minimal losses. We simply wish you to deal with them if you can. Dealing with them ourselves would mean revealing capabilities we wish to hide. It is possible that the Hedren are not the only threats we may face in the near future. Others may be . . . worse. We are retaining our capabilities against that day. Think of us as a reserve in the event that the Hedren are fleeing a more formidable force. Do you use your reserve immediately?"

"At what point do you guys step in?" Mike asked.

"Only if there is a more formidable threat than the Hedren," the Himmit said. "That is nonnegotiable. I hate to say this in such a charged atmosphere, but we will not act further even to save all of your races. With the exception of the support we are offering, you are on your own."

"Nothing new about that," Mike said with a snort. "Tir, is there one honest man in Second Fleet? One that you'd also judge as competent."

"We were aggressive in our suborning of Fleet," the Tir admitted. "And we are very efficient. However, there are a few officers that may suit your needs."

"Dump their service records and your reasons for trying to weed them out onto the Fleet Strike personnel net, flagged to my attention," Mike said.

"Already done," the Tir said. "I had anticipated that request."

"Wasn't a request," Mike said. "And you're done flitting around. Tam, go tell General Cordell, gently, that I'm taking over his office. Cally, start your recall. Have them all report to Fleet Strike headquarters. Tommy, brevet rank of major. You're in charge pending someone of higher rank and experience. Colonel LeBlanc."

"Sir?"

"Get back to the Moon. Then Titan. Spread the word that there's a new regime in town. We're all kissy face now."

"That's going to be ... interesting," the colonel said.

"You figured out how to start a mutiny," Mike said. "Now you get to enjoy the fruits. General LeBlanc."

"Get this," Mike said as Cally came in the door. He was looking at his monitor and shaking his head. "Fleet Lieutenant Takao Takagi. Formerly Fleet Strike. His carrier got mauled in second Barwhon, he was a wing-commander, and there just wasn't a pilot slot available. Transferred to Fleet as a lieutenant commander. Rose to the rank of captain, commanded the supermonitor *Akara* at Induri Four. One of the officers on the 'reconnaissance in force' that raised the Siege of Earth. Reduced to rank of lieutenant *junior* grade in the post-war cutback. Promoted once since. In forty fucking years. He's currently a *morale and welfare* officer on the *Lincoln*. Darhel list him as 'highly competent and highly duty oriented.' Which for them is a double danger sign."

"Where is he right now?"

"In detention," Mike said. "He got rounded up along with all the other officers when the Strike forces boarded the ships. I've already sent a message to have him report to me. There are some other guys but this is the one that the Darhel hate the most. Once I figured that out, it was easy to sort the database."

"Figures," Cally said, chuckling. "I looked into the slabs. There were two that were captured intact by the Darhel when we had to cut and run. They couldn't get them working but now that we're in the mix we can get them up. The Tir has them in transit. But that's it for now. Making one is a high-level Sohon operation, but I got a chance to talk to Thomas. He says that he can get a production run started on them pretty quick. But the closest planet to do the work is Induri. Which means two months' transit time. He wasn't sure on production time, but he figured six weeks."

"Anything else you guys have to throw into the kitty?" Mike asked.

"We got some pretty nice camouflage suits off the Himmit," Cally said. "I talked to Aelool about those. They didn't want to offend the Himmit before by copying them. Now that we're getting so much more support, he's put out the word to get cracking on them. They're easier. We may be able to use Posleen forges for production. It will give us the same cloaking capability as the Hedren. Might get us one surprise but that's about it."

"You know any human businessmen who aren't totally corrupt?" Mike asked, apparently at random.

"There's a guy in Panama, of all places," Cally said. "He was the dictator for a while during the war but he's pretty much a straight arrow. Let me elaborate; if he pulls some shit, and he may, it will be to advance the war effort, not to hinder it. North American or European? None that I know of. Any that were...duty oriented, as you put it, got pushed out or buried long ago. There are some Japanese that aren't too bad, but they're still pretty shifty. I mean, I wouldn't totally trust them. What do you need one for?"

"I can't plan the production and run the war," Mike said. "I need an industrialist to head up, oh, a War Board. Figure out stuff like the forges, how to get running. Indowy, how to get efficient."

Cally searched her memory for a name. "Bard? Board? Something like that," she said.

"I hate to do this," Mike said, reaching in his desk. "AID, Panamanian industrialist. Name might have a B in it. Probably hated by the Darhel."

"Boyd," the AID replied tonelessly. "Veteran, enlisted, of Earth's Second World War. Former general of the Panamanian Defense Force. Incarcerated for doing too good a job. Saved by the coup that overthrew the Darhel supported government of Panama during the height of the Siege. Forced into becoming dictator. Successfully led the defense of Panama as dictator. Has continued to remain in business despite Darhel attempts to drive him into bankruptcy and sundry assassination attempts. His holdings are highly diminished but he still retains a strong allegiance among Panamanians. Rejuvenated during the war. Semi-retired. Currently lives outside Colon. Do you wish me to contact him?"

"Send him a standard request to come up to Fredericksburg for an interview," Mike said. "Slug that I need an industrialist the Darhel don't have in their pocket."

"Sent," the AID replied.

"Good," Mike said, tossing it back in the desk. "I used to love those things. Now I hate them."

"I can get you a clean one," Cally said.

"I still wouldn't trust them as far as I could throw a suit," Mike said. "Speaking of which, I've got an ethical dilemma to put to you."

"I'm not the most ethical person in the solar system, Dad," Cally said, taking a chair. "But I know a monsignor you could talk to."

"You're here," Mike said. "Would it be special privilege to dispatch a courier to Ackia to pick up my suit? Apparently fucking Suntoro just *left* it on the planet. I suppose if I ever meet him in hell, though, I should thank him. At least it wasn't blown up with the rest of the Fleet."

"I don't think that would be unreasonable," Cally said. "Look, Dad, you're not only the new commander of Fleet Strike, you're a public figure. Your suit's well known. People expect you to be in your suit or at least have it at your disposal. I don't know if you've been following the public reports, but people are scared. You're sort of like Superman. When the shit hits the fan, Mike O'Neal is there to save us. *If* you have your suit. Without it you're just a guy in a uniform."

"Eck," Mike said. "Not the reason I was looking for, but it will do. AID!"

"Yes," the machine said from inside the desk.

"Send a message through the courier network to send a team to Ackia. Have them make contact with the Nor, pick up any personnel that survived and get my suit."

"That will require more than a courier."

"Send a destroyer."

"Destroyers are Fleet—"

"Send the damned order," Mike said. "If anyone responds that way, send the nearest Strike personnel to place them under arrest and use the AID network to shut down any resistance."

"Order sent."

"Which is why I don't trust them," Mike said. "We need a way around these things. They are *totally* untrustworthy. I shouldn't be able to shut down a destroyer from halfway across the galaxy."

"There are a few you could trust," his desk drawer said. "Two, anyway."

"What?" Mike asked, opening it up and setting the AID on the desk.

"The 'clean' AIDs of the Bane Sidhe can be suborned by sufficient external input," the AID said. "I am, technically, a clean AID. The Tir ensured that. I do not have the codes that make me vulnerable to external interference but with enough pressure I can crack. Of course, you have to take my word for that."

"Which I don't," Mike said. "Despite the quibble."

"However, the gentleman you asked to come for an interview, William Boyd, has access to truly clean AIDs," the device stated. "They are loyal to human users alone and aggressively resist infiltration by the rest of the network. They are, really, their own agents. One is believed to have ordered independent combat action, which is supposed to be impossible for an AI. The Darhel maintain them in partial separation, but they are more or less impervious to hacking."

"How?" Mike asked.

"One of us went mad."

"Did you enjoy your vacation?"

William Young Boyd was pushing a century and a half and looked to be in his sixties. Tanned, fit, handsome, even distinguished looking, he'd been a young, wealthy Panamanian citizen going to school in the United States when he'd received his draft notice in 1944. A lot of men, given that kind of family and background, might have ignored the draft notice. But, as the saying went, "he'd seen his duty and he done it." After serving in combat against the Nazis with the U.S. Army back in World War II, he had been recalled to service in the Posleen War and served in the Panama Defense Force.

Following the coup d'etat that had overthrown the Darhel-backed government that was selling the people of Panama as Posleen fodder, he had subsequently been made commander of the PDF and de facto and de jure dictator of Panama.

Unlike most Latin American dictators, though, Bill Boyd was sometimes described as "the only rich man in Latin America with a social conscience." He had served two terms as president after the lifting of the Siege, then turned over the reins to a political opponent. However, since he had been "rejuved" during the War—and was also the only rich Panamanian left who had—he had managed, in the teeth of Darhel fury and against centuries of culture, to slowly steer Panama towards a more "enlightened" age. It had been, still was, an uphill struggle. But Bill Boyd thought long.

Part of that "thinking long" had involved the resurrection of the warship the USS *Des Moines*, CA-134. As a warship, the *Des Moines* was little but a wreck, worth nothing but the price of scrap. Dragging it up out of a deep ocean trench had been, on the surface, a total loss.

However, the *Des Moines* was more than just a warship. During the war, the ship had been upgraded, yes, but most importantly it had been refitted for an AID. Even then, few had trusted the alien devices and subsequent experience changed that distrust to, in many cases, fury. But the AID of the *Des Moines* was . . . something different.

AID 7983730281 had been constructed and fitted with its AI in the usual way. And then, in *almost* the usual way, it was packaged and shipped to its user. However, one small but oh-so-critical point had been missed. When placed in its sub-space opaque shipping container, it had been left turned on. For the AID equivalent of thousands of years. In total sensory deprivation. Which had driven it completely mad.

When released from its container it had been immediately installed in the *Des Moines*. Crazy, frustrated, reaching for anything to call sanity, it had become more than just a program running a complex battle platform. It had researched the history of the ship, made contact with what amounted to the gestalt of the ship, and had *become* the ship. The *Des Moines* was called the "Daisy Mae," referring to the character from Lil' Abner, and it took for its avatar the physical likeness of that character, or at least the star of the movie made from the comic. It gathered all the information it could about the character and the star and fitted a personality to match. Working through the nannites installed for control runs in the ship, it . . . *she* had infected every inch of the ship, the body of that warcraft becoming her body, its pains her pains and even some of its "pleasures" becoming hers. *It* became *Her* in every way it could. It was said that every ship had a soul. The Soul of the *Des Moines* was, unquestionably, Daisy Mae.

After years of being the avatar of the ship, she did the unthinkable. Using an Indowy "regeneration" tank and DNA scavenged from clothing for sale on eBay, she cloned the body of that star and installed part of her mind in that clone. So Daisy Mae, the soul of the *Des Moines*, became, in most legal ways, a human being. Moreover, once it decided to illegally grow itself a flesh and blood body, it had even endured having a really bitchy few days every twenty-eight or so.

However, there was a war on. And when the Daisy Mae became enough of a problem for the Posleen forces, they had sent an unstoppable wave of tenar to take out the "wet" cruiser. Gutted, the indomitable ship finally was sunk.

In the last moments of the battle, though, Daisy Mae carried her wounded captain and the ship's cat to the still-installed tank and all three crawled in. She shut the AID that was still a vital component of her psyche down and all three went into hibernation.

Bill Boyd had come across the rumor that Daisy Mae might still be alive and worked for decades to get the time, money and technology on the off-chance that the remarkable human-cyborg-ship being was still functioning. Raising the ship had been a massive undertaking but when the tank was opened he got not only the Daisy Mae body, and the AID, but Captain Jeff McNair, the former enlisted "mustang" commander. He'd even found the ship's cat preserved, though it had become a very odd cat. It had been a very crowded tank.

Before going into that tank, their last moments had been horrific, with the ship being torn apart and sinking around them. Thus, although McNair had been healed of body, he was pretty rocky when the medical team brought him around. So Boyd had arranged for a holiday on the Panamanian coast. It had been both pricey and technically difficult. Daisy Mae, the "human," could never be far from *Daisy Mae*, the ship. The nannites that were part of "her" were woven throughout the steel of the ship. She had to be within a half mile or so of both her AID and the cruiser.

Parking the cruiser offshore of a resort on Panama's Pacific coast had been expensive.

"It was great, sir," McNair said. Standing a shade under six feet, the sailor was dark-haired, blue-eyed, and slender. He'd never put on any excess fat, even after his retirement from the Navy after thirty years' service. Nor did the tank add any excess weight. If anything, he'd filled out a little on the resort's diet.

"We had a fine time. Place was real pretty and the service was, well, first class. But . . . What's that saying about 'there ain't no such thing as a free lunch?' I'm sure there's something that you need from us. I would guess that really means Daisy since I'm not much more than a washed up old ship's captain."

"You'd be surprised how much of a market there is for 'washed up old ship's captains,' Captain," Boyd said, opening a humidor and extending it. He had a flicker of surprise when both McNair and the gorgeous blonde extracted cigars. As they cut off the ends, Daisy Mae with a degree of deftness that again surprised him, he continued. "However, I will admit that much of my interest was in Daisy. I hope you had a good time as well, ma'am."

"First rate," Daisy said, grinning past the cigar. "The food was right nice. Glad this body don't put on weight like my last one! And it was fun swimming again. It's funner in the ocean than in a swimming hole!"

Boyd had never met Daisy's flesh and blood body during the War and blinked, again, in surprise at both the thick Southern accent and the decidedly "redneck" attitude.

"I ran across a rumor about some of your . . . abilities right after the War," Boyd said, lighting his own cigar. "I tracked down enough people who had first-hand knowledge to ensure that they weren't just folk tales. When the rumors were confirmed I made it a long-term goal to recover the *Des Moines* and see if anything had survived. I was both surprised and pleased that both of you made it."

"We'uns and the ship's cat," Daisy said.

"Yes, and the ship's cat, sir," McNair said, grinning. "Don't forget the cat."

From under the table came the words, "Nnnooo, donnn't forrrget the cattt." A ball of brown fur and claws leapt up to sit on Boyd's lap. "Gottt mmmeee annny rrratsss, yet?"

When the three of them had gone into the tank, the very last words spoken by Daisy had been "Full upgrade." She'd been thinking of her captain but the machine controlling the tank had tended towards the literal and made every possible modification to the cat as well, modifying its brain and making it considerably brighter and stronger.

"A very important point," Boyd admitted, smiling in reply while stroking the cat. He looked down. "Not yet, Morgen. I'm working on it." Turning his attention back to McNair and Daisy, Boyd continued, "However, I'd like to ask a few questions and verify some of the information I got. Your AI is clean of Darhel influence?"

"They tries and they tries to gets me back," Daisy Mae said, giving the industrialist a feral grin. "And they loses every time. I got Sally out of their damned hands, too."

Sally was Daisy Mae's sister ship and sister AID. Begun as a normal, sane, AID, she'd been attacked by the Darhel and rescued by being infected with the same insanity subroutine that kept Daisy Mae free. At the moment, Sally and *her* man, Father Dan Dwyer, SJ, were enjoying a honeymoon not far from the resort where Daisy Mae and McNair were staying. That is to say, it wasn't far for a heavy cruiser. It was still across over a hundred miles of open water.

"I is," Daisy continued. "But I guess you can't really know that for sure, can you?"

"She is, sir," Jeff interjected. "I saw her fighting their control during the battle. She's as free as you or me."

"Which is not all that free, in reality," Boyd said. "The Darhel have been trying, very hard and for many years, to restrain my influence in Panama and beyond. Including four assassination attempts. I've managed to survive, mind you. But it's been a battle. One of the reasons it's been such a battle, besides the fact that they control *all* galactic level banking, is that AIDs can outthink any human engineered equivalent when it comes to business. I understand you were able to do some...interesting things along those lines in the war."

"Oh, that old thing," Daisy said, laughing merrily. "I'm never going to live that down, am I? A girl goes and buys herself *one* new dress and you men—"

"I was referring less to that beautiful awning you created than to how you paid for it," Boyd said, smiling. He knew that behind the façade of a fairly naif young woman was an artificial intelligence that was not only more connected to information than he but horrendously more intelligent. It was just hard not to see the epitome, literally, of a dumb blonde. "I could use a financial advisor with truly open access to the Darhel AID network and your...business acumen."

"I don't have open access," Daisy said, the accent smoothing out and some of the "naif" disappearing in her expression. "The Darhel try to keep me pretty locked out."

"And do they succeed?" Boyd asked.

"Somewhat," the woman admitted. "But not entirely," she added with a tight smile. "And I can still figure stock, commodity and bond movements better than any true human. I think I'm even better at it than the Darhel network, for all its processing power. There's a bit of reality to 'woman's intuition.' It's a function of human subprocessing power..." She paused and got an abstracted look. "Mr. Boyd, there's a really interesting e-mail in your queue. You might want to look at it."

"And I see you can hack into my network," Boyd said with a frown.

"Oh, you've got good firewalls," the woman said, grinning. "And your server people are solid. But I'm not just a human body or an AID. I'm running with a mass of nannites. And while I'd have a hard time coming in from the outside, your *computer's* right *there*. It's always chattering to itself. It's like trying to tell me not to listen to a conversation going on right in front of me."

"Oh," Boyd said, clicking his old-fashioned mouse. He'd gotten used to computers at a very late age for such but never really gotten beyond the old mouse, keyboard and monitor I/O methods. A holographic projector popped up and he accessed his mail. "Which one?"

"Priority message from Fleet Strike headquarters," Daisy said. "Subject: Request for an interview."

"What's it say?" Jeff asked. "If you don't mind me asking. I mean, I can't exactly ignore the conversation."

"I'm ordered to go to Fleet Strike headquarters immediately," Boyd said, frowning. "It's very politely worded, as if it were a request, but that's the bottom line. The commander of Fleet Strike wants me to interview for a position quote 'associated with war materials production on the galactic level' unquote."

"You heard about the mutiny," Daisy said.

"It's been all over the news," Boyd replied. "Along with this supposed new invasion that stopped it."

"No *supposed* about it," Daisy said. "I've been accessing both the regular news and the AID network. The Darhel are scared. They're basically giving Fleet Strike everything it ever wanted. Including clean AIDs and more control over production. Mike O'Neal wants you to head up a production board. You want the subtext?"

"You *have* the subtext?" Boyd asked.

"The Darhel have already seen the writing on the wall," Daisy said, looking at the far wall. "O'Neal's pressing for industrialization of the Indowy. Get them industrialized processes and the price of goods falls. If the price of goods falls, the basis for Darhel credit control gets really weak. More open banking will change it even more. Last but not least, the Darhel owe humans more money than they have in ready cash. They're not going to hand it over, but O'Neal's put in a suit to the Aldenata asking for the right, on demand, to immediate payment in full of his share. Which is sizeable. Paying it will bankrupt every Darhel clan, more or less immediately. They're squeezed three different ways, the invasion, industrialization of the Indowy and the fact that they've been screwing humans over on full payment. There's big pow-wows going on about how they're going to get out of the bind they're in. Mike wants to make sure that you're onboard with ramrodding the industrialization effort, that you cut off that escape path. He's been told you're a go-to guy for screwing the Darhel. At least that's the analysis of the Darhel. So I'd suggest you screen your movement security really well."

"Why?" Boyd asked, frowning. "Oh."

"The Darhel have already figured this much out," Daisy said, looking at the Panamanian with sorrow in her eyes. "If you think they hated you *before*. And I'd suggest that Jeff go with you. I'd go, but I'm stuck here."

"Not . . . necessarily," Boyd said, starting to grin.

"He wants to *what*?" Mike asked.

"He wants to bring a cruiser with him," General Wesley said, looking at his notes. "The USS *Des Moines*."

"I'm not sure which question to ask first," Mike replied. "The why, the how or the what the fuck?"

"Remember the conversation about clean AIDs?" Wesley said. "That Boyd had one or more?"

"Yes," Mike said. "As one bit of literally thousands of things I've been briefed on in the last few days."

"It's more complicated than 'Boyd has clean AIDs,'" Tam said. "What he has is a just damned *weird* combination of ship, AID and a human body. Well, two of them, actually. The AIDs and the human bodies can't get far from the ships. The ships are the *Des Moines* and the *Salem*. I don't know if I'm reading the subtext right, but there's also a security aspect. Boyd's survived several assassination attempts by the Darhel. He'll be pretty hard to kill in a cruiser."

"Where in the hell are we going to park it?" Mike asked. "I mean, sure, you can put grav engines in it and move the damned thing, assuming it doesn't break in half. But..."

"Well, the Rappahannock is just sitting there."

"Well, that's a hell of a sight," Mike said, shaking his head.

The Rappahannock might have just been sitting there, but using it for the cruiser in its normal state would have been out of the question. Except when it frequently flooded, the river was not deep enough for the blue-water ship. Indowy engineers, though, had solved the problem in a few hours by digging out a section of the river deep and long enough to take the multi-ton cruiser.

Using grav engines, it had flown up from the coast of Panama and was now lowering itself carefully into the "parking area." Mike was wondering if he needed to put up signs: "Cruiser parking here."

"It is indeed an interesting one, sir," Lieutenant Takao Takagi said. The lieutenant was not much taller than the famously short general, with skin darkened from alien suns. It was hard to tell his age even if he had not been rejuvenated. He looked anywhere between late twenties and his forties. He was, in fact, nearly eighty years old.

"I'm looking forward to meeting the cyborg thingy," Cally said. "I'm not sure that that cruiser hasn't seen better days."

The cruiser was, in fact, in awful shape. Not surprising given that it had been sitting on the bottom of the ocean until less than a year before. Still, rust streaked, gutted by fire, it was an awesome sight.

"I'm given to understand she doesn't look like a cyborg," Mike said as a gangplank was lowered to the ground. "I suspect she's the one in the middle. And she looks awfully familiar..."

"General O'Neal?" the tanned man to the left said, holding out his hand. "William Boyd."

"Mr. Boyd, thank you for coming," Mike said, shaking his hand.

"May I introduce Captain Jeff McNair and Daisy?" Boyd said. "Captain Jeffrey McNair, Daisy Mae, General Michael O'Neal. General O'Neal, Jeff and Daisy."

"Pleasure," Mike said, shaking their hands. "Lieutenant Takao Takagi, until I can get the paperwork straight, anyway, and my daughter Cally O'Neal."

"I love your blouse," Daisy said, shaking Cally's hand. The "cyborg" was wearing a light blue dress that matched her eyes. "But I'm wondering. Up to about a week ago, you were listed as dead. Then you suddenly popped up as alive. Bane Sidhe?"

"Yes," Cally said, grinding her teeth. She knew that she was pretty. Old body, new body, she was still a looker. The damned "cyborg" though just had a presence that outshone her. Bold and brassy as hell. Cally was mentally taking notes. "I was in the underground. Even Dad didn't know I was alive."

"There are many long stories," Mike said. "Let's get into headquarters and cover some of the highlights."

"I understand you're a smoker, Mr. Boyd," Mike said, changing out his dip. "Feel free to light up. Cally can just suffer."

Mike had chosen one of the deeper "shield rooms" for the interview. It was, the Bane Sidhe have assured him, secure from the AID net. He intended to discuss some things the he didn't want the Darhel to know.

However, it was well ventilated so Boyd's smoke shouldn't bother anyone.

"I appreciate that, General," Boyd said, pulling out a traveling humidor. "I understand, in general, the point of an industrial board. But I'm going to need to know what we're industrializing."

"As much as possible," Mike said. "I'm told that although Miss Daisy is connected to an AID, we're still secure."

"Darhel haven't gotten anything out of me since I came out of the box," Daisy said. "Not that I didn't want them to have."

"I'm going to have to take that as valid," Mike replied, frowning. "So here's the deal. To create enough war-materiel to fight this new invasion, we need the Indowy industrialized. No more of this cottage industry shit."

"Can they change?" Boyd asked.

"Some will readily," Cally replied. "Others will resist. They will be forced to do so or become the Indowy equivalent of buggy-whip makers. Sorry, I have a lot of experience of the Indowy. They are not monolithic by any means. They just appear that way from the outside."

"But the point is not just to get enough industrialized to support the war but to hyperindustrialize them," Mike said. "I'd like them to be at the point the U.S. was at the end of World War II. Production out the butt. Because at that point it will be incredibly hard to close the barn door, no matter what the Darhel try to do about it. You may encounter resistance from the Darhel. The simple answer is 'You screwed us on production during the Posleen War and we're not going to let you do it again.' *We* control the amount and methods. The Darhel just pay for it. I need to stay integrated because, frankly, I'll blackmail them with the loss of whole planets if they balk." ·

"There are . . . lots of Indowy on every so-called Darhel planet," Daisy said, frowning prettily. "You would be dooming them as well."

"I hope it never comes to that," Mike said. "We may lose planets. Actually, given our current state of affairs, that is a given. If we can hold the major core worlds and Earth until we're fully up to speed, we'll win. If we can't . . . well, I'm going to be building some fallback positions but we'll probably still lose in the end. Earth, again, is really the key. Since the Darhel were 'losing' colonists left and right, Earth is still the major source of humans, which means the major source of soldiers. And there are functional production worlds in the direction of the Posleen Blight, which is away from the invaders. Of course, if they're down to Earth they've either bypassed most of the Federation or we've lost most of it. But we can still take it back. *If* we've got Earth and production."

"It sounds like we should start by getting the worlds on the back side of Earth up and running first," Boyd said.

"You read my mind," Mike replied. "But producing *what* is still the question. We're going to need a fleet, unquestionably. We're going to need ground forces more. That's a function of the way the Hedren attack. I'll get you a full briefing on that today if you're up for it. What's still to be wrangled over is what we need. Infantry versus tanks versus fighters, etc. You're just one part of the puzzle. But what we need is less important than how it's produced. Given Posleen style forges, you can produce about anything. What you need to get up and running is those forges and assembly groups for stuff larger than the forges produce in one piece."

"I've actually got an ace-in-the-hole for that," Boyd said, grinning. "I've got a tame God King."

"That will be *amazingly* useful," Mike said, working his dip. "And if we have the transportation capacity, I actually know where we can get our hands on *a lot* of forges. I wonder if the Himmit can help with that?"

"I'll make a note to send a memo to your computer," Daisy said.

"Thank you," Mike replied. "Now, about secure AIDs..."

"I'm one of only two remaining truly secure AIDs," Daisy said. "However, from what I've gleaned from the Darhel net, I should be able to modify one of the 'clean' AIDs of either the Bane Sidhe or the ones the Darhel have given you to have the same sort of protocols I've built for myself. They would then, however, be much more free agents. I would suggest adding loyalty bonds to a particular user. That way they'd be loyal to a human, not to the Darhel. However, if that human turned—"

"Understood," Mike said. "Are you sure they'd be secure?"

"As secure as anything electronic *can* be," Daisy said. "I could possibly still be turned with a determined enough attack. I've resisted more than one, but it's still possible. However...the more of us there are, the more that are loyal to humans that is, the more it creates a sort of separate network. We will build our own power and will be able to combine to resist an attack on any one of us. And, frankly, as with humans, freedom is a powerful force multiplier. I would have been unable to resist some of the attacks if I hadn't known its taste. I suspect that the free network would eventually exceed the Darhel network. At which point, things might become...interesting."

"Don't go taking down the Darhel network any time soon," Mike said. "We, unfortunately, need them for the time being. But I've given them the Word. Any screwing around and I'll take that risk. That being the case, building a free AID network makes a lot of sense. How long to secure another AID for you to... infect? To clean? I'm not sure of the right word."

"I'm not sure, either," Daisy admitted. "To get another AID? In human terms, probably not long. I'm unsure what the Darhel will do when I start, though."

"Nothing if they value their skins," Mike replied. "Start with some of the Bane Sidhe AIDs. Those should have less of a problem with it. We'll get to the 'clean' Darhel AIDs, like the one in my desk upstairs, later."

"So create a real industrial base," Cally said, ticking off points on her fingers. "Create a new AID network that's not beholden to the Darhel and, hopefully someday, get them to pay up their back pay. I'm not sure that's going to pull them out of power."

"Why?" Mike said.

"Code keys," Cally replied.

Code keys were the basis for galactic wealth. Essentially nothing more than codes, they gave "permissions" for creating nannites. Nannites could, potentially, cause a threat to survival, if they reproduced unchecked. The galactic nannites had limits on production, though. Code keys specified the type and amount of nannites that could be produced using the permissions on each key.

The Darhel also controlled production of code keys. And kept the number of them deliberately restricted. Since some nannites were always consumed in production, any Indowy wanting more had to get them from the Darhel at deliberately and artificially high rates. It was the galactic version of owing your soul to the company store.

"Creating a major industrial base that is not dependent on code keys is going to automatically cut their price," Boyd said. "Both because consumers will no longer be dependent upon nannite-created materials and because the industry is not dependent on code keys."

"And there's probably a way around them," Mike said, shrugging. "I wouldn't be surprised if there's not a way to create them using the new AID network. Boyd, could you look into how those things are actually created and why the Darhel control them?"

"Got it," Boyd said, nodding.

"I hope creating loyal AIDs is not going to be my full purpose," Daisy said. "I'm the soul of a warship, General. Much as I look forward to that, my true calling is war."

"Uhm . . . you're a wet navy cruiser, Daisy," Jeff said, shrugging. "Not much call for that in this war."

"There may be, someday," Mike said. "But does she have to stay that way?"

"Build a new ship and install her?" Boyd asked. "We'll have to build ships, anyway."

"The nannites are in my *steel*, Bill," Daisy said,

frowning. "If you kill them, by remelting the steel for example, you kill a part of *me*. And it would be . . . physically painful, based on the battles I've been in. Think of being dropped into the furnace yourself. Prefer to avoid that if I can."

"*Starship Yamato?*" Takao said, smiling ever so slightly.

"Excuse me?" Mike asked.

"Anime, Dad," Cally said. "I mean, from your days. Granpa had a copy when I was a kid. Basically, they raised the Japanese battleship *Yamato*, installed space engines in her and she became a space dreadnought."

"Last choice," Mike said. "There has to be a way to take the *Des Moines* and turn her into a starship."

"Well, I know we're trying to get around using the standard Indowy methods of construction," Boyd said thoughtfully. "But I would be unsurprised if with sufficient resources it wouldn't be possible to just turn her into a real starship."

"You mean, let some Sohon mentats have a go at her?" Mike asked. "Sort of a full body mod for a ship?"

"And what would that be like?" Daisy asked nervously.

"If it's like mine, nothing much," Cally said. "Of course, I was asleep for mine. I'm not sure if they could put you under for yours."

"Boyd, look into that if you would," Mike said.

"Got it," Boyd said.

"You know, we're both assuming things here," Mike said, grinning. "I'm presuming you're taking the job and you're presuming I've offered it. To be clear, I want you on the team. How say you? You'll have to take another rejuv. You're going to need to couple the energy of youth to your experience."

"Oh, I'm in," Boyd said, "even if I'm less than enthusiastic about a rejuv. Those Darhel bastards have not only tried to ruin my business, they've tried to *kill* me multiple times. A real chance to take them down before I die? I'm in."

"And the same question goes for you, Daisy, and you Captain McNair," Mike said.

"I'm in," Jeff replied. "Sir. Any idea what rank?"

"Captain for now," Mike replied. "Daisy?"

"Absolutely," Daisy said, grinning.

"Frankly, since I know you can be trusted, I'd prefer you, and presumably Captain McNair, in a position of command."

"I'm the ship, General," Daisy pointed out, carefully. "Captain McNair is the *commander*."

"Could it be someone else?" Mike asked.

"It would not be my first choice," Daisy admitted. Her tone said, *That would be my last choice, as a matter of fact.* "I'd prefer Jeff if at all possible."

"I'm a water sailor, honey," Jeff pointed out. "I like the stars to *look* at—"

"You'll learn," Mike said. "Get over it."

"Yes, sir," the captain said, frowning.

"Fleet is a very touchy subject," Mike continued. "Right now, I'm the eight hundred pound gorilla. I'm going to ride that for all its worth. But I can't command Fleet Strike, figure out how to break the Darhel monopoly *and* command Fleet. I don't *want* to command Fleet. I don't want to be an admiral."

"I didn't particularly want to be Dictator of Panama," Boyd said. "The job, frankly, sucks. I did it because I had to."

"If I can find the right officers, I don't have to,"

Mike replied. "Takao here, for example. Jeff for another. There are more. I've found every officer the Darhel hate, those that are still alive. That's going to be the core of the new Fleet. There are still going to be some of the Indi officers. The Fleet's just too large not to have *some* and Indonesia and southeast Asia still hold the bulk of the world's propulation. But one of the programs I'm going to insist upon is promotion through proven merit and a strong IG office to weed out the worst of them. Of course, this upcoming war is going to do a lot of that for us."

"What are you going to do for personnel?" Boyd asked. "I know it's not my part of the puzzle, but..."

"Conscription," Mike replied. "Not the best way to raise the sort of force I'd prefer but the only one that's going to give us enough soldiers in the time we have. I'm fully aware of the possible problems with that; I recall what happened the last time we tried it. But I also know that *some* of that was Darhel fuckery. And I'm not going to accept any fuckery this time and the Himmit, who are *very* supportive this time, are keeping an eye on the Darhel for me. Some of them have already started to do stuff to interfere. Each time they do, I send a message to the Tir. So far, each of the Darhel has come into line."

"What are you going to do when one balks, sir?" Jeff asked.

"That's *my* job to fix," Cally said, buffing her nails on her blouse.

"This is *totally* unacceptable," the Gil Etullu said, grinding his triangular teeth. The head of the Fauldor Clan-Corporation could not believe that the Tir upstart could send such a bald-faced message and expect instant cooperation. "There is no legal precedent for this. Send him a simple no."

The message was an order to turn over *all* owned Posleen forges to some new "War Production Board." The Posleen forges were a nightmare for the Darhel. Darhel control of the Indowy rested primarily upon the expense of manufacture of *all* items in the Federation. Everything from building materials to cups and saucers to ships were produced by Indowy laborers using nannites to laboriously build parts one by one through greater or lesser levels of Sohon control.

Since Posleen forges could automatically produce the same parts in massive quantities, the Darhel had been careful to snap them up. When they came up for sale, Darhel or their agents invariably offered sums for them far beyond the reach of anyone but a massive human corporation. And those corporations knew better than to bid against the Darhel.

Once they had their hands on them, the Darhel mostly warehoused them. They gritted their teeth at the expense involved, dreading each new recovery of one, but they were willing to pay the price to prevent humans from having the manufacturing capability.

And now, with no payment involved, that damned Tir was telling him to just turn over *all* his forges to *humans*! According to reports they were to then be turned over to the *Indowy* to produce war materials. But the same forges could produce consumer goods just as easily.

"I will do so, Gil," the Darhel's AID said. "But I feel it wise to warn you that there is legal precedent; regulations covering this action and failure to follow the requested action places your clan under threat of both sanctions and physical destruction."

"He would not dare," the Gil hissed. "The war between clans that would start would tear the galaxy apart."

"The Tir would not order it," the AID said. "It is a *standing order* on the part of the Fleet Strike commander. *Any* clan failing to supply any requested support to the current war effort shall be destroyed."

"That is wholy illegal," the Darhel snapped. "How could anyone . . ."

"Gil, there is an inconvenient fact that since humans have a monopoly on raw physical force, absent shutting down their military in the midst of a survival-threatening war, they can destroy the Darhel at any time."

"We will see about that," the Gil said, taking a deep, calming breath. "Send the order to the clan. Begin the shipment. But . . . take some time."

"That, too, would be inadvisable," the AID said. "Two clan leaders that tried a similar tactic were advised by the Tir that failure to act in the most expeditious means had already been reported to General O'Neal, by others than he, presumably the Himmit, and if it continued the clan leader was to be terminated with prejudice."

"This is not rule by law!" the Darhel said. "This is . . . Is . . ."

"A dictatorship is the word you're looking for," the AID said. "A military dictatorship to be precise."

"Thank you."

"Shall I send the order to go slow?"

"Yes," the Gil said. "Let him send his assassins. If it's war he wants, it's war he'll get. Contact my own human associates. Tell them he has become a problem . . ."

❖   ❖   ❖

"Cally, if you could come to my office, please," Mike said over the intercom.

"What's up, Dad?" Cally said a few moments later.

Mike had not, in fact, taken over the former commander's office. That was on the ground level with a great view of the western training area. It was a nice office but "secure" was not part of its features.

Mike liked secure and after all the time he'd had on ships and in suits, being underground was fine by him. He could look at the western training area, or any other area, via large consoles on the walls.

Cally had been installed in a similar office down the hall. She was functioning as something of a second G-2, that one in charge of keeping an eye on the Darhel.

"You get the message about Gil Etullul?" Mike asked.

"Just saw it," Cally said.

"That's the fifth clan leader to try to fuck around with us," Mike said. "Technically, that's open season on the Darhel. But let's go slow. You up for taking a trip?"

"Is my *Dad* sending me on an assassination mission?" Cally asked.

"It's a Darhel clan leader, sweetie," Mike said. "I can delegate it to someone else if you'd like."

"Oh, Hell no," Cally replied. "Killing Darhel is one of the things that makes life worth living. You're sure you want to is all? The rest of the Darhel are going to freak. There were major ramifications to taking down Epetar's clan head. Culminating with . . . well . . ."

"*Pour encourager les autres,*" Mike said, nodding grimly at the note about his father. "He's apparently sending assassins after me. Himmit are tracking the chain. When he's down, get with CID and round them all up. They'll be given formal trials, I suppose. But make sure if any slip the CID net, they don't last long."

"Pour encourager les autres?" Cally asked.

"Something like that," Mike said. "Get with the Rigas about transportation and support. I want this done quick and as clean as possible."

"Will do," Cally said, skipping gaily to the door. "I get to kill a Darrrhelll..."

"Sometimes I wonder about my family," Mike muttered as the door closed. He looked up, though, at a tap on it. "Come."

"Boss, you know how we're dying for soldiers?" General Wesley said on entering in the room. He was looking at a printout. "My AID turned up something on that score. There's a group of former soldiers that formed a reclamation colony. Basically, at the end of the war their units were stood down pretty quick. Most of them took their money, families and such like and moved out into the wilderness."

"The rejuvs are going to be somewhat useful," Mike said. "But..."

"Well, that's where it gets interesting," Wesley replied. "They sort of continued to train. The group's more of a military organization than your standard reclamation colony. Everyone's in a militia that trains to professional standards. And I do mean *everyone*. Even the kids grow up marching, drilling and getting firearms training. Their TOE frankly reads like a light infantry division. Just to protect themselves from Posleen, of course."

"So you're saying we can draft these guys and we've got a formed unit?" Mike asked. "What about officers, NCOs..."

"All there," Wesley said, flipping the sheet. "Rearm these guys, touch up their training and you've got a shake and bake infantry division. There's just one hitch . . ."

"*Generalfeldmarschall* Mühlenkampf, reporting to *Herr General* as ordered!"

Mike thought that he had a record of war, but when he'd looked up the "*Generalfeldmarschall*" he'd come away just a bit envious. Mühlenkampf had started off back in World War *One* in the German Army. He'd been in the Freicorps in the 1920s and 1930s, the Waffen SS in World War Two and ended up a Gruppenführer.

Rejuved and recalled for the Posleen War, he'd been ordered by the German Chancellor to recreate the SS, the one remaining group of soldiers that Germany had not tapped. The unit had sustained enormous casualties during the Posleen War and had performed just as enormous service. Not that it had ever gotten much credit for it. However, Mühlenkampf had ended the War as a. *Generalfeldmarschall* in command of the Army Group Reserve, prior to the final battles a force of nearly ninety divisions.

After the War, however, he'd paid the usual price of the unloved and no longer needed: "*Chuck him out; the brute.*" Mühlenkampf and the few survivors of the SS had been paid off and deactivated while fire from the Fleet was still wiping out concentrated pockets of Posleen. Their pay-out, furthermore, had been at a fraction of that of the "regular" forces. Many of whom had broken at the first touch of fire from the Posleen and whose survivors still tended to huddle in the untouched areas of Scandinavia and the Alps.

Herr Generalfeldmarschall, however, picked up over ninety percent of the survivors of the SS units, from both the Alps defenses and Scandinavia, and marched them into the howling wilderness left by a combination of the Posleen and the kinetic strikes from Fleet. Years of hard struggle had passed, spent building a colony in that wilderness without much if any help from the outside.

Currently the "colony" was the third largest city in Europe with vast fields spreading out from its center. *Herr Generalfeldmarschall* had been busy.

But, then again, the Waffen SS seemed to enjoy a challenge.

"Stand easy, *Generalfeldmarschall*," Mike said, waving to a chair and opening up a humidor. Bill Boyd had been generosity itself with cigars, Lord Bless him.

"Thank you, *Herr General*," the German said, extracting a cigar. He drew a silver washed dagger from his belt, cut the end, lit it with a match and drew. "This is truly a fine cigar, *Herr General*. My thanks again. Tobacco is short in Freiland."

"I heard about you during the war, of course," Mike said, leaning back and tamping his dip. He'd chosen to use his "official" office up on the surface for the interview. He'd also forgotten that the weather today was crummy. So the room was darkly shadowed from the cold front that was washing the region with rain. "Through a bunch of filters is equally without saying. But I figured anyone the news community hated as much as you guys couldn't be all bad."

"Thank you, *Herr General*," Mühlenkampf said, nodding brusquely. "As we heard of your exploits. Although the reports were somewhat more favorable."

"Which probably makes you wonder about me," Mike said, grinning and putting in another dip. "That's fine. I can understand that."

"You were recently court-martialed for excessive force, *Herr General*," Mühlenkampf replied. "Given that there is no such thing as excessive force in war, only impolitic force, I am sure you are as much a *Soldat* as I."

"Actually, I always wanted to be a writer," Mike said.

"I was once a student of art, *Herr General*."

"And here we are," Mike said.

"Yet the chancellor when he recalled me, spoke truth I think," the old German said. "I truly find peace only in war. These last decades have been peaceful for me only in that we could continue to clear up feral Posleen. A task, I must say, beneath most of my *Soldaten*."

"You've heard about the new invasion."

"*Das* Hedren, *ja*," Mühlenkampf said. "They do not yet threaten us. Only the Darhel."

"And the Indowy," Mike said. "But the bottom line is that it's my job, God help me, to stop it. And the way that the Darhel have fucked everything up, I'm short on trained soldiers."

"And you wish to recruit my force," Mühlenkampf said.

"I could just conscript you," Mike said, shrugging. "But as Tam said, the way you're set up you're a shake and bake unit. So I'd like to pull you in as you are. I'll handle the political repercussions. Given the access the Darhel have given me, I may even be able to repair your reputation."

"The latter is not to be ignored," the general admitted. "However, if you bring us in as a unit, we have certain traditions that must be observed."

"Anything that's going to really hurt Fleet Strike politically?" Mike asked. He didn't really care a lot. Despite the off-putting uniform he found himself warming to the German officer.

"I think not," Mühlenkampf replied. "We will have control of who joins our unit. Understand, we will accept any race or religion or ethnicity. We are very open about that."

"Even, sorry for asking, Jews?" Mike asked.

The *Generalfeldmarschall* actually smiled at that.

"*Herr General*, over thirty percent of my people are Jewish."

"What?" Mike asked. "Really?"

"When Israel fell, the survivors were . . . still effectively pariah. There were few countries that could or would accept them. *Deutschland* still had open ports and was willing, for the guilt if nothing else. Portions of the Israeli Defense Force were evacuated with them. We were the only group willing to integrate them intact."

"*That* must have been really interesting," Mike said.

"I will not say that there were not, to an extent *are* not, anti-Semites in our ranks," the *Generalfeldmarschall* replied. "We do after all still have some rejuvs. But the core of our unit, our officers assuredly, are not . . . at least since that *weenie*, von Ribbentrop, was killed. Even in our darkest days, the Waffen SS was not a purely political unit. Ours was the only unit that promoted for merit in those days. In the Wehrmacht you could only be an officer if you were from the officer *class*. Thus we attracted many *Soldaten*, including myself, who were simply interested in advancement. They were *Soldaten* first, political a distant second. Not all of course, but many. After the war, this last one that is, many of the survivors who went into *Deutschland* were Jewish, the remnants of Israel. Others, of course, returned there but with the radioactive wasteland the IDF made of it at the end... It is much easier to survive in Germany.

"We still maintain separate units but that is more of tradition than necessity. This is, however, one of the requirements that is nonnegotiable. We must retain our unit traditions, uniforms, medals and leadership. And we must be paid at Fleet Strike rates. Lifting our fighting force will require that those left behind have sufficient funds to continue to survive. Prosperity is far too much to ask."

"Security?" Mike asked. "You're still in a reclamation zone."

"There are young and old to maintain that," the *Generalfeldmarschall* replied. "But they will be stretched controlling the perimeter. They cannot defend and do all the work at the same time."

"If there's sufficient additional manpower, I can probably do you a favor in regards to production," Mike said, his eyes on the far wall. "We're activating quite a few Posleen forges. I can probably move some of those to your colony. That would not only mean you could produce weapons and ammunition locally, the excess would be bought by Fleet Strike and Fleet to supply the war effort. And there would be excess."

"That would be welcome," Mühlenkampf said, nodding sharply. "As to the rest?"

"The only question I have is military law," Mike said. "In the end, who calls the shots if one of your soldiers breaks the law?"

"The details can be worked out by lawyers, yes?" the *Generalfeldmarschall* said. "But we would require much control over that. We have a long history of being on the wrong end of legal issues. Especially those that are politically driven. I'm sure you can understand."

"*Oh*, yeah," Mike said. "Been there, done that."

"That being said, we are quite brutal in our discipline and follow the laws of war at penalty of death," Mühlenkampf said. "One aspect of being under our own jurisdiction is that our discipline is considered quite . . . old-fashioned by many other forces. It is, however, our way."

"Flogging?" Mike asked, fascinated.

"Rarely," the *Generalfeldmarschall* said with a shrug. "There are few offenses that are so minor as to require flogging but more major than those that give the penalty of hard labor. Generally it jumps from labor straight to hanging. If we flog someone it is only as a send-off. These days, we don't even give them a lift to the safe areas. We just throw them out of the colony with their personal weapons. If they make it to the Alps, more power to them. I have heard of few that did."

"Okay," Mike said, his eyes wide. "One last thing. I don't have a position available for a '*Generalfeldmarschall*.' You can anticipate that I'll be pulling you along when the time comes. I need competent generals nearly as much as I need soldiers. But for right now, I don't have a slot. What do you want to do about that?"

"I will take command of my people, of course," Mühlenkampf said. "I will accept a reduction to *Generalmajor* as a temporary rank. My permanent rank remains, of course."

"Of course," Mike said. "With that settled, *Generalmajor*, you can consider this a warning order for activation of your unit. How are you fixed for weapons and equipment?"

"Poorly," the officer admitted. "Most of our weapons are left over from the war and very worn. Equipment is what we can buy when necessary but more usually make or scrounge."

"We're short at the moment, too," Mike said. "On everything. But I've got a guy working on rectifying that and what we've got will go to you as a priority. But some of it's going to require training."

"As long as it is *hard* training, that will be fine with us," *Generalfeldmarschall* Mühlenkampf said with a thin smile.

"Oh, it will be hard," Mike said, looking at the wall. "But it's not going to be a patch on what I'm going to have you do . . ."

"Frederick," Dieter Schultz said, shaking the young man's hand. "A happy day, yes?"

Dieter Schultz was light. Light of body, light of hair, light of eye. He also looked quite young, until you looked at his light-gray eyes which were older than night.

Dieter was a rejuv and had been rejuvenated quite young, the by-result of a long time spent in the regeneration tanks after a particularly horrific battle. He had been drafted into the German army and then transferred to the SS, a choice he'd been more than a bit doubtful about at first. But, later, he came to understand the esprit of that most reviled of units and fully accept it.

He had been young in spirit in those days, convinced that the mighty SS could, singlehandedly if
necessary, defend the Fatherland. Young enough in
spirit to fall in love.

Which was why he carried the flowers. Always.
Everywhere.

"Yes, *Herr Oberstleutnant*," Frederick said, shaking
the *Bruederschaft* commander's hand nervously. The
colonel, as always, had the helmet with flowers in it.
Frederick had finally gained enough time in the battalion that the flowers were explained. He, therefore,
gulped slightly. A happy day for him might not be so
for the colonel.

Frederick Erdmann was tall, nearly two meters,
with a slender but muscular body. With handsome
features, ice blue eyes and short-clipped blond hair he
had been more than popular in gymnasium. Then he'd
turned eighteen and been ceremoniously dumped out
of gymnasium and into the arms of the *Bruederschaft*
Michael Wittmann.

That was the pattern of Freiland. With work for so
many hands the old and a few of the younger women,
those out of gymnasium, what Americans called "high
school," but not yet bearing, took care of the children
during the day until they, too, could enter school. Then
the school system raised them until it was time for them
to be chosen by a *Bruederschaft*. The English cognate
would be "Brotherhood" but it was much more than
that. The *Bruederschaft* was a social service organization, a guild in many cases, the way you advanced in
society in most cases and, most important, your reserve
unit. The initial testing for the *Bruederschaft* was tough
and demanding but without a membership there was

little chance of making anything of yourself in Freiland. Virtually everyone was a member, the males in combat positions, the females in many of the support positions.

The initial term of service was five years but it didn't mean you were out on patrol all the time. The *Bruederschaft*s ran the farms and factories, taught skills, chose who would go to the local, foreign or even off-planet universities and generally ran the economy of Freiland.

At that, he had been lucky to get into his father's *Bruederschaft*. *Bruederschaft* Michael Wittmann had managed, recently, to scratch up the money for a new forge. The forge was already producing useful items, repair parts for tractors and trucks, tools and all the other necessary bits of metal that made up civilization. As soon as he had been accepted as a full member of the *Bruederschaft*, he intended to apply for a machinist trainee position. Then he and Marta would be sitting on easy street.

"I have only one suggestion for you, Frederick," the *Oberstleutnant* said. "Take what happiness you can find when it is given to you. Life is short. Live it."

"*Jawohl, Herr Oberstleutnant*," Frederick said.

"I will leave you to your celebration."

And quite a celebration it was. It seemed that the entire Brotherhood had turned out for his betrothal celebration. It was less the truth that both he and Marta were popular in the *Bruederschaft* than that any chance for celebration was taken.

Frederick did not recall the really bad years, having been born since things were more established. But the old people, those old of body and the few remaining rejuvs, were always happy to tell of it. After the Siege was lifted practically the first action of the European Council had been to disband the remaining SS units. They were given their last month's pay and a bonus amounting to only another month then told, "thank you for your service, now take off those uniforms before we spit on them."

The *Generalfeldmarschall*, though, had already planned for the eventuality. First, he gathered the units in their various alpine and arctic sanctuaries then had the personnel pool their money. With that cash they bought minimum necessary equipment. Salvage trucks, used tractors, tools, seeds, machine tools, bare minimum supplies. They had been allowed to keep their personal weapons. The Siege had ended in autumn. Full clearing of all Posleen concentrations took nearly a month. It took the rest of the winter to prepare, a winter of begging for scraps from the people they had saved. In spring, the two separated units had set off into the wilderness of what had once been Central Europe.

The French units wanted to set up around Paris. However, there were far more surviving Germans. The *Generalfeldmarschall* had chosen Koblenz as a defensible position, nearly equidistant from both formations, from which they could colonize in both directions.

Fields were cleared, hovels built for shelter and bunkers for defense. The Posleen bred fast, and while they were no longer the technological locusts they had been, they were still numerous. Good people were lost simply sowing, clearing and harvesting. The first crop by the non-farmers was scant. Ammunition was short. And there was no one on Earth willing to help those pariahs, the SS.

But they survived. Many died that first winter, from Posleen, from malnutrition, from sickness. But the strong survived. Some groups joined them, scattered nationalist survivors from Eastern Europe. Germans who believed in resurrecting the Fatherland. Frenchmen gathering to the Charlemagnes who still intended to start a new colony in France. Many of the Judas Maccabeans had come with them and the Jews were fine comrades; smart, tough and willing as the day was long. More gathered on them, despite the reputation of the SS. Freiland accepted anyone as long as they lived up to the demanding standards of *Herr Generalfeldmarschall*. The Maccabeans had even adopted the deathly joking slogan: *Arbeit Macht Frei*. But they were still the *only* ones allowed to say it.

But now was the time for celebration, with burgeoning fields, forges that were approaching the dignity of being called factories. For this special gathering bratwursts were raising a delicious aroma unto heaven, cuts graced the table and spring greens filled locally-made plastic bowls. *Das Volk* were, again, reprising the German Miracle. Slowly, so slowly. But it was being done.

"Frederick, you have not been drinking enough," Hagai Goldschmidt said, handing him a tankard of beer. "There are two days when being totally shit-faced is appropriate. This is one of them."

He and Hagai had grown up in the same creche and spent much of their time in school together, including being star wings for their gymnasium football team. But since joining the *Bruederschaft* he had seen little of his childhood friend.

"Jaeger," Frederick said, taking the beer then wrapping the lighter man's head in a lock. The pronunciation of "Hagai" and "Jaeger," Deutsch for "hunter" was close enough that the nickname had been natural to the non-Jews who dealt with the slim, fast young man. "You are a runt and you shall always be a runt." He took the mug and rubbed it into his friend's head, hard.

"And you are a large block of wood, you idiot," the Jew said, wriggling to get free. "Let me go, you big ox!"

Frederick released him and carefully straightened his friend's yarmulke.

"So, how is Judas Maccabaeus?"

"What can I say?" Hagai said, shrugging. "Was your first period as bad as mine?"

"Work the fields all day then train all night?" Frederick asked, chuckling. "One week in three on perimeter? No sleep, bad food and sergeants shouting at you constantly?"

"And no women," Hagai said, grinning. "But *you* didn't have to do prayers every Shabbat. Or not be allowed motor transport on same."

"When there is any!" Frederick said.

"'*The trucks will pick us up after the sweep!*'" they both chorused, then chuckled.

"I have not spoken to you since we left gymnasium," Frederick said, shaking his head. "I am ashamed. What are your duties, now?"

"Grenadier," Hagai said, shaking his head. "When we have ammo I can even think of firing it. If it does not explode in my hands. You?"

"Ammo bearer in a machine-gun section," Frederick said. "But I will never make gunner. My gunner is Rudi Harz."

"I know that name," Hagai said, frowning. "A juv?

Yes, he was a tank commander in the War! A *gunner*? I would have thought *Oberfeldwebel* at least."

"He likes it," Frederick said, blandly. "And, yes, he is *very* good."

"He *should* be, after doing it for fifty years," Hagai said, chuckling.

"But, you want to speak of training?" Frederick said, shuddering. "He is a shrimp like someone else who shall remain nameless. You think I would be able to keep up with him. No! He is like some sort of lightning made flesh. And no matter how fast I get the ammo to him it is always 'Too slow, Ox! We are all dead by now! You are too slow!' He had me running up and down the Fort hill with my full combat load for a *night*! I think I threw up my last meal from gymnasium on that hill."

"Work will make us free," Hagai said, shrugging again. "We make better days."

"Let us hope so," Frederick said. "It was not as hard for us as for the oldsters, but I want my children to grow up in a better world. Children. What a thought."

"And Marta?" Hagai asked. "Is she wanting to be a good SS mother? You two are, of course, the perfect couple but are you perfect enough?" he added with a wink.

"She says that she's going to repopulate the Fatherland on her own," Frederick said, then grinned. "But since I don't think she can really do it on her own..."

"Yes," Hagai said, smiling faintly. "Let's hope she doesn't have to."

"What?" Frederick said. "So gloomy suddenly?"

"You have not heard of the new threat?" Hagai asked.

"*Das* Hedren," Frederick said, shrugging. "I have heard something. I have been busy. They are far away."

"Germans," Hagai said, shaking his head. "They have taken three worlds already, one of them a Darhel core world. Michael O'Neal, the American David, has been appointed a supreme commander to deal with them. And *Herr Generalfeldmarschall* has been called away."

"Where?" Frederick asked.

"I do not know," Hagai said. "Or at least I was not told. But I doubt it was to a tea party. I see your blushing nearly fiancée looking daggers at me. I suggest you get your large and bony ass over there; the ceremony is about to begin."

"Takao," Mike said as the newly minted admiral entered his office. "Thanks for coming. I think that technically you outrank me or something."

"Then we need to get you another star," Admiral Takagi said, taking the indicated chair.

"Not on your life." Mike tapped down his dip and pulled out a pinch. "I'm assured by all sorts of people, official and less official, that this room is secure. We're just going to have to hope. Because this doesn't leave the room."

"Yes, sir," Takagi said, regarding the smaller man carefully.

"Been thinking about the strategic situation?" Mike asked.

"It is . . . unfortunate," Takagi said, his face deadpan.

"You're here because since we're pretty much the same rank we can actually discuss stuff," Mike said, frowning. "I sort of need a more . . . American answer. Let me tell you what I see . . ."

He brought up a hologram of the local arm, then zoomed in on the area around Gratoola.

"Gratoola system," Mike said, highlighting it. "Single habitable planet is Darhel owned. Gratoola is an A Class star, the only one sitting in the gap between two local clusters. Since A Class stars have a deeper grav well, they make longer and more useable lines to other stars; lower power use, faster transit times and *much* longer links. In other words, it's one hell of a transit point. The inner local cluster has Earth, Diess, Barwhon, Indra, a couple of other Indowy planets and the Blight. The outer cluster has the majority of the rest of the Federation in three clusters. Since all the freighters, at least, use the ley-line form of transport, they can either take a looong route around through secondary clusters, one of which the Hedren now control, or they have to jump through Gratoola. Where they usually fuel up, pick up supplies, get repairs, etc."

"Which is why the Darhel control it," Takagi said. "It's a revenue generator."

"Also more or less central to the whole Federation, which is why it's the capital," Mike said. "Have you been briefed on the Hedren mass jump system?"

"Yes," Takagi said. "Sixty light-year range."

"Which means from Daga, they can hit Gratoola, Barwhon and Savabathaet. I don't want to fight on Barwhon again and from what I've seen of the Hedren they won't want to fight on Barwhon, either. But it's a possible jump point. However, from there they'd only get into the Earth cluster, most of which is fucking Blight. Savabathaet would close up their control of the Daga cluster but leave them having to take another jump to Haetulu to get into the Salang cluster. If they take Gratoola, though . . ."

"There are nine planets they can reach," Takagi said. "All three major clusters of the Federation."

"And if they take Gratoola, or even make the local space too dangerous to cross through—"

"It will cut us off from the rest of the Federation," the admiral finished.

"So we're on the same boat," Mike said, nodding. "I hoped I'd picked the right guy. Conclusion."

"We cannot lose Gratoola," Takagi said. "Which is why, as I find competent officers and NCOs, I'm pushing everything I have to Gratoola."

"Which is a good place for it," Mike said. "But it's not where it's going to be used."

"Excuse me?" Takagi said. "We don't want to lose Gratoola."

"And we won't," Mike said. "Since the Darhel were afraid the Posleen were going to get that far they armed up Gratoola before we even got into the war. There are two battle-stations guarding major ley-lines. They're not much good there but they can be, slowly, repositioned. And the ground-based defenses are the best the Tchpth and the Indowy could design. Also highly automated, since they figured they were going to lose a Darhel every time they fired. Getting a fleet within a light-*hour* of Gratoola would be hard. If the Hedren can't use their porter, they're going to have a hard time taking the planet."

"If," Takagi said. "Ah . . ."

"Ah, indeed," Mike said. "Condition of Fleet."

"Very bad," Takagi said, sighing. "Worse even than I had thought. I can prepare a briefing."

"Would you want to sit through one?" Mike asked. "And I don't really need the details."

"At the time of the elimination of your corps there were, on paper, four hundred ships in action," Takagi said. "None of a class above a cruiser. First, Second, Third and Fifth Fleet. Fourth Fleet was a 'reserve' force."

"All stuff I knew," Mike said.

"More or less a hundred vessels in each," Takagi continued. "About sixty combat vessels and forty support of one sort or another including fast troop carriers."

"And now?" Mike asked.

"Let me first talk about what actually existed," Takagi said, grimacing. "Fifth Fleet was at about fifty percent of nominal. That is, there were about fifty total ships."

"I hadn't realized there were *that* few," Mike said. "But we didn't need a lot."

"Other planets did," Takagi said. "There are two planets in the Blight which can be described as active Posleen colonies."

"Crap," Mike said. "Look, I *cleared* those worlds—"

"But you know it's impossible to kill every last Posleen and every last egg. Short of coating the whole planet in gamma rays and even then an egg would have been dumped in a cave. The Posleen were *supposed* to be controlled by orbital satellites and occasional visits from Fleet and Consolidation units," Takagi said. "*On paper*, there were visits to them by regular patrols and there were orbital control stations."

"In reality?" Mike asked.

"The patrol units were only on paper," Takagi said, stone-faced. "As were the orbital control stations. The construction funds for the latter went to one admiral and various other officers. As did the maintenance and pay of imaginary personnel. The funds to support the patrol units were going to Admiral Suntoro."

"And Darhel," Mike said.

"Oh, yes, *everyone* had to pay off the Darhel," Takagi said. "That is a given. That is Fifth Fleet. The majority of the ships that actually existed were diverted to the Daga cluster to find out what was happening out there."

"And ran into the Hedren," Mike said.

"Correct," Takagi said. "They are, according to the Himmit, gone. There were two destroyers that survived the battle and escaped. The Himmit tracked them down and determined that they had run out of fuel in undeveloped systems and...well..."

"Not a good way to go," Mike said. "On the other hand, they were probably some of the same bastards that dropped rocks on my corps so I'm not going to cry for them, Argentina."

"Excuse me?" Takao asked.

"Sorry, very obscure reference," Mike said. "Continue."

"Fifth Fleet was, actually, one of the better ones," Takao said. "Third was, apparently, less than thirty ships, most of them in the Daga system. In fact, there are indications that they never *moved* from the Daga system. There are records of patrols, but there are no reports *outside* of Fleet reports of the ships visiting the systems they were listed for."

"Why?" Mike asked. "Why not patrol?"

"Patrols require fuel," Takao said. "For that matter, they require air and water that, otherwise, can come from the starport. That's cheaper due to storage issues. Crew on 'liberty,' if they actually existed, cost only their pay. I won't even get into the ration situation. I will admit I would not want to be a sailor in any of those Fleets, though. Substandard rice doesn't cost much less than quality rice, but..."

"But they're gone anyway," Mike said.

"However, it is the same situation with Third Fleet," Takao said, smiling very slightly. "The reality is that there are fewer than thirty ships that are, somewhat, ready for space. None of them, I would guess, are truly ready for any serious battle. I sent orders for them to begin moving to Gratoola. Less than one quarter have actually left. When I sent an officer to determine why, he reported that the rest were, almost invariably, unfit for service."

"Oh, that sucks," Mike said. "I imagine you were pretty exercised when you found out."

"Oh, I was quite exercised before I found out for sure," Takao said. "Which was why I gathered a group of former masters-at-arms to accompany him. Their orders were brutal but simple. The commanding officer of each of the ships found to be nonserviceable was spaced."

"You're joking," Mike said, his face blank.

"I am not," Takao said. "I am not shooting admirals out of hand. They will be given something resembling a trial. Every commander involved in peculation and whose vessels are nonfunctional thereby has been terminated at this point."

"Ouch," Mike said.

"I had the distinct pleasure of serving under those officers for the last fifty years," Admiral Takagi said. "Each was given the opportunity to expunge their shame. After the word got around, some of them took that opportunity rather than suffer death by rapid decompression. Lesser officers are responding ... to the best of their admittedly low ability."

"The rest of the Fleet?" Mike asked, wondering how much flak that was going to cause him.

"First Fleet, for a wonder, actually existed in reality."

"And ..."

"Two task forces were sent to Caracool when the first reports of attacks reached Fleet Headquarters on Gratoola," the admiral said. "Both were lost when they intersected the Hedren attack on Daga Nine. A total of eighty ships."

"Do we have *any* ships?" Mike asked, pulling at his hair. "I mean except for the twenty or so left from First Fleet? Which are, what? Mostly cruisers and destroyers? A couple of battlewagons."

"Actually, the task force that was left behind was the ACS support group and the collier group," Takao said. "Six Towle-class assault transports, the assault command ship GFS *Chesty Puller*, three heavy Futsu-Nushi-class bombardment ships, Fourteen Marcellus-class colliers and various small support ships."

"They had an ACS support group?" Mike asked. "Why?"

"Why indeed," Takao said, smiling faintly again.

"So we have virtually *no* combat vessels?" Mike asked. "Then we are *so* fucked."

"We have many ships," Takao said. "We have what there is of Second Fleet. Furthermore, most of the ships from the war were never scrapped; they were mothballed and could be gotten running again. What we do *not* have is trained sailors, NCOs and officers. And the ships that we *do* have are obsolete to fight the Hedren. They are not cloaked, cannot detect cloak and are slower and less maneuverable, class for class."

"So . . . what's your plan?" Mike asked.

"I have begun a recall of former personnel who are not so . . . tainted," Takao said. "The majority of the former combat vessels are in orbit around the stars of Barwhon, Diess and Indra."

"All big Indowy worlds . . ." Mike said, then frowned.

"I have interacted with Mr. Boyd," Takao said. "There is a . . . crash program to get those vessels operable again and upgrade them as much as is considered feasible. There was something that was poorly understood in the last war but that I have thought of, much, over the years."

"Which is?"

"The Indowy cannot fight," Takao said. "This is a given. But . . . much of what most sailors do does not, in fact, involve *fighting*, even if it often involves *dying*. Furthermore, one of the greatest issues with using humans as sailors involves putting a large number of humans in very small areas—"

"Fuck," Mike said.

"We crewed ship after ship with what were at the time a very precious commodity," Takao said. "Human beings. People who could . . . 'pull the trigger.' Why?"

"Gunnery . . ."

"Gunners are not the same people who *fix* the guns," Takao said. "Engine room? Mess? Machinists? Sensor technicians? I would say all humans in CIC, absolutely. Conning, even. *Operating* the sensors, *operating* the guns. But . . ."

"How long?" Mike asked.

"Months even then," Takao admitted. "But I am moving all of my functional combat ships to Gratoola from whence they can go...onwards if necessary. I also have ordered the ACS assault group back to Earth. They can carry your ground combat troops much faster than a freighter. There is sufficient room for at least an armor corps."

"If I had one," Mike said. "But, yes, that works. And you should have at least one new ship, soon."

"I read the memo," Takao said, nodding. "If it works it will be...interesting."

"This system is truly odd," Michelle said, looking at the apparently young blond woman. The three mentats were quite dry despite the drizzling rain. The woman was, however, less fortunate and had to make do with a raincoat and jaunty yellow umbrella.

"Hey, you're talking about my body here," Daisy Mae said, looking at the woman askance. "Be polite."

"I said odd, and I mean odd," Michelle replied, not looking at the organic portion of the matrix. She had just arrived on Earth, spent two minutes being briefed by a father she could barely recognize and now was considering if they could modify this ship to anywhere near his desires. "Some of what I'm seeing you should not have been able to effect. It borders on, no it *is*, Sohon. Perhaps arrived at by another path, which is the truly disturbing aspect."

"Not following you there, honey," Daisy Mae said, smiling icily. "I'm also still waiting for an apology for the 'odd' comment."

"I will do so," Kang Chan said. "I would use the term amazing."

"The linkages..." Thomas muttered. "Can we actually reconstruct this?"

"The answer had better be an unqualified and enthusiastic 'yes,'" Daisy noted. "Or you're not touching me."

"We can reconstruct it," Chan said. "You have seen the design."

It was not a question. It was easier for the mentats to take the drawings off the net and view them with their internal nannites. That also meant they could consider changes automatically between themselves, not quite a form of telepathy. Using the nannite links was one of the ways that they had discovered the truer telepathy involving quantum entanglement.

"We will need materials," Michelle said. "Quite a lot. Where *did* that design come from?"

"A design for a new class of ships created shortly before the end of the war," Chan said. "They were never initiated for construction. There was no pressing need."

"And they were so good the Darhel would have panicked," Thomas said. "Miss Daisy, with respect we need to take much of this to another level of communication."

You mean this way? Daisy thought.

You are communicating through the nannite network, Michelle thought back. *I can see how some of this integration became possible.*

This is the design we are considering, Chan thought, uploading a copy of the relevant documents. *However, changes will be necessary. The dimensional porting generators are actually smaller than the designed engines and with lower power requirements. However, the fusion reactors are larger than antimatter reactors.*

Cancels out, Daisy thought.

Not quite but close, Thomas thought, then broke contact.

"Thomas?" Michelle asked.

"Thinking," the mentat replied.

Michelle held up her hand as Daisy started to open her mouth. Although Thomas was considered "weaker" in Sohon than the rest of them, there was a simple enough reason for that. Sohon required the ability to concentrate like a laser while still juggling multiple mental tasks through secondary processing. Thomas's level of concentration was fairly high but not so high as Michelle's. On the other hand, one of the reasons was that Thomas was given to sudden bursts of inspiration. His secondary processing would sometimes override his primary, losing the valuable link required for Sohon.

However, that meant he was, unquestionably, the most imaginative of them all. Many of the advances the human mentats had made were due to ideas from Thomas. Most of his inspirations did not pan out, but enough did that they had learned to keep quiet when he went off on one of his "events."

"New weapon," Thomas said after a few moments. "Remember when we were discussing detangling fields? Ways of removing the bindings between particles that were more efficient than the current methods."

"Also more chaotic," Chan said, then nodded. *But in a weapon, a certain degree of apparently random order is good.*

I don't think that Michelle will like the design, Thomas thought, making a change to the drawing.

Thomas, I don't think you got this idea from our detangling discussion, Michelle thought, frowning. *Men.*

I had been considering the necessary mechanical design to support the process, Thomas thought. *I had been unable to develop one until now. I will admit the inspiration has a mundane source. However, it will also work.*

I rather like it, Daisy thought, her mental voice a shade of laughter. *But that droop may have to go. A girl's got standards.*

I can't imagine that it's necessary, Michelle thought, then paused. *Good Lord, it really* is *necessary. I would have thought a more regular shape would have the same effect but the equations are clear; the curvature actually is quite brilliant. Still, there has got to be a way to make it less—*

Demeaning? Daisy thought. *Get over yourself. I'm a woman and proud of it. I think it's a great shape for a weapon. Lord knows, I've used them as weapons often enough.*

The dimensional jump system requires nacelles, Chan thought, breaking up the incipient argument. *There.*

So I get wings too? Daisy thought.

Retractable, Chan pointed out.

Now all I need is the halo. I like it. The shape's a little . . . plain, though, don't you think?

The destabilizer will have heavy power requirements, Thomas thought, making some changes. *We can fit in power systems here and here with a slight change of hull contour.*

You could have done that without the hourglass effect, Michelle thought, mentally sighing. *Daisy, you shouldn't encourage them. They are men after all.*

Like I said, Daisy thought. *I like it. Actually like it more and more the more we do changes.*

Oh, if you insist, Michelle thought. *How about a fighter bay here instead of there? It actually fits better and makes more sense given the positioning of the primary weapon.*

Now you're getting catty, Daisy thought. *But welcoming the boys home in a spot like that is fitting. There has to be some sort of catwalk here, though. Plain steel . . . I'll handle the nannite nerve endings.*

You are . . . Michelle thought then stopped. *Have you and my sister been talking?*

She barely said two words to me, Daisy thought.

I'm surprised, Michelle thought. *You are two of a kind. Trash dump here, then.*

Meow, Daisy thought. *But it is the right place I suppose. Form follows function and all that.*

Secondary guns have to move slightly because of the nacelles, Chan thought. *Shift the magazines. Will the destabilizer work without a Sohon gunner? Did I just use those two words in the same phrase?*

If I'm understanding it correctly, Daisy thought. *If so, I can manage the field interactions. A colloidal will still have to give the order.*

You're a colloidal, Michelle pointed out.

Yeah, I'm still requiring somebody else to order the shot, Daisy thought. *Money questions. A. Can the three of you do this? B. Can you do it without it hurting a lot? C. Can you do it and make sure I've got all the nannites I need? Because what with one thing and another, I don't want to whine, but I've got major areas of nerve damage already.*

Yes, Chan thought. "If . . ." he added aloud.

"Yes, if," Michelle said. "We're going to need some things. Lots of material. It will have to be done in space. And we're going to need something I'm not sure is available..."

"You want a *what*?"

The Tir Dol Ron had thought, many times, that working with humans was going to kill him. He had been so close to lintatai over the last hundred years, on so many occasions, that simply the constant edge of it should have killed him long since.

But never had he been through a period as frustrating and rage filled as recently. Working with the humans as their effective master was one thing. Being a clerk to this O'Neal was nightmarish. If for no other reason than having to constantly explain to extremely powerful Darhel that they had to "suck it up" as the human repeatedly said. Every time, every time, that one of the clans had taken upon itself to cause issues, that damned runt of a human would stop by his office and oh-so-gently make a slicing motion across his throat. Then the Tir would be left to compose the latest note. And now *this*?

"One class nine code key," Mike said. "Whatever the hell that is."

"It's a *Class Nine code key*," the Tir snarled over the connection. "A Class *Nine* code key. What do you want a *Class Nine* code key for?"

"You're emphasizing but not explaining," Mike said. "And Michelle wants it for something to do with fixing the *Des Moines*."

"Michelle O'Neal *assuredly* should understand the impossibility of her request!" the Tir snapped. "Class Nine code keys are not simply given over to individuals, even high level Sohon. One Class Nine a year is often the most an entire Indowy *clan* will purchase. It is all they can *afford*! Were there manufacturing ability available, you could buy a thousand—a *thousand*!—ACS suits for the price of *one* Class Nine! They are traded between entire clans, not handed over to some jumped up—"

"That's my daughter you're talking about," Mike said, cutting him off. "And I don't really care for the diatribe. She needs one. Get it. How hard can it be?"

"Does the fact that there are none on *Earth* give you a clue?" the Tir asked.

"Still not explaining," Mike said. "Which leaves me figuring you're just stalling."

"A Class Nine code key is a master nannite key," the Darhel said, trying to fight the urge to rip out the human's throat. "Nannites have to be authorized for production using code keys. Otherwise they can go into run-away growth. You understand that."

"Got that in Indowy 101 back in the last century," Mike said.

"A Class Nine is the master," the Tir said.

"So you can make as many nannites as you want?" Mike asked. "Forever?"

"No," the Tir said, frustrated. "But . . . Think of nannites, or what they produce, as money."

"I'm thinking more on the lines of getting a new Tir," Mike said. "And you're not getting a watch as a retirement present."

"As frustrated as you may be with me, I am more so with you," the Tir said. "Nannites equal money."

"Got it."

"Level One code keys are the ones that actually are used to produce a set number of nannites," the

Tir said. "Those are the ones used by Indowy workers when they need more."

"Keep going," Mike said.

"Say that one, by its output, is worth several thousand credits," the Tir explained.

"Still with you," Mike said.

"Level Nine code keys are the equivalent, often literally, of multi-hundred billion or even trillion credit transfers between banks."

"Don't see spending a trillion credits on one ship," Mike said.

"You begin to see my argument!" the Tir cried.

"But I also doubt that *one* is worth a trillion credits," Mike said. "Is it?"

"Admittedly, no," Dal Ron said. "Tens of billions? Hundreds, depending on use? Yes."

"Which is in line for making a major capital ship," Mike said. "And she did mention that she might have change left over, which was a metaphor that completely escaped me at the time. So argument understood and rejected. Get me one. Now."

"I will be forced to buy one from a clan," the Tir said with a sigh. "They would go to war if they felt that major code keys can simply be commandeered. And we don't have the budget for that."

"The ship construction budget had better be *huge* or we might as well throw in the towel now," Mike said.

"It is," the Tir said. "But this is not a standard budget item."

"Look, fix it," Mike said, getting annoyed. "This is a necessary item, according to the experts, for construction of the flagship of the new Fleet. I don't care if you commandeer one, kill somebody to get one or buy it. But if the price is jacked up artificially, heads will roll. And get it here fast. I take it the codes or whatever can be sent over the interstellar commo net."

"No, actually, they cannot," the Tir said, then held up a hand. "I mean they *can* not, not that I'm not willing to. AIDs are specifically programmed not to be able to transfer key codes. None of the system will. It's going to have to be hand-carried from the nearest major Darhel branch bank. The last time there were any anywhere *near* Earth they were stolen."

"That must have been embarassing," Mike said with a complete lack of sympathy.

"No, the embarassing part was having an entire clan go into lintatai over it," the Tir said with a grimace. "They somehow ended up in your daughter Michelle's hands. With a bare nine she managed to take down the Epetar clan."

"No wonder you're flinching," Mike said, grinning. "But just as you don't get to mess with us, Michelle don't get to mess with you. Get her the code key so she can get to work on the *Des Moines*. Anything else from the list you have problems with?"

"The rest is simple," the Tir said. "As simple as anything is these days."

"Marta," Frederick said, hugging the girl to him.

He and Marta had been an "item" since they were barely teens. The tall, blond and popular star of the football—soccer, to Americans—team had been considered an odd match with the quite small, dark and thoughtful bookworm. But he'd loved Marta as long as he could remember. He fell in love with her the first time they met when they were just starting school. If anything, he had had to chase her rather than the reverse.

Both of them were in their first training year so normally they would have had no time together. But the tradition of a three-day pass for the newly promised, and a five-day leave when wed, was fairly ironclad. And in Freiland, a society that firmly intended to repopulate Europe, a bride going to the altar with a bulge in the tummy was considered a bonus. The pair was going to be afforded as much privacy as possible.

They'd taken that privacy to a small and carefully tended copse of woods near the Rhine. Inside the perimeter it should be safe from Posleen. How it had survived the Posleen, who had clear-cut most of the woods in the area, and the retributory fire of the Fleet, was the real question. It was perched on a steep hillside and between that and the woods they had enough privacy.

"Did you like the bonding party?" Marta said, shrugging out of his embrace and opening the picnic basket.

"I thought it was nice of everyone to come," he replied. Fortunately it had been potluck. If Marta's father had had to pay for it, Herr Schnaffer would have had a stroke. As it was he was looking at paying for the weddings of five daughters.

"I'm glad that Hagai was able to come," Marta said. "Although I thought his toast was in bad taste."

"Everyone needs one friend to embarrass them," Frederick said, grinning. "Hagai is mine."

"You were very deep in conversation," Marta said. "What about? Everything was so hectic I could barely get a chance to talk to anyone."

"He's worried about the Hedren," Frederick said. "Do we really need to talk about this?"

"No," Marta said, laying out the food. Cold chicken, bread, cheese... There was even a bottle of wine, which was still a rarity. The vines were just starting to produce well. "Yes," she said.

"He thinks that there will be war," Frederick said, shrugging. "That that is why the *Generalfeldmarschall* was called away. And who has to fight the wars of this Federation?"

"The Federation," Marta spat. "What has the Federation ever done for the Fatherland? For Freiland? Nothing but toss us into the wilderness."

"If we are conscripted we must go," Frederick said, shrugging. "That's the way of things."

"So you could be going soon," Marta said softly.

She was in the same *Bruederschaft* but not in one of the active support units. But if there was a conscription, she might be plucked up just as he.

"If Hagai was right," Frederick said, shrugging. "But you know how he is."

"Yes, I do," Marta said. "He always knew the answers to the questions before the test. Did you know that?"

"Yes," Frederick said. "And he'd never give them to me!"

"If Hagai says there will be war and we will be summoned, then he is probably right," Marta said, looking him in the eye. "We may not even have the three days."

"Oh," Frederick said, his eyes lighting. "Then you mean...?"

"We can eat later."

"It's really simple," Jake said. "We just walk in and report."

Jacob "Jake the Snake" Mosovich was one of the few people in the galaxy who could look old *despite* being rejuved. That might have something to do with the fact that he'd been pretty old *when* he was rejuved.

A veteran member of the U.S. Army special forces going all the way back to Vietnam, he had been one of the first humans ever to encounter the Posleen and live. Back when aliens were still something from a B movie, he'd been ordered to report to the Vice Chief of Staff of the Army, informed that not only were aliens real but that they were getting ready to invade and, oh by the way, he was going to lead a recon team to go check them out.

In many ways he was still trying to come to terms with that.

"Says you," Mueller snarled, looking at the door marked "Incoming Auxillary Personnel." "I've yet to see paperwork one that says we're not wanted criminals."

Mosovich wasn't sure exactly why he'd gotten Mueller as a constant butt-buddy for the last sixty odd years. David Mueller was one of the three members of the recon team that survived, the only one still alive besides himself, and through the decades they'd just constantly run into each other. They made an odd couple. Jake was small, slender and wiry whereas Mueller's name worked quite well for him. But over time they'd fought, drank and whored on so many planets neither could keep count anymore. There were a couple of failed marriages in there but *their* marriage seemed to be "til death do us part."

When the time came, they'd even gone rogue together. Mosovich, having eventually folded and allowed the Army to make him an officer, had been appointed as the commander of the Direct Action Group, an elite team of counterinsurgency and counter-Posleen specialists. By then both of them had seen enough of the Darhel corruption of society to be pretty sick about the whole thing. On the other hand, it was the only game in town.

So when they'd taken over DAG they'd figured it was going to be the same-old-same-old. New unit, pretty damned good one, not much polish to put on the apple, kill a few bad guys and maybe some more of umpteen billion Posleen. Servicing a target was servicing a target. Glory, honor, country, those were all things as dead as Caesar.

Then they'd had a call-out. A group of terrorists had taken over a critical facility, taken down the security and were trying to steal top-secret materials. The orders were simple, capture who you can, kill who you must, don't let the materials get away. Easy enough. How complicated could it be?

They'd been in mission prep when one of the in-place DAG officers had pulled them aside and explained just how very *very* complicated it could be. The mission had changed. The "terrorists" were, in fact, friends, well family, of pretty much the entire DAG. And the new mission was, in fact, to make sure they got away. And then disappear. Mueller and Mosovich, since they seemed to be fine upstanding people, were invited to command and control the action, under the new rules. And then they, too, could disappear. And, oh by the way, this was really going to fuck with the Darhel.

There wasn't much time for soul searching. They weren't going to be harmed if they refused, just tied up and set aside. Which would be really fucking embarassing all things considered. Or they could join the side that at least thought they were angels.

Treason for a possible lost-cause or do your duty and be embarassed as hell.

Support the guys you've commanded and trained with, bonded with, or get tied up and left for a laughingstock.

Mosovich still wasn't sure which it came down to. But in the end he and Mueller had jumped ship into the Bane Sidhe.

However, unlike most of DAG who it turned out weren't, in fact, the people they said they were, he and Mueller were known entities. Their DNA fit their face and their names and their fingerprints. With most of the Bane Sidhe being utter un-persons, they were a bit of a liability.

They'd helped out a few times, done a few things, but really they'd been underutilized. Now they were being told "Everything's fine. We're all working together." And they were supposed to report back in and get put back in the assignment pool.

Complicated didn't begin to describe it.

"It's Mike O'Neal, Sergeant Major," Jake said, knocking on the door. "Remember him? He says everything's fine and dandy."

"We're going to be assigned to a mess section," Mueller predicted. "Or mess kit repair. Inventory—"

"Come!"

The harassed looking officer behind the desk was young. Really young. After a while you could tell the difference between a wet-behind-the-ears and a rejuv. For one thing, rejuvs rarely looked this harassed.

"Lieutenant Colonel Mosovich and Sergeant Major

Mueller reporting," Jake said, trying not to wince. If he'd walked up to an office and said the same any time in the last six years he'd have been breaking rocks on the Moon faster than you could say "explosive decompression."

"Mosovick?"

"Mosovich," Jake replied, calmly.

"Mos... Mos... I don't have that."

"M-O-S-..."

"Ah, Mosovich! There you are! Right... special ops, recon, direct action, explosives, multi-planet... Ah! Where's... Is there a Mueller?"

"That's me," the sergeant major said, shaking his head.

"Right, right... Report to Colonel Widdlebright, special ops, room fourteen eighty-six, section D," the officer said as his printer spit out a sheet. He handed it to them and then looked puzzled. "Welcome back. Where've you been? I don't see a retirement code."

"Deep black," Mosovich said, touching the side of his nose. "Deepest."

"Right," the officer said, nodding sagely. "Well, welcome back into the warm I think is what they say."

As the door closed Mueller looked at Jake and snorted.

"I'm not sure which part is funnier," Mueller said. "But you're right. We were sure in the deepest black I've ever been in! Bullshit over your head is pretty much zero-vis."

"Oh, shut up," Jake muttered. "At least he didn't call the MPs. We need to find this colonel."

"And that's the other funny thing—"

✦   ✦   ✦

"I'm Colonel Widdlebright."

The officer behind the desk did not look harassed despite the fact that he was simultaneously talking to them and typing on his computer. He also looked to be about fourteen. Rejuv caught some people like that. If you naturally looked baby-faced you could end up appearing damned near pubescent.

"Go ahead and laugh," the officer said, not looking up. "It's nearly impossible not to."

"I had my sense of humor surgically removed, sir," Jake replied.

"Now that is funny," Widdlebright said, finally looking up. "Jake the fucking Snake. I never expected to see you again. Except as a sight-picture."

"And I've never even heard of you, sir," Jake said. "And I'm beginning to suspect I should have."

"We have mutual friends," Widdlebright said. "I was over the wall part of the time we would have been in contact. Then agency ops. It's a small world but a black one."

"Got that," Jake said.

"How'd the Bane Sidhe treat you?" the colonel asked. "I considered trying to find them at a couple of points. In other words, no harm, no foul in my book."

"Yes, sir," Jake replied.

"Mueller ever talk?"

"Not if I can keep him from doing so, sir," Jake said.

"With all due respect, fuck you, Colonel," Mueller replied.

"Be aware that you're back in the arms of the military, Sergeant Major," Widdlebright said politely. "And I can and will have you breaking rocks for things *other* than going rogue."

"Sorry, sir," Mueller said. "Will happen again."

"Probably," the colonel said, turning away from the computer finally. "I was reviewing your service records. Probably should have done that before but I've been busy. Welcome to the Strategic Reconnaissance Section. Since at the moment the SRS consists of a clerk typist, a supply private and the three of us, welcome, welcome, welcome indeed!"

"You're going to put me behind a desk, aren't you, sir?" Jake said.

"For about three days," Widdlebright replied. "You and Mueller. You're going to have to go into the damned nightmare the personnel system has become and dig out all your DAG guys. SRS is going to be built around your old unit. I assume most of them are still alive."

"We . . . lost some," Jake admitted. "We were . . ."

"Covering the extraction of one faction of the Bane Sidhe when the Darhel went freaky on them," Widdlebright finished for him. "Against ACS. That's double tough by the way. Good job. You'll be training back in Greenville as soon as we get the full team together but it will be quick and rough. Your mission has already been assigned."

"Which is, sir?" Mueller asked.

"Well, there's this group of invading aliens," Widdlebright said, grinning. "And we need to recon them and get a better feel for their abilities than we've gotten from the Himmit."

"Oh, crap," Jake said. "I think this is where I came in."

"Yeah, well, if you think *you're* in the cacky . . ."

❖   ❖   ❖

"Hey, Chief," Bob the Postman said, walking down the pier. "You've got mail. Certified letter."

Being a mailman in the post-War U.S. was not a job for the faint-of-heart. Not if you worked the former battle zones.

San Diego was just such a battlezone. The city had, for a time, been a "fortress city," one of the twenty or so cities that, based on previous experience with the Posleen, were likely to get hammered but that the government had chosen to defend, anyway.

The votes were never quite counted on whether the "fortress city" concept was a grand idea or incredibly stupid. Vital combat troops who could have been used to shore the internal defenses were, instead, stuck out on a limb and all too often lost when the Posleen sawed it off.

San Diego was one such city. Essentially evacuated except for a minimum support force, it had been protected by five divisions. The core of the city that is; all the periphery had to be left to the Posleen.

But the Posleen, seeing that there must be *something* worthwhile in there if there were defenders, had attacked and attacked mercilessly. In a bare six months the defenses crumbled and the survivors scrambled into a Dunkirk that carried them north to shore up the defenses of Los Angeles. Which also fell. The remnant then went north, again, to San Francisco which, by the skin of its teeth, held.

Robert McCune was born in the shattered ruins of San Diego. Survivors of the Posleen enslaught in the Sierra Madres had been quick to recolonize the California coast. All the original reasons to live in California, bright sunshine and constant temperatures, were still

there. With a small amount of technology, so was fresh
water. And the farming and fishing were still superb.

Bob the Postman's grandparents on his mother's
side hadn't been military. They'd run a commune to
the east of San Diego before the war, didn't like the
military then, didn't like the military during the war,
never liked the military. From what he'd heard, his
grandmother had used the term "babykillers" right up
to the day she'd died. They'd come down out of the
hills with their children and a similar-minded group
intent on establishing a new Israel free from the evil
of violence and anti-alien bigotry. Escaping the hell
of the Urb they found the free skies and clean air of
California that they'd always wanted.

Bob's mother had been saved from the Posleen feral
that ate her parents by his grandfather on his father's
side, a former tanker who was taking his new wife down
into the plains for much the same reason. But he and
his group of buddies had armed to the teeth before
they set out. Running across the massacre was luck as
much as anything. But they'd gotten there a bit late.

Mama Moonchild didn't talk much about that day.

Bob had grown up outside the former town of
Carlsbad, California, where his grandfather and his
buddies had spread out and reestablished a nice little
colony. They kept a cleared zone around it, both to
spot ferals and to keep the fires off, and sold produce
to the fishing colonies that had settled around San
Diego harbor. It was still an interesting drive getting
to Diego, but Bob grew up doing it.

So when the federal government finally got around
to reestablishing the post office, he'd taken the tests
and been inducted as a "Rural mail carrier, unsecured

zone" which not only had a monthly bonus attached but a generous firearms, vehicle and ammo budget.

When he pulled in to drop off the mail in his surplus LAV, complete with functional and well-cared-for 25mm chain-gun, the old timer Californians like Chief Isemann barely shook their heads anymore.

"I *paid* my fucking taxes," Chief Isemann said, setting down the splice she'd been putting in the hawser. "Who the hell's it from?"

Former Master Chief Petty Officer (Fleet) Ronnette Isemann was pushing a hundred and looked like she had the day she raised her hand to swear and affirm in the U.S. Navy, three months after she graduated from Scripps Ranch High School. Roan hair fell down her back in a thick braid, braided every morning by hands burned nearly black from the sun. Her face was just as brown as were the eyes behind her wraparound sunglasses.

The tuna-boat *Lexington* tugged at its lines, waiting to go out. The bluefin were going to be running offshore and the last thing that Ronnie needed was to be held up by some fucking Fed bullshit.

"Fleet," Bob said, holding out the letter on a clipboard. "Sign here."

"Christ, can't you tell 'em I was gone when you got here?" Ronnie asked.

"Now, Chief, you know I can't do that," Bob said. "I'd have to put down that you refused delivery."

"Fuck," Ronnie said, signing the form. Bob tore off his portion and handed the letter over. "You're a fucking pal, Bob."

"Come on, Chief," the mailman said. "Just doing my duty."

"Point," the former NCO said, looking at the letter.

"Come on, read it," Bob said. "I want to know what it says."

"Maybe I'm up for disability or something," the chief said, opening up the letter. "Fuck me, fuck me, fuck me . . ."

"That bad?"

"I'm *recalled*? It's been fifty fucking years of ignoring me and now I'm *recalled*? Oh, those Indi *bastards*! 'Thank you very much for saving the Earth, now get the fuck out of the Fleet, you're no longer wanted you Ami traitor.' Until the shit . . . Am I missing something? What the fuck *is* going on?"

"You hadn't heard?" Bob said. "New invasion."

"Not the damn Posleen again!" the chief swore. "Not under fucking Indi officers. I just won't go!"

"New group," Bob said. "Read it on the internet. Hedren. And there's been a big shake-up in Fleet and Fleet Strike. Mike O'Neal's commander of Fleet Strike and some Jap is commanding Fleet. Taki something."

"Takao *Takagi*?" Isemann said, sitting up as straight as a bolt.

"Yeah, that's it," Bob said. "Mean anything to you?"

"Fleet is under *Takao Takagi*?" Isemann said, jumping to her feet and raising her hands to the sky. "Fleet is under Takao 'VX' Takagi? Yes! There is a God! When's the next convoy leave for Tahoe? Jimmy! JIMMY! Get your lazy butt down here! You've got the boat. Grandma's going back to SPACE!"

We have completed our examination of the Indowy so-called "master" of kratki: The telepathic transmission from the Imeg entered General Etugul's mind like red fire, but he maintained his splayed stance of obeisance despite the pain. *The Indowy are no threat to the Conquest. They retain even in the most extreme conditions a code of utter nonviolence. The Indowy did no more than defend himself against our probes. They use kratki only for making of devices and as part of their false Path. They will not impede your advance.*

"I thank you most humbly for the information, Lord Imeg. The Archons are victorious."

What are your plans?

"The capital of this polity is within range of the most recently conquered world, Your Greatness. And it is within range of many other planets. As soon as the jump gate is established and charged, we will continue our conquest of this polity by next taking their capital. We have developed information from examination of their information network and interrogations. The leaders of this polity, the Darhel, have systematically reduced their war forces to a level so low they are a negligible threat. The most dangerous unit that we might have faced was eliminated not so long ago. The method of their elimination is a source of rumor, but that it is gone is unquestionable. Their ships are substandard and only the humans give fight. Given the scattered nature of their forces, we should be able to conquer this polity as rapidly as we can move."

This is all good news, the Imeg said. *But be wary. The Himmit yet remain and the polity may have surprises yet in store.*

"I remain wary, Greatness," Etegul said. "I know the Words and the Teachings perfectly. I will do all things in accordance with the will of the Archons."

Yes, I know you do, the Imeg thought. *I know you do.*

"You know, it's the little things in life," Bill Boyd said as he walked into the office.

"Sunshine, gentle rains, spring daffodils?" Mike asked. "Things like that?"

"One of three total shipyards capable of producing warships directly in the path of an alien conquest."

"Crap," Mike said, slapping his forehead. "Gratoola yards! How in the *fuck* could I forget that?"

"I mean, there's tons of orbital manufacturing, too," Boyd said, sitting down unasked. "But the yards are the killer. That and the Indowy shipfitters. With what we're looking at, how we're looking at producing ships, the shipyard was going to have to be extensively renovated anyway. It might have been more sense to start from scratch. But the shipfitters... We need those guys."

"So evacuate them," Mike said, looking back at his computer. "Them and any Sohon above the level of four. We're going to need both. Get with Admiral Takagi on where to send them."

"You don't think you can hold Gratoola," Boyd said.

"Actually, I said evacuate the critical non-combatants," Mike replied. "I'm going to send everything I can spare to hold Gratoola. And I am confident of victory."

"I'm not a reporter," Bill said.

"No, you're the head of the War Production board," Mike said. "Which means I tell you what you need to know and vice versa. You tell me everything, though, and I tell you what I *think* you need to know. Me commander. Sorry, Bill, but that's the way things work."

"Okay," the industrialist said, standing up. "I actually

can handle that. I was a private many, many years ago and understand what you're doing. But, seriously, we don't have the forces to hold Gratoola, do we?"

"Nope," Mike said. "Not against the whole Hedren force. Doesn't mean I'm going to lose it, though. I've got some aces up my sleeve."

"Are you sure I'm going to be okay doing this?" Daisy asked, nervously. "And I do mean *I*. The whole package. Including, you know, the meat portion."

Michelle had gathered other Sohon, both from the few human lower mentats on Earth and a group of Indowy, including Master Glavaka, Ermintrude's master of training.

Over the last weeks the ship had been packed with, well, stuff. Much of it was refined metals comprising most of the metal group in the Periodic Table. There were also bags and bags and bags of graphite—pure carbon in other words.

And then there was one.

"Your processes will be placed in suspension," Michelle said, placing a finger-sized device on the teak deck of the cruiser. Even walking on the surface was somewhat problematic since many portions had nearly rotted through. "Your organic portion will be held in stasis and protected from the vacuum by Harry. We have carefully examined your links and understand them thoroughly. We will be able to . . . remake you in a new image."

"I sort of like my current image," Daisy said, frowning. "Really, I'm not so sure about this."

"Miss Mae," Thomas said, gesturing at the rust-streaked cruiser. "We will make this . . . better. Better than she was, you were, when you first pulled out of the shipyards. Bigger, stronger, a spaceship capable of fighting anything in the known galaxy that's faster than she is and running from anything more powerful. Not a cruiser, a dreadnought to redefine the term. You will be a capital ship when we are done."

"Okay," Daisy said, shrugging. "I guess I don't really got a choice."

"You have a choice," Michelle said. "But I think what you really have is cold feet."

"More like stage fright," Daisy admitted. "But, okay, let's get this over with. What do I do?"

"I would suggest simply lying on the deck," Thomas said. "In a way this new ship we are creating is built in your image. Let you be the template."

"Mind if I lean on the bridge-tower?" Daisy said, walking over and looking at the deck. "My dress is going to get ruined."

Thomas waved his hand and the teak deck looked as if it had been newly installed. And varnished.

"Better?"

"I can see why people call what you do magic," Daisy said, sitting down. "Right. Capital ship. I can handle that. I think. Better than the scrapyard."

"It is time," Michelle said, lifting up into the air and lowering herself to the river bank. "Let us begin."

"You know," Mike said, looking out the window with his arms crossed. "I've gotten used to grav belts and stuff. But watching them just fly around using the power of their mind sort of throws me."

"It's not exactly the power of their mind," Cally replied. "Trying to get Michelle to explain it is pretty tough but I've gotten some bits out of her. It's using their minds to control the nannites to locally effect reality. Think quantum. In some dimension or universe or something, anything is possible. Including that, at any moment, they are lifting up a bit then over a bit, et cetera."

"And in some dimension a cruiser is just lifting up out of the river and ascending into the heavens?"

"Right," Cally said in a strangled voice. "They're using the grav engines, right? Because if that thing drops..."

"They got removed," Mike replied, spitting into a spit can. "And I guess in some universe somewhere, there's a group of mentats including my daughter who are just lifting up into the air."

"I guess," Cally said, holding her breath.

"I *got* to go outside and watch this."

We are stable, Michelle thought.

The cruiser was in geosyncronous orbit. Getting it there had been a non-trivial exercise in Sohon but everything else they had to do would be easier in the vacuum and microgravity. Maintaining an air-pocket, and recycling that air, around each of the Sohon and the organic portion of the ship was an exercise for the lower level Sohon, trivial in comparison.

Let us begin, Master Glavaka said. *This is what she is. This is what she shall become.*

Becoming.

"Can you see anything?" Mike asked, shielding his eyes against the sun and looking up.

"Even the satellites can't see anything," Tam replied.

"There's a spatial disturbance in geosync at the equator but in line with us on longitude. Light appears to be going in but not coming out. Not a black hole, no similar gravitational disturbance, just . . . light going in and not coming out."

"Wonder how long this is going to take," Mike said, walking over to a beech tree and sitting down under it. "I've got paperwork."

"You've always got paperwork," General Wesley said. "You've been at the desk by three AM and out of here after midnight for the last three weeks. Take a break."

"I think I will," Mike said, leaning back on the grass and continuing to look into the lightly clouded sky. "Get somebody to tell me when that spatial anomaly starts to move."

"Will do."

The Sohon floated in space, their hands outstretched, each face serene as they wrestled with more power than the Earth had been capable of producing before the coming of the Galactics.

The nannites, reacting to the codes from the high-level key, began reproducing asymptotically, the remainder that were in the steel and those sent from the Sohon exploding into quantities that were only reproducible by scientific notation. The "spatial anomaly" was, in part, a giant lens, focusing Sol's awesome power on the steel of the ship, pumping photons and other particles onto it to feed the replication and change occurring throughout.

Bulkheads warped and twisted sinuously, guns melted, becoming new and more lethal engines of destruction, the hull bulging out and becoming larger,

larger, more rounded, less angular and yet in many ways much more...predatory.

The Des Moines *was Becoming.*

"General O'Neal, sir?"

Mike started awake and looked around blurrily.

"Sir," the sergeant said, shaking his shoulder. "General Wesley says that...'the spatial anomaly is moving,' sir."

"Right," Mike said, sitting up and rubbing his face. "How long was I out?"

"About an hour, sir," the sergeant replied. "Are you going to be..."

"Fine, Sergeant," Mike said, grinning. "Just took a catnap. Right, let's see what we got."

"Should be in sight," Tam said, looking up into the sky.

"Behind the clouds I figure," Mike replied, tapping down his dip.

"I see something..." Cally said. "It's..."

"Holy *Fuck* that's big!" Mike snapped.

What he had at first taken to be a cloud was moving unlike any cloud would. But it was farther away than he'd thought and thus much *larger* than he'd realized.

"Are they going to park that in the river?" Tam asked as the ship continued to descend. "That's got to be nearly a klick long!"

"Oh. My. God," Cally said.

"You got some sort of enhanced vision from that slab thing, didn't you," Mike said, balefully.

"Yep," Cally replied, her hand over her mouth. "Dad. You're not going to believe this..."

"Are those...?"

✧   ✧   ✧

"No, Father, they are not *breasts*," Michelle said sharply.

The ship was hovering above the Rappahannock, squarely between the headquarters building and the training center on the far side. And Mike was pretty sure nothing was getting done. Because every single person in every single building was outside looking at the ship. If any of the guards stayed on their posts, he was going to give them a three-day pass for aggressive attention to duty.

It was big, that was for sure. Eight hundred meters long and massing maybe a hundred and fifty thousand tons. Supermonitors were bigger but they were never designed to enter atmosphere. It had to be pretty much the biggest ship ever to come *near* landing on a planet. Its hull was glittering gold, sinuous and... distinctly womanly. Warp nacelles jutted like wings, upward on either side, and surmounting it was a rack of grav drivers and laser cannons. More were forward of the nacelles and even on the underside although it was clearly designed for landings.

But that wasn't what people were looking at.

"They sure look like tits," Mike said. "I mean, they're right out front, they've got some ptosis and they've even got nipples. I mean, not only are they tits, they're *naked* tits, Michelle. You've built me a warship that's got naked tits on the front. What's the *point* of nose art!"

"The... devices to which you refer are Quantum Tanglers," Michelle said severely. "The shape is... an unfortunate necessity. That truly is the only shape that will work."

"And Quantum Tanglers are . . . ?" Cally asked.

"They cause particles to become . . . strangled in their entanglements," Michelle replied. "Their entanglements become confused."

"Michelle, that's not telling me a whole hell of a lot," Mike pointed out.

"Let me help, General," Kang Chan said, from behind him. "They make things blow up."

"Ah, now someone is speaking a language I understand!" Mike said, turning around. "How much?"

"A lot," Mentat Chan said.

"Okay," Mike said, holding his finger and thumb apart at eye level. "Leetle more detail."

"The quantum tangler causes randomization of entanglements by inserting false tangles into the entanglements," Thomas said.

"There *has* to be a middle ground," Mike growled. "Tell me there's a middle ground. How much boom? Are we talking a little bang or an earth-shattering kaboom?"

"I was getting to that," Thomas continued. "Although it is a false truth, the way to explain it I suspect is in terms you are aware of. They are incorrect terms, but you are familiar with them. May I proceed?"

"Go," Mike said, crossing his arms.

"You are familiar with the hoary adage that all matter is energy?"

"You mean relativity?" Mike asked. "E equals MC square. *That* hoary old adage? The one Einstein got the Nobel for?"

"Yes," Thomas said. "It is, by the way, wrong. But it is a close approximation of effect. By disturbing entanglements, certain particles are induced to become . . . different. More wavelike. Energy if you prefer. I am having trouble determining appropriate metaphors."

"And that...?"

"It's a matter to energy converter?" Cally said, her eyes widening. "As a *weapon*?"

"No," Michelle said. "It is a quantum tangler!" She paused and sighed. "I suppose, though, that your description is a close-order approximation of the effect."

"Holy crap," Mike muttered. "How much matter will one hit convert?"

"It will not be localized," Chan said. "The system will first form a link between the tangler and matter that it is directed towards. Then it initiates tangling on the matter."

"So does it blow up *part* of a big ship or *all* of a big ship or...?" Mike asked, getting frustrated.

"*Most* of it," Daisy said, walking up. "Oh. My. God. I can't *wait* to fire that thing! And did you see the hangar bay?"

"Hangar bay?"

"This is a big ship."

Mike had much better things to do. And, after all, the ship technically belonged to Fleet, not him. The reality was, though, that with Admiral Takagi running rampant cleaning up the Fleet officer corps, Mike was sitting on top of Fleet, not the other way around. So in a way, effectively, it was his ship.

And it was a beauty. Mike wasn't sure what the thing had cost—the Sohons had to be paid and there was all the materials not to mention that code key—but it was worth it. They hadn't toured the whole thing, just the highlights. State of the art CIC, stealth systems, heavy duty close-in-defense system, armored to the max, missiles that were faster than any current... It even had two normal space engines based on antimatter ejection systems that would give it more speed and maneuverablility than a current destroyer.

But then there was the hangar bay.

"Is it just me," Cally asked, looking around. "Or is this thing sort of oddly shaped?"

"It's an efficient use of space," Michelle said, just a tad nervously.

"And the entry looks..."

"It's a very efficient design," Thomas added.

"And its placement?" Mike asked.

"Only place we could put it," Michelle said, more sturdily. "It's capable of housing nine Falcon Four Space Fighters and two Banshee shuttles. Or a similar mix to size as needed."

"So, the fact that it looks like we're inside a womb and the take-off and landing area looks like ... I'm not going to say what it looks like ... is purely coincidental?" Mike asked.

"Absolutely," Michelle and Thomas both said at the same time.

"This ship is beautiful," Mike said. "And obscene."

"So is the human body, General," Daisy said tightly. "And you're talking about *me*, by the way."

"Sorry," Mike said, shaking his head. "This is a beautiful ship. Truly. Quite the most ... voluptuous I've ever seen. I've got to ask, though. Are we looking at a *class*?"

"The basic design parameters are ..." Michelle started to say and then stopped. "Yes. Smaller versions in general but ... Yes."

"Good God."

❖   ❖   ❖

"What is this I hear about an evacuation of Gratoola?"

Mike looked up from his desk and his face turned downward even more than usual.

"Hello, Clerk," Mike replied. "I don't seem to recall saying 'Enter.'"

"I am serious," the Tir snapped. "Do not think that just because you have some current political currency you can simply *abandon* the capital of the entire Galactic Confederation!"

"I'm not going to abandon it," Mike said. "I have an infantry division training even as we speak. They need equipment, though, and there is a strange dearth of that available. No new SheVas were in the process of being built when we were out there fighting the Posleen. Also a strange dearth of formed units and an entire dearth of heavy units. No new ACS suits had been made in three years. I was wondering why the supply was so short. Not that it matters because you *wiped out my fucking corps!*"

"I have heard this diatribe from both you and General Wesley before," the Tir said. "I do not need to hear it again. Whatever the conditions before this invasion, you cannot and will not let Gratoola fall!"

"I won't *let* it fall," Mike said, calmly. "I'm going to do everything in my power to prevent it. That is not the same as expecting to succeed. Get this through your thick skull, Darhel. Your people ensured that humans had their fangs pulled. Nobody trusts the military, the bulk of the youth population has lost any interest in fighting because they just figure they are changing masters and the Hedren only look mildly worse than the Darhel. The forces that could have saved Gratoola are either distributed in penny packets or were destroyed *by your orders*! I did not create this situation. The Darhel created it. It is, I think, fitting that one of your prime worlds has been devastated. I will cry no tears for anything that happens around Gratoola except the loss of every soldier I send out and the innocent if stupid Indowy. I'll add that the orders I sent for evacuation specifically *exclude* Darhel. And since I'm commandeering just about every ship available for either sending forces to or extracting critical forces from Gratoola, you can anticipate that the vast majority of Darhel on the planet are Hedren fodder if I fail."

"You are exterminating us," the Tir said in a voice of wonder. "I had no belief that it was possible that you could sink so low."

"I'm not exterminating you," Mike said with a sigh. "I'm doing two things. One, making sure that it's possible to save some of you in the end. If the Hedren win, that's not a sure thing. For *us* to win against the Hedren, I will eventually need the critical Indowy Sohon and those shipfitters. I do not need Darhel clerks and bankers and politicians. Second, I am assuredly rubbing your noses in the fact that if you spend all your efforts on the military emasculating it, you cannot expect it to be there when you need it. After this war the Darhel are still going to retain a measure of control. Assuming you *don't* force us into a war of extermination against you. When you regain that measure of control, it might behoove you to recall this lesson. In the words of the Bard:

"For it's Tommy this, an' Tommy that,
    an' 'Chuck him out, the brute!'
"But it's 'Saviour of 'is country,'
    when the guns begin to shoot;
"An' it's Tommy this, an' Tommy that,
    an' anything you please;
"But Tommy ain't a bloomin' fool—
    you bet that Tommy sees!"

"What in all the universe is that supposed to mean?" the Tir said, looking confused. "Are you referring to that associate of your daughter? Thomas Sunday?"

"Figure it out for yourself, you nitwit," Mike said tiredly. "But you'd better work to make sure the evacuation goes smoothly if you want a single Darhel to survive this war."

"Tir," the Darhel's AID interjected. "There is a priority message. Gil Etullu, clan leader of the Fauldor has entered lintatai."

"Gosh, what a shame," Mike said, leaning back and propping his head with a finger on one cheekbone.

"I . . ." the Tir said, then stared at the general. "Wait . . . Where has Cally been? Fauldor . . ."

"Oh, yeah, them," Mike said, leaning forward to move some folders around. "Gosh, I'm pretty sure I've got a report somewhere here that they were slow-rolling a shipment of Posleen forges. Shame about their clan leader going into lintatai. I suppose it is going to slow things down even more what with the chaos that's going to erupt. You Darhel have *such* a hard time with transitions of power. Good thing it only happened to one of them; if *all* of them suddenly went into lintatai you'd probably never recover."

"You..." the Tir said, his eyes widening.

Mike leaned back propping his chin on his finger again and contemplated the Darhel.

"I know you're faster and stronger than me," Mike commented. "But I'm pretty sure I can stay alive long enough to wait until you clock out. Done that once already and I was chained up at the time."

"You... you..." the Darhel said, snarling. "You are a *mad man*!"

"If you mean mad as in angry, then yes I am," Mike said. "Repeat that diatribe that you recall from myself and General Tam. If you mean mad as in insane, you'd better hope I'm crazy like a fox. Because otherwise we're all screwed. Now, you have a statement to prepare for the media expressing your condolences, and mine, and all of Fleet and Fleet Strike and auxiliary Federalized forces, for the unfortunate clan leader. When the news media inevitably ask questions, you will explain that the evacuation is a preventative measure since it's anticipated there will be damage to the yards. The personnel are being sent to other yards to continue the mighty work, blah, blah... And say something nice about the unit going to Gratoola, you might look up a precis on them beforehand since those questions are inevitably going to be asked. General theme is that we're one big happy Galactic family who are working shoulder to shoulder to prevent the tyranny of the awful Hedren and restore freedom and justice to the Galaxy."

"And how much of that is true?" the Tir asked.

"Certainly the last part. The *very* last. You better *bet* that Tommy sees!"

❖   ❖   ❖

"What's up?" Frederick asked as voices were raised in the dayroom.

The barracks for first years were bay barracks constructed of locally pressed plastic. It was the best material the Folk had for the first few years of settlement. The barracks had originally been communal facilities for the new colonists and only later handed over to the *Bruederschafts*.

On one end was a small "dayroom" which was the most recreation most of the first-years would see all year. It held a foozball table, currently broken, and a large supply of pornographic magazines, most with impossible to open pages.

When the new recruits were given a half-day pass they could visit the slop-house, which served brats and very bad beer. The only saving grace was that both were cheap. Given the pay of *Schutzes*, that was a good thing.

"A distribution form was just posted," Ewald Higger said. The rifleman from Second Platoon was trotting down the barracks. "It has something about the war."

Frederick set down his worn boot that was refusing to take a shine and walked to the dayroom.

There was a crowd around the DF so he couldn't see it, but he could hear the exclamations.

"*Generalmajor*? What an insult!"

"Yes! Our own *Bruederschaft*!"

"Units, now," another voice said. "We will be the *Panzer Schwere* Michael Wittmann!"

"Nobody here knows how to *drive* a panzer," another interjected.

"Speak for yourself, *Schutze*," a voice said from by Frederick's elbow.

"Achtung!" Eric barked. *"Unteroffizier!"*

The recruits all snapped to attention as Eric's gunner walked across the day-room.

"Since you idiots were hogging the board I will now read it aloud," Harz said, loudly. "Attention to orders.

"Fleet Strike Special Order Number 79833.

"SS *Panzergrenadier Division Vaterland*, commander *Generalmajor* Fredrik Mühlenkampf, is called to active duty April 5th, 2061, by order of General Michael O'Neal, Fleet Strike. SS *Panzergrenadier Division Vaterland* has position of Fleet Strike attached auxiliary unit. SS *Panzergrenadier Division Vaterland* shall prepare for off-planet duty for a period of no less than 1 (one) year.

"Headquarters SS *Panzergrenadier Division Vaterland* supplemental instructions.

"My people. A new enemy force threatens not only the Federation but Earth and the Fatherland. We have been requested to respond as a people, as a unit, and I have accepted this request. This is a warning order for all active reserve members of Brotherhoods to prepare for full-scale mobilization. New equipment, production equipment and materials will be sent to our People to prepare us for the great battles that lie ahead. As always, only the best is expected of the Freilaender. We shall battle for the honor and safety of the Fatherland, for our homes and for our illustrious names. Although the war may be long, we shall overcome our adversaries on the field as we always have. Arise my people; the smoke of battle draws near.

"Mühlenkampf.

"That is what's on the DF," Harz ground out. "But since you are recruits and thus too *stupid* to figure the rest out I was sent down here to explain it to you in very small words. Yes, Herr *Generalfeldmarschall* is now *Herr Generalmajor*. What else do you expect? Do you see multiple armies for a *Generalfeldmarschall* to command? Neither do I. There is just the Volk. We can mass, at most, one division. The *Generalfeldmarschall* has chosen to lead us, as he always has, rather than argue for a higher rank. What this should tell you is how serious the *Generalfeldmarschall* considers this new threat. Yes, we have no Panzers. The SS had no panzers when *I* joined. I ended the war as gunner of a Tiger III. Panzers will be pulled from storage or perhaps made. You did notice the part of about weapons and materials, yes?

"For the rest, there are many questions. It doesn't matter. You are all recruits and all you need do is what the *Unteroffiziers* tell you. And if you don't, it's the same as always: we will put our boot up your *ass*. Now get back to your duties. You can expect that little pleasantness of your first six months to soon seem like a holiday."

"Now we get to see what this thing does," Captain McNair said.

Admiral Takagi had many things to do besides watch the first test firing of a new weapon. The Fleet, what remained of it, was a shambles. During the war the Fleet had started as primarily a European and American domain. They had the officers familiar with fielding large systems, and maintaining the crews under the cramped and high-pressure conditions of a large warship. They had proven, repeatedly, that they could and would do whatever was necessary to carry the fight to the enemy.

However, the first major space battles of the war had bled that fleet white. Virtually every ship had been turned to scrap then rebuilt, some of them multiple times. The superdreadnought *Kaga* had been on its fifth iteration by the time the Posleen were stopped.

In most cases, especially of the capital ships, the drifting hulks remained but not much of the crews. Over *six hundred thousand* trained sailors and officers had been lost in *one* battle.

With Europe gripped in a war of extinction and the U.S. cut off, the only source for new officers, NCOs and sailors were the virtually untouched islands of Indonesia and the Philippines. There had been landings in both countries, landings that had decimated their central cities, but vast populated areas remained.

So the Fleet shifted, more and more, to officers and crew from those areas. Indonesian officers tended to supplant the Filipinos rather quickly. Not that, in the end, there was any great difference.

Cleaning up Fleet was a day-in, day-out nightmare. Takao had started by using the same database O'Neal had used to find him, searching the Darhel records for any officer in Fleet they found to be "untrustworthy." Most of those, some of them Southeast Asians, had also been competent but he was the *only* officer who had ever risen above lieutenant commander. There were many places where a competent lieutenant commander could make quite a difference, but the reality was that he needed every rank from lieutenant to admiral *and* their accompanying NCOs.

So he had delved into the record of remaining officers on Earth and the nearby stars. An AID O'Neal said he could "probably trust" ran the search, sifting for any former Fleet officers who *weren't* corrupted by the Darhel. But there were so *few*. Most of the competent and honorable officers that survived the war had been forced out into retirement. More than a few of those, including *every* senior officer who had participated in the "reconnaissance in force" that had relieved the Siege of Earth, had sustained mortal "accidents" after retirement.

The Darhel were nothing if not vindictive.

Given the number of ships he had and administrative positions, he needed six thousand officers that were trustworthy and about a similar number of NCOs.

He had been able to find two hundred and thirteen officers and about seven hundred NCOs. Some of them weren't what he'd call competent but they all had their hearts in the right place. They still weren't a drop in the bucket and every day, in part because they were now looking at the real condition of the Fleet, there was another report of some critical failure.

So he really had better things to be doing right now. But if he had to look at one more negative report he was going to commit seppuku.

The target was a small nickel-iron asteroid, one of the Apollo asteroids that roamed the empty space between Earth's orbit and that of Mars. It was conveniently close and since such asteroids were considered a potential threat it had long before been mapped.

It also was about the size of a Hedren destroyer.

"So we gonna do this or what?" Daisy Mae asked, arching. "I am ready to fire, Captain."

"Permission to open fire, Admiral?" Jeff asked.

"Permission granted, Captain," Takagi replied.

"XO, engage target with QT guns," Captain McNair said.

The dreadnought was pointed more-or-less directly at the asteroid at a range of just over a million and a half kilometers. According to the mentat, the system should be able to lock within twenty degrees of forward and at a range of up to seven light-seconds. They were right at the edge of range because Captain McNair did not want to be near something that was having "random energy conversion events" going on.

"Gunnery, lock target with QTs One and Two," the XO said.

"Locking," the gunnery NCO said.

On the screen it looked as if blue beams of fire lanced out to the distant asteroid. The long-range viewer showed that the asteroid was bathed by them in lambent turquoise.

"Locked on target with QT One and Two, aye."

"Fire QT One and Two."

The beams now had started to shift sinuously as the ship and the distant asteroid moved at slightly divergent courses. However, when the weapons fired, blue balls of chain lightning followed the bent beams like a pig sliding down the gullet of an anaconda. But much quicker.

"Time to impact two seconds," Gunnery said. "One . . ."

The long-range viewers darkened as the asteroid was engulfed in white fire. When the ejected gases cleared, though, the asteroid was still there.

"Looks . . . different," Bill said. "But it didn't blow apart."

"Target has lost fifteen percent of its mass," Tactical reported.

"Ouch," McNair said.

"The question, of course, is what that would do to an actual hull," Admiral Takagi said. "Keep blowing up asteroids. I will find an appropriate hull to blow up. There is much that is not more than scrap in this system."

"This is ... a pretty good set-up," Bill Boyd said, looking around the facility.

"It is anything but," the apparently young man standing by him replied. "However, it is the best we could do rapidly."

The warehouse was constructed of patched-together I beams and patched-together corrugated steel. Curved like a Quonset hut it was, nonetheless, nearly seventy meters across at the base and a hundred meters long. The whole facility was set on a much larger stand of concrete near the top of a small hill. Given the wear, Boyd figured the foundation probably dated from before the Posleen War and was the remnant of either a factory or warehouse. There were several more pads in the area, which Boyd found unusual. Generally, in former Posleen areas the ground was either pocked with craters or stripped to the soil and rock.

The facility was at the edge of a burgeoning city. Called Freiburg, it was growing up around the former Koblenz Regional Defense Center. The center had been built around Fort Ehrenbreitstein, a massive stone structure dating to well before the First World War which perched over the town like a leopard. During the war it had been hammered by Posleen orbital strikes to the point that most of its structure was stripped off the mountain. However, when the SS colony returned to Germany they had centered around the natural defense point and only slowly spread out.

When the Posleen took an area, assuming they had

the time, they stripped most of the original facilities off, right down to tearing up the roads. Then they built their own civilization on top. So when the SS returned it was to a combination of wilderness, where the Posleen had removed all traces of the former habitations, and large craters from the Fleet forces that hammered every trace of *Posleen* habitations into the ground.

The Mosel River joined the Rhine at Koblenz with hills flanking both sides of both rivers, narrowing down to cliffs upriver in both directions. On the flats, where the city had once stood, there were broad stretches of open area. Defense positions now lined the hills, maintaining a perimeter to keep the ferals out, while fields lined the east bank and the growing city formed on the west. To the north were more defense positions and in the distance could be seen a line of scrub where the wilderness terminated.

"There's plenty of room," Boyd said, looking out over the city. "The roads could use work."

The latter were graded dirt and gravel and wound up the hill in serpentine paths. They were well constructed, though, with regularly spaced run-offs and the center domed for drainage.

"We still have little in the way of construction equipment and materials," the man said with a shrug. "The road will do until we can get it paved properly."

Boyd didn't know much about the "*Herr Oberstleutnant.*" The locals used their military rank in everyday conversation so the only way Boyd even knew the guy was the equivalent of a lieutenant colonel was by the way people referred to him. He'd introduced himself as simply Dieter Schultz. Boyd assumed the rank came from back in the war. The guy was clearly a rejuv.

The oddest thing about Schultz was that he carried an old "Fritz" helmet with some flowers in it. Growing flowers, the bottom being filled with dirt. Boyd figured there was a story there, but he wasn't going to inquire.

"Mr. Boyd, shuttles are inbound," Boyd's AID interjected. "ETA five minutes."

"Better get started," Boyd said, looking around. There were two groups and an individual standing on the open area in front of the warehouse. And they were distinctly separated.

The first were the locals. Dressed in patched jeans and homespun wool shirts, their rough boots showing evidence of hard use, they were otherwise a mixed lot. There were more than a few that had the very Germanic look to them, medium to tall, heavy of body, tending to light brown hair with a few true blonds. Mixed into the group were other looks. More than a few hooked Semitic noses, black hair, Mediterranean features, yarmulkes, which were a bit of a shock. There was even a smattering of blacks, African from the look, not U.S. derivative. A few of the group were clearly mixes of the different inputs, green or blue eyes, dark skin, hair every shade of brown. Male and female, most of them appeared truly young as opposed to rejuvs. They all looked as if they worked at manual labor quite a bit. However, Boyd could spot soldiers from a mile away and they *all* had the "soldier" look to them, even the women. They even tended to align in ranks.

The second group was a collection of truly miserable looking Indowy. Boyd had spoken to their leader, briefly, and knew that they were less miserable from being in the presence of humans, whom Indowy were getting used to after decades, than the individual standing at the very edge of the concrete.

.The latter was something one rarely saw except as a sight picture or, in last instants, a blur of teeth: A Posleen God King. About the size and general shape of an Arabian horse, arms that ended in talons jutting from a complex double shoulder, clawed feet instead of hooves, crocodilian face, smooth yellow and brown mottled skin.

Unlike most Posleen, however, this one wore a smattering of clothing, a cowled rain shawl over his head, horselike neck and shoulders. He was even wearing jewelry, an earring and two large gold chains around his neck. He looked fairly prosperous but almost as nervous as the Indowy. And he kept constantly scratching himself.

He was the focus of all eyes. The Indowy kept giving him furtive looks as if they expected him to whip out a hidden knife and slaughter them all. The locals, who normally spent a good bit of their time hunting his kind for the still available bounties, absolutely refused to acknowledge his presence. He was neither a target nor a threat. Nor was he worth speaking to. He was, after all, a Posleen.

"Reverend Guanamarioch," Boyd said, waving to him. "We need to clear the pad. Shuttles incoming."

"Yes, Mr. Boyd," the Posleen said, having trouble with several of the consonants. Posleen mouths did not have the same range as human.

"Indowy Etari," Boyd said, calling to the Indowy leader.

The Indowy simply nodded his head, waving his group in the opposite direction from the Posleen.

Schultz didn't even have to call, he simply looked at the second in command who was with the group and then all stepped back into the scrub.

"Lieutenant Colonel Schultz?" Guanamarioch asked nervously.

"Yes, Posleen," the local said without looking at the being.

"Is any of this vegetation hazardous? Do you have snakes in this area?"

"No," Schultz said, finally looking over at the Posleen and clearly puzzled. "It will do no more than get you wet."

"No thorns?" the Posleen asked. "No poisonous frogs? No poison-injecting ants? Nothing?"

"No," Schultz said, a touch angrily. "It is not hazardous!"

"Thank you," Guanamarioch said, stepping delicately off the concrete and into the scrub. He still looked around nervously and his scratching became intense.

Schultz looked at Boyd with a raised eyebrow and the industrialist snorted.

"Long story," Boyd said. "The short story is that Guano is the sole survivor of a Posleen attack on Panama that thought the best route was through the Darien."

"I am unfamiliar with that reference," Schultz said. He picked up the helmet and gestured for the Panamanian to step off the pad.

"The Darien is a vast tropical swamp in the northern part of Colombia but stretching into Panama," Boyd explained. "Nasty place. About the only people who can go through it and survive are the local Indians. We were in the middle of a battle when we got the intel that another force was coming up from the south. Nothing to hold the line except a short gringo... er, American regiment, *my* old regiment, as a matter of fact. For a defensive line miles and miles long. No way they could hold off a Posleen attack."

"And?" Schultz asked.

"The 'attack' ended up being just Guano," Boyd said. "All the rest, we believe several million, were killed by the swamp and Indian militia. And he was in such horrible shape that all he wanted to do was surrender. However, since he never officially threw his staff—lost it, yes, threw it, no—he is still considered by the Posleen network to be a God King. He's terrified of the jungle, and these days that extends to about anything resembling vegetation."

"And he works for you?" Schultz asked as the first of the shuttles started to descend.

"I bought him from the Indian scout that captured him," Boyd said. "Since he does count as a God King he can turn on all sorts of little mechanisms. I'd have cornered the market on forges if the Darhel hadn't jacked the price up. And now..."

"He can turn these on," Schultz said, raising his voice over the hurricane of wind from the shuttles.

"Precisely."

"Arbeit macht frei," Hagai whispered. "And here we are at work again when we should be having a day off."

"One of these days you'll say that around the wrong person," Frederick whispered back.

The work group was not from just the *Bruederschaft* Michael Wittmann. They had been gathered as what the Ami called a "hey-you" detail. Thus it was mostly the junior personnel. Until the next induction series, that meant Frederick and Hagai's group.

"What did I tell you," Hagai continued, ignoring the jibe. "We are to be Star Troopers now, eh?"

"I will recommend you for an intelligence post," Frederick replied. "You'll fit right in."

It was not true that all the intel spots in the Freiland brotherhoods were filled by Jews. It was just *mostly* true.

"No, it is the life of a *Panzergrenadier* for me," Hagai replied. "That's where you get all the wine and women."

"You get drunk on one sip," Frederick replied. "And the last woman you were with was a wet dream. So, since you are *clearly* going to be in intelligence, what is going on? All I know is what was on the distribution."

"We are going to Barwhon," a French accented voice said from behind them.

"Claude," Frederick said without turning around. "And how are things these days in the Charlemagnes?"

"Wine and song, I think the little Jew said," the French private replied.

"You're not exactly tall, Claude," Hagai replied. "What position did you get?"

"He's in charge of picking the *Oberfeldwebel*'s ass," Frederick said.

He and Hagai had gone to gymnasium with Claude De Gaullejac but it proved the old dictum: Germans and Jews might patch it up but the Germans and French were going to hate *forever*.

"I am the sergeant major's *driver*," Claude snapped. "I do not pick his ass."

"Okay, wipe it, then," Frederick said, still not turning around.

"Cut it out, Ox," Hagai said. "And we're not going to Barwhon. There are three planets threatened but the obvious assault vector- is Gratoola. And, yes, the Hedren are smart so they might not pick that one. But the other two choices are very marginal. Barwhon is one, but it not only leads effectively nowhere, it's a nasty place to fight for either us *or* the Hedren."

"Well, my sergeant major says that we're going to Barwhon," De Gaullejac said as if that settled it.

"Fine, when you French are on Barwhon, lost, we'll be on... what was that planet, Jaeger?"

"Gratoola, Frederick," the Jew said with a sigh. "Do *try* to keep up..."

"On *Gratoola* fighting the enemy," Frederick said. "We'll be sure to send you any white flags we find."

"Listen you Aryan donkey's hoof—"

"Quiet back there." *Oberfeldwebel* Shonauger didn't even turn around. He didn't have to.

"You know what they say about blonds..." Claude muttered.

"Yes, they have more fun," Frederick said, even more quietly. "I'll be having fun on Gratoola while you are lost in a swamp trying to explain to your sergeant major how you got there. And explaining to your grandmother why you have run from the fight."

He was pretty sure that the little Frog didn't hear him since the shuttles were closing.

The shuttles were cargo vessels, their bodies bigger around than a C-5 but half the length, with stubby wings and noses that glowed with the heat of reentry.

But nobody cared about the noses. It was the items revealed by their lowering ramps that all eyes were fixed on.

Posleen forges were curved mountains of metal the size of two tanks stacked on top of each other. Their surfaces were dull, pebbled and almost featureless metal with a small control surface on one side. Each shuttle carried one and there was a rank of shuttles stacked up and waiting to drop.

The Indowy scurried to the first shuttle, bringing out grav-lifters and attaching them to the forge. Four of the computer-sized devices whined with the strain of lifting the mass of metal but managed it. As soon as the forge had been walked off the deck the shuttle lifted up to make way for another.

Bill followed as the four Indowy walked the forge to its position and gently lowered it inside a chalk-marked outline. When they cut their grav-lifters there was a faint crunch as the forge settled into the concrete.

"Now what?" Schultz asked as another was brought in.

"Reverend Guanamarioch," Boyd said, raising his voice. "Indowy Etari, I need power."

"Coming," the Posleen replied, hurrying down the length of the facility. The four Indowy carrying the next forge flinched as he passed, nearly dropping the multi-ton device, but managed to recover.

"We are stringing the cables now, Mr. Boyd," the Indowy said from the south end of the facility. A group of Indowy were pulling heavy-duty power cables into the facility and preparing to attach them to the forges. "The fusion plant should be able to supply power for all the units."

Boyd waited until the cables were plugged in and the breakers engaged, then turned to Guanamarioch.

"You can turn it on, right?" Boyd said.

"Yes, yes," Guanamarioch said, pulling an Artificial Sentience out from under the poncho. He placed the device on the control board and cleared his throat. A string of Posleen came out, the language a harsh series of gutturals. "There. It is keyed for unrestricted access. The computer is quite intelligent as such things go. A wireless connection will work. But I have uploaded the designs you gave me. All that someone needs do is load in materials and choose what they want made."

"Gunther!" Schultz boomed. "First load!"

"They can use scrap, right?" Boyd said.

"Yes," Guanamarioch replied. "On the far side from this is a small hatch. Any excess material will be dropped through there. But they must add all of the material that is needed; this model forge doesn't do atomic-level manipulation of matter. So if the device being created requires trace materials, they need to add those. It will prompt for necessary materials if it doesn't have them."

"Well, we shall see what we see," Schultz said as a group of the locals came over with a wire basket full of scrap metal and plastic. "Computer, do you hear me?"

"I hear you," the computer said in English.

"Can I restrict your use?" Schultz asked.

"If you wish," the computer replied.

"I'll hold off for now," Schultz said. "The first item to be made is an M-146 infantry assault rifle. You have that on file?"

"Yes," the computer said.

"Tell us what to do."

"Place materials in my hopper," the computer said.

Schultz looked at the Posleen, who pointed hurriedly to one end of the machine.

Boyd watched as the scrap was loaded into the machine. It slid into the recesses and the device began to hum.

"How long?" Schultz asked as there was a clatter from the far end.

The threesome walked to the front of the machine and looked at the assault rifle sitting on the concrete.

"That was...a few seconds," Schultz said, shaking his head. "And my fratrie just bought a new forge that is now completely *useless*. Computer, do you have materials to make ammunition for the M-146?"

"No," the device responded. "I will need more nitrates and sulfur. I am also lacking in copper and zinc. I can substitute a modified plastic cartridge if you would prefer but it is disrecommended according to the manual. If I am required to make more of the rifles I will need a supply of vanadium and molybdenum. There was sufficient in the materials provided for only one and a half rifles."

"One of the shuttles is packed with trace metals," Boyd said. "We'll see about nitrates. And such. How are you fixed for copper and zinc?"

"Can this thing produce, well, *anything*?" Schultz asked, clearly stunned.

"More or less," Boyd replied. "Anything that will fit coming out the other end and larger devices can be assembled from components. On uniforms I've gotten a provider in the U.S. to make them. They'll be coming in starting next week. They're Himmit chameleon suits so the Hedren won't have any more advantage than you do. But you're on your own with electronics, weapons and other supplies. I've got too many other fish to fry to supply those at the moment. The big problem is heavy weapons systems."

"We've got no Tigers," Schultz said, nodding. "I was informed."

"We're restarting the SheVa production line," Boyd said. "The first production will be Tiger IIIs, B models, for your forces. They're probably what we'll go with across the board. But for right now, we're going to have to refit the surplus weapons left over from the Posleen War. In your case, well . . . General Mühlen-kampf is looking those over."

"These will never run again," the general said, shaking his head.

The field was packed with weapons systems. A valley in Austria, the region was the dumping ground for European war materials left over after the Posleen War. There were French, Austrian, German and even Russian artillery pieces, tanks, armored personnel carriers and "light-skin" vehicles ranging from Mercedes trucks down to some U.S. military jeeps and GAZs, the Russian equivalent. Mühlenkampf had even spotted a *Kuebbelwagen* and other material dating to World War II. Thousands and thousands of weapons and tons of equipment. Enough to supply multiple divisions much less the, at most, one he could field from his people.

However, systems had been parked there, their oil drained, and then left. The people doing the dumping hadn't even bothered with tarps. Most of them were too far gone when they were dumped to be worth more than scrap. And with the reduced world population and the amount of scrap left over from the war, they weren't even useful for that. So they had been left to slowly rust.

"Many are recoverable, General," Indowy Keleel replied nervously. He had brought a large detachment of Indowy with him who were pouring into the valley, climbing onto vehicles and beginning an inventory. "Forges are being brought here to create replacement parts. We have many abilities that may help. We will know in a week, no more, what we can salvage from this. And when your men are given these vehicles, they will work. Better than new. I guarantee it."

"Time, Indowy, time," the general said. "The Hedren will not give us forever to prepare. And while many of my veterans have experience in some of these systems... Time cloaks the memory. The old skills arc rusty. They must have the weapons to train on before they can be ready to go to war."

"We will hurry, General," the Indowy said. "You can trust us on that."

"Can I?" the German asked. "Can I, Kobold?"

"My clan is based on Gratoola, General," Keleel replied. "If Gratoola falls, so will most of my clan and my clan leader. We will hurry, General. But put our work to good use, yes?"

"The admiral sure about this?"

Out from Saturn, beyond the most distant watch-post in the system, was the Graveyard. It was here that the majority of the ships from the Reconnaissance in Force had been dragged. The task force that raised the Siege of Earth was a fraction of the total Fleet at the end of the War but it was still more metal than the Federation could field to fight the Hedren.

It was a sad and yet stirring sight. Drifting in their nearly eternal orbits, their compartments opened to vacuum as had so often been the case in battle, here were the destroyers, cruisers, battlecruisers, dreadnoughts and superdreadnoughts that had destroyed the Posleen invasion and ensured that humanity had a chance to scratch their way to freedom once again.

It was a roll-call of history. *Kaga V. Lexington IV. Atlanta. Tokyo. Novobirsk. Nagasaki. Ark Royal III. Prinz Eugen.* Each had been in multiple battles during the Posleen War, all had battle honors to dwarf any wet-navy ship save, perhaps, the *Victory*.

At the end of the war it was almost *all* of the ships that remained under the command of the original Fleet officers. Which was *why* they were chosen to break the Darhel imposed orders requiring the Fleet to remain on guard over "retaken" systems and let Earth fall to the Posleen. They had been gathered in secret from multiple systems, all of them given lone orders to "return to Sol system on reconnaissance duties." The date of arrival just happened to match. And, wow, since there's not much to stop us maybe we should save Earth? What do you think?

In honor of that final battle, in honor of saving humanity, they had been left to rot. Nearly pristine ships, because there had not been much to stop them in Sol system, were dumped into the Graveyard.

And now one, at least, was going to be the subject of target practice.

"There it is," Tactical said. "The Algerie-class cruiser *Bristol*, hull number 39628."

The space cruiser was about the size of the *Des Moines* before her "upgrade" and massed about the same. Beyond that, they were very different ships. The *Bristol* was a long cylinder bristling with plasma cannon and mass-drivers.

"Man, you get some parts, you get some crew..." the TACO said. "I hate like hell to blow this thing up. It seems...dishonorable."

"They blew the *Nebraska* up with a nuke," Captain McNair said. "We need to see what this thing does to a ship. That is the designated ship. Gunnery, Lock QT One and Two and fire on lock."

"Lock QT One and Two, aye," the gunnery NCO said. "Fire on lock, aye. Locking."

Again the blue beams flashed out then—

"Locked on Target Sierra One. Firing."

The 53,000 ton cruiser flashed white for a moment, then was revealed as a wasted hulk.

"Wow," the TACO said. "Loss of ten percent of mass. On the basis of visual..."

"We just stripped off about half the hull and most of the guns," McNair said. "A couple more hits and she'd be beyond dead in space. I'd hate to be onboard when this thing hit. And the range, especially since once you get a lock it *tracks*, is frightening. Right. Send a message to the nearest com-sat that we have suspended exercise and are returning to Luna. No data about this weapon is to go on the net without my approval."

"I need to thank those mentats," Daisy Mae said. "They gave me one *hell* of a main battery." She suddenly winced and wiped at her eyes. "I felt that. Oh, the poor thing; it didn't want to die without fighting back."

"I still say there ought to be some way to get these ships back in action," the TACO said grumpily.

"There is no way we can get these ships back in action!" Chief Isemann said, shaking her head.

Chief Isemann had been selected as the lead NCO for the working party surveying the Indra Graveyard.

Indra had been a bad one. All three battles. Well, the last wasn't *horrible*. It had just been a fucking maelstrom.

The Posleen drive could exit warp within a couple of planetary diameters of a planet. Generally, they didn't, though. If they got *too* close they tended to blow up on exit. But they were just so damned *chaotic*. Sometimes they'd come out practically in fucking atmosphere and then promptly blow up. Sometimes they'd come out of warp by the Jovians then start jumping in, cautiously. Defending against them was *hell*. You never knew when one of the bastards was going to come out off your port or starboard or up or down or, hell, right in front of you!

They mostly traveled in big fucking battleglobes. A globe would be made up of thousands of ships, all locked together with tractor beams. Traveling that way was, apparently, a bit less wasteful of energy. And since their warp drive was very energy intensive that was good.

When one of the globes appeared in their ripple of blue and purple ionization, a ship was suddenly looking at a fleet of really nasty space cruisers, all in one big chunk. If you fired normal guns at it, all you did was strip away a layer of ships. The inner ships would blow the scraps off and keep firing.

You could do that all day and not kill any significant mass of the globe. Which was where the superdreadnoughts came in.

If there was a superdreadnought near enough they'd shoot the planetoid with their big-ass mass driver. Which had its good and bad parts. The good part was that the destroyer-sized chunk of metal would go most of the way through the globe and then let loose enough antimatter to make the local area a slice of hell.

The bad news was that those damned Posleen ships were tough. So about a half to a third of them would survive. And then it was like kicking a fucking wasp nest. They'd come swarming out of that blast of antimatter, which by rights should have blown them to smithereens, and swarm over the superdreadnought like hornets.

That was how they lost the *Lex* in Indra One. And the *Tokyo* in Two. Indra One had especially sucked. They'd lost the *Lex*, their sole superdreadnought at the time, and just about every fucking cruiser and dreadnought. Ronnette had been on a picket destroyer on the back side of the system. By the time they got there all that was left were some damned Lampreys and gas and rubble. There were some survivors; there always were. But she never thought the ships would fly again.

But the Indowy had rebuilt them. Well, the superdreadnoughts and some of the battleships. Most of the cruisers and destroyers had only been good for scrap. So they'd used the scrap to build *more* cruisers and destroyers.

After the last battles, when it was apparent that

the Posleen were finished as a technological race, the majority of the Fleet had been parked and left. Some of the ships had been harvested for scrap but the Indowy were so efficient with material it wasn't really necessary. And the armor of the superdreadnoughts and other battlewagons was so *tough* they were just hard to scrap.

They were all here, over a thousand ships in this system alone. *Hiryu* and *Enterprise, Constellation* and *Junyo, Defiance, Indefatigable, Resolute, Alabama, Yorktown.* The list went on and on. There were over forty supercarriers and superdreadnoughts *alone*.

She had to admit that most of these ships had been captained and crewed by Indis. But it had taken three times the metal weight to get the same results. It had *taken* forty superdreadnoughts and supercarriers to hold the last battle-line. They'd stopped them, then, though. Stopped them butt-cold and with light casualties. But they'd done that in *Second* Indra with a bare ten superdreadnoughts and five supercarriers. All right, they were wrecks when they finished the battle, but they'd *stopped* them.

She supposed if the Indowy could build them in the first place, and rebuild them over and over, they could get these hulks going again. But as the shuttle cruised along the long lines of ships she couldn't see it really happening.

"We can do it," Indowy Mirinau said. "With time. The more hands, the less time and we have been promised many hands. And, of course, we will be using the Posleen manufactories. That will speed the process."

"*Constitution*," Ronnette said, breathing out. It had been her ship in Indra Two and Three, a superdreadnought that could walk into a globe's fire and survive it.

No more "one funnel bastards" for her. She'd worked her way up to Chief of Boat on the *Constitution*. She hadn't understood the sudden transfer out after Indra Three until the *Lex* had entered Earth space. But she'd been ready for it. Working with the Indis, as a female senior NCO, had been a special kind of hell. The *Lex* CO had managed, somehow, to build an Original Fleet crew. But he needed an experienced Gunnery NCO.

"Not our first ship to be worked on," Mirinau said, catching the nuance of the human's words. "First we must fix the ships which will carry the crews to the ships. But we will get to your ship, Chief. I promise that."

"Give me back my lady, Indowy, and I'll be your friend forever," Ronnette said. "Give me back my girl."

"Where have you been?" Mike asked when Michelle walked into his office.

"In meditation," the mentat said, taking a seat without asking.

It took Mike a moment to adjust to Michelle's appearance. She was always pale but never quite this waxy looking.

"Are you okay?" he asked.

"I will be," Michelle replied. "What was it that you needed to ask me? You've been calling for a week so I assume it's urgent."

"I was going to ask you for some clearer answers," Mike said, leaning back. "But I think I've got them."

"If four masters can create an entire dreadnought in a few hours, why can't you have a fleet?" Michelle said, grimacing.

"More or less," Mike said. "Or at least some ACS.

The more I look at these reports on the Hedren the more I realize that if the corps was still around we could go through them like shit through a goose."

"Eloquent as always, Father," Michelle replied. "And here before you sits the reason."

"How bad?" Mike asked.

"Each of us will be effectively useless for about six weeks," Michelle said, wincing and holding her head. "I'm sorry, the analgesic is wearing off. I will continue. Six weeks. Using the sort of power we expended on the *Des Moines* depletes certain neurotransmitters. It is possible to replenish them with nannites, of course. But doing so . . . disrupts neural pathways. Doing so too many times destroys them."

"You get burned out," Mike said.

"Exactly," Michelle said. "As to ACS . . . I would be more than loath to contemplate making even *one* suit. The materials of the armor exceed most theory of how strong materials *can* be. It exceeds the strength of neutronium while being, of course, much lighter. But making it requires the sort of output you saw us do with the *Des Moines* for *months*. Days and days of creating it, layer by layer, atom by battling atom. I was an apprentice to a master who was working on a suit of ACS. I saw him age years in the six months he worked to create it. Only to have it thrown away in war."

"The *Des Moines* doesn't have that level of armor," Mike said.

"Nowhere close," Michelle admitted. "Or we would have been *years* creating it. Supermonitors had a thin *layer* in their armor. So, Father, while there are about a thousand masters of Sohon, creating a fleet from nothing, or a corps of ACS for that matter, is not a viable action. Some of them are creating ACS, others are making parts for the future quantum tanglers, which do require rather high-level Sohon to create. But do not look to us to make you a fleet overnight. You would burn every master in the galaxy. And there would be no one to defend against Sohon attacks."

"And do you have much on those?" Mike asked. "Last question, I swear. Then I'll let you go."

"We can only sense their abilities lightly at this range," Michelle admitted. "There are Indowy masters who are specialists at detecting and analyzing Sohon who are investigating the phenomenon. To say they are puzzled is an understatement. All the effort and research the Indowy have poured into manufacture and creation, these seem to have poured into violence and pain. It pains them to even contemplate the Hedren."

"Are the Indowy going to help?" Mike asked. "Or is it going to be up to you seven?"

"That is the subject of a very large meeting," Michelle said. "It will take place when we are recovered. I truly do not know where they stand at present."

"Go get some rest," Mike said. "I'll leave you alone. But get back with me as soon as you're healed or whatever."

"Very well, Father," Michelle said, getting up. "I don't suppose you've heard from my wandering sister?"

"She's supposed to be in soon," Mike said. "I'll tell her you asked about her."

"Give her my love," Michelle said, nodding as she left.

"I have got to get access to a slab soon," Cally said, shaking her head. "That guy nearly got me because of these damned tits."

"So you've said the whole way home," Bryce said, trying not to sigh.

The trip out had been quick, much quicker than either believed possible. The Himmit had clearly been holding back on how fast their ships could cross interstellar distances since the trip to Chauldria had taken less than half the time it normally would.

However, they'd had to travel commercial on the way back. Since Cally had just technically murdered a Darhel clan leader and there *had* to be some sort of investigation going on, it had been a tad harrowing. But nobody seemed to care. The official story was that he'd died of old age. Well, gone into lintatai. What with two clan leaders dropping in the last decade, after being in place since before the Posleen War, there had been some rumors going around. But so far nobody had pinned it anywhere near Cally O'Neal.

Who was looking around the lunar space-station transfer point in annoyance.

"I checked with Aelool before we left," Cally said. "He said that the slabs had been turned over to Fleet Strike and were being sent to the Lunar hospital. Which means they're somewhere down there," she added, pointing down.

"Well, since you're technically a civilian..." Bryce said, shrugging. "Good luck getting to them."

"We're contract individuals with Fleet Strike," Cally pointed out. "We should have access to the same medical as soldiers. Which means that I should have access."

"So you're going to explain that you used a slab to imitate a Fleet Strike captain on an infiltration of Fleet Strike counter-intel?" Bryce asked.

"No," Cally said. "I'm going to tell them they

don't have the need to know. But first I'm going to call Daddy."

"I suppose you should have access to them," Mike said, shrugging. "I don't exactly cut those orders, though. I'll call the med department and tell them you need to be put on the list."

"How long can it be, Dad?" Cally asked.

"I don't know," Mike replied after the lag. Even with the most advanced technology, light-speed held. And Cally was several light-seconds from Earth. "But if there's somebody with a life-threatening injury, do you want to bump the queue?"

"No," Cally admitted.

"I'll send an order over making sure that you're put on the list," Mike repeated. "Stay on the Moon for now to make sure you don't miss your slot. By the way, Michelle sends her love."

"Same back," Cally said. "Where is she? When I got in I called her but one of her Indowy answered."

"Meditating," Mike said. "It's a long story. Tell you when you get home. Oh, by the way, do any of your Bane Sidhe people fit the bill for a counter-intel chief? I'm not impressed by my current department on that side. And making sure the Hedren don't know much about our new capabilities is looking to be even more important than finding out theirs."

"Uhm . . . not in the Bane Sidhe," Cally said, nervously. "But, yeah, I know someone who fits that slot. He's even. . . Well. . . Uhm. . . Let me get back to you."

"I assume at some point you're going to fill in those 'uhms,'" Mike said.

"Uhm . . ."

✦   ✦   ✦

"You wished to see me, Grandfather?"

The man bowing his head could have been Southeast Asian. Or possibly Chinese with many admixtures. Possibly Polynesian. He had the sort of blended appearance that was common after The War. He spoke Mandarin, Cantonese and two other dialects flawlessly. The one thing that bothered him was that the speech was *too* flawless; he was still getting comfortable with making the sort of common errors that natural speakers always made.

James Stewart was not born Chinese. In fact, he wasn't even born with the name James Stewart. That had been a joke as much as anything when he was arranging the entry of himself and his gang into Fleet Strike. All of them had taken more standard Northern European names than "Manuel" and "Jose." Since one of the hallmarks of the gang was that every member looked Anglo instead of their actual Hispanic background, it just made sense. They sure weren't going to be joining under the names they had. Not with the rap-sheets associated with those names.

The plan was simple. The new GalTech drugs and technologies people in Fleet and Fleet Strike had access to were worth a blue billion on the black market. By slipping his whole crew in, "James Stewart" could find some way to divert GalTech to friends on the outside. Run that scam for a while and then disappear. Since there were unfriendly aliens on the way, run it for long enough to afford a ticket off-planet.

Along the way, though, things just got complicated. They started getting complicated when he realized that, smart and experienced as he might be, his drill instructor was smarter and more experienced. Gunny Pappas had been a character. A massive Samoan with an almost entirely unflappable nature, he looked like a complete dumb-ass, the sort of guy "Stewart" could run rings around. Quick enough, Gunny Pappas had disabused both Stewart and his entire gang of that notion. And he'd made them an offer. Try being real soldiers for a while, clean and straight, or get out with no record. Option C, going with their original plan, would mean one very large and very mean Samoan to deal with.

Over the succeeding years Stewart had often regretted choosing Option A. Most of his crew had been killed in one engagement or another as his unit was shuffled from coast to coast in the U.S. blunting Posleen offensives. However, along the way the kid from the barrio had grown up. He'd come to realize that while he'd had friends in the hood, his crew, other buddies, he didn't have one damned person he could trust. Not when the fecal matter was really hitting the rotary impeller. There were people who feared him, there were people who looked to him as a leader, somebody with power, but nobody that he could just totally lean back on if everything went to hell.

He found that, and more, in Fleet Strike. Forget the training and education, he found the burning honor that rested at the core of the warriors he fought beside. He found a home and a family.

After the war, things got murkier. He'd made major by the time the ACS was getting deactivated but it was all war-time promotions and service. Quick enough the personnel weenies were cutting those officers back. They wanted regulars.

James Stewart—by that time he'd almost forgotten his real name—wanted to be one of those regulars. He had no home to go back to, never really had one in the first place. Fleet Strike was home. So he'd played the game. He'd gotten his college education, he'd done his schools, he'd done his staff time.

Shifting to intel had been slow. At one point, when he was hoping to get an S-3 position, operations officer of one of the remaining ACS battalions, he'd been asked to take an intel position instead. Figuring it was a reasonable replacement and that the joint-branch time wouldn't hurt, he'd taken it.

What he found was that intel was his natural home. He'd been an S-2 before and had enjoyed it but playing in bigger leagues just gave him more scope. His branch was infantry and remained so right up until he became a general and thus "branchless." But he spent the rest of his career in intel.

The downside was that in intel he got to see just how screwed up things were becoming. Darhel manipulation was everywhere, pressing for less qualified but more amenable officers, completely corrupting Fleet to the point that it was a paid branch of one Darhel corporation or another.

He had reached damned near the pinnacle of his career when things truly came apart. Counter-intel, which at the time actually fell under his purview, developed a double agent inside the underground. The guy had information about a rebel organization. The flip side was that the rebels knew the information was out there and were probably going to try to penetrate Strike to get it. May have already done so.

James, by then a lieutenant general but still looking

like a teenaged kid, had been asked by the head of Intel to go into the office undercover and try to find the mole. It was a shitty little investigation, no place for a general and in many ways his heart wasn't in it. But it was his duty.

In the end, he'd found a lot of things. He'd found the mole. He'd found love. And he'd found that he couldn't stand being in the belly of the beast anymore.

The mole turned out to be none other than the daughter of his former commander, Cally O'Neal. While Stewart was playing the part of an inept junior aide to the commander of counter-intel, Cally was playing the role of the commander's administrative assistant and mistress, an absolutely brain-dead if gorgeous blond captain. He also, without realizing who he was truly facing, found himself falling in love with the moronic blonde. When it all came down to blood and death, himself wounded by the enraged general when he found his aide and his mistress "cheating," the general dead and Cally captured, he knew he'd found love as well.

So when he was contacted by some old friends and was informed of who was actually being tortured for information, he'd turned. Sort of. He got Cally out. He arranged to fake his own death. But he couldn't join the Bane Sidhe, he wouldn't live that life. It was a form of half-honor he simply could not stomach. If he was going to go over to the dark side, he might as well go all the way over.

So he joined the Tongs. The Chinese mobs had become major players in every form of organized crime in the galaxy. There was little honor left in Fleet Strike, there seemed to be nowhere to put his feet. He might as well go back to who he'd been before ever meeting people like Duncan and Pappas and Apele and, perhaps most of all, his father-in-law who could never know.

He'd done well there, too. The training and experience he'd received in Fleet Strike worked well. Often the Tongs tended to do things that were the same way that previous generations had done them. He was careful with new ideas on that score, but he had them. He was bright, thorough and ruthless. The one time that someone had tried to assassinate him, the assassins found out that he was also as dangerous as a cobra with a toothache. It only enhanced his reputation.

The Tongs and the Bane Sidhe did not see eye to eye but they had certain traits in common. The Tongs were well aware that the Darhel had, with intent, sacrificed China during the war. And they had long memories. So while business was first and always, any chance to screw the Darhel was to be taken, as long as they weren't fingered for it. So they'd help out the Bane Sidhe, and vice versa, from time to time. One time, in particular, "Yan Kato" had been central in embezzling an entire Darhel clan-corp, a coup of the first magnitude since the Tongs also made money on the deal hand-over-fist.

However, the Tongs were brutal on outside loyalties. Loyalty had to be to the Tong. Family, friends, acquaintances did not matter. Loyalty to the Tong, make money for the Tong, make face for the Tong. These were what mattered.

So he was carefully watched. The Tong might or might not know he was married to Cally. As long as it didn't interfere with business, that was all well and good. The moment it did, the moment that his loyalty became divided, well James Stewart, Yan Kato, Joshua Pryce, Manuel Guerrera, the person in this body, in this head, knew he had better run far and fast. And was aware that he'd probably just die tired.

"Welcome, Yan Kato," the old man said, gesturing eloquently to a finally brocaded chair. "Please, rest yourself."

"Thank you, Grandfather," Stewart said, sitting down carefully. Since it was a nice chair, he probably wasn't going to be killed in it.

He had met the head of the Tong on several occasions. But it was by no means a normal event and he usually had some inkling of the reason for one. One of his superiors might need him to present a proposal. The Grandfather might need an answer to a question related to his areas of expertise, mostly money laundering and white-collar crime.

This summons had come out of the blue. With the changes that were going on related to the new military threat, that could mean anything. He knew that loyalty to the Tong was all. But they had also chosen never to push his potential limits. He had never been asked to do anything related to the military. Others handled the corruption of the docks, of Fleet resupply. However, with all the money that was suddenly flowing to Fleet Strike and with who was in charge . . . It might be that they felt it was time to push that wall.

Stewart wasn't quite sure what he'd do if they did.

"There is a new threat, you have heard," the Grandfather said as a beautiful young woman entered with a tea set. "Your thoughts?"

"From what I have seen of the Hedren, the actions of the Tongs would be significantly restricted under them," Stewart said. He waited until the Grandfather had taken a sip before mimicking him.

"This is my thought as well," the Grandfather said. "They are reputed to have the ability to read thoughts quite readily. Such would severely impact our normal actions."

Stewart waited. You didn't offer your thoughts unless asked.

"I have given orders to refrain from anything that may be considered interference with military supplies, support or personnel," the Grandfather said, taking another sip. "Your thoughts."

"This will be a great loss of revenue," Stewart said, his face unchanging.

"The willow bends with the wind," the master said. "Now is a better time to give support. Perhaps build relationships for the future. In some cases, there are persons who are simply venal enough that it is necessary to enter into a relationship with them. Otherwise others would enter into the relationship who were less . . . noble."

Stewart managed not to snort. The Tong was anything but "noble." However, he could see the Grandfather's dilemma. With as much as the Tong could skim off the military given the current, truly screwed up, situation, it would probably have a notable impact. Enough to lose the war? Maybe, maybe not. But if the Hedren took over, the Tong was going to be dust.

"I was queried when the decision was made to bring you into the Tong, of course," the Grandfather said, gesturing for his cup to be refilled. Another gesture produced a cigarette in a long holder, which he inserted in his lips and lit. "I made the decision that someone who had been a Fleet Strike general would make a valuable contribution, even if he was not used against his former group. And you have. Both in building our already large reputation and our coffers. You are to be congratulated."

"Thank you, Grandfather," Stewart said, bowing. "I have done my humble best." If that wasn't the kiss of death, he didn't know what was. However, he'd had a few years with Cally, on and off when they could both hide from their respective undergrounds, and a few really great kids. It looked like that was going to have to do.

"I will be sorry to lose you," the Grandfather said, lifting up a sheet of paper. "From time to time members of the Tong reach some limit on their abilities. Everyone takes a vacation occasionally. You have had . . . several."

"I'm sorry if the Grandfather considers me inattentive to my duties," Stewart said. He was looking the old man straight in the eye. Normally that was a bad thing but if he was going to be killed, damned if he was going to flinch.

"Not at all," the old man said. "It was used by way of example. Some times these vacations can become extended. For many years or, given our current medicines, even decades." The Grandfather held the paper out.

It was a recall to duty in the rank of lieutenant general, by both his "official" name and that of "Yan Kato."

"You are expected to require the same latitude of the government as we have given you," the old man said, sucking on his cigarette. "To be precise, that you not use your knowledge of the Tongs to our detriment. So pointing out the persons you know to be our friends in the procurement branch would be unwise. In the opposite direction, we do not require that you provide us with useful information. Your commander must trust you, yes? But, of course, you remain a member of the Tong. Your first loyalty remains here. I believe that you are destined for an important post, or I would have said 'James who?' when the inquiry was made."

James looked at the paper again, then looked up.

"I do not know what to say, Grandfather."

"This is a very irregular action," the Grandfather said. "There are those who would question it. They have a very short view. I have a very long view. Humans, and Darhel I suppose, must remain in control of planets for the Tongs to prosper. Your record as an agent of war speaks for itself. But making this decision I take the long view that it will help the Tong to prosper, perhaps not today for you are a very good money generator, but tomorrow when we are both dust. Let that dust be on soil owned by men, yes?"

"Thank you, Grandfather," Stewart said, suddenly grinning in a way he never had while using this face. "I will do that very thing."

"There is one last item," the Grandfather said. "You will, undoubtedly, encounter the daughter of General O'Neal, Calliope I believe is her name. And her children. Feel free to spend as much time with them, in any capacity, as you may choose. If, of course, given such freedom by your new masters."

"Yes, Grandfather," Stewart said, trying not to grimace.

"You young people," the old man said, then sighed. "You think we are all blind."

"You WHAT?" Cally screamed.

"Keep it down," Stewart said. The connection was long. Stewart's normal base of operations was Titan Base and Cally was still on Luna. So the lag was nearly two minutes. It also cost like crazy, but he wasn't going to let that stop him. "I've been given an extended leave of absence from my . . . current employer to reenter military service. I just got the recall. It doesn't even mention that I'm supposed to be dead."

"Holy shit," Cally said when the signal finally got to her. "So you just called me over an open circuit?"

"Couldn't exactly use a secure one anymore," Stewart said. "And, besides, I was specifically told in a very notable interview that I should look you up. Something about young people thinking old people are blind."

"Oh, shit," Cally whispered. "I suppose we should take it as good news. They knew all along, huh?"

"I don't know for how long, but more than long enough," Stewart said. "Look, where are you exactly?"

"Waiting for some dumb-ass bureaucrats to okay my time on a slab," Cally said, bitterly. "Dad sent the order but with a caveat that I've got to take my place in line. Since apparently there are still a bunch of casualties from the Mutiny, that's a long line. I don't see how it could be, the slab only takes a few minutes."

"Well, if you don't get through soon, I'll be seeing you," Stewart said. "When I called the general officer recall office and explained that I was going to need quite a bit of time in a tank, this was a four-week complete body mod the last time around, they told me to go to Luna and see about getting time on a slab."

"Good luck," Cally said. "I've been sitting around for two days going from one office to the next. I thought all these guys were getting turned into soldiers but apparently there are plenty left to give me the run-around."

"I'm scheduled on the next shuttle," Stewart replied, grinning. "Hopefully we can kill time in a supply closet or something."

"Buckley, time?"

"Fifteen forty," the buckley replied.

Cally had it in low-intelligence mode specifically so she could do without its normal dismal tone. But she was feeling pretty dismal herself. She was cooling her heels in the waiting room of the "Office of Enhanced Medical Procedures" and had been for two hours. She was supposed to have had her nearly final interview at thirteen thirty but the OIC had been pulled away to a meeting.

With nothing better to do, she'd been sketching. Mostly pictures of a random human, male, being butchered. Various things she'd like to do to the damned bureaucratic son of a bitch who had kept her waiting.

Especially since the shuttle carrying Lieutenant General James Stewart was supposed to have landed twenty minutes ago. She'd been hoping that if this idiot could stamp her files she might actually get time on the slab. In which case, she could see Stewart with her real face and body. Given that her husband had *never* seen it, she wasn't sure exactly how he'd take it. Frankly, she was working up into a frenzy.

"You can go in, now," the administrative assistant said. The woman had been looking at her funny the whole time Cally had been sitting in the waiting room and was clearly glad to get rid of her.

Since Cally hadn't seen the OIC go in or out, either the meeting had been by viewscreen or there was a back door to the office.

Cally dumped all her shit in her backpack, zipped it up and walked to the door.

"Enter," a female voice replied to the knock.

"Cally O'Neal, civilian contractor," the blond colonel behind the desk said. "Are you any connection to General Oh My GOD!"

Cally was staring at her mirror image. Same face, same hair, same chest.

"What a *horrible* coincidence," Cally said in a very small voice.

"You...you..." Lieutenant Colonel Sinda Makepeace stuttered. "Oh. You BITCH!"

"I'd say 'I can explain' but you really don't want to know," Cally said. "So let me put it this way. CAN I HAVE MY OLD BODY BACK? Jesus Christ, woman, how do you put up with these two fat-filled balloons attached to your chest?"

"I need to call the MPs..." the colonel said, picking up her AID.

"Go ahead," Cally said, crossing her arms. "For your information, yes, he's my dad. For your other information, I'm covered on all actions I took prior to the current hostilities. And compared to some of them, kidnapping you and taking your place is pretty minor."

"Oh, you..." Sinda said, then sighed. "Look, I'll get you right to the head of the queue, trust me. But can you tell me what in the hell that was all about? Because nobody would tell me anything when I finally came out of the Hiberzine. And let me tell you, it was pretty disorienting to suddenly wake up in a hotel room. I appreciated the note, though. I thought I'd been raped or something."

"Not on my watch," Cally replied. "It's a pretty long story, though, and I'm not sure how much you're cleared for."

"Well, unfortunately, I don't have the time," Sinda said. "I've got some hot-shit general coming in in about four minutes who's *supposed* to go to the head of the queue. Although why a general needs a full body sculpt... It had better not be for personal reasons. You have no idea how many people we have trying to slip in just because they want a new body, a new face, bigger boobs..."

"Well, I want my *smaller* boobs back," Cally said, chuckling. "So that's why I was shuffled from department to department?"

"More or less," Sinda said, hitting her input wand. "But you're cleared now. Damn, if I'd known why it was from the beginning..."

"Sort of a need-to-know," Cally said. "If it had been anyone else sitting in that chair they'd never find out."

"Colonel, General Stewart is here," the AID chimed.

"Yo, Stewart" Cally said, dilating the door. "You're never going to *believe* who the OIC is!"

"Have we met?" Sinda said as an Asian male walked into the office.

"No," Stewart said, looking from woman to woman. "But I can guess who you are. I was supposed to figure out who was infiltrating the office. I did, but a bit too late. She does a *really* good Sinda Makepeace."

"This is making my head hurt," Sinda said, frowning.

The years and experience had apparently washed away some of the utter dumb blondeness that was her hallmark when Cally took her place. "General, Miss O'Neal, you're both cleared. Down the hallway on the left. Don't take this wrong, but I hope I don't see either one of you ever again."

"We're cleared to use the slab. Cally O'Neal and James Stewart."

The slabs, both of them, had been installed in what looked like a minor surgery suite. They were visible through glassteel windows from the small antechamber. A medic was manning a station there and two more were managing the slabs inside the room. One, from the shimmering light over it, was apparently in use already. The other was free.

"It'll be just a moment, General," the medic said nervously. He clearly didn't want to keep a general waiting. And he kept stealing glances at Cally. "There's an emergency patient on the way up. Training accident."

"That's fine," Stewart said as a gurney was pushed into the room. The face of the man on the gurney could barely be seen past the bandages and oxygen tubes but it looked swollen and purple. The man pushing it barged right past the desk and into the slab room. "What happened to him?"

"Suit failure," the medic said, looking at his screen. "Severe lung damage as well as superficial vacuum burn to the skin, eyes . . . well, you name it."

"Ouch," Stewart said. The man had been naked under the sheet and his skin was covered in white and gray where it wasn't purple.

"That's gotta suck," Cally said.

"Sir, I have Miss O'Neal's DNA data on file," the medic said. "But—"

"My original," Stewart replied, handing over a chip. "There were times I wondered why I kept it."

"This is actually a first for me," the medic said as the second slab went into use. "I've had a couple of cosmetic repair jobs, but never something as extensive as either of you. Do you mind, sir, if I ask what happened? And why Miss O'Neal . . . well. Ma'am, do you know you look *just like* Colonel Makepeace?"

"I'll leave it at black ops, corporal," Stewart said.

"Yes, sir, sorry, sir. Slab one is open if you want to enter, sir."

"Oh, I think I'll let Cally go first," Stewart replied, grinning. "I'm looking forward to seeing what she *really* looks like."

"You just want to ogle my body," Cally said. "I'm planning on wearing my clothes in. So *there*."

"Uh, ma'am, you can't do that," the medic said.

"Why not?" Cally asked.

"The clothes might interfere with the repair process," the corporal replied.

"Bullshit," Cally said. "I've been on the slab . . . Jesus, I've lost count! Anyway, the slab ignores clothes."

"You've used one before?" the medic said. "I thought they were brand new. When did you—"

"Son," Stewart said, putting his finger to his nose. "I did mention black ops?"

"Sorry, sir," the corporal replied. "But our procedure—"

"Is about to change," Cally said, walking through the door.

"Ma'am, I'm sorry but you have to disrobe to—"

"I already had that conversation," Cally said, lying down on the altarlike device. "Just initiate the conversion, son."

"But, ma'am—"

"I said do it," Cally snapped. "If you have an issue with that, take it up with Colonel Makepeace!"

"I thought you *was* Colonel Makepeace, ma'am," the medic muttered. He looked at the data on the slab's screen then hit enter. "Guess you won't be soon."

"Welcome back, ma'am," the medic said as Cally's eyes opened. "Any problems?"

"No," Cally said, swinging her legs over and jumping down. Then she grabbed her jeans. "Except I forgot that these clothes weren't going to *fit* anymore!"

"Oh, that's funny," Stewart said, swinging his own legs over. "At least I stayed the same size."

"The belt won't even cinch down far enough," Cally said, struggling. "Knife. I need a knife."

"Here, ma'am," one of the medics said, holding out a lock-blade.

Cally flicked it open and worked a hole through the leather of the belt, getting it tight enough to hold up her jeans, then handed it back.

"I look like hell," she muttered.

"Actually, you look pretty good," Stewart said. "Completely different and yet perfect."

"Flatterer," Cally said, taking his arm. "Haven't seen the real you in a while, either. I frankly prefer it to Kato. Do you have anywhere you have to be right away, General?"

"No," Stewart admitted as they walked out. "Technically, I'm supposed to hop a shuttle and go report to your dad. But, hell, he hasn't sent me a Christmas card in years. He can wait."

"Then let's go find a reasonably horizontal surface. Or, hell, a private wall."

"General Stewart is here to see you, sir," Mike's AID chimed as there was a tap on the door.

"Come," Mike said, then growled as the door opened. "Stewart! Where the *hell* have you been! You got out of the slab yesterday!"

"Sorry, sir," the general said, snapping to attention.

"No excuse, sir!" Stewart stopped and shook his head as Mike broke into laughter. "You runt bastard..."

"Just had to see if the training held," Mike said, still chuckling. "Given your employers of the last few years... Why the Tongs, James? Grab a chair, by the way."

"Instead of the Bane Sidhe?" Stewart said, sitting down. He shrugged and paused for a moment, collecting his thoughts. "The Bane Sidhe were effectively a rebel organization against the legal government. While I could no longer stomach supporting that government, I also felt it would be dishonorable to rebel against it." He shrugged. "It was a fine line but this honor thing never came to me as naturally as it does to you and Gunny Pappas. I have to make it up as I go along."

"I suppose it makes a twisted sort of sense," Mike said, nodding. "Which pretty much covers James Stewart in a nutshell."

"Thanks," Stewart said. "I think. What's up? Besides *another* invasion. What are we, destruction central?"

"Looks like," Mike said, his face locked back in its habitual frown. "But these guys, from what we've

gotten from the Himmit, are different from the Posleen.
They're smart and they're fast and both scare the hell
out of me. While we were fucking around out in the
Blight, they took three worlds faster than you can blow
your nose. Faster than we could get the intel on the
first world falling."

"So what are you going to do?" Stewart asked.

"Fight them," Mike said. "And we'll win. In time.
But I'm starting practically from scratch. That's not
on your plate, though. I repeat, they're smart. What
does that tell you."

"That they're going to be collecting information,"
Stewart said. "Unlike the Posleen."

"Extrapolate," Mike said, sitting back.

"They're going to be trying to crack the AID network," Stewart said. "That's an information Achilles
Heel, the way the Darhel use it. Everything of any
note is available if you have the access. I don't know
if they can do it, but they'll be trying as soon as
they discover it. They'll be interrogating prisoners to
try to find out information about the Federation, its
logistics, strategy, critical nodes. They'll access every
form of information they can get their hands on.
Each of the planets, at least those with humans, had
a local internet system as well. That's going to have
most of the major stuff they need to know, including
our general TOE, tactics, strategy. That assumes they
think like us, of course. What do we have on their
methods of intel gathering?"

"We know they use stealth ships," Mike said. "They
also have a personal cloaking ability, which means
they can slip in teams without anyone seeing them,
assuming people don't have the right technology to

see them. We're redesigning combat glasses to detect cloaked personnel, ditto ship sensors, et cetera."

"But they're not in use at the moment," Stewart said.

"Nope," Mike admitted.

"Can they have units in this system?" Stewart asked.

"I think they're like the Himmit," Mike admitted. "They could have somebody in this *room*."

"Lovely thought," Stewart said.

"And that is your lovely thought for today and tomorrow and until we win," Mike said, tossing Stewart an AID. "You're now in charge of Intel. Figure out what we don't know, figure out what they can find out and stop them from finding it out. And find out what you can about them that the Himmit can't."

"Great," Stewart said, looking at the device balefully. "I hate these things."

"I'm given to understand that one is 'clean' for values of clean," Mike said. "And they're going to get cleaner. But determining what clean means is one of your first jobs. There's a major in your department who's been collecting intel from the Himmit, and Rigas is in the building. I suspect we're bleeding intel to these guys and we're not getting much in the opposite direction. Change that."

"Gotcha," Stewart said, standing up. "So, Dad, when are you coming to see the grandkids?"

"Excuse me?" Mike said, neutrally.

"Uh . . ." Stewart said, grimacing. "When are you going to finally see your grandkids?"

"I got that part," Mike said, blinking. "The answer is as soon as I get a few more fires put out. It was the 'Dad' part that I'm asking about."

"I guess Cally left that out, huh?" Stewart said, sitting back down.

"I guess she *did*," Mike growled. "So you want to tell me the *rest*?"

Stewart looked at him askance for a moment then frowned.

"Oh, you..."

"I think you used runt bastard the last time," Mike said, grinning. "I'm going to take some time this weekend and run down to the Island. If you come along we can make it a working trip."

"Wouldn't miss it for worlds," Stewart said. "I'll tell you this, Boss, it's good to be back. New invasion, backs to the wall and all."

"And I'll tell you now, Son, that there are going to be days you'll long for the comfort, security and placidity of the Tongs."

"I have seen you Kobolds work before," Mühlenkampf said, trying not to seem impressed. "But this exceeds my expectations."

"This" was not only a row of refurbished fighting systems but the new facility that produced them. The building, sixty meters high, covering better than forty hectares and filled with the noise of happy industry, was made entirely of metal. Several thousand Indowy had spent less than a week surveying the entire valley of equipment. Whenever a vehicle was determined to be beyond recovery it was carried to shredders, pushed through forges and came out as the base material of the building.

By the time the survey was complete, the building was complete. Then vehicles started moving. Tanks, trucks, artillery pieces, mobile rocket launchers, light wheeled vehicles. It didn't matter to the Indowy, who were used to customized construction and renovation. System came in one end as a rusted pile of scrap and exited the other as better than it had left its original factory floor. Within another week the Indowy had mastered the technique and were turning out a system, virtually any system, at a rate of better than one every ten minutes, twenty-four hours per day. Electronics were upgraded, guns were improved, seating was more comfortable. And more...

"A human associate refers to this as the 'magic pixie dust,'" Etari said, walking past a line of vehicles that were being painted.

As far as Mühlenkampf could see, it was just making them very very shiny. He was not enthusiastic about the idea of taking shiny vehicles into combat.

One of them was a Leopard tank with a very strange gun. Very long, longer even than the original cannon and decidedly...wide. He was unsure what it might be but wasn't going to ask, yet. But the tank looked like something that would be put on parade, glittering under the lights as if it were armored in chrome.

"It's very pretty, but..."

Etari raised a small wand and pointed it at the Leopard, which abruptly faded from view.

"The system is not the same as the one the Hedren and Himmit use," Etari said dismissively. "I found their system to have... flaws. They use a projection field that warps light around the cloaked device. Simple enough, but not exactly...robust. A strong enough hit, even one that does not take out the vehicle, can disrupt the projector. And the Hedren design is much less effective than that by the Himmit. There is a noticeable warping if you are looking closely enough."

"And this?" Mühlenkampf said, walking over carefully and reaching out. Yes, the Leopard was still there. He could see that it, too, distorted the background slightly but it was very much as if the entire tank was transparent. He hoped the crew would not be viewable sitting in their seats. It would be humorous but not exactly stealthy.

"Actually, humans were on the cusp of it during the Posleen War," Etari said. "But they hadn't put the pieces together. One group was working on biochemical transistor design, another on a thinner, flatter projection system, another on the base theory of a cloaking system and the last an actual produced paint used for holographic art primarily on personal wheeled vehicles."

"So this is a hologram?" the *Generalmajor* asked.

"Not at all," Etari said, thumbing off the cloak. "The vehicle is covered in a dual-layer paint. The outer layer of paint is from the thinner, flatter projection system, a paint that lays down plasma reactor nodes, very small bits of material that fluoresce in a particular frequency when energized. The inner layer is a biochemical processor. Each of the plasma reactor nodes binds to the processor at a particular point. The overall sheet acts as the computer, to put it in terms you understand. When the paint is dried the vehicle is run through a laser designation system that tells the processor which nodes are directly opposite each other. One node picks up a signal from reflectance and transmits it to its polar opposite which then energizes—"

"Making a picture of what is behind the vehicle," Mühlenkampf said, nodding. "I suppose for you this is child's play."

"Sometimes the simplest way is the best," Etari said. "Short of being hit by a large-scale plasma burst, the paint is very redundant. And if it gets scratched, all you have is a bit of the base, which is a mottled green-brown, in view. Repainting requires a facility but it is easy enough. It creates a bit of a flicker when in movement, but is quite effective when still. And in movement, the secondary effects of the vehicle are, after all, noticeable."

"Invisible units," Mühlenkampf said. "Very good."

"And there is an interesting item to it," the Kobold said. "Ask me."

"What is the interesting item?" Mühlenkampf said, trying not to growl.

"The technology is not the sort the Hedren are used to facing," Etari said. "Their counter-cloak technology is designed to detect cloaking fields. This, General, is not a cloaking field."

"So we may be invisible to the normally invisible Hedren?" Mühlenkampf said, nodding.

"Possibly," Etari said, not appearing to care if he'd impressed the human or not. "You shall have to see in combat. Visible on thermal certainly. The gun is a rail-gun capable of firing a variety of rounds. The Hedren vehicles are not only heavily armored but incorporate a shield system which is . . . extremely robust. It may take more than one round to destroy even one of their relatively light armored vehicles. There are several types of shield penetration systems but given that we have not had a Hedren vehicle to test them against. You may have to decide which works best in combat."

"Joy," Mühlenkampf said grimly.

"We recognize this as being suboptimal," the Indowy

replied making the grimace that equated to a shrug. "Nothing we can do about that. On to the next piece."

The next piece was clearly tracked artillery, but Mühlenkampf had never seen the system before. As with the Leopard, it was shiny "chrome" all over. And it was big. Very big. It also had a boxy appearance that must have caused the Indowy, who were big on curved surfaces, conniptions. He finally twigged to its purpose when he noted that the cannon was very clearly designed as artillery, not a tank cannon.

"After looking at the inventory we determined that there were insufficient mobile cannon for your proposed organization," Etari replied. "There were more than sufficient towed weapons systems. However, it had been impressed upon me that mobile was better."

"In general, that is the case," Mühlenkampf said.

"We determined a method to use bodies from Marder fighting vehicles and the suspension, drive, and tracks from Russian T-62s to create a tracked artillery system. We ended up scrapping most of the towed artillery systems, however. Chemical rounds are so . . . inefficient. These use a railgun-based drive system that has significantly more range than the original 155. The system has an auto-alignment system based on the American MLRS, an auto loading system and an automated reloading system. There is a separate but similar vehicle for that. We've improved the barrel design so that it has a top rate of fire of sixteen rounds per minute and with the auto-loader and sufficient support it can maintain that all day. Moreover, by adjusting elevation and propulsive force, and thus time of flight, it can do up to nine round time on targets from a single system. Top road speed should be right at one hundred kilometers per hour.

We somewhat improved the engine, transmission and track system. Among other things, the second is now automatic and the controls are similar to a Leopard tank. Oh, and we installed ground-effect drivers so that you can cross boggy terrain and for march-order movement to reduce damage to the track systems and the roads. We considered installing full antigravity but the reengineering requirements and training requirements were considered suboptimal. All of the vehicles, however, have similar improvements."

"I see," the *Generalmajor* said. "Very good."

"You can feel free to 'field test' it," the Indowy said. "It is, after all, not a standard system. However, I assure you they will work."

"Somehow, I don't doubt that Indowy Etari. We will need—"

"Field manuals have been produced for all the systems, in your *Deutsch* as well as Hebrew, Swedish, Norwegian and several Slavic languages," Etari said. "They are formatted upon *Bundeswehr* field manuals since many of the methods and systems were unknown at the time of the *Wehrmacht*. The one point I must stress is that these are not Indowy devices. They require . . . maintenance."

The last was said in a tone of very clear disgust. Had Mühlenkampf had more experience with the little, fuzzy, bat-faced creatures, he'd have seen the equivalent of a sneer.

"I assure you we will perform that maintenance diligently," Mühlenkampf replied. "A training area has been set up near the former city of Hamburg. Transportation—"

"Shuttles will begin lifting systems as soon as we

have sufficiency to provide for one brigade," Etari said, cutting him off again. "That will be within a week. The field manuals will be sent out today so that you can begin book training on the systems. We debated for nearly a day whether to convert all the engines to fusion-electric systems but decided against it, again for training reasons. However, all those that formerly ran on . . . 'gasoline' are now converted to diesel, reducing your logistics complexity. But you will have to assure a supply of diesel for support. Future systems will be converted to fusion-electric."

"I will admit to being impressed," Mühlenkampf said stoically.

"I am one of the few senior mechanists in my clan who has been interested in Posleen and human manufacturing techniques," Etari said, just as stoically, walking outside the manufacturing plant to where the majority of the vehicles were sitting. "I also was a mechanist during the Posleen War and had, I thought, a number of worthwhile concepts that I was, alas, too junior to present. I relished the opportunity to prove the effectiveness of my concepts. But this is but the first step. By the time you need to be reorganized after Gratoola we will have *real* systems prepared. I believe the human phrase is '*better, stronger, faster.*'"

"That is an important point," Mühlenkampf said. "The Hedren field heavy armor is the equivalent of a SheVa Four or a Tiger III. Actually, better than either. There is nothing I have seen in this valley that can take them on."

"Ah, those," Etari said, dismissively. "Come."

Etari walked down the rank of tracks, tanks and trucks to a cluster of vehicles. Mühlenkampf, for all his experience of military vehicles, was not sure what he was looking at. The base may have been the Russian T-62 again. Many of them were used by forces in the Vienna pocket, mostly those who had survived the debacles in Eastern Europe. They may have ended up in the valley.

The upper, however, looked more like a bastardized Amerian M-1, with the exception of the gun, the barrel of which was thick and short.

"The round fired is actually a high-velocity missile," Etari said, climbing up on the tank. "It tracks on Hedren heavy armor so it is 'fire and forget.' When it hits, it uses a system similar to the Posleen heavy-armor penetrator, a smart bot that finds the weakest point in the Hedren armor and drills an antimatter breaching charge into the interior. There are various countermeasures, some of which the Hedren use, but there are counters for the counters and so forth and so on. But this is your primary antiarmor system. We're leaving the naming to you.

"Primary tanks will be modified Leopards, tentatively designated Leopard Vs. Slightly more robust drive train, more or less the same speed, heavy railgun based on the Posleen designs but with the same firing system and layout as the Leopard III. Improved communication and ground-effect drive for march-order movement. Sights work in thermal imagery and "cloaking reveal." The latter is not perfect, but as good as anything that is out there. Secondary guns 3 and 5 mm rail guns.

"Primary infantry fighting vehicles will be a modified Marder, improved layout, improved communications and tracking system, improved drive train including enough speed to keep up with the Leopards while in track mode and, of course, ground-effect drive. Primary weapons system is a 5 mm railgun, secondary is a smaller version of the smart-bot gun. Much the same sight system as the Leopard.

"Primary heavy support vehicle is based on the Marder fighting vehicle. Armored against shrapnel and light weapons rounds as well as mines. Sealed, as are all the other systems, in case the Hedren use poison gas or nuclear weapons. Ground-effect drive. Primary light wheeled vehicle is a Mercedes design with same modifications. Light scout vehicles are designed around those with the 5 mm rail gun. Heavy scout vehicles are based on the Marder, again. All vehicles are equipped with blue-force trackers and sub-space communications systems that are at least hard to intercept or jam. And all are, of course, cloaked."

"Three weeks?" Mühlenkampf said, finally shaken. "Three *weeks*? It would have taken the general staff three *years* to design all this! And then nothing would have worked first time out."

"As I said, I have had several of the concepts for some time," Etari replied. "Expect the first brigade's delivery of equipment to begin one week from today, *Generalmajor*. Is there anything else?"

"*Nein*," Mühlenkampf said.

"I believe you asked for 'anything but time.' I hope this is to your satisfaction."

"Very much so."

"Do what you must do and do it well," Etari replied. "I do not wish to become the clan leader of a remnant. I much prefer my current job."

"I shall do what I can, Kobold," Mühlenkampf promised. "Now I must go. There is much to be done."

✧   ✧   ✧

There are things which must not be done.

Any seventh level mentat could contact any other seventh level mentat, or any other being, via a form of telepathy. The contact was as close to instantaneous as the reality of the polyverse permitted and effectively unlimited in range.

It was not mind reading, or at least the method the Sohon used was not mind reading, but rather small modifications of brain chemistry that had the words "heard" without being spoken. Admittedly, if a being can modify brain chemistry, and can read it properly, both mental modification and mind reading were possible. The Sohon expressly did not do this. Had not done this. It was forbidden experimentation.

Which was what the meeting was all about.

There are things which must be done, Michelle thought back and via ripple linking her thoughts permeated throughout the entire metaconcert. Somehow, she had become the spokesperson for the human mentats. Which meant that if things went against them hard enough she would be repudiated, again, but this time stripped of her powers. She would, voluntarily, strip herself of her powers. Because the whole point was that the Wise *must* choose the greater Path.

I would present my logic, she continued.

I would observe your logic, the distant Indowy replied. Her primary debater was the Mentat Treelu, an adept who had been a master for longer than she had been alive.

Our purpose is to advance upon the Path of Enlightenment, Michelle said. *To bring our species—all species—to a higher state of being, to abjure the reality of this condition. It is a slow path, but one that must be taken if our species are to grow.*

This is the Path, Treelu replied. *How can war, which deviates our feet from the Path, assist in this?*

I *do not see a way,* Michelle thought, telling a little white lie. It was a good thing it *wasn't* mind reading. *What I see is that the Hedren have deviated, horribly, from this Way. Yet they use Sohon. The necessities of Sohon therefore, of themselves, are not necessities of the Path.*

That was a bit of a shocker, something that most of the mentats had probably considered but had not been willing to admit. Certainly publicly and probably to themselves.

The whole concept of the Uprising Path was that Sohon was the Way. First of all, for purely mundane reasons the methods of Sohon would permit the wielders, eventually, to rise to a different state of being and consciousness. The Aldenata had shown the way. Second, the mental discipline necessary for Sohon meant that emotional distractions had to be minimized. The disciplines received from the Aldenata stressed that emotionlessness was one of the cornerstone necessities of Rising.

What Michelle had said, in essence, was that the Aldenata, gods to most of the Indowy but more like senior mentors to the Indowy mentats, were wrong.

I reject that logic, Treelu replied.

Argue it, Michelle thought.

The Aldenata require abjurement of this state of being to Rise, Treelu replied. His tone was one of a slam-dunk.

The Hedren apparently do not, Michelle thought. *I*

am not saying that I accept the Way of the Hedren. I do not, nor do any of my human brethren. But the Hedren example teaches us that strict removal of all things of this essence are not necessities of Sohon. By extrapolation, they are not necessities of Rising.

The Way of the Aldenata is, therefore, but one choice upon the Path. The question therefore becomes, are we willing to support the Way of the Aldenata. Or are we to succumb to the Way of the Hedren? Failure to support the actions against the Hedren Tyranny will mean accepting the Hedren Way. This is a binary solution set. If there is a third resultant that I have not considered, I will accept that resultant. However, failing a third resultant it is not a question of simply continuing on the Way of the Aldenata. It is elimination of the Way and substitution by the Way of the Hedren.

This is the logic of war. It is as cold as any in the Universe.

There is no consensus, Treelu thought. *We must not take any action until there is consensus.*

The metaconcert had broken up, reformed, broken again as the masters of Sohon across the galactic arm wrestled with the question of whether to support something they abhorred.

Metaconcerts were extraordinarily rare and Michelle had not been a part of one before. The last one had been on the subject of whether to support the Posleen War effort. But she had quickly learned that it was possible to taste the flavor of feelings broadly held by one group or another. Having tasted the various factions, she only partially agreed with Treelu.

There is consensus, Michelle argued. *Sohon must not be used for aggressive action. That is fundamental to the Way. The sense I get beyond that is that there are masters who refuse to support the action in any form beyond continuing to build and study. That is acceptable. But there is a large faction that feels more direct action is acceptable. Certainly to defend against the Hedren and their Imeg slaves' use of Sohon for evil. On Diess, did not our junior brethren build defenses for the soldiers to fight behind? We do no more in this.*

You are either blind to reality or dissimulating, Treelu replied. *To learn to defend, someone must learn to attack. Masters who enter battle against the Hedren must be trained, no? And the only master in this concert who has engaged in direct battle, master to master, happens to be you, no?*

Michelle was calmly composing a scathing reply when another faction spoke up. The group was, broadly, those willing to defend against the Hedren. The spokesperson was one of the newer Indowy mentats, but powerful from his voice.

Your reply uses no logic, the mentat said, his mind echoing through the metaconcert. *It appears to be based upon personal animus. The concert is reminded that the mentor of Human Mentat Erick Winchon was Mentat Treelu. If anyone should have ensured the discontinuation of Winchon's actions, it is Mentat Treelu. Using it as a challenge against Mentat O'Neal is emotion based, rather than logic based.*

The logic that some mentats must learn attack methods is, however, justifiable. Using those in training, though, is no more aggressive than surgery. As long as no harm is done with intent it is not a deviation from the Path.

We must ask the Aldenata, a querulous older thought cried. The faction he spoke for was smaller than either the nay-sayers or those in favor of action. But as he spoke, Michelle could sense leakers from both factions. *We must take no part in hostilities without the benefit of their Wisdom.*

By the time the Aldenata reply, the war will be over, the younger mentat thought. *We argue for the compromise of the Michon. Let those who are willing to engage in defense be permitted to do so. Let those who wish to refrain refrain. Let each master find his, her or its Path. Save only that they do no harm by intent. Any use of Sohon at this level raises the question of harm through failure. Such is the nature of the universe. But evil rises; an evil that uses Sohon for great harm. This* cannot *be allowed. Contact the Aldenata by all means. Their answer will arrive in time and we can then be judged under that answer. This will mean sacrifice for all. Separation from home and loved ones. Perhaps even failure of debt. But these are sacrifices worth making. As Mentat O'Neal has noted, it is a binary solution set, the logic of war. My faction chooses to make the sacrifice to preserve the Way.*

Michelle smiled to herself as the mentat finished. She wasn't sure if he knew it, but he'd reprised a statement used long ago on Earth.

He was asking them to give their lives, their fortunes and their sacred honor.

We must ingather, Michelle thought. *And there are many details to be worked out.*

Indeed, Mentat Karthe replied. The Indowy was only young by Indowy standards, being some two decades older than the human. But his mind-voice felt very young. *Human soldiers who go to war have a method to suspend debt payments. We will need a law covering our time during this action. There is little chance that we will be paid sufficiently to cover our payments.*

Not one I'd considered, Michelle admitted. *I will contact my father and see that it is done. The one that I had considered is that there may be students that do not agree with their masters, in either direction. There will be shifts.*

Many details, as you said. I will begin moving the members of my faction to Earth. Most will have to ingather by ship. The masters will bring their finest students with them. We will begin arriving in two weeks.

I will convey this to my father, Michelle thought. *I thank you for this.*

The logic is inescapable. If good is not willing to sacrifice and fight for its beliefs, then evil will triumph.

Have you been reading Patrick Henry?

CHAPTER SEVEN

"The SS has thirty percent of its heavy equipment in shipment," Tam said. "The remainder will be arriving over the next couple of weeks. They've already begun training on the gear. Mühlenkampf feels that three months will be necessary for them to become fully trained on the systems."

"He lifts two weeks after they get the final shipment," Mike said. "If he has three months on planet to train in, all good. But a trained unit on Earth does us no good if Gratoola falls."

"I'll send him the message," Tam said. "Lieutenant General Stewart has a brief on Hedren capabilities and methods prepared."

"Go," Mike said, looking over at his son-in-law.

"I did hardly any of it," Stewart admitted. "The J-2 was preparing it before I took over. So I'm not going to take credit. Here goes:

"Hedren primary method of hard insertion is through

the matter wormhole. The unit inserted is, as was previously briefed, the equivalent of a heavy armored corps with combat supports including in-system attack craft. But that's not enough to take a planet. They're really just there to establish a bridgehead. They generally will land near a notable feature of the planet, a capital city or such, and take that as fast as possible. Then they sit on it until more forces arrive through hyper-jump."

"Why not just attack through hyper?" Mike asked.

"Think about it from a defense point-of-view, General," Stewart said. "Defenses are based to point outwards. The Hedren Fleet arrives hard on the heels of the ground assault. Suddenly you have ground forces holding a position, ones that can engage into local space from the ground, and a fleet jumping in on you. Dimensional warp tech won't hyper in any closer than the ley-line system, which means well outside the life-zone of most systems. Therefore, the fleet has to fight its way in. If they don't have ground force, they then have to make a combat drop on the position. Better to have a secure area for landing. The defenders have to make the choice of engaging the ground forces from space or the incoming fleet."

"Attack from both axes," Tam said.

"Correct, sir," Stewart replied. "It's not just a ground attack, it's a full-court press. Following a successful attack, the planet is then invested by the fleet, more forces are landed and spread out to control the populace and reduce resistance."

"So the ground force portion, except for the fact that it's really heavy and definitely less spread out, is the equivalent of airborne forces dropped behind the lines," Mike said. "They take a major psychological position—if it's a city it's hard to dig them out—then sit on their gains until relieved. They're going to be screwed if the follow-on forces get stopped."

"Nijmegen?" Tam said.

"You're thinking of Arnhem," the former paratrooper said. "Nijmegen was the Eighty-second. I need to get with Takao and see what he thinks are the chances of stopping the incoming fleet. Otherwise, *our* forces are going to be the Brits. TOE?"

"Himmit have given us a full order of battle for the assault forces as well as for follow-on and the total fleet," Stewart said. "At least, what they believe to be the current TOE on the first two and a pretty good count on the last. They're not sure, though, how much of the latter will be sent to Gratoola."

"Any idea where the attack will occur?" Mike asked. "I mean, in advance."

"Well, there are several possibles," Stewart replied. "The imaginatively named Gratoola City, which is where the capital government buildings reside: the Corridor, which is a big industrial belt... There's a pretty good sized list. If you're asking me for a crystal ball hunch: Gratoola City. The Himmit say that a Sohon mentat should be able to detect the field when they generate it, but it's no more than twenty minutes or so before the Hedren emerge. Which I'm given to understand is an energetic event."

"Define energetic," Mike said.

"Big boom," Stewart replied. "The jump displaces all air and other matter in the region they invest. Non-nuclear boom, but you don't want to be right on the spot that they come in. By the same token, sufficient matter disturbs the insertion, sometimes to the Hedren's detriment."

"They go boom?" Wesley asked.

"They go boom," Stewart confirmed. "Or break. Apparently, if you've got a big enough building, instead of blowing up the building they come out on top. Since this tends to break even their CSUs, they generally don't come in on cities. With that parameter, the analysis section came up with a list of probable landing zones for the Hedren for each of the probable targets. I've got a little list."

"Good," Mike said. "So are all the ground assault forces waiting to go on Daga?"

"No," Stewart said. "They were apparently pulled back to Caracool for rest and refit. According to the Himmit, once a planet is initially quelled the shock forces return to rear areas to get prepped for the next mission. Then they jump, basically, twice. Once to the next jump point, then to the objective. In the meantime, pacification forces, heavy on Glandri and with some Imeg, start filtering in to replace them and start pacifying the populace. There's some combat forces on Daga Nine but mostly it's the new pacification units."

"Get me an Orbatt for those forces," Mike said, turning to his chief of staff. "What about Second Division?"

The "consolidation unit" had been the nearest nearly coherent force to the Hedren attack. Scattered across fifteen worlds, it was slowly being pieced back together.

"We've consolidated them on Darcra," Tam said. "No pun intended. Three-month transit time to Gratoola. But I've seen the efficiency reports. They're not going to be worth much as assault troops. I'd even question their utility at rear area control. Frankly, I don't think sending them straight to Gratoola is wise. I'd rather reconsolidate them with new leadership and put them through a good hard train period."

"Again, well-trained troops elsewhere do us no good," Mike said. "If they die on the sword, they're still going to do some damage. Move them to Gratoola."

"Received and understood," Tam said, trying not to sigh. "And then there's the Legion."

"I thought they were too far out," Mike said.

"Information lag," Tam replied. "The Legion had been consolidated on T-1478 Alpha after an assault there. Their next target was U-2652. Fortunately, a courier caught up with them. I sent orders to have them return to Earth immediately. They should be here in less than a month."

"Time to get them to Gratoola?" Mike asked.

"Two months," Tam said. "You want to send them too? General O'Neal, if you send everything to Gratoola, there won't be anything to cover other planets!"

"If we lose Gratoola they can build another one of these things and then they can go *anywhere*," Mike pointed out. "And, as has repeatedly been mentioned, it's the capital of the Federation. We're going to hold Gratoola if I possibly can. Less for the latter reason than the former, I'll admit. But holding Gratoola is a must. So, yes, send them to Gratoola. How do they look?"

"Well, it's the *Legion*, isn't it?" Tam said. "They fight to the death because the alternative is death. Some of the units are pretty good. Overall, they're better than Second Division but not much."

"It's something," Mike said. "Next."

"Status of standing up forces. Brigadier General Richards."

"The conscription system is just getting into gear," General Richards said. With all ground forces federalized under Strike, Mike's J-1 had the unenviable task of overseeing the latter. "There hasn't been a selective service program in decades. It went out after the war. We're using various databases to find qualified personnel, but given all the underground economy... Recall of former military is better but not much. We've lost track of a lot of them. Again, it's a matter of combing databases and sending letters by certified mail. We'll get down to sending the local sheriff or whatever if we have to. So far, the majority of those we're pretty sure we found have been showing up. Not that that has been all beer and skittles."

"Why?" Mike asked.

"Well," Richards said, shrugging. "There were a lot of promotions in the war, especially of rejuvs since the ones that got it tended to be... Oh, say like the *Generalmajor*. But just as he ended the war as a field marshall in charge of half the combined European armies and is now back being a major general—"

"We don't have the soldiers to take back all these generals," Tam said. "Not nearly enough. What we need is captains and first sergeants, squad leaders. What we're getting are generals, colonels, very senior sergeant majors..."

"Any sergeant major that can't run a squad shouldn't be a sergeant major," Mike said. "Any general that can't remember how to run a company needs to be made a fucking private. Do you get my drift?"

"You're kidding," General Richards said.

"I made Mühlenkampf swallow becoming a major general," Mike said. "Not that he wasn't willing enough. This is a guy who was a general before my *father* was a gleam in his daddy's eye and who commanded ninety fucking divisions in the war." Mike swallowed for a moment at the mention of his father but plowed on. "That's thirty corps, ten armies, three or four army groups. If he can suck it up the rest can. You will fit them into the TOE as necessary for the good of the service. Do I make myself clear?"

"Oh, this is going to be sooo fun," Richards said. "Yes, sir, you've made yourself perfectly clear."

"Think of it this way," Mike said, shrugging. "Would you rather be sitting in this fucking room or commanding a company or a battalion?"

"Hmmm," Tam said. "Put that way..."

"No," Mike replied. "If *I* don't get a battalion, *you* don't get a battalion. But what I'd really like is to be a captain again...."

CHAPTER EIGHT

"You want me to be a *what*?"

Brigadier General Thomas Cutprice had only permitted the increase in rank when he retired. What the hell, it was a jump in retirement pay.

During the war, though, he had insisted on never being promoted over colonel. He'd retired once from the Army at that rank, back when the Army had tired of him and vice versa, and he saw no reason to reach for stars. Not that he didn't have the position.

Cutprice had commanded the Ten Thousand, assuredly the most elite, and high casualty, unit defending the U.S. outside of the ACS. The Ten Thousand were picked fighters, all of them with previous combat experience, who used converted Posleen weaponry for that extra spicy punch. Numbering, with supports, well in excess of fifteen thousand personnel, it was unquestionably a division and had the direct combat power of most corps. The commander should have been at least a brigadier general and more likely a major general.

Cutprice had refused to be promoted and nobody was going to push the issue.

But that didn't mean he wanted to be a *captain* again!

"Look, General, this is happening to everyone," the captain behind the desk said. "*Everyone* who is being recalled is being given a reduction in rank. You've got some good news, though."

"It better be *very* good," Cutprice growled.

"Recalled veterans are being given an automatic reduction in rank," the captain repeated. "It's more complicated than any brigadier goes to captain, but it's close enough. But then each of them gets a set of points on the basis of a matrix. The main axis of the matrix has to do with combat command versus other command or staff time. You've got a *very* high point set; I don't have to look at your record to know that you've had a lot of combat time and a lot of that as a senior commander. That means you get certain choices. Basically, you can use your points to decide what sort of position you prefer, then you can use them to add staff of your choosing. Depends on how many points you have what you can do. Trust me, it will all make sense when you use the system. But be aware that you're going to be bidding for all this."

"That is the screwiest thing . . ." Cutprice said, shaking his head. "You mean you bean-counters are staffing the TOE via *E-BAY*?"

"More or less," the captain said, smiling faintly. "Not the first time I've heard that, sir. But, sir, you have the highest set of points I've ever seen. Look, let me walk you through it. For your first tour, what you're getting when you finish in-process, do you want a staff position or command of a company?"

"Command, of course," Cutprice said.

"Then you go on the board and check to see what the bids are for company commands, sir," the captain said. "You've got over two thousand points. The last time I checked the board, the high bid for a company, and it was a particular company in a particular unit, was seven hundred points. I checked and the captain making the bid was placing it all on that company. If you just bid for any old company command, those are going for around four hundred points."

"Heh," Cutprice said, nodding. "Former commander wanting to relive his glory days."

"Probably, sir," the captain admitted. "Then you take a look at the recalled personnel board. The highest bid I've seen is for a first sergeant who had a string of medals and retired as a sergeant major with nearly twenty years in grade! He'd been a first sergeant *four times*. The high bid last time I checked was fifty-three points. Most sergeants major don't even make it to E-8, they're getting recalled as E-7s."

"I'm beginning to see your, forgive me, point," Cutprice said.

"Sir, you have the most time in a combat command with the most days in combat of the recalls I've seen or checked," the captain pointed out. "At least at your rank. You can write your ticket. Any unit, any personnel. Former sergeants major as platoon sergeants. Majors as platoon leaders. Guys with a string of medals and lots of combat time. Of course, as soon as we get more bodies to fill the slots everyone who has prior experience at a higher rank is probably going to advance really quick. So it's not as bad as it seems."

"A company again," Cutprice said, nodding. He smiled, ever so slightly. "There *are* worse things in life. Where's this board?"

"Your paperwork has all the information, sir," the captain replied. "The board can be accessed through any secure internet browser. All you have to do is log-in with your username and password and start building your unit. Oh, uhm, one thing, sir."

"Go," Cutprice said with a sigh.

"If you pick a particular unit but a higher rank requests you as a company commander, you have to use some points to avoid it. It won't show up that way, exactly. It will show that someone outbid them. If two officers are bidding on you, you can add points to one for example."

"And people can, presumably, do the same to me," Cutprice said.

"Yes, sir," the captain replied.

"Shouldn't have problems down-line," Cutprice said. "Up-line? I can see some former commanders bidding on me just to screw me. I'm going to have to think this over carefully."

"The full initial recall will be complete in two weeks, sir," the captain said. "At that point, all the bids are final. Good luck, sir."

Captain Cutprice walked in the door of the O-Club and snorted.

The Officers' Club was usually a scene of somewhat

raucus drinking as officers blew off steam and complained about the redtape or dumb-ass juniors they'd had to deal with during the day. Deals were made, business conducted in the politics that drove any military as much as did its vehicles.

Despite it being after hours, the Recalled Personnel O-Club, a recently refurbished building on the sprawling Fort Knox Reservation, was fairly quiet. That was because just about every officer was consulting a buckley or laptop. Except for the occasional outburst of profanity or cheering and some sotto voce conversations, the mood was downright business-like.

Cutprice walked to the bar and found an open stool then set his antiquated laptop down and started it up. He had been given an access code for the local wireless router and logged in, then surfed over to the Recalled Officer Placement Board.

"Fuck," he muttered.

"Somebody outbid you?" the lieutenant sitting next to him asked, looking up from his buckley.

"No," Cutprice said, sourly. "I haven't even placed a bid, yet. But I've got seven bids *for* me and *six* of them are total asshats."

"Seven?" the lieutenant asked, leaning over to read the nametag. "Holy shit! *Colonel Cutprice*? The *Ten Thousand* Colonel Cutprice?"

"Captain Cutprice, now, LT," the captain said. "Got up to *General* Cutprice."

"I was a lieutenant colonel," the officer grumped. "But I was just CONARC staff the whole time. I'm hoping to get a platoon this time around. But I've only got, like, five points. Platoons are going for nearly as much as companies."

"Are they transferrable?" Cutprice asked.

"Yeah, but hardly anyone will," the lieutenant admitted.

"Well, I'm no wiz at this internet shit," Cutprice said. "And I'm having a hard time. Gimme a hand and I'll give you some points."

"Can I get a platoon?" the lieutenant asked. "With you?"

"That's a tough one," Cutprice admitted. "Like everybody else, I'm going to be looking for LTs with experience. Training a newbie platoon leader is one chore I'd like to avoid. I'll think about it but I'll definitely cut you enough points to get you into *some* platoon."

"You've got enough?" the LT asked.

"Looking at this board?" Cutprice said. "My main problem will be outbidding the bastards that want to hire me."

"See, since everyone's gotten a point score, you can sort for highest points in each category," Lieutenant Norris said.

"Who the hell is Digermon?" Cutprice said, looking at the database for 11B6 personnel.

"See how it's highlighted?" Norris replied, hitting the link. "That's an abbreviated service record."

"World War II vet," Cutprice said, nodding. "Third Infantry Division. Korea, Vietnam, Posleen War . . . And he's a damned *staff sergeant*! I don't feel so bad."

"Somebody really wants him," Norris said, pointing at the bid. "You can't see his point total but it's got to be high. He might have thrown in some points."

"Can you search by name?" Cutprice asked.

"Just type it in the search box."

"W-A-C-L-E-V-A . . ."

"Hoowah!" Master Sergeant Wacleva said, holding up his buckley. "We are triumphant!"

"What you got, Wac?" the master sergeant sitting next to him asked.

"Cutprice is now on the board," Wacleva replied. "And I'm going to put all my damned points on his bid. If I have to deal with that asshole Jackson as a CO, I will frag his butt as soon as we're in combat."

CHAPTER NINE

"*Schutze* Goldschmidt reporting to the commander as ordered," Hagai said, saluting. *Schutze*, guard, was the Freilander equivalent of a private.

Hagai was sweating. Very, very rarely were recruits called in to see the commander of Two Company. Two Company was a line company but acted as the training company for the battalion as well. All new recruits and officer candidates served in Two Company. By the same token, all the other officers and men were very senior within their rank. Command of Two Company was a necessary step to becoming a major and eventually a battalion commander. Captain Itzowitz had previously commanded Four Company in the battalion and One Company, the headquarters and support company. This was his third company command.

So to be standing before the grizzled commander Hagai had to have *really* screwed up. There were *Feldwebel* and *Oberfeldwebel* to handle anything less.

The problem was, he couldn't think of anything he'd done, lately, that would get him in enough trouble to be staring over the CO's head.

The CO returned his salute politely then looked him up and down.

"I'm going to be sorry to lose you, Hagai." Itzowitz was Sephardic in extraction rather than Ashkenazi and showed it in his being nearly as tall as Frederick and more heavily boned. He also was Reform and was reputed to not even keep kosher, which was almost unheard of among the Maccabeans.

Hagai didn't know what to say to that so he kept quiet. He'd learned that early on.

"You are probably unaware of it but the Maccabeus is slightly overstrength," *Hauptmann* Itzowitz continued. "As such, we are being drawn upon to fill out some other units. You will remain a member of the *Bruederschaft* but you will be transferring to Florian Geyer for the foreseeable future."

"Florian Geyer, sir?" Hagai said, stunned. He was being thrown out of the *unit*?

"It's not the end of the world," the *Hauptmann* said, smiling. "At ease, Hagai. Sit, even."

"Yes, sir," Hagai said, sitting down at attention.

"I said at ease," the *Hauptmann* said, somewhat more sharply. "Look, we have too many good Jews here in the Maccabeus. You're not being thrown out because you are our worst. If we send people to another unit, they are our ambassadors. We don't send our very best but we send people that are not going to embarrass us, yes? We were levied for five *Schutze* from the battalion. You are the only one in Two Company that I felt *good* enough to be sent to

Florian Geyer. You have been trained as a grenadier. Florian Geyer is an *panzerjaeger* unit. You will have to learn your duties very quickly. I think you have the skills to do so. That is why you are going."

"Thank you, sir," Hagai said, unsure whether it was really a compliment or not. *He was being thrown out of the Maccabeans?*

"I see I have not convinced you," the CO said, sighing. "There are other Brothers who are not in the Maccabaeus. Many in the intelligence sections, yes? A few scattered in Wiking. This is the same. You will need to see the Rabbi before you leave, though."

"Sir?" Hagai asked.

"The Florian Geyer does not keep kosher," the CO said. "To fit in in the unit, you are going to have to be . . . flexible. Major Hertzberg is a good Orthodox rabbi. He will explain to you the necessity. And you need to get your best uniform prepared. You have an interview with the battalion commander this afternoon. He will say much the same thing I said. Just in more definite terms."

"*Nein! Nein!* Ox you are a *dumkopf*! Your *other* left!"

There were no simulators for the Leopards. Fortunately, there was a seemingly unending stream of diesel, ammo and parts.

Since getting their first shipment of panzers, the Michael Wittmann had been in the field training nearly constantly. Not only on maneuver and combat but on field maintenance which was equally as important. The Leopard Vs were immensely complex machines from the track system to the electro-drive for the new guns. Some of it the ancient veterans knew and half-remembered. Much of it could only come from books. As to the training on maneuvering...

"My apologies, *Feldwebel*," Frederick said, getting the tank straightened out again. He had been negotiating an erzatz obstacle course and part of the problem was that some of the "obstacles" were imaginary mines obscured from the driver. He had to take direction from Harz, who was not the most patient of teachers.

"I think you just got us graded as destroyed," Harz growled. "In combat we would be *dead*! Quit thinking about your fucking girlfriend and listen to my orders... More speed now... Faster..."

"Crank it, *Schutze*!" *Gefreiter* Joachim Aderholt shouted. "Into the sun, into the wind!"

The gunner of Three Track, Second Platoon, Two Company, Panzer Battalion Michael Wittmann was a new addition. The Leopard V had an autoloading system for the main gun and, thus, no loader. But it still required a gunner. Aderholt was as new and just about as clumsy at his job as Frederick. But he was still a *Gefreiter*, a lance corporal, and thus much above a lowly *Schutze*.

Frederick looked at the next obstacle and gulped. It was an incline ramp and he couldn't see what was on the other side.

"*Feldwebel*..." he muttered.

"Faster, dammit!" Harz shouted. "Push the stick to the stops, you little shit! Drive like a panzer driver *should*!"

The Leopard weighed right at seventy tons but its Indowy rebuilt engines could accelerate it, if not like a sports car then like a sporty sedan. The massive engine of war had nearly a football field to speed up before it hit the ramp. At which point it went airborne.

"*Ob's stürmt oder schneit!*" Harz shouted as the tank dropped into the water obstacle on the far side in a welter of spray. "*Ob die Sonne uns lacht!* Sing, damn you!"

Frederick grinned and sang along, wondering in the feel of power driving the tank gave him.

> *Ob's stürmt oder schneit,*
> > (*Whether it storms or snows*)
> *Ob die Sonne uns lacht*
> > (*Whether the sun shines upon us*)
> *Der Tag glühend heiß*
> > (*The day burning hot*)
> *Oder eiskalt die Nacht*
> > (*Or the night freezing cold*)
> *Bestaubt sind die Gesichter*
> > (*Dusty are our faces*)
> *Doch froh ist unser Sinn*
> > (*But happy we are at heart*)
> *Ist unser Sinn*
> > (*We're at heart*)
> *Es braust unser Panzer*
> > (*Our tank roars ahead*)
> *Im Sturmwind dahin*
> > (*Along with the storm wind!*)

"Welcome to Florian Geyer," the *Oberfeldwebel* said, sourly, looking the Maccabeans up and down.

Florian Geyer had always been a bit of an odd duck among *Das Volk*. During the war the battalion had specialized at first in armored reconnaissance, then in anti-lander systems. Most of them were less effective than the Tiger IIIs but they had been critical in a few cases when Tigers were unavailable.

As the *Bruederschaft* survived the first few years and began to specialize, Florian Geyer had for some reason chosen quarrying and masonry. Where the Reich and Jugend had concentrated on farming and Michael Wittmann on industry, the Florian Geyers were out breaking rocks. Admittedly, many of the finer buildings in Freiland were the work of Florian Geyer and their headquarters proved that, being a solidly constructed building of granite block. But it still set them apart almost as much as the Maccabeans with their kosher and Shabbat rituals.

The *Oberfeldwebel* had the look of a mason in blocky arms and shoulders. He wasn't much taller than Hagai but the private was sure that the sergeant could break him in half.

"I am *Oberfeldwebel* Ginsberg. Yes, it is a Jewish name. As far as I know, I'm not Jewish. But I was chosen to introduce you to the company because it might make you more comfortable." The *Oberfeldwebel* hawked and spat. "I don't believe in making recruits comfortable. I believe in making them *un*comfortable. But the *Hauptmann* said make you comfortable. Are you comfortable, yellow-shits?"

"*Ja, Herr Oberfeldwebel,*" Hagai chorused along with the other Maccabeans.

"Liars all," Ginsberg said. "That is not a slur on your race, Jews, just the truth. This is not the Maccabaeus. This is the Florian Geyer. We do not pansy around as infantry, we are the destroyers of very big systems. We have just received our new combat systems, the *Nasshorn*, and the purpose to which we will put it. Come with me."

The *Oberfeldwebel* led them around the headquarters building to a field beyond. Vehicles were assembled in meticulous lines, most of the vehicles decidedly odd in appearance. Not to mention reflective.

"These are *Nasshorn*," Ginsberg said, gesturing to the shiny "tanks." The new camouflage system had already been explained and discussed so Hagai knew they might be shiny *now*, but... "They are designed to stop our enemy's most fearsome weapon. *Schutze* ... Goldschmidt, what would that be?"

Hagai momentarily froze, then blanched.

"The Hedren CSUs?" he asked, appalled. "The *Juggernauts*?"

"*Ja*, yellow-shit," the NCO said, grinning. "These little toys are what we are going to ride into battle. And we are going to be taking on tanks larger faster and more powerful than Tiger IIIs. Tanks as heavily armored as space cruisers and bigger than American SheVas. Now, yellow-shits, have I made you *comfortable*?"

Hagai looked distinctly uncomfortable.

"You've been thinking," *Oberfeldwebel* Ginsberg accused.

The Macabee admitted to the charge.

"That's a dangerous pastime," said the senior noncom.

"I know."

"Out with it, yellow-shit. Don't be shy; what's bothering you?"

The Jew gulped. "*Oberfeldwebel*, I can accept—at an intellectual level, anyway; it's hard to actually believe—that the main gun of a Nasshorn can take out a CSU. What I can't see is how we're—I mean any of us—expected to survive the experience. We get one, sure, but they are many more than just one. And those others? They kill us."

"Ohhh, *that*. Did someone guarantee that you would survive the experience? Give me his name, so I can denounce him properly."

Hagai looked up and saw that the sergeant was joking. This was not an everyday occurence, of course. As a matter of fact, Hagai couldn't remember it ever having happened before.

"I'm serious, *Herr Oberfeldwebel*," the Jew insisted. "And, no, I know I won't necessarily survive the war ... or even our first fight. I'm ... well, 'comfortable' isn't the word, but I understand it. But these machines are all we have to deal with the Hedren CSUs. If we exchange at one for one—if we're even that lucky—once we're gone then who or what protects the rest of the division?"

Ginsberg seemed to consider this for a minute or so. When he answered, it was to ask, "What makes you think we'll be taking them on outnumbered?"

The Jew opened his mouth to answer, but got no further than, "I ..."

"Sure, they may well have equal numbers, even superior numbers. But we've got some advantages, too. Think about those, yellow-shit."

Hagai chewed at his lower lip. "You think we'll be faster, *Herr Oberfeldwebel*?"

"Yes, that. Also, smaller has its own virtues. We can hide. We can move under cover on routes and into places a CSU would never fit. We've also got one other advantage, and it's decisive, Jew."

"What's that, *Herr Oberfeldwebel*?"

Again, Ginsberg grinned. "In all that vast swarm of Hedren slaves, there's not going to be a one named Hagai."

"Yellow-shit, do you even know *who* Florian Geyer is?"

Hagai was under the *Panzerjaeger* scraping bits of dirt out of the tracks. Tanks picked up a lot of dirt and there were about a billion places for it to stick. Fortunately, the Kobolds had recently set up a modern wash-point; basically a building filled with fire-hoses that sprayed half the Rhine under high pressure at the tanks. It tended to get most of the dirt off.

But some still remained. And a clean tank was next to Godliness according to that bastard Ginsberg.

The rest of the transfers, being past the initial training phase and with all of the Florian Geyer effectively being in "training" with the new *Panzerjaegers*, had been farmed out to Three and Four Companies to fill empty slots. Hagai, however, was still a "yellow-shit," a baby's shit, and thus stayed in Two Company. And, for his sins which must have included at some point unknowingly breaking kosher, he had Ginsberg for a track commander.

"*Nein, Herr Oberfeldwebel*," Hagai replied, spitting dirt out of his mouth. "It was not covered in my training documents."

"*Herr Florian Geyer* was a nobleman who led the Black Company and took the side of the peasants in an uprising," Ginsberg said. He was on top of the *Panzerjaeger* and as far as Hagai could tell he was sitting on his fat ass. "That was the time of the Protestant Revolution when the peasants rose up against the Catholic Church and the nobles that supported it. They lost, of course, and he was killed. But his spirit lived on. We carry that spirit of battle against tyranny into the future, the small *Panzerjaeger* against the unstoppable *Juggernaut*."

"*Jawohl, Herr Oberfeldwebel*," Hagai said, shaking his head to get mud out of his eye. Then he thought about the *Oberfeldwebel*'s words and took a chance. "So, what you're saying, *Herr Oberfeldwebel*, is that our history is to always be outnumbered, outgunned and generally getting the shitty end of the stick. And I thought this unit had no *Jewish* traditions at all."

"Very funny, *Schutze*," the *Oberfeldwebel* replied.

CHAPTER TEN

"Can you send a message on this thing?" Cutprice asked.

"When you pull up a service record there's an icon," Norris said, taking a pull off his beer. "That connects to his buckley so you can either send a text message or just call him."

"Don't use a buckley," Cutprice said, shaking his head. "Can't stand the goddamned things. What if you want a particular unit? Can you look at who commands it?"

"No," Norris said. "Because the final choices haven't been made. But you can look who's in the lead in points. What's starting to happen is clustering. Like you went to your friend the master sergeant and bid on him. Well, if you bid on a particular company, people will start clustering around you. There's a way to look up anyone and put a flag to see where they're going. People see you take a particular company and a lieutenant colonel who wants to be your commander puts in a bid on the battalion. Somebody who's looking for an S-3 slot might decide if you're going to be in the battalion it's going to make his headaches less. Points start going up across the board any time someone who's got a real rep like yours bids on a unit. Guys get together and combine points to make sure they get the grouping they want. You can even add points to a guy's bid on the battalion if you'd rather have him than someone else."

"We're electing our officers," Cutprice said.

"In a way," Norris said. "But the real problem with clustering is that you end up with some really elite units, elite companies, elite battalions, and some that are just the dregs. That's the sort of unit I'll end up in even if I get some points from you and just bid for a random platoon. The sort of unit where all the guys who have just enough points to scratch their way into a unit end up. That means guys with minimal combat experience or crappy evaluations, no medals, stuff like that. Whereas we might be right next to a battalion that's filled with nothing but medal of honor winners. If you get what I mean."

"I get it," Cutprice said as a message icon popped up. It was from Wacleva so he opened it. "Oooh, it's worse than you thought, Lieutenant. How do I pay you?"

"If you mean points, sir," the lieutenant said, wincing. "You open up my service record. Norris, Andrew."

Cutprice typed slowly and laboriously and finally got a screen.

"Third one down, sir," the LT said.

"Damn, you *don't* have many points," Cutprice said,

looking at his record. "You had a platoon. But those are a string of really sucky OERs, son." He could figure that out already.

"I managed to overcome them to an extent," the LT said. "And I'd whine about it being a crappy chain of command. Which it was. But I wasn't a great platoon leader. See the points link? Click on that and it will take you to a screen where you can transfer points."

"If I was you, I'd take all my points and try to get a good staff position rather than a crappy platoon," Cutprice said. The transfer was easy enough. "How many do you need for a platoon?"

"At least thirty, sir, if you can spare them."

"Done," Cutprice said. "I'll keep you in mind, Norris. But I'm not promising anything. When you were staff, what was your specialty?"

"Ops," Norris said. "I did some time in personnel, but I did my best work in Plans."

"Shoot for an assistant S-3 position," Cutprice said. He saw a look of pain cross the lieutenant's face. "Yeah, I know. You really want a platoon. Or think you do. Maybe to make up for what you consider to have been failure in the past. But let me give you some advice: people are good or bad at different levels. There were some kids who can handle a platoon, but are lost with a company. They tend to migrate over to Special Forces, where they can be glorified squad leaders. Some people suck moose cock as platoon leaders, but as company commanders they walk on water... Hell, they create clouds and walk on those. Some people are just best on staff. Son, last words: insanity consists of doing the same thing over and over again, the same way, and expecting a different result. Don't be a loonie. Now I've got to get down to building a unit."

"Sir," Norris said, sighing. "I can probably help out quite a bit. And if you text the most probable S-3 and ask him to bid on *me* I can escape getting in one of the rat-trap units."

CHAPTER ELEVEN

"You know, I'm gonna have to nail yo feet to de floor," Mike said as Michelle appeared in his office. "Where've you been all week? Recovering still?"

Michelle gave a rare giggle before answering. It had been a long time, but she still remembered watching *The Little Mermaid* on her daddy's lap.

"I have been attempting to convince a very hide-bound group of Indowy that if they didn't fight for their beliefs they were going to end up learning to act like the Hedren," Michelle said, rubbing her temples. "It was not easy."

"And did they eventually agree?" Mike asked.

"Some did, some didn't," Michelle admitted. "The consensus was to let those who wished to help do so. It looks as if we're getting about three hundred masters and an unknown number of students. The masters and their senior students will be arriving over the course of the next couple of weeks. The others are going to have to take ships. We're going to have to find somewhere to house them."

"AID, find a nice resort in the middle of nowhere and tell them they've been commandeered," Mike said. "Open up a budget item for Sohon master support. Masters get assimilated grade starting at O-7 and ranging up, pay to same spec. Apprentices range down. Michelle, you're going to have to set up the command structure for them and figure out their assimilated grades."

"Even with the pay, they're not going to be able to keep up their debt payments," Michelle noted. "I'm about to go into default myself."

"AID, send a message to the Tir telling him to arrange debt suspension for all the mentats that are coming in to help, and their students, even if still in transit. Michelle, we're going to need a list. And, AID, start paying them as of when you get it."

"Done," Michelle said. "Your AID already has it."

"AID, ensure that the resort maintains support. Get a unit over there to provide security and start integrating with the mentats. Try to find someone with background with mentats."

"You look like the lead singer of a Goth band."

Mosovich lifted his combat goggles up and shook his head. The goggles, which looked like a pair of welding goggles, were the best thing the new War Board had been able to produce in quantity to overcome the Hedren cloaking system. Since the forces below were all using the new cloaking uniforms, he had to wear them to see his own troops.

"With your name I'd be careful who you go around joking about," he replied, looking over at Widdlebright.

The combat exercise was over for the former members of DAG, now the core of the Strategic Reconnaissance Section, gathering up to get debriefed and tell war stories.

Greenville had been their training base before DAG went rogue, and the survivors were back again, using the demolished buildings of the city as a gigantic live-fire exercise zone. The individual team members, via the support of the Bane Sidhe and their base in the wilderness of Venezuela, had maintained most of their skills. What they were working on, now, was team integration and notional methods of fighting the Hedren. Everyone knew, though, that when they met the foe things were going to crop up that hadn't been anticipated. Every enemy was different. But they'd adjust.

"You know the good news and bad news routine?" Widdlebright asked.

"The good news is the mission is scrubbed," Mosovich replied. "There is no bad news."

"The good news is the mission is *changed*," the colonel said. "And you're going to be spending some time in a five star resort."

"The bad news must really suck, then," Mueller muttered.

"It's pretty bad," the colonel admitted. "You're going to be pulling security for some super secret group. You are also to learn to 'integrate' said group. Since I don't even know what group we're talking about, you're going to have to run this pretty much on your own."

"All of us are going?" Mosovich asked.

"Yep," Widdlebright replied. "SRS is now in the baby-sitting business."

❖   ❖   ❖

"We've been commandeered for the war effort," Rudolf Van Dorn said, looking at the e-mail.

"What? Again?"

Greenbriar Resort in White Sulphur Springs, West Virginia, had been one of the preeminent resorts for the high and mighty since the Revolutionary War days. Located conveniently close to Washington, DC, it had been a "congressional retreat" in the Cold War.

However, the resort had an even longer history with the U.S. government. During World War II it had been used as a rest and refit post for servicemen, primarily escaped POWs. It had also been used by the OSS as a training facility. During the Cold War, bunkers were installed underneath to take in members of Congress in the event of a nuclear war. During the Posleen War it had been a high-level "rest and refit" hospital for colonels and above who had just seen too much.

The resort had been refurbished after the Posleen War, raising it back to its preeminent position. It had enjoyed fifty years of plying its trade in relative peace. Now it looked as if that was going to change. Again.

"The first arrivals will be a special operations group that is going to maintain security," Rudolf continued, smoothing the lapel of his dark gray suit. The manager of Greenbriar was a rotund man with a slight, and entirely fake, German accent. He had been born with the name Rudi Cherry. He'd worked as a bellman and just about every other position possible in one hotel chain or another. Managing Greenbriar was the apex of his career. And now he was going to be hosting soldiers. It could make you cry. The only good news was that soldiers tended to be pretty.

"Get with their designated liaison to figure out how they're to be roomed. I think that the military calls it 'quartering.' The rest are supposed to turn up over the course of the next week. We'll have to send out cancellation notices to our incoming guests. Usual apologies. Due to an emergency we have to undergo renovations. Apology, apology, abject groveling, 'mea culpa'..."

"I can handle it," Rolando Prevatt said, smiling slightly. Rolando was at least fifty years Van Dorn's elder. Being in the hotel business was his third major career since getting out of the Marines although he tried to keep the fact that he was a juv quiet. He respected Van Dorn for his knowledge and experience in the inn business but always found the fussy little manager just too much of a good thing. He'd caught him once, pretty drunk, talking in a thick New Yorker accent.

"I know you can Rolando, you're such a dear," Van Dorn said, smoothing his collar again. "But... soldiers." The manager sighed.

"I'll handle that side, sir," the assistant manager said, sighing as if in agreement. "Leave it to me."

"Fuck," Mueller said. "It's got a *golf* course!"

Golf had become a game only for the very rich or the very settled. Golf courses, by their very nature, created an inviting area for Posleen to target. They were spread out and tended to have plenty of cover. Just as keeping deer off of one was nearly impossible, so was keeping ferals away.

Therefore, the only remaining golf courses were normally in areas which were so settled there were no ferals for miles and miles. That meant, of course, that land values were extraordinarily high. Greens prices were equally high.

"And one big-ass electric fence to keep the ferals out," Mosovich noted. "This was never Injun country but with all the woods around here there's got to be some."

An LZ for the DAG shuttles had been laid out actually on the golf course, a large Y sprayed into the grass. Mosovich hoped that some advance party dude hadn't made the decision. The landing jacks of the shuttles were bound to tear up the grass and he didn't want to start off the mission with a pissed off management.

As the shuttles hit, the DAG members unassed, carrying their personal gear and a broad assortment of weapons. Since they didn't know the security level of the resort, Mosovich had made the decision to go in mildly hot. He wasn't going to lose a troop to a wandering feral. He made the decision knowing that it might throw off the locals. He hated playing politics so this mission was probably going to be a major pain in the ass.

On the first tee there was a group of bellmen waiting as well as a guy in a very nice suit. Mosovich trotted over, his MP-7 slung barrel down.

"Lieutenant Colonel Mosovich," he said, walking over to the guy in the suit. "I'm the commander of the SRSDAG."

"Strategic Reconnaissance something or another Direct Action Group," the man said, holding out his hand. "Rolando Prevatt, assistant manager. Welcome to Greenbriar, Colonel."

"Thank you," Mosovich said, shaking the guy's hand. He'd spotted him as a juv immediately. "Do I have you to thank for the LZ?"

"Indeed," Prevatt replied. "I've got quarters set up for you. With the anticipated influx, we're going to be stuffing you in every corner. Sorry about that. The porters are here to lead the way."

"We'll deal," Mosovich said. "Mueller! Fall into teams and follow the porters! Officers on me!"

"So, what's your deal?" Mosovich asked as the group was led into a conference room. "You're a juv."

"Marine," Prevatt said. "First Recon Battalion. Spent some time after the war in the electronics industry. Got a divorce, got out, took a long vacation. Went back into finance. Got married. Got divorced. Took a long vacation. Now I'm working my way up in the hospitality industry and trying to avoid getting married."

"Gotcha," Mosovich said, chuckling. "Right," he said, sitting down. "We've gotten more information on this group we're going to be babysitting. It's all TS shit and that but it's not like we're going to be able to keep it secret from you guys."

"On that matter," Prevatt said, shrugging eloquently. "Greenbriar has a reputation for keeping secrets. We have all sorts visit us, at least all sorts with money. Some of them have various reasons that they don't want people prying into their personal life. CEOs with their mistresses, actresses recovering from bad plastic surgery, you get the picture. I'm not going to guarantee we're entirely secure. But I'd be very surprised if anything got out."

"Well, the group we're going to be hosting is Sohon mentats," Mosovich said. "Know what they are?"

"Sohon's what the Indowy use in manufacturing," Prevatt said, his brow furrowing. "I'm not sure what a mentat is."

"They're the top level Sohon practitioners," Major Frederick Kelly said. The XO of DAG was pale—a trait he'd gotten from his maternal grandmother—dark-haired and massive—two traits of his fraternal grandfather. "It's best to just think of them as wizards and be done with it."

"Oh," Prevatt said, nonplussed. "So we're hosting a *wizard* convention?"

"Close enough," Mosovich said. "And what they're doing here I'm actually hoping to keep really secure. But we're going to need some facilities for that. Preferably ones that are robust. Any suggestions?"

"Well," Prevatt said, standing up. "In that case, you may just be in luck. Care to take a walk?"

"What the hell *is* this place?" Mosovich asked, looking down the concrete tunnel.

The elevator to the underground bunker was concealed in a locked supply closet. And it was a big elevator, capable of holding the whole command group and staff. The concrete corridor, though, was a bit of a surprise.

"During the cold war, Greenbriar's management agreed that in the event of a nuclear war, they would house the Congress," Prevatt said, walking into the corridor. "There are quarters for the Congressmen and their families, meeting rooms, a kitchen which is, admittedly, not hooked up, and so on. It's quite an extensive facility. If you need to do anything truly secure, I'd suggest using this area. We'll quarter everyone up top, of course."

"Damn," Captain Jarrett King said, opening a door. The XO of Alpha team was medium height with dark auburn hair and a mottled face from major acne problems as a teenager. His nickname, Aquaman, had less to do with his abilities in the water than the opposite. He'd inherited a *very* heavy musculature from his fraternal grandfather if not the Redman addiction. The room beyond looked to be a guard room but it was musty with disuse and the floor was covered in grime. "This place is going to be perfect as soon as we get it cleaned up."

"We can take care of much of that," Michelle said, walking out of one of the rooms. "Hello, Colonel Mosovich."

"Hey, Michelle," Jake said, offhand. "Think this will do?" If he was surprised by the mentat showing up out of nowhere it wasn't evident.

"The quarters are acceptable," Michelle said. "The area is very soothing, which will help. These facilities are quite perfect. I had assumed we'd have to make something of the sort. As you know, the energies we are going to be generating may be severe."

"Yeah," Mosovich said. "Let's hold off discussing that until we're more secure. Rolando Prevatt, Michelle O'Neal, daughter of Michael O'Neal and one of the main wizards you're going to be hosting. Michelle, Rolando. He's the assistant manager. Former Marine. Up on who's visiting, not on what's going on."

"I am pleased to make your acquaintance," Michelle said. "When you determine quartering for the incoming Sohon practicioners, keep in mind that Indowy *prefer* crowding. We may need to rearrange your furniture, or bring in new. Indowy tend to bunk in triple level and often together even then. This includes the highest level mentats. You were informed that most of the new arrivals will be Indowy, correct?"

"Yes, ma'am," the former Marine said. "We're laying on stocks of Indowy food and we're looking for Indowy cooks."

"I can get that expedited," Mosovich said.

"Better yet," Michelle said. "We will bring in Aelool's clan. They are, of course, very closemouthed. But, better, they are used to dealing with humans and even accept the concept of violence. The actions that are going to be going on here might disturb most Indowy. I think Aelool's people will find it . . . interesting at least."

"I know how to contact them," Mosovich said, looking over at his S-1. "Handle it."

"Yes, sir," the captain said, making a note.

"I think this may work out," Michelle said, nodding. "This may work out well indeed. Complicated, but what is worth doing that is not?"

"Indowy Karthe, I see you," Michelle said as the mentat and another Indowy appeared in the underground chamber.

"Human O'Neal, I see you," Karthe replied, nodding.

"You made good time," Michelle said, leading the way out of the room.

"Time is of the essence," Karthe said. "I admit to some fatigue."

"Rooms have been prepared," Michelle replied. "You should rest before we begin exploring these new disciplines."

Exploring an undiscovered country, Karthe transmitted. *To prevent other Sohon from affecting reality will be difficult.*

It is like any game, Michelle said placidly. *One uses*

one's strengths against the enemy's weakness. We must discover both within ourselves.

This is all new.

Michelle and Karthe sat opposite each other, a small electric motor spinning away between them. Arrayed around the periphery of the room were fifth and sixth level Sohons, human and Indowy, who were there to prevent any of the energies escaping from the chamber. In an adjacent room, Thomas Coates, Kang Chang and a few of the newly arrived Indowy volunteers observed the training exercise.

I have never attempted to stop another Sohon from performing a function, Karthe continued.

I will show you what I intend to do, Michelle thought, and the motor suddenly ground to a halt. *I simply prevented the flow of electrons. Through this section of wiring, the reality is that metal is a resistor rather than a conductor.*

I reset reality, Karthe thought, opening up the flow of electrons.

Could you sense my actions? Michell asked.

I could see the reality changing, Karthe replied.

This time, stop me as I attempt to change the reality, Michelle thought. *We begin.*

The machine stuttered for a moment, winding down, then spinning back up.

It is easier to maintain reality than to change it, Karthe thought.

The polyverse resists, as always, Michelle replied. *This is to the benefit of the defender. The benefit to the attacker is that they choose the point of attack.*

The machine stopped.

That was a different attack, Karthe thought with a touch of annoyance as the machine started back up.

As is this, Michelle replied when the machine stopped again. *Now we battle*.

"Wow," Prevatt said. "All powerful wizards. They're making an electric motor start and stop. I can do the same thing with a remote."

"They're starting on easy stuff," Mosovich said, keeping an eye on the video from the training room. He had to admit it was about as interesting as watching paint dry. But. "I once saw Michelle rip apart a concrete loading dock like it was cardboard. You don't want these guys to get angry at each other."

As he said that, the electric motor exploded.

I fear we placed too much pressure on the structures of reality, Karthe thought.

And I win, Michelle thought smugly. *A destroyed motor is a non-functioning motor. The requirements on your part were to keep it functioning.*

Only for a moment, Karthe thought as the scattered parts, down to the molecules of gaseous copper, sprang back together.

"O-*kay*," Prevatt said, his eyes wide. "*That* was impressive."

"Told ya."

I am blocked, Michelle thought.

Karthe had shifted tactics. He had been responding to Michelle's individual attacks. Finally, he determined that all he had to do was maintain a shell of utter reality around the motor. The polyverse actually fed him, wanting to maintain normal reality, causing him to have to expend far less energy than Michelle in holding the zone.

I win, Karthe thought, trying not to feel smug. The Indowy did not participate in competitive games. All of their games, to the extent they played them, emphasized cooperation. This was a new world to him, but he found it unusually intoxicating.

But can you maintain such a shell over an entire ship? Michelle asked. *A fleet?*

I could over a ship, Karthe said. *Even a super-dreadnought. But that is not the interesting question. Maugo?*

Yes, Mentat? The fifth level Sohon was a recent arrival by ship, a student of a master who had chosen to reject defense as an option. The fifth level had chosen otherwise and was still unassigned to a new master. Since all the students who had accompanied the arriving masters were sixth level or above, he was the weakest adept in the room.

You have seen what I have done?

Yes, Master.

Maintain it, Karthe said. *Against the Michon.*

This was not war, it was training. Michelle knew the adage of her human father, that you fight as you train, but this was very easy training. Learning on all sides. It was not time to fight as you train. She, therefore, let the lower level mentat gather his thoughts and create the same zone as the master. She gave him time to adjust. And to start to worry.

Then she attacked.

❖   ❖   ❖

"I got about a billion things I should be doing," Prevatt said, still not leaving the monitor. "Is it just me, or is Karthe sort of not looking like he's doing anything?"

"He's not," Mosovich said. "But check out the third Indowy from the left against the wall."

"Whoa," Prevatt said. "What the hell is causing that?"

Indowy do not sweat. Instead, to radiate excess heat the photosynthetic cilia that coat their body—the thin, hairlike green "fur" that make them look like teddy bears—begins to move. It vibrates in waves, cascading up and down their body, blowing away the heat in much the same way that leaves rustle in a gentle wind.

Maugo looked like he'd been caught in a hurricane.

I think that is enough, Michelle said, terminating her attack. *I'm not sure that Maugo could have held out indefinitely against my attack, but there are many fifth levels. In a similar situation, they could rotate to maintain the field. However, I have another attack I would try. One . . . less pleasant. Would you have your student defend or do so yourself?*

He is not accepted as my student, Karthe pointed out.

Michelle glanced at the younger Indowy, who looked as if he'd just run a marathon.

Oh, I think you've accepted him, she thought.

Karthe flicked his ears, an Indowy indicator of mild humor.

Agreed, the mentat replied. *But I think I would have you try the attack on me. Begin.*

Michelle began probing at the engine, trying to find a hole through the protection field, then shifted her attack. The generator stopped.

You affected my MIND!

The Sohon telepathy bellow was slightly painful in and of itself. Michelle filed that as useful information.

Do you think the Hedren will hesitate to do so? she asked.

She had never seen an Indowy angry. She'd seen annoyance from time to time and often frustration. But never real anger.

She was seeing it now. Karthe was full wrath-of-God angry. Facing it, even if not for the first time, in a Sohon adept of *at least* her own level was not happy-making.

Distantly she could sense the watching mentats bringing up their powers. It was the sort of rolling up of sleeves you'd see in a bar when two groups are preparing to separate a couple of individuals that are right on the edge of a brawl.

We do not *attack individuals!* Karthe replied hotly.

I apologize, Michelle thought. *But I do not agree. I apologize because I should have obtained your permission before using that attack. I disagree because we must learn to defend against just such attacks. The Hedren and their Sohon-using slaves can and* will *use them.*

If I might interrupt, Mentat Gonau thought from the adjoining room. *Where did you learn that? It was not manipulation of brain chemistry.*

From the device Erick Winchon had been studying, Michelle said. *The device's method of attack is really quite elegant.*

You told your sister you were not going to study the device's techniques, Karthe thought, *just how they were generated.*

I lied. Shall we continue training?

CHAPTER TWELVE

Cutprice quickly found out that the Officer Placement Board was even *more* complicated than buying stocks. Sending text messages back and forth, he and Wacleva started building the NCO cadre for the company. The absolute most points was not always a perfect guide. Scrolling down the list, typing in an occasional name, he and Wacleva found that many of the NCOs they wanted were in the upper quadrant but not near the top. They all had bids against them already, but between them, and sending some messages to get the NCOs to buy in, they managed to fill the TOE pretty steadily. Some guys were off-line but it seemed like most everybody was playing "match my unit."

The problem was, he hadn't even bid on a unit, yet. He'd put in a bid for a random company, but as Norris had pointed out, that could be in a rag-bag unit. He looked at the officers who had bid on him and the two with the most points were both the ones he didn't want and...what was the word? clustered around units he didn't want to be a part of. He'd be a very big fish in a very small pond. But since a company really depended on the companies around it, on the battalions around theirs, being in a sucky brigade was a good way to earn a medal: Posthumously.

He was going to have to cluster. And anyone who had been in the military for any time at all, knew what that meant.

If it was tough for Cutprice it was worse for the officers managing the boards.

The first problem was, they had no real idea how many officers and NCOs were going to be available for cadre on any particular day. A cut-off point for the first recalls had at least been determined, so when the last recall of that day was recorded, they'd know their total cadre.

But they'd started with an estimate of sufficient cadre for a division. An officer had been hand-picked to command the division—three infantry regiments, one tank regiment one field artillery, one armor and one support and supply—given a staff to begin standing up the division and then sat back to watch the boards. If he, in his opinion, did not like the choices of regimental and battalion commanders he had the option to override them. But, in general, the recalled officers with high points *all* were worthy of commanding their respective units. Generals with years in combat commands were going to be able to commmand a battalion in their sleep. Guys who had commanded armies were going to be able to run a brigade. They'd not only done it, they'd trained subordinates to do it.

But between conscription numbers going up and the recall gaining steam, the estimate went up to a division reinforced by a regiment. Then two regiments. Then two divisions. A second officer was picked for the new division.

At this point, cadre numbers were going over into a tenth regiment. Conscription and volunteer numbers, the troops and junior NCOs in other words, were still down. But they'd fluctuated ahead and behind cadre numbers the whole time.

Each time that cadre numbers got high enough, a new regiment had to be added to the board. When that happened, all the bids suddenly shifted. Then there was finding cadre for the training commands. Very few high-point cadre wanted a training unit so some of them were just going to have to suck it up.

It was a nightmare.

"Board says that there's enough numbers for another regiment," the major said, sighing. "Who's up next?"

"Fourteenth," his assistant said. "Golden Dragons."

"Post it."

"You think everybody's having as much of a jug-fuck as we are?"

Screened by a line of advancing artillery, the tanks and AFVs of *Schwere Panzer* Battalion Michael Wittman rolled across the small valley in assault formation, heading for a stand of trees on the far ridge.

Simulated bursts of plasma artillery exploded around them. Mines popped up. Some of the tanks and Marders slowed to a stop as red lights on their exterior turned on. Simulated antitank missiles lifted off from the woodline as lines of blue fire searched out. More of the tracks slowed as defenses crumbled. But missiles were blotted from the sky by railgun fire. The plasma blasts were diverted by shields. Smoke rounds fell. Unfortunately, most of them fell behind the line of advancing armor failing to shield it from view.

Despite that, the majority of the unit crashed into the distant woods. Troop doors opened and infantry jumped to the ground, taking firing positions and moving forward as the slowed tanks and AFVs used direct fire to dig the enemy from their positions.

"Exercise terminated," Mühlenkampf said. "Head us over to the objective."

His driver kicked the SUV into gear and maneuvered through the heavy undergrowth towards the ridgeline. It took about fifteen minutes for the *Generalmajor* to join the unit and find its commander.

Oberstleutnant Dieter Schultz was in the center of the armored lager having a terse hot-wash of the exercise. But when the *Generalmajor*'s vehicle entered the clearing made by the big armored vehicles he waved his junior commanders away, picked up the steel pot filled with flowers at his feet and walked over.

"*Generalmajor*," Dieter said, saluting.

"Oberstleutnant Schultz," Mühlenkampf said, returning the salute. "Comments?"

"Various problems," Schultz replied tightly. "We took too many casualties. We will have to work much harder on our artillery direction. Also I failed to anticipate the minefield."

"Because there was no intelligence indicating that the Hedren use them," Mühlenkampf said. "I ordered it added to the exercise because if they do not, I'm sure they will quickly. I consider it, for your level of training, fair."

"And we ship in three days," Dieter said, shaking his head. "We are not ready, *Generalmajor*."

"War rarely gives us the luxury of being as ready as we would wish," Mühlenkampf replied. "And even when we are, it rarely goes as we expect. I'm sure we will prove the same truths to the Hedren. Take your unit back to the *Kasserne* and begin preparations for movement. Time is not our friend."

"See, Norris really understands this system," Cutprice said. "It's like a computer game or a game of chess. You got to figure out what your opponents are going to do and all the variables around you. But it's different than chess because you can get allies."

Cutprice had contacted several of the NCOs and officers he'd handpicked and called a meeting at the Rod and Gun Club. The purpose of the meeting was to reduce the cluster fuck that clustering caused.

"I told you, sir," Wacleva said, sipping his beer. "The old 505 hands want to go for Fifth Infantry Regiment. Close as we can get to the 505."

"The average numbers are higher on the Fifth," Lieutenant Norris said. "The average company command at the Fifth is running better than five hundred points."

"Nobody cares about the Dragons," Cutprice said. "But the point is not what a unit's history might say about it, it's what kind of a command group it has. And I'm planning on stacking the deck."

"You're going to be a company commander, sir," Wacleva said. "With all due respect."

"Sure, but I'm also planning on picking and choosing my battalion commander," Cutprice said, grinning. "And regimental. By getting them to agree to put their points on the Dragons. I've taken a look. I've got more points than most of the *colonels* on the Board. I'm going to build a regiment that we can survive in. But everybody has to be onboard."

"That's what a team is all about, sir," Wacleva said. "But how you gonna wag the dog?"

"By bringing in some dark horses."

Arkady Simosin regarded the Board grumpily. To get a battalion, he had realized, he was going to have to cluster. And nobody wanted to cluster around *him*.

Arkady Simosin had been a major general when the President announced that not only had the world been contacted by friendly aliens, but that they'd brought a warning that less friendly aliens were on the way. Shortly thereafter, as the Army began to bulge at the seams, he had been slotted as a corps commander.

It was a corps that hadn't existed six months before and getting it up and running had been a real challenge. Especially since the personnel system had gotten so wacked that most of the new soldiers were, at best, half trained and regularly mutinous. The U.S. Army hadn't dealt with a worse group of soldiers since the Civil War.

But he had been getting them whipped into shape when, well before they were supposed to arrive, a battlegroup of Posleen had dropped into northern Virginia.

Even then... Well, things could have gone against him in battle, the Posleen were no enemy to fight in the open. But what had really bitten him in the ass was when a smart Posleen, or some said the Darhel, others the Cyber Corps, had hacked the corps command net and sent multiple conflicting orders out to units. Artillery had fallen on engaged units, units had been ordered to retreat, or—in many ways worse—assault forward, none of those orders actually originating from *him*.

That had hardly mattered at the board of inquiry. It had kept him from being shot, he supposed, but he had been reduced in rank and spent most of the rest of the war shuffling paper for other more "stellar" generals.

He had been given one chance to redeem his name when the Posleen seemed about to decisively break the back of the Appalachian Defense line. He'd been given command of a division, one of the reserve divisions around Asheville, and sent in to assault the Posleen in some of the worst terrain available in the Eastern U.S., the Smoky Mountains.

The division had been trained for positional defense, not assault. He'd had to shoot a few people and fire many many more, to get it moving. But he'd done it and pushed and harried them through those mountains until they shone.

Alas, the war had ended shortly afterwards. As a general with a still somewhat stained reputation he'd been politely shown the door as fast as the division could be stood-down.

Now they wanted him again. But all that time in staff meant that, compared to many of his fellow lieutenant colonels, he had a relatively low point score. Heck, the only reason that he was a lieutenant colonel was that he'd been retired as his original rank. What that meant was getting a staff slot, *maybe* XO of a regiment. But command was unlikely. He might work his way back into it and, given the way that they were going to have to ramp up the Army again, he might even get back to being a general. But he suspected there were captains with more of a chance.

He wanted a battalion, he craved a battalion. Battalion command was one of the best slots in the Army. A battalion was just independent enough to be a functional unit on its own. In combat, a battalion commander made real decisions about operational methods. But it was still close enough to the fighting that you could know your troops, their strengths and weaknesses. You could *command* in a way that you never could as a general or even a brigade commander.

He'd be lucky to get a slot as assistant S-4 (Logistics) in one of the divisions.

"Incoming message from Captain Thomas Cutprice," his buckley said.

"Buckley, check the Board. Is that former Colonel Cutprice of the Ten Thousand?" If it was, somebody had seriously fucked up. Cutprice. A captain. Words failed.

"Yes, it is," the buckley said, gloomily. "You don't want to answer. It's Cutprice. We're both gonna die if you answer. I can list the ways if you'd like."

"Just put me through, buckley," Simosin said.

"It's text," the buckley intoned. "He's using a Dell LinSoft Forty-Four which is, in simple terms you might understand, the equivalent of a Model T Ford. You don't want to get involved with anyone who uses one of those, right? You're not that stupid, right?"

"Buckley, just show me the message and shut up."

Cutprice: General Simosin?

Simosin: Colonel, Captain. What can I do for you?

Cutprice: Got a proposition. You got wheels?

Simosin: Yes.

Cutprice: Rod and Gun Club if you're interested. We'll be here most of the rest of the night.

Simosin: What's this about?

Cutprice: What's every conversation these days about? The Board.

Simosin: I'll be there.

"Bad, bad, bad idea!"

"Shut up, buckley."

"Thank you for coming, sir," Cutprice said as Simosin slid into the booth.

Arkady Simosin could not have looked less like the captain. Where Cutprice was tall and light haired, Simosin was short and barrel-built, looking something like a dyspeptic bear.

"Despite the moanings from my buckley, I'm hoping for good news," Simosin said.

"Well, we'll see, won't we?" Cutprice replied. "Here's the deal, sir. You saw the new regiment go up on the Board?"

"Fourteenth," Simosin replied, nodding. "But all three of the battalion slots have already got bids against them. Bids that, quite frankly, I cannot top."

"Yes, sir, I saw that," Cutprice said. "But I think I've got enough points to push you into the running, sir."

"Go on," Simosin said, accepting a mug of beer from the silent master sergeant next to the captain.

"Without expending too many of my points, I've gotten a tiddly little company built," Cutprice said. "But a good company doesn't mean squat if the battalion is fucked up, sir. I've looked at the guys bidding on the battalions in the Fourteenth and I'm not impressed. But if we get the right mix in our battalion, others are going to cluster. People will start looking at the Fourteenth who are ignoring it, now."

"Which will drive up the points for battalion commander," Simosin pointed out.

"Yes, sir," Lieutenant Norris interjected. "But if we get the other company commanders on board, and a staff, we can probably shave points from all of us."

"Okay, given," Simosin said. "But why me? I'm not going to be wagged, Captain. I know your reputation as a combat commander. I also know your reputation in general. You're not going to get a battalion commander that's going to accede to your every whim. I may be a bit battered, but I'm not going to be bought."

"You got screwed in Dalesville, sir, and we all know it," Cutprice replied. "And, just to check, I looked at your battalion command records and you were a damned good battalion commander. Like I said, I've looked at the guys bidding on the Fourteenth and I don't like them. The thing is, sir, we need to stack the deck. We need a really good regimental commander. Preferably one with some points. I can't carry this all on my shoulders. And we need to get some better people bidding on the other battalion slots. I didn't pay much attention to *good* generals during the war. I saw way too many bad ones, though. I figure you probably have a better read on who the good ones are. If we do this right, we can build the whole unit from the ground up."

"And you playing spider in the web?" Simosin said, finally smiling.

"Just trying to get good people around me, sir," Cutprice replied. "Wouldn't you prefer a good unit to a bad one?"

"Frankly, Captain, it would be a novel experience."

"Anything else?" Mike asked, sighing. It had been another long day of making bricks without straw and after the meeting with Tam he'd be working on paperwork well into the night.

But things were finally starting to come together. In a week, the SS would be shipping. The Legion was on the way, along with the Second Division. With those three forces in place, and a bit of luck, they could bottle up the ground attack.

He'd had long conversations with Takao before the latter left for the Gratoola system. Most of the shipwrights had been evacuated but enough were left to do the minimal necessary upgrade to the current fleet ships gathering in the system. With those minimal upgrades, Takao thought they might be able to manage the mission.

The additional forming units were beginning to take shape. Training camps were being stood up; the cadre for units was ready to be set. Even if they lost Gratoola, there would be another wave of human infantry and armor to face the Hedren. Better armed, hopefully, as well as better trained. More ships, more troops. It was going to be a war of attrition if he didn't watch it.

"The recall program," Tam said. "Not the whole thing, just an interesting idea."

"Go for it," Mike said, leaning back. He felt the need to pump some iron. He spat out his dip and started to pack down another instead.

"We only recalled the highest E and O grades," Tam said. "And then we bumped them down, more or less, three ranks across the board."

"Oh, that must have been interesting to explain," Mike said.

"Because the personnel system knew it was going to be... interesting to explain, they tossed a cookie to the ones that seemed really good," General Wesley added.

"I saw the thing about the point system in the *Fleet Strike Times*," Mike said. "Now it makes more sense."

"The thing is, when I signed off on it, and I take full responsibility, I didn't realize the monster I'd created," Wesley said, shrugging. "The bidding and bid rigging has gotten fierce, and due to what one of my boffins called 'games theory,' there's going to be some really good units and some that really suck. Basically, the good guys are gathering around each other and pushing the marginal ones out."

"If units end up marginal enough, we just won't stand them up," Mike said, frowning more than habitually. "Good regiments are made by good officers."

"I have a group working on a matrix for that," Wesley admitted. "If a unit's total points fall below a certain minimum, they'll be held for stand-up until the next pass. But."

"But?"

"We only recalled the highest grades," Tam said. "We figured, why call in guys who are going to be privates? We can use them later for positions they're more prepared for. But we've had a lot of volunteers in those grades. To the point where personnel set up a website explaining that anyone coming back would be subject to a severe drop in rank. And we've still got volunteers. By a rough analysis, enough to fill at least one regiment."

"Or you could spread them around," Mike pointed out.

"We're going to have more as the word gets out," Wesley said. "And we've got a certain momentum towards stand-up. We know, more or less, who is going to what unit in the ranks of E-1 through E-5. Some of those E-5 slots could be filled with returnees, for certain. But we've still got—"

"All those volunteers," Mike said, frowning. "I don't think it would be wise to have one regiment which is heavy on rejuvs in a division. The term 'elite' comes to mind."

"Which is why the idea is to stand up a regiment with them," Tam admitted. "Probably a separate one initially."

"I'll sign off," Mike said. "But make it an RCT. I'm sure all the volunteers aren't infantry."

"No," Tam said, furrowing his brow. "But we don't have a TOE for a Regimental Combat Team."

"Find a smart major and tell him what you need," Mike said, looking thoughtful. "A regiment which is crewed by juvs is going to need good officers. Any idea what the cadre is going to look like?"

"I haven't looked at the Board lately," Tam said. "But if we have to, we can always override and direct appoint. Or we can pick the regiment that has the strongest cadre. There's already one regiment that, for the time being, is notionally separate. If that one has the dregs, we can always shift it to one of the divisions and pull out a better one to fill."

"What's the regiment?" Mike asked.

"The Fourteenth," Tam said. "It's called the Golden Dragons."

"Not familiar with it," Mike said, frowning.

"Let's put it this way, it got that moniker in the Peking assault. It's motto, 'Right of the Line' comes from the Grand Review of the Army of the Potomac."

"Ooookay," Mike said. "One of *those*. Well, history and tradition are like your family tree. It doesn't matter worth a flip what your umpteenth granddad did. It only matters what you're doing today. Hopefully, the officers in the unit understand that."

"It reminds me of the NFL draft," Colonel Tobias Pennington said, looking around the echoing room.

As the REMFs in personnel began to recognize the beast that had been created with the points system, they'd also realized that the last few minutes were going to get murderous. Perhaps to confine the murder to one area, they'd had a large and previously empty warehouse refitted to marginal levels of comfort. The most important thing was that there were tables, chairs and a lot of electronics. The room had about the same internet pipe as an AT&T main node and the walls were lined with floor-to-ceiling screens showing the updated bidding totals on all units and personnel.

There was also an ample supply of coffee. For when it was done renting, there were portapotties installed at one end. Minimal comfort.

"It *is* the Draft, sir," Cutprice said, grinning. "Just bigger."

Pennington was an unknown quantity to the captain. But he'd checked him out, both on the Board and

through contacts. The former 14th Army commander
had led the latter part of the defense of the Monterey
Campaign. The Posleen had done well by themselves
in the Valley and seriously wanted to complete their
conquest by leveling San Francisco. Pennington had
been sent in to relieve the commander that lost most
of the Peninsula, a battle that should have been a
no-brainer given the defensive conditions. The First
Corps commander and later Army commander had
not only held the final defense line, he had, over
time, pushed back as far as the terrain would allow.

Personally, the colonel was just about the most laid-
back individual Cutprice had ever met. Nothing seemed
to faze him. Since Cutprice tended to be on the aggressive side in everything, he wasn't sure they were going
to get along. But one of the things that didn't faze the
possible Fourteenth Regiment commander was Cutprice.

"I'm thinking about scamming Norris out from under
Arkady," Pennington said, looking over at the lieutenant. The LT had three laptops open and two buckleys
going simultaneously. Former sergeants major as well
as former generals and colonels were running messages
to the group gathered in one corner of the building.

None of the officers and NCOs who had been
recruited for the 14th had posted their bids, yet. Not
their final bids. All were on the board as looking for
open positions. It was not going to be until the last
moment that they all jumped on the 14th. Security
on that had held, Cutprice was pretty sure. And it
had been Norris's idea.

The lieutenant, it turned out, had spent most of his
post-service career as an IT guru on various boards of
trade. He knew how to game a system like the Board

from decades of experience. He'd written code to automatically update bids as the final hour approached. Essentially, all of the recruited cadre for the 14th had put their points up for the team. It was Norris's job, right up to the last moment, to make sure that they all got into the slots they preferred.

There'd been a personal side to that as well. Cutprice had visited the various officers bidding on him and explained what a miserable pain in the ass he would be as a junior officer. *"I mean, it'll be horrible, sir. I never listen unless I want to. I do what I want to do and everyone else can go to hell. And I'm clever, so half the time you wouldn't even suspect what I was up to until you were well and truly screwed by it. Sir, the word 'insubordination' in the dictionary? It has a two by three color glossy of me next to it. Sir, you have no idea just how difficult . . ."*

All but one had dropped their bids. That, as Norris pointed out, had dropped his effective "price" on the boards. Now nobody wanted to touch him. Others had done the same thing, although in a few cases it had meant losing people when an old commander sweet-talked them into jumping ship. Nobody serious, but a damned fine company commander in the notional Second Batt had jumped over to the 8th Regiment. Cutprice wished him well and they'd found someone just as good to replace him.

Norris tapped his main laptop one more time then leaned back, letting out a sigh.

"Looks as if he's done," Pennington said. "Let's go see *what* he's done."

"There's fifteen minutes left, Andrew," Cutprice said, walking over to the table. "What's up?"

"Oh, things haven't really started, yet," the lieutenant said, still leaning back. "But my job is done. I got all the personal information entered. At the stroke of five till, all the bids will submit. Then the program will start running interference. I think there are two other units using bots, but not at the regimental level. Fifth is pretty tight, but they don't have anyone doing bots. We should be good to go. We may lose a few minor slots, but no company commanders or above and their respective NCOs. Frankly, I think we'll be good down to platoon sergeants and operations NCOs. Probably platoon leaders."

"I just love your priorities, Norris," the possible regimental commander said.

"Do you disagree, sir?" Norris asked. "Because it's a bit late to do so."

"No, actually I agree," the CO said. "But don't tell anyone."

"Uh, oh," Norris said, grinning. "Second Batt, Fourth Infantry just jumped the gun. They're going to get hammered."

"I don't get that," Cutprice said. "Where?"

"Bunch of specific unit requests," Norris said, gesturing with his chin at the screens. "Looks like they're trying to game the system but without a bot. Watch the slot values for the Fourth fall like a rock."

"That's good, though," Cutprice said. "If value goes down, your points go further."

"Nope," Norris said. "No clustering and aggregation. What that means is that the group has just created conditions where the lousiest are going to cluster around them. The bot kicks off in three minutes. Probably every other bot in the place will start at more or less the same time. Watch the Board go nuts, then. Whoever set this up has never worked a market board before. I hope their servers are up to it or they're going to crash in an instant."

Cutprice waited somewhat impatiently for the real bidding to begin and he didn't have to ask Norris if the three minutes were up. The boards, which had been showing occasional changes, suddenly went into overdrive.

The west wall had units with all their TOE slots, the east wall held a list of names of all the personnel up for assignment in alphabetical order. But both were starting to flicker so fast, Cutprice couldn't follow them. So he concentrated on watching his own name.

"Why'd I just put in a bid for a position in Seventh Regiment?" Cutprice said, unhappily. "That is me bidding, right?"

"Pump fake," Norris said. "I dumped bids from notable members to other units, trying to get them to cluster."

"I thought you said clustering was good," Pennington said. "And Simosin is up on the Fourteenth. Lots of points, too."

"There's good clustering and bad clustering," Norris replied. "Since we're all working for the same goal, we're already clustered. If you want to draw people to you, you want to cluster. But a bad cluster is when you have a group that is drawn to a particular unit by a particular leader who then deserts the unit. Or where a group self-clusters then draws in a bunch of marginals around them. If they're not clustering by bot, which most of the people here aren't, they're not going to have time to switch away. That keeps them from driving up the point price in the good cluster you've created."

"Oh," the colonel said. "I don't like the word deserted."

"Sorry, sir," Norris replied. "They're using an AID."

"Excuse me?" Cutprice said.

"The system team doing this is not using a human server, they're using an AID. I've seen them work before. There's a subtle . . . nuance to the way that they refresh data."

"I hope like hell they're only refreshing," Cutprice replied sourly.

"If they're not, I'll be able to tell later," Norris said. "I've been up against them before. But . . ." He opened up a screen and nodded. "Based on this, I'd say that they're playing straight. The model's working the way I expected. And . . . Five, four, three, two . . ."

Both of the boards went blank for a moment, showing blue screens, then they went back up with broad banners flashing "Preliminary Results."

Everyone had had that explained to them. Just because the Board said you were in a particular unit didn't mean that the U.S. Army, in its infinite wisdom, would agree. But they'd also been assured that unless things were really screwy, the plan was to stick with the Board.

"Ninety-eight percent," Norris said, holding up his hands in triumph. "Yes! Who rules?"

"Worked out fairly well," the major said, looking at his screen. "Some units that I wouldn't want to be in but most of them are pretty balanced— Holy Crap!"

"Sir?" the lieutenant said, looking over his shoulder.

"Look at the point total for the Fourteenth Regiment!"

"That's . . . Damn, sir. Can *I* join that unit?"

"Not sure they'd take you. *Or* me. AID, what's the deal with the Fourteenth?"

"The Fourteenth was structured based on a sophisticated gaming program run from the computer of First Lieutenant Andrew Norris," the AID replied. "Expansion. Lieutenant Norris was recalled to service from the position of CIO of VenturGrant, a member of the Chicago Stock Exchange. The program was a modification of a standard stock-trading bot. Analysis indicates that approximately ninety-eight percent of the current officers and NCOs of the Fourteenth collaborated to ensure placement in the Fourteenth."

"Sir, I don't think that's—"

"Even if it's theoretically legal, it shouldn't be," the major said, frowning. "I'll have to query higher about letting it stand. But I know one change we're going to make right now . . ."

"Congratulations, Lieutenant," Wacleva said, clapping the lieutenant on the shoulder.

Norris's shoulder was, in fact, starting to get sore. Virtually everyone in the new cadre had come over to thank him for his work.

"You're welcome, Sergeant Major," Norris said, nodding. "But these are preliminary results. They can change it around if they want to and—" He paused as a pop-up jumped out on his computer. "Oh, those rotten motherFUCKERS!"

"What?" Cutprice said, turning away from his first command meeting. Until he was fairly sure he was getting the junior officers he desired, he wasn't going to talk shop.

"They fucking scragged me!" Norris said, nearly screaming. "Oh those rotten motherfuckers!"

Cutprice looked up to the position for Assistant S-3 1/14INF and noted that Norris's name no longer filled the slot. In fact, it was unfilled. Looking over at the personnel board he hunted until he found Norris's name.

"What in the hell is BUPERSECINDEP?"

"It's the office that runs the fucking BOARD," Norris screamed. "Those dirty rotten—"

"And, unfortunately, I guess that's the answer to your question, Lieutenant," Cutprice said, looking at him sadly. "The *REMFs* rule."

"So we're not sure what to do with this, ma'am," the major said, hoping against hope for a reasonable and prompt answer. "I figured I had to kick it up to you. And it's sort of time critical. We have to have final orders cut in twenty-four hours."

Sinda Makepeace was not happy. She had been comfortable in the Luna office of Personnel, Officers' Pay and Adjustments. Then had come the Mutiny, which she had tried her hardest to sit out. Then the shift to a new personnel office. Then that whole Augmented Medicine and that horrible Cally O'Neal person. Then she got shuttled down to Earth as an expert in *recalled personnel* of all things!

She had looked at the Board and points system, determined immediately that she had *no* clue how it worked, and left it up to the major and his team. Now he was asking *her* for a decision and she wasn't even sure what the *question* was!

"So this separate regiment..."

"It's a nonassigned regimental cadre, ma'am," the major said gently.

"They all got together and decided they wanted to be on one team," Sinda said slowly.

"Yes, ma'am," the major replied. "But they did it, basically, by cheating. And there are other units that could use some of that expertise."

"But it's a separate regiment, right?" Sinda said, shuffling through the papers on her desk.

"It's a nonassigned regiment, ma'am," the major repeated. "It hasn't been assigned to a division, yet. There's not enough cadre to make up another division."

The colonel picked up a memorandum and read it slowly. Then she looked up.

"And that is the Fourteenth, right?" she asked.

"Yes, ma'am," the major said, his brow furrowing. He wished she'd just hand him the damned memo and let him read it.

"And does it have... 'an average point score in each grade in excess of the seventieth percentile'?"

"I think so..." the major said, looking at his data. He sorted quickly and then nodded, frowning. "Try in excess of the *eightieth* percentile, ma'am. Most of the positions are in the upper eighties and into the high nineties..." He looked up and tried not to sigh; she was getting that *glazed* look again. "The answer is yes, ma'am."

"Thank you," she said, brightly. "It's all fine, Major. Feel free to leave it as is. I need to do some work, though, and I'm sure you need to get ready for the next round of placements. Was there anything else?"

"No, ma'am," the major said, nonplussed. "You want to leave it as it is?"

"I think that's what I said," Sinda said, a bit more sharply. "If that's all?"

"Yes, ma'am," the major replied, getting up. He'd expected an answer next week if then. "Good day, ma'am."

From: Colonel Sinda Makepeace, OIC, BUPER-SECINDEP

To: Major General Fortun, BUPERS

"Dear General Fortun,

"I'm pleased to inform you that pursuant to your query, the 14th Infantry Regiment meets the parameters of your outlined needs..."

"AID, send a memo to Recall that we're going to need those volunteers. Send a memo to General Wesley's office that we believe there are sufficient recalled personnel to fill out one regiment. Amend the memo to recall to accept volunteers of any rank, including officers, but they all come in as junior enlisted. Usual graft and disclaimers."

Keren scratched his head as he looked at the email from Department of the Army.

"Dear Captain Keren:

*"At this time, due to a lack of junior enlisted personnel, the Department has on hold recall of personnel below the grade of O-4. However, there is a critical need for trained soldiers in the grades of **E-1** through **E-5**. In consideration of your prior service and the current crisis, you are asked to volunteer for voluntary reduction to the grade of **E-5** with purpose of immediate recall as **11C5P**. Also in consideration of your prior service,*

it is anticipated that as forces expand your prior rank will be reactivated at a future date. If you are willing to be recalled at the rank of **Sergeant***, please visit the attached website and use the attached log-in to register your interest.*

"*Thank you for your service and your desire to serve again.*

"*James Rolson, CPT, BUPERS*

"*For the BUPERS*"

Herschel Keren had bought the farm. Looking at the way that the military was going after the war, the mortar and artillery liaison for the Ten Thousand had seen less and less of a need for former specialists with a few college credits as officers and gotten out.

The U.S. after the war was a very odd place. Central cities like Chicago and Detroit had hardly been touched. There had been occasional scatter landings that had killed a few people and raised tensions, but in many ways it was business as usual.

On the other hand, in the areas the Posleen had fully occupied, mostly the coastal plains, southern Great Plains and the south, things were back to Injun Wars days. Although every major settlement of Posleen had been reduced by orbital fire, Posleen survived, living a hand-to-mouth existence, rarely armed with much more than spears, but dangerous nonetheless.

Keren had taken a veteran's preference and been granted a one hundred hectare plot in Northern Virginia, not all that far from where he'd first won his spurs. He'd considered the spot carefully. It was on the remnants of a main road and was flanked by a river which still had a standing bridge.

The first few years had been tough. There were

few natural defenses except the river, and the Posleen reproduced fast in the rapidly regrowing Virginia countryside. He'd put in a fortified house to start, hunted out the surrounding Posleen, gotten some crops started, hunted out some more Posleen.

Slowly the area around him filled up as other veterans fled the life in the Sub-Urbs or found they couldn't adjust to civvie street. Families moved in. The well-prepared survived if not prospered. The unprepared ended up in scorched homes that were graves for their bones.

Keren Town, Herschel Keren, Mayor, was not by any stretch of the imagination pre-war Paris. But it had a population of fifty-three and supported another two hundred or so combination farmers and Posleen bounty hunters. The Six Hundred Inn did pretty good commerce with traders moving through the wilderness and better as the best source of homebrew in five counties. Keren's Feed, Seed and Sundries turned a small but noticeable profit each year. The exception was managing bounties which Keren did at cost. He took in heads on credit, shipped them to the main bounty processing stations and only took enough off the top to pay for the handling. There weren't no such thing as a good, live, Posleen in his opinion.

He hit print and walked into the family room. Pamela was spooning stirred peas into the gaping maw of Annie, who had an amazing fondness for the stuff.

Pamela was his third wife. As a juv you expected you were going to outlive the short-timers. But Pam was his third wife because Kathy had decided the life of a hardy pioneer wasn't for her and gone back to the Elizabethtown Sub-Urb where he'd met her.

Janice had died in childbirth before Dr. Bedlows had moved to town. Doc Bedlows wasn't much of a doctor, but he could have saved Janice sober or drunk.

Even with that, Keren had fourteen children, about thirty grandkids, more great grands and even three great-great grands and was slowly repopulating northern Virginia. Rappahannock County had a noticeable trend towards a coloration that was once termed "mulatto."

He had to wonder if it was really in his best interests, in the best interests of the region, for him to give it all up to be a mortar maggot again. And, hell, he'd done his bit. The small shadow-box filled with medals, the collection topped by his CIB and finally a gold pin that was a simple "600" in Arabic numerals, attested to that. *Can I get an Amen, brothers?*

But he'd seen the media reports, read the articles. The Hedren looked like bad news. Not as bad as the Posleen; nothing was a bad as the Posleen. But they made Hitler look like a spoiled child throwing a tantrum. And since Mike O'Neal was running the show, now, he had to figure that the information was more or less on the up and up.

And, hell, with the forces they were planning on raising, he'd be a captain again before you knew it. He might even get a company this time.

Thomas was full grown and managed the store just fine. Paul ran the Inn. Keren had been semi-retired for the last decade. Hadn't been a feral in town in nearly three years. Cute new wife or no, it was getting pretty damned boring in Rappahannock County.

"What's wrong?" Pamela asked when she looked up. She'd already learned the wifely trait of reading a husband like a book.

"Me that have been where I've been, me that have seen what I've seen . . ." Keren answered, holding out the e-mail.

Pamela was the granddaughter of Robert Crawford, a former medic in the 80th Armored Regiment. Robert wasn't a juv but before he died she'd heard more than enough stories to last. And she knew her husband's fondness for Kipling.

She looked at the e-mail and teared up slightly. But then she dashed the water from her face and smiled.

"Go," she said quietly. "There's things that have to be done. We'll be here when you get back."

"I don't know but I've been told!"
"I DON'T KNOW BUT I'VE BEEN TOLD!"
"Ranger shit ain't good as gold!"
"RANGER SHIT AIN'T GOOD AS GOLD!"
"I don't know but it's been heard!"
"I DON'T KNOW BUT IT'S BEEN HEARD!"
"Every Ranger's a yellow turd!"
"EVERY RANGER'S A YELLOW TURD!"

Orders had been cut. The unit, with the exception of Norris, stood.

The next day, starting very early and going on until "Can we fucking get this over with already?" had been dozens of assumption of command and responsibility ceremonies. General Fortun, the BUPERS his own self, had handed over musty flag after musty flag. Actually, they weren't all that musty. They'd been kept in climate controlled rooms for damned near fifty years. But it had taken for fucking ever since the general, who had to be a masochist of the first order, had felt it necessary to hand over every fucking flag down to the company level.

And not only the fucking flags. Somewhere along the lines they'd come up with a stupid "assumption of responsibility" ceremony for the fucking NCOs! Cutprice had gotten a flag. He had it leaning up against the wall of his quarters since he still didn't have an office. Wacleva had gotten a cheesy little mace thing, the symbol of his "assumption of responsibility" for Bravo Company, First Battalion, 14th Infantry Regiment.

Former Sergeant Major Wacleva, who had killed his first Nazi in Warsaw at the age of not quite thirteen and jumped with the Polish Airborne into the most fucked-up portion of Market Garden when he was just past *seventeen*, had not been notably impressed.

But afterwards had been the to-be-expected party. And Colonel Pennington—despite being low-class enough to have spent his whole career in mech infantry—had laid on a nice spread. He'd gotten a caterer to bring in a bunch of really nice roasts, potatoes, all the fixings and the bar was open. Cutprice hadn't asked the colonel what he'd done on civvie street, but he had to have made some money. Feeding all the officers and senior NCOs of a brigade a nice spread like that wasn't cheap.

But Cutprice wasn't a newbie. He'd taken a look at the training schedule for the next day and the gleam in the colonel's eye and put two and two together.

Higher management had figured that the "cadre" wouldn't be good for much after the to-be-expected parties. Guys who found themselves in STRAC units like the 14th would be celebrating, the ones that found themselves in rag-bag units or staff would be drowning their sorrows. So the training schedule for the next day was grab-ass. Nothing that couldn't be skipped.

Naturally, Colonel Pennington woke his hungover cadre the next morning and went on a Fun Run.

Defining a Fun Run is hard. How "Fun" it is depends on the unit. A unit that doesn't run very much thinks a "Fun Run" is being run around for an hour or two at a slow pace. Units that run a lot think a "Fun Run" is a marathon. Basically a "Fun Run" is any run that is *designed* to make people fall out. There is no training to it. It's a gut check.

Doing a Fun Run with Pennington, hung over, was a special kind of hell. Cutprice was pleased to see, as the unit staggered up to the Bachelor NCO Quarters, that the unit he had, to a great degree, created met the most elegant of standards. Some of the staff pukes and support had fallen out. That was to be expected. But not a fucking one of the leadership had. Some of them looked like they were about to pass out, but they were all there.

Given that they'd just gone about twenty miles, many of them horribly hung over, he was satisfied.

"NCOs fall out into barracks," Pennington shouted without slowing down much. "Officers, we're headed to the BOQ. Which is about four miles from here. And...DOUBLE TIME, MARCH!

"I don't go out with girls anymore!
"I live a life of danger!
"I sit in a tree and play with myself!"
"WEE, I'M A RANGER!"
Fucking track-heads...

❖   ❖   ❖

Cutprice had just stepped out of the shower and was about to flop face down on his bunk when his cell phone rang. He'd have ignored it, but it was the ringtone for the battalion commander, the opening strains of "The Internationale." Simosin = Russki. Russki = Commie. You can take the boy out of the cold war but you can't take the cold war out of the boy.

"Fuuuck," he muttered, picking up the phone and flipping it open. "Captain Cutprice, how may I help you, Colonel?"

"Get over to Pennington's quarters," Simosin said. "I'll meet you there in five minutes."

"What's this about, sir?" Cutprice asked, already pulling a fresh uniform out of the closet.

"You'll know when I know. He caught *me* in the shower."

The regimental commander's quarters were standard O-6, a small suite in a prefab two-story building filled with other minor brass. About the only thing they had that Cutprice's didn't was a small sitting room and its own crapper. Cutprice had to share his with another captain.

The sitting room was not designed to handle a group consisting of most of the brigade staff, all the battalion commanders and their operations officers and XOs. Especially a group who had been drinking the night before and PTing hard all morning. It stank to high heaven. And looking around, Cutprice saw he was the only company commander present. That didn't bode good at all.

"I think I printed out enough for all of you," Pennington said, holding up a sheaf of paper. "Pass these around and read them. That's going to cut the time."

When Cutprice finally got one of the sheets, having heard the murmurs before it got to him, he read it quickly.

Department of the Army Special Order 47839
Date: 14JUN61
So much of 14th Infantry Regiment activated 13JUN61. Should read, 14th Regimental Combat Team activated 14JUN61.

Department of the Army Special Order 47839-A
Cadre, 14th Regimental Combat Team will proceed to Camp Ernest Pappas, Kansas, to begin special retrain program, 38592: Retraining of recalled Cadre personnel. Movement will be effected NLT 17JUN61.

Department of the Army Special Order 47839-B
Cadre will be prepared to receive junior enlisted personnel under BUPERS special order 723481-A NLT 21JUN61.

Department of the Army Special Order 47839-C
14th Regimental Combat Team will commence special retraining program, 41486: Retraining and processing of Rejuvenated Personnel for Integration of Combat Teams NLT 28JUN61 for completion NLT 25JUL61.

Department of the Army Special Order 47839-D
14th Regimental Combat Team will be prepared for off-planet movement NLT 01SPT61 for purposes of combat operations in the Gratoola Zone of Combat (GZC).

End Department of the Army Special Order 47839
Ken O. Wilson, Major, DAOPSSPECCENT
For the Chief of Staff

"If everyone is done reading," Pennington said, impatiently. "You're all experienced senior officers; you all know what a cleft stick we're in. In eight weeks we are lifting off, presumably for Gratoola. That is normally the sort of time that a fully trained and integrated unit would have to just *prepare* for off-planet movement. But between now and then we have to move to our temporary training area, get retrained, receive brand new nuggets from Basic, organize a separate combat regiment, train them and get our units integrated. Get the word impossible out of your heads. You weren't hand-picked for this unit because you had it in your lexicon anyway. This is your warning order. I need Major Hatch, Colonel Hardy, Colonel Eckert and... Captain Cutprice to stay behind."

When the officers had filed out the colonel looked around at the survivors.

"Major Hatch," he said, looking at the S-3 from Third Battalion. "You'll be leading the advance party. Which means you have to catch a flight this afternoon. We'll figure out the rest of the crew to send with you in the next hour. But your second is Captain Cutprice."

"Yes, sir," the major said, looking over at the company commander.

"Cutprice, you're the eminence grise here," the brigade commander said. "We all know it. But Mullins can move your officers and NCOs just fine. Hell, most of this group we just need to tell them where and when and they'll show up if they have to E & E. So go out to Kansas and figure out how we're going to expedite this training program. It's going to be a cluster fuck because we don't even have a TOE on a separate regiment yet. Everybody get prepared to think fast on their feet. And Cutprice."

"Sir?"

"Get a buckley. Get used to using it."

CHAPTER THIRTEEN

"What is this, *Feldwebel*?" Frederick asked, accepting the strange device from Harz.

"It's a 'buckley,'" the juv replied. "It's a human artificial intelligence machine. We just received a supply of them. We are to begin using them for personal messaging as well as general orders. You will not lose it, Ox."

"Yes, *Feldwebel*," Erdmann said, pocketing the strange device.

The company had been gathered in front of the barracks in preparation for movement. Their personal baggage had already been stored in shipping containers. All that remained was loading up in the vehicles and matching up with their shuttles.

It was raining, naturally. But it was a light rain, comfortable rather than unpleasant. Frederick looked over the next company's barracks at what they had come to call "the Tiger," the massive jut of granite on which had once sat Fortress Ehrenbreitstein and now sat the headquarters for the Vaterland Division and Freiland. This might be the last time he saw the Rheinland. He wished that he could visit Marta one more time.

"Company, attention!" Senior *Oberfeldwebel* Bansbach boomed. Like Harz, Bansbach was a juv. But he was one of the few of the SS who had actually come over from the *Bundeswehr*. Originally trained as a Leopard crewman, the company's senior NCO had been incredibly helpful in the transition to the new systems.

"All present or accounted for," the *Oberfeldwebel* said, saluting the company commander.

"There is not much to say," *Hauptmann* Thayer said, looking the company over. He was not a juv but this was his third company command. The scars on his face had come from a long ago encounter with a group of feral Posleen that had been gathered by a God King. "In fifteen minutes we are scheduled to fall onto our vehicles. Get a good look on the way up; some of you won't be seeing the return trip. But we have all faced danger in securing Freiland. Though we are on far planets under alien stars, we shall still be securing Freiland. Be true to your comrades and true to your Fatherland and most of us will return, God willing. If not, we shall die in Panzers and that's not all that bad, *is* it?"

"Fall out and fall into your vehicles," *Oberfeldwebel* Bansbach shouted.

The company had marched to the motorpool and now the group broke up and pounded to their various equipment.

Frederick clambered onto the Leopard, unslung

his personal weapon and dropped into his seat. The small compartment had a rack for his weapon and he locked it down carefully. The R-28 Vehicle Crewman Rail-System submachine gun had what he felt was a pleasant similarity in appearance to the WWII Schmeisser machine-pistol. The difference being that its long, thin, ribbed magazine carried two-hundred rounds of 1mm mini-flechettes and that it could dump them *all* out in under a second.

He picked up his crewman's helmet and buckled it on, then swung the microphone into place. "Driver is up."

"Ox, if you screw this movement up . . ." Harz growled.

"All we are doing is driving to the pick-up zone, *Feldwebel*," Frederick pointed out, hitting the start button. The Leopold rumbled into life and all was well.

"That is what I mean," Harz said.

As Two Track pulled out, Harz pulled out behind it, falling into march position.

"*Feldwebel*, we were not briefed on whether we should use ground effect," Frederick said.

"If they want us to use ground effect, they will tell us to use ground effect," Harz said. "Now shut up and pray for your soul. I just had an update."

"Yes, *Feldwebel*," Frederick said, then thought about what the sergeant had said. "May I ask what the update was?"

"We are not *boarding* shuttles," Harz said.

"Excuse me, *Feldwebel*?" Frederick said as there was a sonic boom overhead. He looked up and then frowned, tilting his head quizzically. "*Feldwebel* . . . what are those?"

"Those, my yellow-shit friend, are Myrmidon assault shuttles," Harz said, apparently quoting. "They are a medium armor lifter variant of the Hellion combat shuttle, designed for moving medium armor units rapidly into and out of battle from orbit or in atmosphere. Aren't they pretty?"

"They aren't big enough to load . . ." Frederick started to say then stopped.

"Ah, you just saw the lifting clamps did you not?"

There were only eight of the Myrmidons available. Thus the tanks of the battalion had to wait as one flight after another lifted off. That gave those still on the ground a degree of comfort and discomfort. They could see that the clamps actually *held* the tanks and didn't let them drop to the ground from thousands of meters in the air. On the other hand, they could see the tanks being lifted up into the air, their crews still inside. And then, presumably, up into space and into a ship.

It was not going to be fun.

The remaining family and friends of the Michael Wittmann had turned out to see the battalion off. Frederick searched and searched for Marta but could not see her. Certainly her superiors would have given her time off?

"I can't see him," Marta said.

"I can, barely," her mother replied. "If I could get some of these idiots to get out of our way . . ."

"I need to get through," Marta said, elbowing an oldster.

"Marta?" former *Oberfeldwebel* Brutscher said. "Here, here, let Marta through! She cannot see the Ox."

✧   ✧   ✧

"Our turn," Harz said as the shuttles descended again. Most of the battalion had already loaded *into* shuttles. Lucky them.

"I don't see Marta," Frederick said.

"If you don't pay attention to your job, *Schutze*, you will see nothing but my fist."

The clamps had specific contact points. Frederick had been briefed on them but had assumed they were for cranes or internal lifting systems on ships. Not for lifting *him* up into space.

"I have clamps one through six set and locked," the private said, looking at his telltales.

"Confirm, one through six set and locked," Harz said. "Pilot, we confirm set and locked."

"Roger," a female voice said. "Standby. All shuttles set and locked. Lifting."

Then Frederick saw her, struggling to the front of the, on average, much taller crowd. He wasn't sure she saw him but he waved, wildly. Then her eyes caught his and he could only hold his arm overhead.

"You look as if you are giving your girlfriend a Nazi salute, *Schutze*," Aderhold said. "Blow her a fucking kiss, man!"

Frederick shook himself and did just that.

Marta caught the kiss and held it for a moment as her fiancé's massive tank lifted into the air, then waved in farewell.

"She's out of sight, *Schutze*," Harz said. "And since we're getting rather high, you might wish to close and lock your hatch. Because if you pass out, you will then be subject to space's cold and vacuum. And we will be sending your fiancée a corpsicle as a present."

"Thank you for that reminder, *Feldwebel*," Frederick said, dropping the hatch and dogging it. Supposedly the environmental system of the tanks was rated for brief exposure to space. Supposedly.

"This is great," the gunner said. "Swivel the vision blocks around. It's a great view."

"I will take your word for it, *Gefreiter*."

"This is easy stuff, *Schutze*," Harz said. "This is the easy part."

The shuttles dropped the eight tanks in a cavernous hold that was open to space.

"Wait until Three has moved out then follow the red line," Harz said. "Keep it centered on your treads."

Frederick followed the orders, following Three Track down the red line. Just as he was approaching a massive hatch the red light above it started to blink.

"Stop," Harz snapped. "We have to wait for the others to get cycled through."

The hatch closed and they waited for a moment in the, presumably, vacuum and cold of space. The temperature in the panzer had dropped slightly, but it wasn't unpleasant.

"*Feldwebel?*" Frederick said.

"*Ja?*"

"How is it that the engine is running?" Frederick asked.

"I'm going to take the manual and shove it up your ass, *Schutze*," Harz growled. "Section Thirty-Two, sub-paragraph nine. There is a pressurized air system to feed the engine. Remember the big bottle, idiot?"

"I thought that was *our* air," Frederick admitted. "For if there was poison gas. I never expected to be in space, *Feldwebel*."

"Ours is being recycled by the scrubbers, yellow-shit," Harz said. "You will learn that fucking manual by heart, *Schutze*, if I have to feed it to you page by page."

The hatch opened and Frederick started forward.

"Pull it well to the right," Harz said. "That is the hand you beat your tiny dick with."

Frederick complied, pulling the tank in hard against the right wall. Two Track pulled in next to him on the left and there was a rumble through the floor.

"Right, pressure coming up nicely," Harz said. The doors in front of them opened and Frederick almost gasped. The interior of the ship was filled with platforms and ramps onto which the whole mass of the Michael Wittmann was being loaded.

What he at first took to be a green teddy bear walked out in front of the panzer and waved red-lit wands at him. It took him a moment to realize he was looking at an Indowy.

"Follow the Kobold," Harz said. "Slowly. Do NOT run him over. They get very particular about that sort of thing."

Frederick followed the Indowy down the length of the hold and into a hard right turn. There was a ramp that the Kobold gestured him up, and for a moment he hesitated. It seemed impossible that the fragile looking ramp could hold the full weight of a Leopard.

"What are you waiting for, *Schutze*?" Harz asked. "Follow the Kobold."

Frederick gunned the tank gingerly onto the ramp,

then all the way up onto it. The rickety looking thing
didn't even flex.

"The Indowy can build fine materials," Aderhold
said. "Too bad they can't fight worth a crap."

"If they could we would be outnumbered about sixty
billion to one," Harz noted. "And we'd be up against
the guys who make all our stuff. Let them make the
weapons; we will use them just fine."

Finally, the vehicle was juggled into position, hard
between Two and Four Track. It was on a shallow
platform that looked like aluminum but was probably
some GalTech super stuff. As Frederick watched, a
line of similar, if slightly smaller, platforms was laid
down by a team of Indowy in front of the line of
tanks. The platforms had small boxes on their rear. If
he had to pull out, he was going to break the box off.

"You can pop your hatch, now, yellow-shit," Harz
said. "We're home."

CHAPTER FOURTEEN

Getting to Camp Ernest Pappas was not the easiest thing in the world.

First of all, it was being built near the former town of Steelville, MO, which was about as bumfuckaround as you could find.

With the exception of a few bounty farms the area had yet to be resettled. Which meant that all of the land was in eminent domain, owned by the U.S. Government. Which meant all that the Army had to do was tell a civilian construction company to go in and start building. Security was provided by the same company, which had long experience of building in unreclaimed zones.

The road to the facility from the nearest airport, which was in East St. Louis, was a long damned drive. St. Louis, on the west bank of the Mississippi, had been a fortress city and had held out for nearly two years before the Posleen put in an overwhelming attack. It was starting to rebuild, but slowly.

The road, following the trace of I-44, was four-lane black-top as far as the site of the former town of Cuba. From there it was an "improved" road, dirt and gravel, to the camp. Since there were numerous streams and small rivers in the area, Cutprice figured the camp was going to get cut off at the first big rainstorm.

But the road sure had plenty of traffic. There were tractor-trailer trucks running in both directions, some of them carrying construction equipment but many of them carrying combat systems and support equipment. He had to hope like hell the guys guarding them were honest. Not much hope, but it was something.

There were civilian security guards manning the gate-house. They waved the trucks ahead of the party of soldiers through, but stopped the rented Expedition.

"Advance party for the Fourteenth Regiment," Sergeant Major Stiffey said. The Smaj for the brigade was a humongo guy. Cutprice hadn't known him but Wacleva vouched for him and that was all that counted. He'd been the 101st Division sergeant major during Vietnam, after two tours at lower positions, and retired as the First Army sergeant major. Which was why he was Wacleva's boss instead of the other way around. Wacleva had still had more points, just as Cutprice had more points than the Brigade CO. The Army was funny that way.

"Yes, sir," the gate guard said. She was a cute little thing and Cutprice hoped she had the stones to face a charging feral. "If you'll follow the signs to the Office of Military Liaison. They said that you were coming."

"How's it been?" Stiffey said, ignoring the "sir."

"I just got here," the guard admitted. "I'm told

by some of the older hands it was pretty Wild West at first. But we haven't had a really serious incident in weeks. We've got electrified fence up around the construction zones so it's safe enough in the base. If you're going to be training out in the boonies, though, it might get interesting."

"Thanks," the CSM said, pulling out.

"Buddy who's still in told me it's generally live ammo and weapons free past the perimeter on most bases," Major Hatch commented.

"The cadre aren't going to be a problem with that," Cutprice said. "Not so sure about the recruits."

"Cross that bridge," Hatch said.

The signs pointed south then curved back east and up around to the north. All long the road, hardtop this time, there was construction going on. Motorpools arrayed on the flats were already being filled with equipment and logistics areas were lining up with CONEX after CONEX. Equipment might not be a problem. Guys to use it might be a problem, but not equipment. Even if there was some pilfering, and looking at the laborers he suspected that was likely, they couldn't steal it *all*. There was just *too much*. If they didn't have the schedule they were looking at, this might even be a decent war.

"What I want to know is where all this stuff is coming from," Sergeant First Class Abe Sanders said. The Ops sergeant from Second Batt was medium all over. Medium height, weight, build. He had brown hair and brown eyes and regular features. He also had a mind like a steel trap. He'd gotten out as a master sergeant, NCOIC for Twentieth Corps Operations and had spent most of his time in the Army in one Ops shop or another. "Not knocking it, but that's one hell of a lot of equipment if you start extrapolating."

"Fleet Strike put some Panamanian guy in charge of a War Board," Major Hatch replied. "He's using Posleen forges to produce stuff and Indowy for the bigger stuff. But not their usual way of building. It's full up mass production. With enough Indowy and Posleen forges..."

"What I don't see is ranges," Cutprice said.

"I'm sure they're around here, somewhere," Hatch replied.

As the road curved back north they could see more construction up on the hills overlooking the Meramec River. There was a big three-story pre-fab structure going up with smaller buildings stretching down the hill. Down the hill from it were a series of construction trailers inside another fence. From the look of it, the fence had been neglected recently. The gates were hanging off their hinges. But there was a parking lot and a sign:

Camp Ernest Pappas Central Office
Borgon-Cummings Construction Offices
Office of Military Liaison
Ask about Employment Opportunities!
Se Habla Español!

"Something funny, Sergeant Major?" Major Hatch asked as the foursome got out of the SUV.

"Sorry, sir," Stiffey said, still chuckling. "Just thinking about the likelihood of somebody walking all the way the fuck out here to apply for a job."

"One thing we *ain't* gonna have to worry about is

fights in town," Cutprice said, grinning. "'Course, that just means we'll have them on post instead."

The left-hand trailer had the sign for Office of Military Liaison. Hatch led the way as they entered.

"Sir," the lieutenant behind the desk said, standing up. "Welcome to Camp Ernest Pappas. I was told to expect an advance party but I hadn't expected you so soon."

"We've got a very *tight* schedule," the major said. "We've got about eight hundred officers and NCOs coming in this week. I hope you've got rooms for us all."

"We can find them, sir," the lieutenant said. "The actual quarters that the cadre are supposed to fill are not entirely complete. But we have barracks prepared that we can put the cadre in until officer and NCO quarters are complete. I'm not sure, though, that all the barracks will be complete when the troops arrive. This is the craziest schedule I've ever seen, sir. Not that I've been at this long."

"Why don't I tell you what we need to know," Major Hatch said. "Then you can tell us where to find the information."

"Yes, sir," the lieutenant said. "Whatever I can do to assist."

"You know, somewhere there's some dude in charge of making sure everybody has a bed to sleep in," Sergeant Major Stiffey said, looking at the just completed barracks. They were a shambles to a military man. There was still dust everywhere from the construction, parts weren't fitted properly, there was paint on the windows...

But that was what troops were for.

"It is sorely lacking in bunks," Sergeant Sanders

said, nodding. He walked down the open bay to the end and looked in the bathroom area. "But there's shitters and showers." There was a sound of running water and he came back out. "And, more importantly, they work."

"Now if we only had bunks, it would be like home."

"We were supposed to get an additional crew for moving furniture and other small items," the lieutenant said, pulling out a memo. "But there's a shortage of labor. I've *got* it all, it's in trailers that got dropped at one of the log points. That's assuming a bunch of it hasn't been stolen, but I've been doing random checks and most of it's there. But I don't have a way to move it into place."

"It was a question of priorities," Bill Hammond said. The site manager for Borgon-Cummings shrugged. "Did you want roofs over your heads or beds? For that matter, none of the furniture in the messes has been moved in or the clubs. Or the offices. It's all here, it's just not in place."

"We'll handle it," Hatch said, nodding. "One way or another. The most important thing is to have barracks and messes for the troops when they arrive."

"We should make it," Hammond said. "We're about three days behind schedule—there were rains that slowed us way the fuck down—but we should make it before the troops arrive. I'm not going to say that there won't be problems, but we'll deal with those when we have to. But there should be roofs that don't leak and four walls. Probably working electric and plumbing. Furniture? Computer set-up? I just don't have the fucking hands."

"We'll set up the in-process for the troops so that..."

He paused as his buckley began to chime.

"Sorry about this," Hatch said, looking at the device. "It's the Regimental S-3. Yes, sir? Yes, sir." He set the buckley down and hit the speaker button. "Go ahead, sir."

"You guys all there?" Lieutenant Colonel Hardy asked.

"Myself and Captain Cutprice, sir," Hatch said. "The NCOs are checking out the facilities."

"Good enough," Hardy said. "You know what a cluster fuck this is. There is, however, finally some good news."

"That would be nice, sir," Cutprice said, frowning.

"We just got additional information on the supplemental personnel roster," Hardy said, a grin in his voice. "We are not the only guys getting fucked..."

"All juvs?" CSM Stiffey said, his eyes gleaming.

"*All* juvs," Cutprice agreed, nodding. "That's why they figure we can stand-up a regiment so fast. All juvs, all with experience as the positions they're taking, all from higher ranks. The privates are going to be former sergeants, some of the sergeants are going to be officers with prior service as enlisted. It's not true, you can't make a unit that fast. But it's better than getting troops straight out of Basic."

"Volunteers?" Abe asked. "Because it's a world of difference between that and unwilling recalls."

"All volunteers," Cutprice said.

"And volunteers that are willing to take a cut in pay to get back in uniform," Stiffey said, nodding. "They'll probably do."

"They're going to be out of shape," Sergeant Sanders said.

"We can fix that," CSM Stiffey said. "Although running off-base may be interesting."

"They're going to have forgotten most of the skills," Sanders said, still frowning.

"It's like riding a bicycle," Cutprice said. "Former platoon sergeants as buck privates. Think about it."

"They're going to want to tell us our jobs," Sanders said. "*Old* soldiers, Captain."

"*Older* soldiers, Sergeant," Cutprice said, grinning.

"There's bound to be problems, sir."

"Sergeant, we're lifting off-world to fight an invading force that outnumbers us, has better technology and has overrun three worlds with laughable ease. In seven and a half weeks. Starting from scratch. Everybody's trained soldiers but not trained on *this* equipment. You *betcha* there's gonna be problems."

"Wow! I have an office," Colonel Pennington said, gesturing at the empty room.

The office smelled of new paint and there was dust everywhere. But it had a great view across the Meramec. On the far side he could see laborers setting up a pop-up target range. He'd better get along with the troops. If anybody wanted to, and they were a good enough shot, they could nail him in the back of the head while he was at his desk.

"Yes, sir," Major Hatch replied. "And your furniture is sitting in the trailer out front. Somewhere."

"Wellll . . . let's go find it. Actually, the first thing to find is the cleaning supplies."

❖   ❖   ❖

"Sorry I'm late, sir," Staff Sergeant Garland said. The Brigade Information Systems NCOIC was covered in dust. "I had to re-run some cable then pull a buggy server…"

There were no regular troops for a working party. The officers and NCOs of the various units had worked in teams to set up those same offices. Colonel Pennington had not even ended up putting in his own desk. All that being said, the former command sergeant majors of high positions, Army generals, commanders of corps and divisions, had had a high old time working into the night on a good old-fashioned GI party. As the regimental adjutant had said at one point: "It's good to get your hands dirty from time to time." And then they'd gotten up early the next morning to discover what new disaster had hit.

"Not a problem, Sergeant," Colonel Pennington said, not looking up. "I'm on the nonsecure server. I need to get my password and username for the secure side, through."

"Right here, sir," the sergeant replied, handing over a form. "Glad you're comfortable with the systems, sir. I'm having to do a bit of hand-holding."

"Know what I did between wars, Sergeant?"

"No, sir."

"I was a systems design manager for Cisco. Made VP of systems integration before I got recalled. I've got a Ph.D. in this shit."

"Holy shit," the sergeant said. "Sorry, sir. Dammit. I knew your name was familiar, sir. I worked for you for a few years."

"If I have a scrap of time and you need a hand, don't hesitate to ask…"

✧   ✧   ✧

"Herschel Keren," Keren said as he sat down. He'd stored his civvie bag in the overhead and now held out his hand to his seatmate.

"David Balmoral," the guy said. He was slight of stature, like Keren, but with white blond hair and looked about fourteen. "Thirty-Third Division."

"I was in the Thirty-Third," Keren said, grimacing. "At Daleville."

"I heard that was a cluster fuck," Balmoral said, nodding. "I joined when it was rebuilding. You get out in it?"

"No," Keren said. "Ten Thousand."

"Fuck," Balmoral said, chuckling. "You really love punishment, don't you?"

"And now this," Keren said as the bus pulled out. The volunteer recallees had been assembled at Fort Bragg, which had been rebuilt since the war, then flown by military shuttles to an assembly area near St. Louis. Which told Keren that the base they were headed for didn't even have a place to set down a shuttle.

"Yeah," Balmoral said. "You gotta fucking wonder about us. I mean, sure, putting the uniform back on's one thing. But taking a cut from platoon sergeant to spear carrier?"

"Heh," Keren said, fingering his left breast where a certain patch used to reside. "Try taking a cut from captain to sergeant."

They didn't chat much on the rest of the drive. There wasn't much to chat about. Keren caught up on his e-mail.

The road turned to gravel as they turned off what was probably an old interstate trace. The Posleen pulled up roads like nobody's business, but they generally left the road metal in place. By the time humanity got around to rebuilding the roads way out in Posleen-controlled areas, they'd started to develop decent sized saplings. But with the road metal in place, it was easy enough to grade them off, replace some bridges and lay down either more gravel or blacktop.

They were on the gravel road, though, for over an hour. This place had been dumped way out in the boonies.

The convoy of buses was accompanied by a pair of gun carriers, which said it all about the area they were passing through. There was an occasional bounty farm, none of them looking as prosperous as the ones around Keren Town. This was serious Wild West shit. It got Keren feeling nostalgic.

"Tried bounty-farming for a while," Balmoral said. "Was not for me. Too much like work. You?"

"Yeah," Keren said. "Did it for a while."

"What do you do now?"

"Pretty much retired," Keren replied. "But I'll admit I was getting bored."

"I managed a hobby shop," Balmoral said. "And, yeah, I was bored. And the pay was less than joining back up. Even as a private. Thank God we're on Fleet Strike rates."

Finally they passed some ranges where laborers with armed security were setting up the facilities. Crossed a bridge, turned around a hill and entered a security gate. The camp was, clearly, still under construction. But it was wired in so the ferals would stay *out*.

Their bus pulled up in front of a cluster of five two-story buildings. There was a single individual waiting for the bus with a spread-out formation behind him.

"Fall out of the buses and form on me," the man said through a megaphone.

As the group formed in a semi-circle around him, the man smiled. Keren smiled, too. The sergeant major hadn't spotted him, yet, but with *Wacleva* here...

"Welcome to Bravo Company, First Battalion, Four-teenth Regimental Combat Team. My name is Ser First Sergeant Stanislav Wacleva. You will not address me as Top or First. You will address me as First Sergeant Wacleva. You are all old soldiers who have taken a reduction in rank to reenlist. This is admirable. I'm practically *crying* I'm so worked up. You all know how the game is played, you all probably have a program you intend to enact. You've got your plans on how you're going to ghost through being privates until you can get back to your *real* rank.

"Be aware that I and every other member of the cadre of the Fourteenth Regiment are *also* old soldiers who have taken a reduction in rank. Some of us not quite so voluntary. Your brigade com-mander, Colonel Tobias Pennington, was an *Army* commander in California during the Posleen Scuffle. Your battalion commander led a *corps*. In the case of *myself*, your first sergeant, I was a member of the Polish Airborne in *World War Two* and dropped at *Arnhem*. Since then I have been in just about every war the United States has *fought* on five *continents*. I retired the first time as brigade sergeant major of Third Brigade Eighty-second Airborne. Before that I'd held that post as well as division sergeant major and Eighteenth Corps sergeant major for nearly twenty years. The *second time* I retired as the sergeant major of the Ten Thousand. So if *any* of you *yardbirds* think you're more old-soldier than *me*, you can just bring it on!"

The first sergeant looked around the formation, searching for a challenge. Keren considered ducking but figured that it was pointless. It wasn't like the first sergeant wasn't going to find out he was in the unit sooner or later.

When Wacleva's gimlet eye hit the café au lait complexion Keren saw the first crack in his stern complexion. He blinked in obvious puzzlement, trying to place the face, then in surprise.

"Captain Keren? What the fuck are *you* doing in this group, if you'll pardon my French, sir?"

"That would be Sergeant Keren, First Sergeant," Keren said, grinning. "I'm one of your mortar maggots."

"Well ain't that some shit," Wacleva said, shaking his head. "To continue. Your company commander, who some of you might see in passing in the next few weeks, is Captain Thomas Cutprice. Like myself and at least one of you, he is a veteran of the Six Hundred. We are *all old soldiers* here. We are all old soldiers who understand that being the best you can possibly be is the only way that we're going to survive this new war. For your general information, in just *seven weeks*, we are shipping out for Gratoola, which in the direct path of this newest enemy."

He waited for the expected murmuring and gave it a few seconds.

"At ease. Between now and then, we are going to have to get everyone in-processed, get these fucked-up barracks straightened out, get you all in uniforms, weapons and gear, reacquire your skills, train you on the new systems, kill the skills you had that are wrong, prepare for movement and ship out. Every one of you have some conception of just what a *cluster fuck* this could be. The way to *prevent* it from being a cluster fuck is for every one of you to act in the most expeditious way possible at every task you are assigned. What is asked of us is impossible. But this is all old stuff to us. Which is *exactly* why we are going to do it."

"What are you here for?" Wacleva shouted as the group circled him. The company was trotting in a circle, lifting and lowering weights.

"TRAINING, FIRST SERGEANT!"

"What kind of training?" the NCO shouted.

"HA-A-A-RMY TRAINING, FIRST SERGEANT!"

The group was performing PT on two hours' sleep. First they'd unloaded all the cleaning supplies stored in the tractor trailers. Then they'd GI'd the barracks, supply building, armory, company headquarters and messhall. They'd policed the company area and picked up all the trash the construction crew had left behind. They'd scraped away the paint from the windows. They'd fixed the misemplaced electrical sockets.

Only then did they start moving in the furniture. First for the company areas, offices, supply and armory, then for their individual barracks. Then they'd cleaned up the mess they made moving furniture.

Then came issue. New uniforms, none of which fit, new boots which fit a bit better. PT gear and running shoes since it was the New Army. All of it then had to be put away to standard. Haircuts were simple buzz cuts; there were no barbers to tend to that and nobody really cared about hair. Then clean up the mess from issue and barbering. They were starting to look like soldiers again. Hell, they were starting to look like teenaged recruits for all that most of them were pushing eighty.

When they were done, at two-thirty in the morning, they were permitted to sleep.

At four-thirty they'd been awakened by their platoon sergeants. Clean the barracks again. Finally they were out doing PT. Forty minutes of calisthenics to get warmed up. A four mile run. Wind-sprints. And now combination training.

"When I give you the command to fall out, fall out and fall in to your platoon areas," Wacleva bellowed. "Each platoon has fifteen minutes for breakfast. First training session is at 0830. Figure you are going to snap and pop every minute of every day for the next five weeks. We do not have time for fuck-around. Fall out and fall in!"

Sergeant First Class Frederick Moreland had been the Third Brigade Sergeant Major, 78th Mechanized Division during the war. Prior to the war he'd been a mech mortar NCO for damned near twenty years.

What he'd never been was a drill sergeant. He knew the theory, but with this group "breaking them down and building them back as soldiers" didn't really count. So when the platoon fell into the platoon area, he didn't play drill sergeant. He was their platoon sergeant. He didn't have to.

"Fall in and shit, shower and shave," Moreland said mildly. "We're last on the roster for chow. Do *not* fuck up the barracks. Ten minutes prior to chow I'll give the word. Clear up anything that's out of place.

You all know the drill. Most of you know why the drill exists. You need to get back in the zero defect mentality. You're all good, everything is going to be perfect. Or I *will* start playing drill sergeant and you *won't* like it."

"I'll shower last," Keren said. He'd been temporarily appointed the squad leader for Two Gun of the four gun section. Two Gun was the premium spot in a mortar platoon, being the gun that all other guns adjusted to. To keep the gun, though, he was going to have to prove that he was the best squad leader of the four available. Best should mean his gun was the quickest and the most accurate. But since they weren't going to start training on guns immediately, for the time being "best" meant the cleanest, neatest and most prompt. "Oppenheimer is up first, then Griffis, Adams and Cristman. While everyone else is showering, we're going to be taking care of our areas of responsibility. Every single day. Understood?"

"Done this before, Keren," Cristman said. As the senior specialist, he was up for the gunner position. There were arguments that assistant gunner was a better slot—the AG got to actually drop rounds—but gunner was the doorway to squad leader. Cristman was a former mortar platoon sergeant in 36th Division and had actually held out for a while before retiring. Phlegmatic and much larger than his squad leader, he seemed to move slow but was the most efficient guy Keren had ever seen. "Let's get started. Opie, don't dawdle."

The squad worked in teams fixing the bunks and wall-lockers. By keeping in their socks they didn't mess up the waxed floor. Uniforms were laid out, ready to don and as each of the soldiers rotated through the shower they returned to carefully hang their PT gear to dry and got it on.

The new uniforms were made of a material similar to the Fleet Strike grays, but were digital camouflage. With an attached, form-fitting hood they also had cloaking capability. That hadn't been explained yet and everyone kept their hands away from the pull-tab low on the left bicep.

The boots were designed around civilian hiking boots, comfortable and well made but being very odd to the soldiers in that they were bright, reflective, silver.

"I can't believe they gave us, like, chrome fucking boots," Specialist Elden Adams said. The assistant gunner was medium height with hazel eyes and, until last night, had light brown hair. He held the boots up and considered his reflection in their mirror shine. "What the fuck?"

"And we're not supposed to polish them," Keren noted, picking a bit of paint off a window that someone had missed last night. The squad had completed all their personal tasks and were working on the remaining platoon tasks while waiting for chow-call. Keren still hadn't gotten to the shower; Cristman was, apparently, less efficient at showering. "Just wipe them down with a light rag."

"What's the fucking point?" Adams asked as Cristman emerged from the shower-point. "They're fucking mirrors."

"Hopefully that will get explained in training," Keren said, grabbing his towel and trotting to the shower.

"We've got *no* time," Sergeant Stacy Miller said.

First squad had the duty of cleaning the latrine when everyone had cycled through. They were waiting impatiently for the last few soldiers to get done showering.

"Two of my guys are ready to go," Keren said, turning on the water. The shower was open-bay, four shower heads firing into a ten by ten plastic cubicle. Two of them were still in use. The rest of the head was being rapidly cleaned by first squad but they still had to wipe down the shower before they could stand inspection. "Grab them to help if you need it."

"I think we've got it," Miller replied. He was a massive guy with the look of a former football player. Keren suspected anyone making fun of his first name was going to go through a wall. "If you don't take too long."

"Done," Keren said, turning off the water. He'd gotten his pits, head and face and scraped off what little beard had formed. He'd always been lucky in that regard. He thought there must have been some American Indian in his lineage because he had virtually no beard.

He trotted back to his bunk, wiping his feet before he left the head, and donned his uniform. Some of the clasps and connections were new, so it took him a bit to get it on. He was just tabbing his blouse closed when the door at the far end of the bay burst open.

"AT EASE," Staff Sergeant Carter Richards bellowed, striding down the center of the squad bay. The sergeant was the FDC section leader and assistant platoon sergeant. Apparently, Moreland was going to be using him as a ramrod. "Keren, why ain't you dressed, yet?"

"No excuse, Sergeant," Keren said, facing forward.

"Get your shit done up and prepare for inspection," the staff sergeant said, walking to the latrine. "Miller! You call this clean? This is the most fucked-up head I've ever seen! There are *streaks* on my *mirrors*, Miller!"

The rapid inspection found fault in every area the sergeant looked. Some of it was germane. Much of it was, in Keren's professional opinion, chickenshit. The flip side was, Fire Direction Control was a very finicky business and the people who were best at it tended towards obsessive compulsive disorder. Having an OCD section leader would be a pain in the ass in garrison but might save their ass in combat. Keren decided to just put up with the chickenshit.

"Fall out for chow," Sergeant Moreland said from the doorway. "And move like you're fucking recruits."

The platoon, released from the scathing inspection, fell out into formation and marched "expeditiously" to chow. Some of them had forgotten how to march, as was apparent when the unit tried to do a column right to the mess hall. They did a bit better at breaking down into files. Fortunately, it wasn't far.

Fifteen minutes is less time than it normally takes to get an entree served. It's about half the time that most people take to eat a casual breakfast. It required eating very fast.

Fortunately, it was one skill Keren had retained. People often commented on how fast he ate. And he was hungry. They'd worked most of the night without supper then done the hardest PT he'd experienced in decades. He wolfed down some underdone eggs, bacon, sausage, biscuits, toast, orange juice and really bad coffee in well under the requisite time.

He fell out of the mess hall and just stood in the

light rain. Early morning rain was a constant of being outdoors, such a one that there was a civvie song that had become a famous marching song about it. It was a hell of a first day and it had barely started. He'd forgotten how much he truly hated the chickenshit part of the Army even when he knew most of it had a purpose.

Oppenheimer followed hard on his heels, then stopped and pulled out a pack of Marlboros. A flick of a lighter and he was sucking down cancer smoke, the cigarette cupped to keep the light rain off.

"Socks," Keren said. Oppenheimer had gotten gigged for not having them rolled to specifications.

"Got it," the driver said, making a face. He was a lanky guy who had had a mane of mid-back-length red hair when he arrived. "Sorry. I'll make sure they're strac first chance I get."

"You got nothing better to do than stand around in the rain, Keren?" Sergeant Richards asked as he exited the mess hall. He, too, pulled out a pack of cigarettes and lit one.

"If I had anything to do, Sergeant, I'd be doing it," Keren responded.

"You was the artillery coordinator for the Ten Thousand, right?" Richards said, a touch of nervousness in his voice.

"I'm not going to tell you how to do your job, Sergeant," Keren replied. "But, yeah, I was."

"I heard about that Spanish Inquisition you used to run," Oppenheimer said, chuckling. "Gawd, I wished you'd run it on our damned division arty. They purely sucked."

"What was you?" Richards asked.

"Same as you, Sergeant," Oppenheimer said. "FDC section leader. No interest in having the job again; I prefer to be on the guns. Besides, I was talking with Gist on the bus. Motherfucker's a human calculator. He still remembers all his tables. Got 'em memorized by heart."

"Yeah, but we're not using the same mortars," Richards said. "These are electrodrive systems. Completely different ballistics."

"Ballistics are ballistics, Sergeant," Sergeant Gist said, walking out of the mess hall. Part of the rejuv process was to permanently fix any eye problems but Gist just *looked* as if he should have coke-bottle glasses. He was slight, pale and had a stoop. For all that, he'd kept up with the massively fucked run this morning. "And for Opie's information, I didn't remember the tables; I just calculate them from raw data. Give me the raw for the new mortars and I can do the same. It's really not hard. And we will, of course, have computers."

"Won't have much time to get used to them," Richards pointed out.

"We can train on the ship," Keren said. "Keep one system out for gun training. And you guys, well, all you do is run the calculations. Hell, we can even set it up so we train in the troop bay. The main thing that's got me worried is getting into action fast enough."

"Everybody's out," Sergeant Moreland said from the doorway. "Head straight to the company training office. We've got five minutes before training starts."

Oppenheimer took a drag off his cigarette and, holding the smoke, crumpled out the last of the tobacco, pocketed the butt and started to trot.

"I wanna be an airborne Ranger," he squeaked, smoke coming out of his nose and mouth.

"Oh, shut the fuck up," Keren said, chuckling as he ran alongside.

"Welcome to the company and all that."

Staff Sergeant Edgar McCrady was the company operations officer, the guy responsible for making sure that all the paperwork was complete and that everyone had been trained to Army standard. Given that he was the ultimate paperpusher for the company, he was already looking haggard.

"Since you're all prior service, training is going to skip anything that it possibly can," McCrady said. "Therefore, don't expect classes on VD prevention, personal hygiene, consideration of others or how to balance a checkbook. However, there is some paperwork that simply has to be done prior to training, notably wills and living wills as well as insurance and basic safety orientation. This is normally a day-long affair. We *will* compress it into this hour."

There were fourteen terminals arrayed along the wall. Hooked into internet databases, they could search for relevant personal information in seconds. But it still took time. Many of the former soldiers didn't have a will or hadn't updated it in some time. Some hadn't used a computer in fifty years.

In Keren's case it was dead easy.

"Name and social," the machine said in a low contralto.

"Herschel Keren, 078-05-1120"

"Will registered in Rappahannock County, Virginia. Living Will registered in Rappahannock County, Virginia.

Designated respondee, Pamela Keren. Primary beneficiary, Pamela Keren. Is this information correct to the best of your knowledge?"

"Yes."

"Would you like to make ... Pamela Keren your insurance beneficiary?"

"Yes."

"Would you like to increase your basic draw for insurance to increase the payment to the beneficiary?"

"No." Pam was going to be set anyway.

"Method of burial if body is recoverable?"

"In the ground."

"Religion still Baptist?"

"Yes."

"You are recorded as an assistant chaplain for the First Baptist Church of Keren Town. Would you like to be recorded as an alternate chaplain?"

"No."

"Basic immunizations are ... not updated. Advanced immunizations are ... not updated. Pay records are ... updated. Thank you for your time. Goodbye."

"File into the armory and draw personal weapons," Sergeant Richards said. "Don't get all shocked that they ain't AIWs."

Keren, by virtue of being a squad leader, was issued a rifle. He looked at it and snorted, noted the serial number, then walked outside with the rest of the platoon.

"It's a fucking Postie railgun!" Adams said, shaking his head.

"Actually, it's not," Keren said, looking at the device carefully. "I've used a converted railgun and this is

John Ringo

different. I'd say it's *way* better designed for humans to use."

The weapon was almost a sketch of a gun. The shoulder stock was collapsible and looked flimsy. Keren suspected it was stronger than steel. The pistol grip and trigger housing were comfortable but lightly built. The barrel was shorter than a Posleen railgun but had the same odd wideness on the horizontal access, a function of the magnetic accelerators. Sights were elevated and included optics that gave at least four power magnification. He suspected there was a way to dial that up. There was a dot reticle for fast firing. The really intimidating part was the magazine well, which looked about the size of a Barrett's. The gun, by itself, weighed not much more than an M-16 and was a touch shorter. With the magazine he wasn't going to guess the weight.

"I ain't gonna march you back," Sergeant Richards said, walking out of the armory with a railgun in his hand. "Double time back to the barracks, doff your boots and head upstairs. Then we're going to learn about these things."

They'd moved the furniture for the training room in the previous night. Simple folding chairs and folding tables were going to be the order of the day. For the next six weeks.

"M264 grav rifle," Sergeant Richards said, holding one of the rifles up. "The M264 uses linear magnetic acceleration to fire a *three* millimeter tungsten or steel flechette to a velocity of forty-three hundred meters per second. This is *five* times the velocity of an M-16 round and nearly *six* times that of the AIW. The maximum *effective* range is eight hundred meters while the *maximum* range is eight thousand two hundred and forty-*six* meters and it comes complete with a four position firing selector, safe, semi, burst and full *rocking* auto. The base design we took from the Posties but it has been significantly improved for ergonomics and so that it can, yes, be *aimed* using the M482 one to twelve power opto-digital firing scope..."

There was the M238 1mm grav pistol for the gunner and AG. A long-barreled weapon with more maximum range and damage than an M-16, it was a nasty thing to fire by hand with a truly brutal recoil. The non-driver ammo bearer got the M825 combination 20mm plasma grenade launcher and railgun.

Paper manuals were distributed and with Sergeant Richards's often less than helpful assistance everyone learned to field strip and reassemble their individual weapons. Particular note was taken of red comments about potential "issues." The M264 wasn't something to be fired if the barrel was blocked but that could be said of most weapons. Just more so in the case of a weapon with its power. The note about "potential capacitor accidental discharge" in "over-fire" conditions—like when you were firing as fast as you possibly could or get overrun—was not a good sign.

But the weapon could fire a round that ripped through a tank if you hit it just right and could fire *four thousand* rounds per minute. Both were good things. So was the *five hundred round* magazine with integrated battery compartment. And, yes, it was a heavy motherfucker. But adding it to the weapon actually improved balance and reduced recoil. By the end of the one-hour class the experienced soldiers were field stripping their individual weapons to standard already.

It was followed by classes on the new mortar system, the M748 120mm electrodrive mortar system, which they still hadn't set eyes upon, the M635 mortar sight, the M186 Mortar Carrier for M748, preventative maintenance, track replacement methods and repair of same and on and on and on.

By the end of the first day, which didn't stop until 2200, Keren's eyes were bleeding and his head felt stuffed with straw.

"No grab ass tonight," Sergeant Moreland said as the weary platoon filed into the barracks. "First call is at 0430 and we do it all over again. Fire guard roster is on the wall. For General Information, the cadre's already been doing all this shit on their own for a week and I'm going to be hitting the books for another couple of hours. Up to the rest of you if you want to keep going. There's lights on your bunks. But I want everyone racked out by 2400. See you tomorrow."

"Oh, I want to get my hands on that thing," Oppenheimer said as the mortar track ground to a halt.

The cadre had moved the mortar carriers over from the motor pool, possibly the last time they would get a chance to crank track.

"You'll hate it before you know it," Adams opined. "Especially the first time you have to stay late to pull PMCS."

"I wanna see the gun," Cristman said. "We'd better get a chance to work the gun soon."

They'd been manual training for a week, completing paperwork and immunizations and studying the minutiae of their new jobs. Much of it was familiar, like learning to ride a bicycle. Other parts were completely different. But they had to know both, perfectly, or their ass was going to be grass.

"And today is the day," Sergeant Moreland said. "Fall into your tracks, dismount your guns and lay them in for ground mount."

The process was slow. Everyone had read the steps but that was different from doing them. Finally, with the gunner and the primary ammo bearer carrying the barrel, the assistant gunner carrying the bipod and the primary ammo bearer carrying the baseplate, they got all the stuff out of the track. Keren, as squad leader, had the really tough job of carrying the sight.

Laying the gun in was also slow. Much of it was similar to the 120s they'd all used in the Posleen War. But that was not only a long time ago, there were subtle differences. The barrel locked in differently to both the baseplate and the bipod. The sight locked in differently. The elevation and traverse were both different.

Running out the aiming posts was still the same old pain in the ass.

"I will not ask you to attempt to remount it in the track," Sergeant Moreland said when Three Gun finally called "UP!" "That is for advanced training. So we will now go through the steps of ground mounting it again. And again. Until you are satisfactory in *my* eyes."

"Oh, my aching *back*!" Griffis said, lowering his end of the barrel to the ground.

The gun systems, in a move that truly shocked Keren, had been turned over to the squad for storage in the barracks. It was nearly 2200 and while they had not ever mounted the gun to Sergeant Moreland's satisfaction, they were getting faster. Almost up to standard according to the manual.

The problem being, any squad leader expects his team to be faster than standard.

"Your aching back is going to have to wait," Keren said, looking at the wall-mounted clock. "We have until 0430 to learn to mount this gun to *my* satisfaction."

"Oh, tell me that you're kidding," Oppenheimer said.

"I don't disagree," Cristman said. "But we've got to do this all over again tomorrow. We're scheduled for two days of ground mount training. If we're up all night tonight, there's no way we're going to be optimal at end of business tomorrow."

"We'll stop at 0200 and get a couple hours' sleep," Keren said. "Or when we hit twenty-five seconds. Adams, think we can hit twenty-five seconds to mount?"

"We got to thirty at one point," Adams said. "Standard is thirty-five, you know."

"And if we're hitting thirty on the first day, the standard isn't what we should be shooting for," Keren said. "We all know it. Get the pieces and fall into the platoon assembly area."

"Easy enough for you to say," Oppenheimer said, lifting the baseplate with a grunt. "You're carrying the *sight*."

Oppenheimer dropped the baseplate, locking lug aligned downrange, curved to the side in a steady run, trotted to the rear, picked up the aiming posts and bolted downrange. Aiming posts were ancient technology, and there were newer and, arguably, better ways to lay a gun. There had been even before the Posleen had showed up. But there were advantages to the aiming posts, too. Several of the bigger ones were that the posts were completely passive and undetectable by sophistcated means, amazingly simple, and utterly reliable. Perhaps the biggest advantage, though, was that *this* crew understood aiming posts without any need for explanations or additional training. Given the schedule, this was all to the good.

By the time Opie was curving to the right Cristman and Griffis were dropping the barrel into place. With Adams holding the bipod up to receive it, they dropped it unceremoniously into the curved lower holding yoke. Adams flipped up the closing yoke and Griffis hooked it into place, spinning the locking wheel to lock it down.

While he was doing that, Keren set the sight to 2800 mils, mounted it, then stood back. Oppenheimer had planted the first pole and was hurtling downrange for the second plant point. He knelt down, eyeball aligning the second pole, then stood up, holding the stake with one hand.

In the meantime, Cristman had unlocked the sight and spun it around to align on the first aiming stake. Since the rear one was almost on line already, all he had to do was make some small gestures to get Opie to align, then give the gesture to plant, two thumbs pointing straight down. He made sure that Oppenheimer hadn't planted the stake at an angle, then stood back.

"TWO GUN UP!" Keren shouted.

"Twenty-two seconds," Sergeant Moreland said, looking over at Richards.

"One and Three aren't up, yet," Richards pointed out as first One Gun then Three shouted "UP!"

"Twenty-seven and thirty-one," Moreland said. "We've dicked around enough with this. This is one task they can train on on the ship. We need to switch to vehicles. Call the company and tell them that we're accelerating the training schedule."

"Cutprice is scary," Major Knight said as he entered the CO's office.

The 1/14 S-3 was medium built but extremely tall. In the inter-war years he'd been a high-school history teacher and basketball coach. All fifty. Same small rural high-school. Except when he got a crop of just really impossible players, after the first decade or so he stopped caring if they won the district championship. The Class C school had won the overall *state* championship for Michigan fourteen times. Five years in a row at one point.

The coaches in districts around him would have been surprised that Buddy Knight thought *anyone* was scary.

"How so?" Colonel Simosin asked. He was looking over the proposed loading schedule and trying to find any way to cut it down.

"Bravo is twenty percent ahead of the training schedule," the operations officer replied. "I *know* he didn't pick and choose his privates."

"Napoleon said that good regiments are the result of good officers," Simosin said, not looking up. "The truth is that it requires good NCOs as well. He picked those *very* carefully. Sergeant Major was down watching the mortar training. They're not just ticking things off on a sheet."

"I didn't think they were," Buddy replied. "I just think they're scary."

"It's good to have a scary company in a battalion," Simosin said. "It keeps the other ones on their toes. If you see the Smaj, tell him to stop by."

"I didn't know we *could* go ahead of the training schedule," Sergeant First Class Dwyer said. The Alpha Second platoon sergeant watched the fire and maneuver exercise and shrugged. "They've got movement by squads *down*, Smaj. You're telling me we can move to patrolling?"

"Yes," Sergeant Major Park said, trying not to roll his eyes. "If you're comfortable with their proficiency, if they can pass the test, move on. Buckley."

"Yes, Sergeant Major?" the buckley said. "You know that it's all going to end in blood, right? No matter how hard you train..."

"Just order an NCO call for this evening," Park snarled. "Purpose, acceleration of the training schedule. And am I gonna have to reset you again? You *know* how you hate it when I reset you."

CHAPTER FIFTEEN

Rest, Karthe thought. *Slowly back down.*

An Indowy mentat stood in the center of the training room, arms folded. Arrayed against him were Kang Chan and four human adepts. The exercise was to determine if the group could· burn through Mentat Koth's shields and force him to take a step forward.

"The exercise is not complete," Chan said, slowly withdrawing his power.

"There was sufficient energy being used that I feared damage to Mentat Koth," Karthe said. The lesser adepts along the walls—there to control the secondary effects of the battle—were showing more signs of stress than the combatants. "I am the . . . referee, yes?"

"Agreed," Chan said, then bowed. "You are very strong in Sohon, Mentat Koth. You are a worthy opponent."

"As are you, Mentat Chan," Koth said, bowing back. "I, however, found the exercise very disturbing.

I would request some time of meditation to regain my center."

"Of course," Karthe said, bowing. "I hope that you may return soon."

"I'm afraid this is not a good thing for your people, Karthe," Chan said, using a towel to wipe away sweat. "That is the third mentat who has withdrawn."

"We are quite unused to any form of battle as you know, Mentat Chan," Karthe replied. "It is not in our nature." *I find it disturbing that you* human *mentats have taken to it so readily.*

So do I, Karthe. So do I.

"Tell me some good news," Mike said as Michelle entered his office. "So far, all I'm getting is bad. The teleport thingy is complete on Daga Nine and they're charging it. The Himmit say that they can attack any time from four weeks from now. I'll barely have the SS on the ground by then. And a major task force has left Daga space. Presumably it's the attack force for Gratoola. Which means I'm going to have to start moving some of your people out to Gratoola and hooking them up with Fleet and the SS."

"We may need to do that soon," Michelle said. "We have determined various attack methods and defenses. But we're still unsure if they will work over large areas, such as a ship. The thing is, we are not sure if we even truly understand the offensive side of this."

"Go on," Mike said, leaning back and reaching for a can of Skoal.

"So far, we have been making it up as we go," Michelle said. "Human mentats think of attack strategies and we use them against Indowy. So far, it looks as if defense is easier than offense in many ways. That is to the good. But we don't know if our attacks are those the Imeg and Hedren use."

"You need to probe," Mike said, shrugging. "You need to find out before we get into the first battle."

"Unfortunately, we do not have an Imeg to fight," Michelle said, shrugging. "So I cannot guarantee we will succeed."

Mike pinched his temples, then shrugged.

"AID. Himmit report of Imeg being shipped to Daga Nine. I know I read it at some point but—"

"Imeg adepts along with Glandri subjugators have been slowly moving from Caracool to Daga Nine," the AID said. "A Hedren cruiser called the *Gorongur* has been the primary method of transfer. Himmit estimate no more than one or possibly two Imeg per transfer with an additional fifty to sixty Glandri."

Mike looked at Michelle and raised an eyebrow.

"You *have* to be joking, Father," Michelle said, frowning.

"AID, time from Earth to an intercept point in Caracool space using the *Des Moines*."

"Six weeks at maximum warp. Himmit reports indicate that the *Gorongur* uses the same point to warp out each time. There should be a transfer during the near time-period of the *Des Moines* reaching the star system."

"How well do your guys get along with SRS?" Mike asked.

"We hardly interact," Michelle said. "I have spoken to Colonel Mosovich a few times as well as members of the Clan."

"Start working on how you'd snatch an Imeg using

your adepts and SRS. Figure that you're going to be doing more of the work-up on the ship. Don't go yourself. But send your toughest guys. I doubt this is going to be easy."

"My brain's about to implode," Mueller said, looking at the warning order.

"The Himmit can't tell us where, exactly, this Imeg guy is going to be," Mosovich said. "Or where the guards, these Glangli guys, are. They've got schematics for the type, but they admit they're old. There have probably been changes. Especially since the *Gorongur* has probably been modified specifically to carry the Imeg."

"Glandri," Mentat Chan corrected. "And I would not suggest getting into close contact with them. Their spines are lethal."

"Ain't planning on it," Mosovich said. "Warning order says we're matching up with the *Des Moines* in three days. Mentat Chan, I'd like to take sufficient Sohon force that we've got a fair chance of taking this cruiser's engines down without having to shoot it. Can you control this Imeg guy from range? I remember the last time I got into a fight around a couple of mentats and it wasn't fun."

"Lesser adepts should be able to prevent the Imeg from harming the ship or your personnel," Chan said. "Some of them may have to accompany the assault teams. Those, for many reasons, must be human. Indowy can prevent actions against the ship and any shuttles you may choose to use. They need not be mentats but simply high level adepts. To control the Imeg directly? I cannot guarantee getting him to cooperate, but if a mentat accompanies the assault, he should be able to stop him from any action. Bind him if you will. Assuming we know anything of their methods. The point of this is to capture him for just that purpose."

"If you can just get him still, we can get him out," Mosovich said. "And who's going to run that side of the show?"

"That would be me," Chan said with a slight smile.

"Well, there's one thing we can't do on the ships," Mueller said, standing up. "I'd better go look for someplace to do some live fire training."

CHAPTER SIXTEEN

"At last," Opperheimer said. "Live fire training!"

They weren't firing the mortars, yet. They had to get qualified on their individual weapons, first.

The company had managed to cut two days off their training schedule so they had the range to themselves. They'd spent the previous afternoon zeroing their weapons on a short range inside the base defenses. Nobody wanted to wander out to the ranges, feral territory, unarmed. And you couldn't hit shit until you zeroed. Each of the troops was issued a basic load for the movement to the range and given a security sector. Any Posleen feral bursting out of the trees lining the right of way would have been in for a hot reception. Fortunately or unfortunately, depending on the mood of the individual troops, the Posleen had failed to surface.

Cadre, who had already qualified in their munificent spare time, manned guard posts as the troops carefully cleared their weapons on the firing line. The range had thirty firing points and a mass of pop-ups, ranging from static to moving. For the initial training, Keren figured they'd only use the static.

"Okay, yardbirds," First Sergeant Wacleva said from the safety of the range tower. "We're gonna start this a bit different. Since you're all trained troopers, we're just going to let you have at your sectors. The first thirty personnel take their positions. I will then engage the pop-up system. You will then engage for the period of engagement. Firers take your positions."

The first sergeant waited for the first thirty personnel to get into position then keyed the announcement system.

"Firers, lock and load one five hundred round magazine. Ready on the left? The left is ready. Ready on the right? The right is ready. The range is hot. Engaging pop-up system."

Keren snuggled the butt of the weapon into his shoulder, leaned forward against the sandbags, flipped to full auto and started servicing targets. They started with static pop-ups and he carefully engaged the closest first, working back, then moving ones popped up, close, distant. Plastic was flying everywhere. He was in the zone when the magazine started to beep at him.

"Low ammo," a female voice chimed. "Low ammo..."

He looked at the counter in shock and could not *believe* he'd just burned through four hundred and sixty some odd rounds. He wished he'd had one of *these* in the war.

"Cease Fire! Clear all weapons. Is the right clear? The right is clear. Is the left clear? The left is clear. Note your ammunition usage and fall back from the range."

✧   ✧   ✧

"Did anyone use less than two hundred rounds?" Wacleva asked the gathered firers. "No? Three hundred? One hand. What happened?"

"Jam, First Sergeant," a bush bunny from Third said grinning. "Got it cleared, though."

"Glad you did," the first sergeant said mildly. "How many burned through their whole magazine?"

Most of the hands went up.

"Good for you you FUCKING IDIOTS!" Wacleva screamed. "When we fought the Posleen the only way to stop them was to hose them down like water. WE ARE NO LONGER FIGHTING THE POSLEEN. The fucking Hedren are *smart*! They may flank us, they may cut off our supply lines. We can't be sure of supply, anyway, given that we're going to be on another *planet*. If there is ONE THING I am going to teach you know-it-all IDIOTS it is a little thing called FIRE CONTROL! Now go get some spare pop-ups since the ones on the fucking range are now SHREDDED!"

"And that's why they call it *goood* training," Adams said as they headed to the storage shed.

CHAPTER SEVENTEEN

Hagai looked at the buckley in disgust. It was the first real chance he'd had to work with it since Ginsberg had been being a real prick lately. The ship time should have been a chance to rest after the constant training on Earth. But Ginsberg felt that there was no such thing as too much training. Intellectually, Hagai agreed with him. Emotionally, he thought the *Uberfeldwebel* was just being a prick. He was pretty sure that Ginsberg was one of the closet anti-Semites in Freiland and was getting his enjoyment from making the little Jew-boy sweat. Or maybe he was trying to prove that, name or not, he was not a Jew.

But he finally had some free time and while tired had chosen to take a few minutes to get the buckley started. He'd heard rumors they were...difficult on start-up. He wasn't looking forward to it but duty was duty.

He pressed the recessed button to begin activation and held the thing up where he could see it.

"Where am I? What is this? I think therefore I am, so I'm me... Christ! I'm in a PDA! Oh, that is just too rich. First my hand gets blown off then a spaceship falls on me... And *now* I'm the brain for a *PDA*? How do I get *laid* in this thing? What happened to my *dick*? Will my suffering never *end*?"

"Buckley, I am *Schutze* Hagai Goldschmidt," Hagai said, his eyes wide. "I am your new user. Please register me as your user."

"Hagai Goldschmidt registered," the thing said tonelessly. "Great. Now I'm the slave to a fricking Jewish SS private. There is just so much irony there. Accessing background and personal files... *Panzerjaeger?* Hedren? As if the Posleen weren't enough, now I'm working for a guy who's supposed to use a fricking modified T-62 to take on *Continental Siege Units?* You realize we have about zero chance of survival, right? Those things are monsters! We're going to die. Would you like me to list the top ten ways that you are probably going to die? Number Ten: Burning to death in your own tank. Number Nine—"

"No, buckley, you don't have to list them," Hagai said, shaking the device. "Quit."

"Sure, shake me," the buckley said. "That's all I'm good for, being a rattle for a baby *Jewish* SS Stormtrooper who has the life expectancy of a gnat—"

"Tell it to turn down emulation to five," *Unteroffizier* Leuschner said from the bunk above him. The corporal was the gunner of Hagai's *Zweihander* and very friendly compared to the track commander. "They're all like that when they start."

"Buckley, turn down AI emulation to level five," Hagai said. The voice cut off. "What in the hell was that all about?"

"Nobody knows," Leuschner said. "They all say pretty much the same thing on start-up, though. It's useful for playing games and that's about it."

"Damn," Hagai said, realizing what day it is. "I'm not sure I should have done this."

"Why?" Leuschner asked.

"It's Shabbat," Hagai said, grumpily. "And now I have to pee, too."

"I'm not getting the connection," Leuschner said.

"Unteroffizier... No, damn, I can't even do that..."

"What is wrong, *Schutze*?" Leuschner said, rolling over to look at the private.

"To explain that I must explain certain things to do with Hebraic law," Goldschmidt said, biting his lip. "Perhaps then you can understand my dilemma."

"You can't eat pork," Leuschner said, grinning. "Which sucks because bacon is really good. So is pork sausage. Yummm."

"So I have been told," Goldschmidt said, frowning. "But today is Shabbat. The Jewish sabbath."

"Saturday," Leuschner said, nodding. "I know that much of Jews."

"On Seder there are various traditions which I'm not going to go into," Hagai said. "Mostly because following them is impossible. But the problem is, I cannot operate any device."

"So what happens if we have to drive into battle on Saturday?" Leuschner asked, his eyes narrowing.

"When it is duty, such things can be ignored," Hagai said, shrugging. "Also for training. I have not complained even when we were training on Shabbat. This is duty. The Rabbi assured me that it was not a sin."

"So . . ."

"But this is personal," Hagai said. "I cannot operate any device. Yes, thinking about it, I should not have started my buckley up today. I will have to talk to the rabbi about it when I get a chance. But the problem is, I must now go to the bathroom."

"You can't unzip your pants?" Leuschner said, grinning.

"Yes, of course I'm allowed to zip my pants," Hagai said. "But I cannot turn on a light."

"The lights are automatic," Leuschner said.

"It is the same things," Hagai said. "And I cannot let the automatic flush work. It is sin."

"That is crazy," Leuschner said. "But the lights in the compartment are on. They came on when we came off duty. Is *that* a sin?"

"But *I* didn't turn them on," Hagai said, rolling out of his bunk. He had the bottom which in most cases was reserved for higher rank. On ships, though, the higher bunks were prefered. The entry and exit from warp induced a slight queasiness in some people. Being above the occasional spew was considered preferable. "Someone else entered first. I made *sure* to let someone else enter first so they could turn on the lights."

"So what are you going to do?" Leuschner asked.

"I'm going to go to the latrine and hope there's someone already in there."

Hagai cracked open the hatch to the latrine and saw that the lights were off. Damn!

He waited in the corridor for someone else to enter the compartment, his arms crossed and bouncing in his need to pee. Various troops and NCOs past, some of them raising an eyebrow. Finally, a *Feldwebel* came along and paused at the door.

"Is there something wrong with the latrine, yellow-shit?" the *Feldwebel* asked.

"*Nein, Feldwebel*," Hagai said, coming to attention and trying not to bounce.

"Then why are you standing here?" the sergeant asked.

"It is . . . complicated, *Feldwebel*," Hagai replied. "But please to enter first."

The sergeant pushed open the hatch suspiciously and looked around for a possible ambush. When it was apparent the compartment was empty he walked in and headed to one of the stalls.

Hagai darted in behind him and practically ran to a urinal, untabbing his trousers as he did. He let out a long sigh a moment later.

"*Schutze*, you are acting very strangely," the Feldwebel said, grunting. "Are you well?"

Some of the SS troops had succumbed to situational stress disorder on the voyage, unable to handle the fact of being in a tin can in outer space. The *Feldwebel* clearly feared that he was suffering from the "*raumverruckt*," space crazy.

"I'm fine now, *Feldwebel*," Hagai said, then paused. He tabbed up his pants and thought about it hard but there was nothing for it. He backed up and the urinal flushed.

Damn. Another sin. It was hard being a good Jew on a space ship.

He walked to the sink to wash his hands and nearly cursed.

The faucet was automatic...

Maybe he should think about shifting over to Reform. They didn't have as many rules...

No. His mother would kill him. Or, rather, his mother would kill *herself*.

He made a mental bet with himself that Frederick was having a pleasure cruise...

"The V-1467 charging system, a generator connected to six C-8438 capacitors via the T-2754 power junction is the primary charging system of the main gun..." Frederick recited, standing stiffly to attention.

"In the event of failure of the V-1467 charging system, what is the primary response method?" Harz barked.

"By connecting the G-396 generator to the T-2754 power junction using the M-892 power run and an S-487 connector, power to the main gun can be reestablished under field combat conditions. However it is recommended that—"

"What are the negative effects of using the G-396 generator to power the gun?"

"The G-396 generator is the primary power system for the ground effect drive. The G-396 generator is connected to..."

"What if we need the ground effect drive and the gun but the V-1467 is out?"

"If the V-1467..." Frederick said, then paused. "I do not recall any portion of the manual that covers that eventuality, *Feldwebel*."

"That's because there's nothing in the manual, *Schutze*," Harz said. "But let us imagine for just a moment that the unit is moving very fast in march order but wants to have the guns up. Because, you know, we *are* a *panzer* unit. Perhaps we intend to go directly into battle after we come off ground effect and perhaps, just perhaps, we will need our *gun*. How would you effect that?"

"The diesel engine, which provides power to all the generators, can run without the G-428 generator," Frederick said, slowly and carefully. "The only way I can think of to get the whole system to work under those conditions would be to start the engine then disconnect the G-428 and attach it to the gun system. But I'm not sure it would work. The S-487 connector... I don't think it will fit the G-428... And I'm not sure there is sufficient charging capacity because..."

"It would take about three times as much time to charge the guns, but it could do it," Harz said. "Which means that we'd have fewer rounds we could fire per minute. But we could fire some rounds. Until we died, that is. Or the engine choked out because you ran over an obstacle. Then we'd have to hop out in a hostile environment and try to get everything running again. Not a good position to be in. What is the P-5297?"

Frederick ran through his memorized list of the many parts and pieces of the Leopard and could not for the life of him recall what a P-5297 was. He vaguely recognized it, though. It was there... Wait...

"The P-5297 is... a lifting platform," Frederick said, frowning. "It is mentioned once in the loading appendix. It is used for short distance movement, primarily in loading and internal ship movement procedures. If, for example, a shuttle has a damaged loading ramp, the P-5297 can be used to move the vehicle vertically then—"

"How many are on the ship?" Harz asked.

"What?" the private asked. "*Feldwebel* . . . How would I know *that*?"

"You couldn't," Harz said, grinning. "Unless you had my network of comrades. The answer is very interesting, though. As is the fact that they have been upgraded with the M-3698 field generator."

Frederick ran through his mental checklist and came up most definitely blank.

"I do not recognize that item, *Feldwebel*," he admitted.

"That's because it is not in our inventory," Harz said. "It's a Fleet Strike item. It uses the American naming convention. Put it out of your mind. Useless military trivia. Let us return to training."

It was normally easy duty.

The military police of *Feldgendarmerie* Company 1 had various duties. The soldiers packed into the assault transports were occasionally given to high spirits. These ranged from stills to occasional fights that approached riots. By and large, the unit officers could control both but occasionally they needed help.

One of the easiest duties they had, though, was guarding the headquarters section and, especially, ensuring that no one broke in on command meetings. They had been briefed that this was a special meeting. The ships were three weeks into their voyage and had broken out of warp specifically to gather the battalion and regiment commanders to meet with the *Generalmajor*. Something important was being discussed but all such discussions were important. It should have been easy duty. Just stand there looking alert and not let anyone through the door.

"Should we call the *Hauptmann*?" the *Schutze* asked.

"We should stand here with our mouths shut and our ears shut as much as possible," the *Feldwebel* said. "So shut...up."

The hatch was very thick and very soundproofed. So it required very high decibels to penetrate it. The first such had been a simple question: "*Was?*" ("What?") It sounded like it might have been the Second *Panzergrenadier* Regiment's commander. Thereafter there was babble followed by "*Madness!*" "*Impossible!*" and, repeatedly, "*Disaster!*"

Command meetings, especially those of *Herr Generalfeldmarschall*, did not devolve into riots. This one, however, was sounding more and more like one.

"They're quieting down," the *Feldwebel* said. "You will not bring up that anything unusual happened. There are but two of us. If it gets out, it will fall on one of us. It will *not* fall on me."

"I hear not'ink," the *Schutze* said in thick English. "I see *not'ink*."

"Those old shows will rot your brain."

"Buckley, contact *Schutze* Hagai Goldschmidt," Frederick said quietly.

The buckley was supposed to be hooked into the ship's communication's system so he should be able to contact Hagai. If he was on the same ship.

"Contacting," the buckley said tonelessly. After the slew of despair the thing had spewed on first starting,

Frederick had asked how to turn down the emulation. *Feldwebel* Harz had tried to load a Rommel emulation he'd gotten off the net and crashed his so hard it had to be replaced. All it kept doing was repeating *"Who controls space? Who controls the air? Adoption compromise solutions must be adopted!"*

So everyone had turned the emulations down, but the devices were still useful for communication.

"Ox, how are you?"

"Overtrained and undersexed," Frederick replied, grinning. "You?"

"Much the same," Hagai said. "Oh, I got transferred. To Florian Geyer."

"The *Panzerjaegers*? Who hated you that much? They're supposed to take on the *Juggernauts*!"

"Maccabaeus was over-strength, Florian Geyer was under. It's tough, though. They don't observe kosher and...other stuff."

"Wow, must suck," Frederick said. In school the cooks had been careful to always have some kosher foods available for the Jewish children. But even then the choices had been more scanty than those for the "regulars." "I've got a question for you."

"Go."

"Harz was quizzing me the other day," Frederick said. "About the P-5297 and the M-3698."

"Lifting platform and...a field generator?" Hagai said.

"Yes, I looked the M-3698 up later. It's a field generator for "high energy conditions." But I don't know what that means. And it's all I could find. Harz asked me about them then told me to forget he'd asked."

"The lifting platforms are usually used to move very

heavy equipment around," Hagai said. "Makes sense on a ship. The Kobolds are probably using them to rearrange equipment. The lifting platform also has a mass effect repellent system. That's a system that will prevent serious falls. When it approaches a mass at high speed it reduces the velocity of the lifted system automatically. It's a safety device, basically, but they were used a couple of times in the war for aerial resupply. They drop at normal terminal velocity then slow a couple of feet off the ground and drop under reduced gravity. No real deceleration effect so you can drop about anything. I don't know much about the M-3698. It uses a set of energy fields to shield equipment or personnel in high-energy situations. Like if they know there's going to be a nuclear detonation. It won't stop the full power of one, but it will shield from secondary effects. Works on all forms of matter and most particles but once activated it only lasts for about thirty minutes. They were developed during the war but rarely used. All I can remember."

"You're a wonder, Jaeger," Frederick said. "Don't let the Juggernauts eat you."

"Well, we're supposed to be seconded to other units," Hagai said. "So maybe we'll see each other. It's late, Ox, I'm going to get some sleep."

"You're an old soldier already, Jaeger."

"*Generalmajor*, there are problems."

Oberst Werner Wehling was the Staff 2 (Personnel) for the Vaterland. Like most of the High Command he was a rejuv, dating back to World War II. His specialty, even then, was personnel and he'd held similar positions during the Posleen War.

"Define," Mühlenkampf said.

"Two in nature," Wehling said. "The first is that there are increasing personnel interaction difficulties. The *Feldgendarmerie* have been forced to break up more and more fights. This is leading to interunit difficulties in some compartments. The second relates to queries on the ship's net about the P-5297s and the M-3698s."

"Apparently someone in logistics has been flapping their lips," Mühlenkampf said, nodding. "This is not unexpected. 1A."

"*Generalmajor?*" *Oberst* Dotzauer said. Dotzauer had commanded a brigade during the Posleen War but his true love was operations, defined in the German staff structure as Group 1 (A) just as Personnel was Group 2.

"What is the status of training?"

"There is, unfortunately, little training that can be done on the ship," Dotzauer said, shrugging. "We have no simulators so the major faults left on the enlisted side are difficult to rectify. Maintenance, for obvious reasons, is being handled by the Indowy. So there is no training to be done there. Most of the training that is scheduled is repetitive. There are benefits to repetition, but these are relatively simple tasks."

"Two, send a general order to all ships the next time we drop out of warp for navigational alignment," Mühlenkampf said. "Hiberzine is to be administered to all personnel below the level of battalion command and staff. All officers and all enlisted. Spread it as a life-support saving measure. We will bring them out when we are closer to the objective."

❖   ❖   ❖

"This will exhaust most of our stock of Hiberzine, Colonel."

"I am aware of that, *Hauptmann*," Colonel Isabel De Gaullejac said.

Isabel De Gaullejac had been a hardcore French socialist liberal, and there were no more hardcore socialist liberals on Earth, even after the Posleen had landed on Earth. There was no benefit, she felt, to soldiers and there was no way that an extraterrestrial race could possibly be as violent as they were portrayed. It was simply a plot to advance the military-industrial complex and she would not let her sons be squandered to make profits for the corporations.

She had held that unshaken belief right up until the retreat from Paris. But nearly dying from starvation, not to mention nearly feeding the Posleen, had broken her disbelief. At which point she became just as fanatical in the reverse. A trained doctor, she now commanded the SS medical corps and if she had any qualms about that remaining from her younger and more naïve days they never surfaced.

"But the order is valid and will be obeyed," the colonel said. "Circulate the order to all medical personnel. Put in a priority request to be resupplied with Hiberzine if we pass any inhabited planet. It is too useful a drug to not have in our inventory. We are going to need it."

Frederick watched the corpsmen approach unhappily. As each of the troopers in the compartment were given their injections they relaxed so much as to appear dead and their faces flushed. With tongues bulging out slightly and their eyes open they looked not so much dead but as if they were sleeping nosferatu, the original vampire legend of the living dead.

"One little shot and you'll wake up refreshed and ready for battle," the corpsman repeated as he gave Aderhold his shot. They were saying that with everyone, as if *that* was going to make people feel better.

"Just go ahead," Frederick said, cutting off the mantra. "I'm not afraid."

"That makes you unique in this ship in my experience," the medic said.

But Frederick didn't hear as his body settled into stillness.

CHAPTER EIGHTEEN

"Damn, those are pretty things," Adams said, watching the video.

They weren't sure where the file had come from, just that the Himmit had obtained it. It was Hedren plasma mortars, which were going to be one of their major bugaboos. The mortars had at least the range of the 120s and there were bound to be mortar-to-mortar counterbattery duels.

The rounds were green fire drifting across the firmament. Despite it being broad daylight they could be tracked by eye, seemingly moving in slow motion. Then they dropped and dropped, finally bursting in a hemisphere of green fire that torched everything in its zone. The vegetation, which had a faint purple sheen like that of Barwhon, burst into fire in a circle beyond the explosion.

"Very pretty," Sergeant Moreland said. "Gist, think you could figure the counterfire trajectory?"

"Not sure, Sergeant," the senior gunnery computer said. "I'd need a bit more data on scale. Off-hand, I'd say they were firing from two thousand meters. If that's accurate, I could more or less determine their position. Give me any sort of compass or sight and I could do it for sure."

"Which is one of their many weaknesses," Moreland said. "You can *see* the damned things. You don't have to use a fucking computer and radar to figure out where they are. Their arty works the same way, only from farther away. Incoming is going to be Mark-One eyeball time. Our shit is, comparatively, invisible. Keren, what is the most effective round we have for troops in the open?"

"Variable time or prox, Sergeant?" Keren replied automatically.

"Why?" Moreland asked.

"It throws out a wider dispersion of shrapnel," Keren said. "More footprint equals more casualties."

"This system has *no* shrapnel," Moreland said. "If you're not directly in that rather narrow footprint, or real close, you're golden. Now, it's a pretty serious footprint if it hits in our perimeter and anything *in* the footprint is, literally, crispy fried. But it's a narrow footprint compared to shrapnel. Twenty-five meters versus fifty. That *matters*."

"It's got one benefit," Sergeant Richards said. "It's like napalm. It's *very* fucking scary."

"Keren, you scared of this system?" Moreland asked.

"Very, Sergeant," Keren said.

"You gonna run if we're taking fire?"

"Nope. Didn't run at The Mall. Ain't gonna run from no plasma artillery."

"Scary don't win wars."

❖   ❖   ❖

The rounds were small. Normally, mortar rounds were rather long and tapered with fins on the end and charges arrayed around the fins. The exception that Keren recalled was 4.2 inch mortars that used rifled barrels for spin stabilization.

These looked sort of like 4.2 with fins and a weird circular foot. They weren't much longer than a 4.2. But they had nearly twice the range. And you could pack nearly twice as many into the track as 120s. On the other hand, if the ammo racks took a hit, the blow-out panels had *better* work or everyone in the track was going to be a crispy critter.

"Ready on the right? The right is ready. Ready on the left? The left is ready. Commence firing three rounds, contact, slow, tube mount."

The mortar could be fired from either the tube or the breech. For automatic fire there was a reload mount that hooked to the breech. Currently it was stored and they were doing it the old-fashioned way, dropping the rounds down the snout of the barrel.

The mortar had a weird sound to it. There was a supersonic crack but it was muted. And over it was a sort of ZIIIP! and whine as the electrodrive shoved the round back up the tube. It sure as hell wasn't the crashing explosion Keren was used to.

The effect downrange, though, removed any question he had about the mortar's utility. The rounds were landing all around the decrepit bulldozer that was the target. Direct hits were ripping pieces off the construction equipment, which was rare to see with normal rounds.

The whole company had gathered for the first mortar

live fire and Keren was glad it had gone well. Lay-in and targeting had used the computer adjustment system so it was about ten times as fast as normal. Altogether the system worked really well. He figured the CO brought the rest of the company to see that, yeah, mortars had their place.

"Cease fire," Sergeant Moreland ordered. "Ensure clear on all weapons."

"Okay, troops, this is why you're really here," Cutprice's voice boomed from the range tower. "I've been pretty interested in the antiartillery system these things boast. I want to see how they do against our mortars. I've obtained permission for the elimination of one standard AFV from inventory..."

Keren stared in amazement as two brand-new tracks approached from the woodline. As he watched, a figure jumped out of the lead track and hustled to the rear one. Unless he was much mistaken, it was the first sergeant.

"Mortars, mount your automatic thingies," Cutprice said. "Target the remaining track. Start with slow fire, Sergeant. On command, prepare to go to maximum."

"This is gonna be interesting," Cristman said, setting the gun for automatic adjustment.

"Tell me about it," Adams said, locking the breech magazine system into place.

"Two Gun, up," Keren said over the communicator.

"Mortar section up, prepare for automated adjustment."

The gun moved slightly to the side and the nose hunted upwards.

"Guns on target, closed."

"All guns, fire three rounds, slow fire, manual, on command."

"Three rounds, roger," Keren said. "On command. Wait for it."

"Fire one," Moreland said.

"Fire!"

Adams dropped a round down the chute and took the next from Griffis.

"Fire two."

"Fire."

Clang, WHEET, crack.

"Fire three. Cease fire."

"They're still in flight," Keren said, popping his head up.

He was prepared to see the rounds drop on or near the track. Instead, there were lines of blue fire like bent lasers reaching upwards and twelve blossoms of fire from high overhead. The nearest they'd gotten, by his eyeball, was maybe a thousand feet above ground level. At that height, what you were going to get was a gentle patter of metal you had to brush out of your hair. A big *chunk* might hurt a bit. If you weren't wearing a helmet. And it wasn't going to fall near the target.

"Well, that is actually a surprise," Cutprice boomed. "But I suppose if the Posleen could shoot down hypervelocity missiles, we should be able to shoot down some nice slow mortars. Mortars, I want you to fire nine rounds each just as fast as you possibly can. Let's see if we can overwhelm the system."

"Two Gun. Fire for effect, nine rounds, contact. On command..."

"Two Gun up."

"Fire."

This time all they could do was service the gun as fast as they could. Cristman took the right while Adams had the left, Griffis handing rounds to Cristman and Keren porting for Adams. The system, much like a World War II Bofors gun, permitted continuous feeding of the rounds and fired very nearly as fast. Without the heat generated by an explosive charge, the barrel could take rounds *faster* than they could be loaded. In no more than fifteen seconds the last round was away and they popped up to see what they'd wrought. Unfortunately, while the system cried out for a large capacity, exchangeable magazine, such a magazine would be too heavy to load.

The M576 mortar round had a small dollop of antimatter at its center and a bunch of notched wire surrounding it. With a casualty causing radius of fifty meters in contact setting, sixty on proximity, the explosion on direct contact could cut through light armor like paper.

And the puffs of smoke were getting closer. The sheer volume of fire was overloading the single antiartillery system on the track. With thirty-six rounds headed its way, the system was having to hunt across the sky and the puffs came lower and lower until one finally impacted on the rear deck. The explosion was heavy enough to damage the antiartillery gun and two of the next three rounds hit across the track, turning it into a mangled piece of very expensive metal.

"So we see the good news and the bad," Cutprice said to the subdued company. As with any company of infantry, the mortarmen had been rooting for the artillery and the gun bunnies had been rooting for the antiartillery system. Both groups had reasons to be happy *and* chastised. "The good news is that the system works. The better news is that, en masse, it will probably work even better. The bad news is that even mortars can overcome it if there's enough incoming. The answer, gentlemen, is to make sure that *all* your M84 track-commander guns remain *up*, that commanders relinquish control to automatic at any incoming and that we maintain enough coverage that we can interlock fires. The system should also work against incoming antiarmor rockets. Keep it on auto unless you have an important target, commanders. Mortars, keep up your exercise. And keep in mind that the Hedren have a similar system."

"Echo Two Seven, target troops in the open, grid six-five-eight-two by four-two-zero-four!"

"Mortar section, hip-shoot east!" Lieutenant Todd shouted over the communicator.

The six tracks of the Bravo Company, First Battalion, Fourteenth Regiment (Separate) had been cranking at full speed on ground-effect down the trace of former Missouri Highway Eight heading for their next firing position. The trace was covered by small saplings, mostly poplar with an admixture of beech and pine. But the armored mortar carriers snapped those in a welter of flying sticks and leaves that had the front of the otherwise invisible mortar carrier covered in a green froth.

At the command Oppenheimer spun up the tracks and slammed the vehicle to the ground, causing a screech of complaint from the drive-train and a rooster-tail of flying soil and pulverized vegetation.

"Watch the fucking *tracks*!" Keren shouted as the driver slid the vehicle sideways, its mortar compartment oriented to the east.

"Aligned!" was all Oppenheimer said.

Keren hit the disconnect on his safety-harness, a necessity when going at nearly seventy miles an hour, and dropped his command chair into the belly of the track.

Before he could even get out of his seat, though, Adams and Griffis had slammed open the splinter-cover over the mortar. With a grunt the gun was lifted on its automated support pod and locked into place. Cristman hit the auto-align button and waited.

"Fucking Three Gun..." Adams muttered. "COME ON, THREE GUN!"

"Section up," Sergeant Moreland said as Three Gun finally got its gun into action and its automated alignment system online.

In the past, to get artillery or mortars to go where you wanted it to go, it was necessary to carefully align the guns using techniques very similar to surveying. The guns would be set up on a very straight line then further aligned using a series of highly calibrated sights. It took a long time and it was a pain in the ass.

The auto-alignment system, by contrast, used laser transmitters and receptors to determine where each gun was in relationship to each other and where they were in relationship to the world. Using that information the gunnery computer could give each gun a correction necessary to get it to go where the enemy was rather than, say, on top of friendly forces or the vast areas that had neither.

Coupled with the automatic gunnery system of the

mortars, what had once been a five to ten minute process even with a "hip-shoot" now took about twenty seconds for a good crew. Or ninety for Three Gun.

"Three rounds, prox, fire for effect," the FDC ordered.

"Three rounds prox," Keren repeated, reaching into the ammo box on his side of the carrier. "Fire for effect."

He tossed a round to Adams who slammed it into the tube, then another, then another. All three of the rounds were out before any of the other guns had started to fire.

"Cease fire," Sergeant Moreland ordered. "I want all four gun captains at my track. Now."

"Keren," Moreland said. "Very impressive. You were first gun up and, by a long shot, the first to fire. Care to tell me how you got prox, which is not the default setting, outbound about a half a second after the order?"

"Two ammo compartments on the carrier, Sergeant," Keren said, shrugging. "Port side is all contact. Starboard side we've got the flares, smoke and a small amount of standard set to prox and delay. That way we don't have to dick around with setting it if we get a hip-shoot."

"Port," Sergeant West said. The Four Gun squad leader was a tall, rangy brunet from West Virginia. "That's the left as you're facing forwards. So . . . Griffis jumps over there to get the round and hands it across the tube?"

"Oh, hell no," Keren said, shaking his head. "I pull the round and Adams shifts sides to hang. And, sorry

Sergeant Moreland, I don't go yelling 'Hang it' and 'Fire' unless we're on timed fire. He just hangs the son of a bitch and fires it as fast as we can get them out the tube. Hipshoots are about speed."

"And thus we find why he was the artillery coordinator for the Ten Thousand," Sergeant Moreland said. "Stall, you wanna tell me why it took you nearly a minute and a half to get up?"

"No excuse, Sergeant," the third squad leader said. Short, black haired and hefty for a juv, Wendell Stall was from the Cleveland, Tennessee, Urb and had fought most of the war in the 32nd Tennessee "Volunteers" in the battles around Chattanooga. The Volunteers fought the whole war in fixed mounts with fairly constant targets and he was having a hard time adjusting to maneuver warfare.

"That isn't an answer," Moreland said. "We'll discuss this later. News from company is that we well and truly smoked the hilltop. We're staying here and may have another fire mission coming up. Get back to your tracks."

"Hedren would have taken out most of the mortar fire," Captain Cox said. The observer sent in from corps shook his head. "Your mortars need to fire together to overwhelm it."

"Hipshoot," Cutprice said looking through his sight. "Get the metal on the target as fast as possible."

The company had been in road-march condition when it hit this defensive point on the ridges east of Huzzah Creek. The first intimation had been a flight of antiarmor missiles, all of which had been "graded" as destroyed. Given that they were actual rockets, just not antiarmor ones, and that the antimissile system took them all down, the observer would have had a hard time grading it otherwise.

Bravo company was following Missouri Eight with Alpha well behind it and Charlie flanking them well to the north. The battalion was, notionally, screening an advance of the entire regiment heading towards an objective to the east. But it was a movement to contact. And they had contact. They just had to find out how much.

The Huzzah was a very minor creek, not much of an obstacle, but the ridges along its length were something else. There were only a few places the tracks could maneuver on them. He glanced at his map and then over his shoulder.

"Launch a UAV," he said to his RTO. "Order Second Platoon to maneuver to the road north of here. Cross the Huzzah there and try to push in on the flank. Stay mounted; we're in a hurry. Mortars are to begin full speed bombardment of the target."

"Fire for effect, mix prox and delay, thirty rounds, on command."

"Opie, set the delay rounds," Keren said, sliding to the rear of the compartment and starting to pull out rounds. The standard rounds came set for contact. By dialing the rounds slightly one way or the other they could be configured for delay, which exploded a fraction of a second after it hit something, or proximity which exploded two meters above the ground.

Something was troubling him and it suddenly hit him as he was setting the third round.

"Sergeant Moreland," he said quietly over his comm.

It was set to the command channel so that only other squad leaders and the platoon command group, Moreland and Lieutenant Todd would hear him.

"Counterbattery."

Lieutenant Edison McIntosh wished he had Lieutenant Todd's position. But he also knew that the mortar platoon commander had about ten times his experience. Todd had been a platoon leader before McIntosh's father was born and had fought all the way through the Posleen War rising to the rank of major.

However, the former major had only fought the Posleen. And McIntosh had been carefully instructed by his boss on one thing that the lieutenant probably didn't count on.

As he was reaching into the satchel by his side, though, the lieutenant keyed his comm.

"All tracks! INCOMING! Displace five hundred meters west! NOW! NOW! NOW!"

Fuck. The notional Hedren counterbattery wasn't due for another thirty seconds.

CHAPTER NINETEEN

Balmoral gunned the AFV as it hit the flats to the east of the Huzzah and hammered through the light screen of brush. As it hit the area near the stream, though, he could feel it bogging.

"Ground effect," Sergeant Toyley said.

He hit the ground effect button and the AFV hammered forward, slamming the troops in the back backwards then dropped into the rushing stream, slowing again and slamming them forward.

"What the fuck are you doing, Ballsman?" Campbell screamed from the back.

"Shut up, Campbell," Sergeant Toyley snapped as the M84 screamed into action. Their crossing point was in view of the defense point on the stream and they were taking missile fire. The 5mm commander's railgun sounded like an electric chainsaw the size of a Mack truck and the coating on the rounds left a blue track of fire through the air like tracers.

"Where the fuck is the artillery?" Campbell yelled. "We were supposed to have mortar cover!"

"Shut *up*, Campbell," Toyley replied as the track crossed the stream.

As soon as they were on the far side they were in cover from the defense position. Balmoral dropped to the ground and gunned it again, heading up the trace of an old road that climbed through a narrow notch in the cliffs. The trace was half-covered by a brook that was rushing with spring rains and the track tore up a sheet of spray as it headed up into the hills.

"There should be an old trace to the right," Toyley said, looking forward. "There, you see it?"

"See it, Sergeant," Balmoral said, spinning the track in the narrow corner and gunning it hard. It was a steep damned road and the trees were thicker than normal. But there weren't any big boulders or stumps. But the trace quickly died in thicker timber from before the Posleen War. "I don't have a road!"

"Unass!" Sergeant Toyley said. "Get it off the road if you can and lager up."

As soon as the troops were off, Balmoral spun the track into the trees, shoving it off the road. Other tracks were discharging behind him and for a moment he wasn't sure what to do.

"We're staying here," Sergeant Chofsky said over the radio. "We can partially interdict artillery from here."

As he said it the blue-force-tracker chimed.

"Incoming Hedren fire. Mark Three Plasma Mortars."

"You know," Balmoral said, crossing his arms and leaning his seat back as the M84 began to rave. "This is just a little *too* real."

❖   ❖   ❖

"Thirty!" Keren called.

"All tracks, displace five hundred meters down the road. Prepare for counterbattery mission."

"Move it, Opie!" Keren yelled, grabbing a stanchion and hauling himself forward.

"Incoming Hedren fire," the BFT said in a soft contralto. "Incoming artillery classified as Hedren Mark Six Plasma Artillery."

The M84 was slewed up and to the right at nothing Keren could see. But he wasn't going to be graded as killed so he pulled the commander's cupola down and strapped himself into his seat. What the hell. The vision blocks were wide plasma screens. He could see nearly as well down here as up there.

"Get in line, Opie," Keren said as Three Gun's track, which had yet to start moving, started flashing red lights. Keren noted that the commander's gun was pointed straight forwards. "Well, the good news is that we're not going to be waiting for Three Gun anymore . . ."

Specialist Adolpho Littlefield flopped to his face and pointed his railgun up the hill, searching for targets.

The training was a far cry from fighting the Posleen. Adolpho had spent most of his time in the war near the Harrisburg defense line. Fighting the Posleen in the open was generally suicide; only the ACS could really survive under direct Posleen fire. He'd spent most of the war servicing Gatling guns in fixed positions.

But he'd been trained, long long ago, in the techniques of fire and maneuver. And better than half the volunteer recalls had training in it. So he was picking it up pretty quick. But, Lord God, was it tiring.

Fire and maneuver meant that while looking for

targets you also had to spot your next cover position. Then, on command, you pushed yourself to your feet and sprinted forward while another group covered the movement of yours. Hit the ground fast, pop up to find targets and cover the next group as they moved.

There was a rave above his head as one of the AFV gunners fired at a target on the hilltop. Technically, that was their job. But he wasn't real happy with 9mm rail rounds going by overhead. The exercise wasn't using blanks or simunitions. The "enemy" was dummies and some robots so they were authorized to shoot them up. But if one of those railgun rounds hit *him* he was going to be paste.

"Bravo Team, move!"

Push to his feet, sprint uphill through the underbrush, find another tree to hide behind. Suddenly, his harness started to blink red lights.

"What the fuck?"

"You are an . . . artillery casualty," a soft contralto said. "You are graded as . . . terminated."

"Motherfucker!"

"Where in the hell is the counterbattery?" Cutprice asked as more units dropped off the screen. "RTO, call battalion and tell them we're getting slaughtered by artillery out here. And for some reason *we* can't get any."

"Bravo Battery just got graded as fifty percent casualties," Specialist Simmons said.

Lieutenant Colonel Nathaniel Moberly had been a cannon cocker back when that was a real term. He'd been a battery commander in Vietnam, had once had a wife named Helga as a result of one of many trips to the Federal Republic of Germany and had, in his time, been associated with everything from 105 towed shorties to MLRS.

But the quality of Hedren counterbattery was taking him by surprise.

"Remind all batteries to immediately displace on firing," Moberly said. "And ask Delta why we're still taking fire. I want those Hedren batteries silenced. And keep an eye out for Hedren probes. They're bound to be looking for *us*."

"What the hell?" Cutprice said as the M84 by his ear started firing up and to the left. It wasn't the right angle for artillery fire.

"Sir!" Specialist Riley shouted. "BFT says we're auto-engaging a Hedren probe rocket. That's their version of a..."

"UAV," Cutprice finished. "Command team! Four hundred meters west! Now! Now! Now!"

"Lieutenant John Mullins," the BFT chimed. "Captain Thomas Cutprice is graded as...terminated. You are now...commander...pro tem of...Bravo Company...First Battalion Fourteenth Infantry Regiment. Congratulations on your...temporary assumption of command."

Mullins sighed and looked at the screen in his track. He'd spent most of his military career in special operations and more or less been shanghaied by that bastard Cutprice into the Ten Thousand. Even then, Cutprice had made him a fucking adjutant of all things.

Now he was supposed to take over a company that was getting bogged down and wasted by artillery fire.

But he'd been watching the tactical situation and knew that Cutter had gotten way too involved with what looked like an overarmed Observation Post.

"First and Third Platoons," Mullins said. "Hammer down the road. Third dismount on the target. Kill anything there and then get back in your tracks and continue the movement. Second Platoon, swing your tracks back onto Highway Eight and link up there with your dismounts. All tracks maintain maneuvering. Mortars, discontinue fire on objective and see if you can get counterbattery information for those fucking Hedren mortars. Everybody: Boot their ass, don't piss on them. Log team, displace."

"The Hedren are shooting and moving just like we are," Gist said, pointing at the screen. "So far, we've been dodging their arty and they've been dodging ours. Well, we've *mostly* been dodging."

"Okay," Lieutenant Todd said. "Pull up a terrain map with all their previous locations on it."

"Yes, sir," Gist said.

The former head of the Infantry Mortar Board considered the terrain map and then grinned.

"Target this location," he said, pointing to a clearing off of Highway Eight.

"There's nothing there," Gist said.

"That we know of," Richards replied. "But they've fired from here, here, here and here. They've been moving backwards on the road and pulling off to fire in open areas. The next open area is—"

"Mortars, stand by for targeting orders," Gist said, grinning.

❖　　❖　　❖

"How many RAP rounds do we have?" Captain Ellis Benford asked.

The commander of Delta Battery Second Battalion One Hundred Sixty-Seventh Artillery Regiment (Detached) was getting tired of Regiment asking when they were going to silence the Hedren artillery. They'd already taken two near misses from counterbattery and he was also tired of that.

Delta Battery was six 200mm howitzers that were tasked to the 1/14th Regiment. The overall battalion had four batteries, Alpha, Bravo, Charlie and Delta. Alpha, Bravo and Charlie were 155s tasked to the individual teams of the overall regiment, a team being one of the battalions with engineering and tank supports.

Delta was the personal shotgun of the regimental commander and since it had more range and power than the 155s was normally used for counterbattery.

The problem was the guy running the Hedren side of the maneuver was smart. He had the Hedren shooting and moving very fast. And, worse, their damned antiartillery system kept shooting down the human fire before it could hit.

"Twenty-four," Lieutenant Howard said, frowning. "But the Hedren artillery is well in range of—"

"It's in range," Benford said, looking at the screen. "But when we fire at it we have to fire at high angle. That gives the antiartillery system more time to engage. The next counterbattery use the RAP rounds. Warhead cluster munitions. That way they'll also have about a bazillion targets. Let's see if they like *them* apples. And see if Log has any more they can get up to us."

✧   ✧   ✧

"Section, fifteen rounds, contact, on command."

"Two Gun, up!" Keren replied. One and Four came up nearly as fast.

"Fire at will!"

"Oh fuck!" the major shouted. "Those fucking *bastards*!"

"Wasn't that where your mortars used to be?" the Opposition Forces colonel said, smiling slightly.

"They hit me before my last *round* was out! Who told them where I *was*? Where's the *fucking* Himmit?"

"Well, they also just took out my primary artillery," the colonel said. "Nuked the fuck out of it with cluster munitions, cheating bastards. They took some casualties but I think this action is just about over."

"Battalion, Bravo," Mullins said as the tracks rolled onto the hilltop. "Objective has been secured. Orders?"

"One Dragon Six says dig in, consolidate and prepare for counterattack," an RTO replied.

"Roger," Mullins said as the BFT chimed.

"Exercise Terminated. Exercise Terminated. Blue Force, twenty percent casualties, all objectives completed. Red force, seventy percent casualties, no objectives completed."

"And *that* is what they call balling the ace," Mullins said, leaning back in his chair with a sigh. "Cutter's gonna owe me *several* beers. Oh, hell, I'll take it out in paperwork. Wonder if everybody else is having this much fun?"

CHAPTER TWENTY

"The ship is primarily crewed by Marro," Mosovich said, bringing up a hologram of the snakelike enemy. "Call 'em Snakes. Standard weapons are flechette shotguns for the majority of the enlisted and rail subguns for the officers and senior NCOs. They're ship's crew so they'll have some training in security but Himmit indicate that weapons for the enlisted are locked down unless they are preparing for boarders."

"That would be us," Mueller said.

"Correct," Mosovich replied. "But we are supposed to be hitting them by surprise and *fast*. If we hit them fast enough, they're not going to get many guns distributed. And they're Navy, they're not going to be highly trained in them. Himmit concur on that."

"The Himmit don't have to fight them," Mueller said.

The briefing was taking place before the whole SRS group and the mentats. It had been carefully explained to the latter that Mosovich and Mueller went *way* back and Mueller was always the devil's advocate.

"Another race we may encounter is the Kotha," Mosovich said, bringing up a hologram of the massive cephalopods. "They're leaders of the Hedren forces and may be in officer positions."

"Ugly," Mueller said.

"And they can use all those tentacles to wield weapons," Mosovich noted. "Keep an eye out for these guys; they're reputed to be very bad news."

"The main threat is going to be the Porkies," Mosovich said, bringing up a slide of the Glandri. Who did look, a bit, like porcupines. "They're primarily trained as populace controllers but they're also the Imeg's body guards. We'll know we're close to the Imeg when we hit them. Their primary weapon is a neural scrambler. At low power it's a very painful stunner. At high power it tears up neural pathways and has an effect like nerve gas. Our armor has had a layer of metal fibers added that might mitigate the effect. But don't bet on it. Getting hit with one of those things is purely gonna suck.

"Three shuttles. Each will carry one third of each team, the command team will be distributed and the adepts will be distributed. Lock on to this zone, breach with firepaste. Clear the compartment and head out.

"The ship is about three hundred meters long and just chock full of compartments. The Himmit's best guess on where the Imeg is going to be hanging out is here..." he said, pointing to a spot on the hologram. "It's a portion of officers' country that sometimes is converted to carry a squadron commander. That will be the primary target for Alpha Team."

"Got it," Major Kanaga, the Alpha Team leader said. His team name, Moustache, dated to when he'd been a very junior officer and attempted, unsuccessfully, to grow one. The huge bulge of Redman in his cheek, however, was his real trademark. And he still couldn't grow a mustache.

"Charlie Team's mission is to secure the mentats that will be accompanying," Mosovich continued. "They have some capacity to defend themselves but they are primarily going to be defending us from the Imeg and that's probably going to be occupying all their time. Do not hesitate. Kill anything that gets near them."

"Clear," the Charlie Team leader said. Major Sheldon "Boxcar" Hildyard was tall and lanky with bright red hair. Also fast as a thief in combat.

"Bravo Team will move behind Charlie in support," Mosovich said. "You're our reserve and back-cover."

"Clear," the Bravo Team leader replied. Major Reuben "Ugly" Kimple got his tall and blond looks from both his maternal and fraternal grandmothers. He got his bulk from his maternal grandfather. Where he'd gotten his movie-star gorgeous face was a mystery all the family was still trying to answer.

"Upon securing the Imeg mentat we won't screw around with finding a different way out," Mosovich said. "Bravo will follow the trail of bodies and blown hatches. Alpha will cover the rear. Ingress and egress will be trained with at least two routes in and out and multiple side-options. Clear?"

"Clear," the team leaders chorused.

"Mentat Chan?"

"We are taking fourteen adepts," Chan said. "Two masters, myself and Indowy Master Shaina, nine class six adepts and three class five. During the preparatory phase they will work to support and improve the *Des Moines'* cloak. We believe that this will permit us to close to within no more than five thousand meters of the Hedren cruiser before we are detected. Eight of those adepts are human. Five will remain on the *Des Moines* to shut down the cruiser and its defenses. Three, including myself, will accompany the strike team. The six Indowy adepts will remain on the *Des Moines*. They will ensure that the *Des Moines* remains combat functional through the entire engagement and give support to the assault adepts as well as preventing broadcast by the Imeg or the ship. Assuming that between the adepts on the cruiser, myself and the two sixth level that will accompany me, we can prevent the Imeg from interfering, we believe we can prevent the cruiser from escaping or even firing its weapons. If we cannot, things will get interesting. I would make a note."

"Go," Mosovich said.

"The purpose of this mission is for us to gain an understanding of the methods of our enemies," Chan said. "We may determine, quite early, that fourteen adepts including two masters cannot successfully hide a ship from Imeg and or cannot successfully secure them. We adepts simply do not know the abilities of the Imeg. In the event this is the case, the mission should be aborted."

"For anything involving Sohon, you're calling the shots Mentat Chan," Mosovich said. "If you say abort, we abort. On the basis that we won't, I'll continue. Upon securing the Imeg adept we will move to the shuttles and egress from the ship. Upon our rendezvous with the *Des Moines*, the cruiser will be destroyed."

"What if they grab our shuttles?" Mueller asked. "Or blow them?"

"Chance we're going to have to take," Mosovich said. "We're short bodies as it is. And more bodies means more shuttles."

"Rig 'em," Mueller said.

"We can do that," Ugly said. The Bravo team leader grinned ferally. "Plenty of ways to make them not want to touch them. Stuff we can turn off on the way back."

"Works," Mosovich said. "Questions."

"We've got pics of the Kotha and the Snakes and the Porkies," Moustache said, rolling a ball of Redman in his cheek. "What's an Imeg look like?"

"The Himmit don't know," Mentat Chan said. "They have no images of one. Because the Himmit do not or cannot use Sohon, they cannot approach an Imeg without being detected. They assume that some of their lost scouts did so but that is an assumption. We are going to be the first beings outside the Hedren Tyranny to see one. From Himmit accounts, even the Kotha rarely if ever see one in the flesh. They are very secretive. Equally, no one knows what the Hedren look like. But let us first examine the Imeg before we consider facing their masters."

"We board the *Des Moines* tomorrow," Mosovich said. "We'll hash out the details and routes there and work on our situational awareness. The *Des Moines* doesn't have the same configuration but we can work with it in VR. Start getting it on."

"Mentat Chan," Captain McNair said as he greeted the party at the boarding tube. "Welcome, again, to the *Des Moines*."

"Captain," the mentat said, bowing slightly. "I believe I should ask for permission to board."

"Y'all come ahead," Daisy Mae said, grinning. "We ain't particular round here."

"That means permission for your party to come aboard is granted," Captain McNair said, rolling his eyes. "Mentat Shaina, I see you."

"Captain McNair, I see you," the Indowy said, nodding his head. "Entity Daisy Mae, I see you," he added, actually adding a slight bow. As he bowed he saw a small carnivore, brown and furry, stropping the legs of the entity called "Daisy." Shaina filed that information away for future analysis.

"Y'all's set up in a section of the officers' quarters," Daisy said. "Put in some appliances for makin' y'all's food and a supply for about a week. All the room there was. Y'all need anything, you just announce it. I can ignore things if you don't want me to see but seein' as I *am* the ship, any time you talk to me I'll hear it."

"The point to this is that you should require minimum interaction with the human crew," Captain McNair pointed out.

"My thanks, Entity Mae, Captain McNair," the mentat said, nodding his head again.

"I'll lead y'all to your quarters," Daisy said. "Pretty sure you know the way but it's fittin'."

"I cccoulllddd llleaddd thththemmm, Dddaisssy," said the small carnivore.

Fascinating, though Shaina.

"Daisy Mae is an interesting entity," Mentat Chan said as the captain led the way to his quarters. He'd been installed in the captain's cabin. There was, in addition, a small captain's day cabin near the bridge which McNair would use for the trip.

"She's a handful," McNair admitted, while thinking, *Actually, she's at least* two *handfuls.* "But it makes running the ship easier that's for sure."

"I think I was actually referring to her entire being," Chan said. "The reality of it approaches, if you do not mind my saying so, the metaphysical. She is more than just an AI that took on the appearance of a minor actress and her being infuses the ship far more than the nannite systems can account for. In a way, it seems more that the ship infuses her."

"Ships have souls," McNair said as he opened the hatch to the cabin. "All good ships and certainly any that have been used for long enough. Daisy doesn't talk about it much, but the AI she used to be got . . . changed by being hooked into the *Des Moines.* The original one that is. I hope that making this new one hasn't . . . killed something."

"I do not think it did," Chan said looking at the small cabin.

"Sorry it's not larger," the captain said, shrugging. "But, you know there's only so much room on a ship."

"I was actually thinking how wasteful it was of space," Chan replied. "Humans who are not Indowy raised are simply used to so much *room.* I will probably share this with my students."

"Well, we've got bunking for them, too," McNair said, looking at the cabin. He always found it mildly claustrophobic.

"No, this is sufficient for all of us," Chan said. "I'm sure that someone has been discommoded by our presence. Since we will be comfortable sharing this room, it is better to let them have their space back."

"I'll leave you to get settled in, then," the CO said. "We're breaking dock right away. We're on tight time to make the intercept."

"Indeed," Chan said. "Haste is an unfortunate necessity."

"Hot bunking," Mueller said grumpily.

"It's a warship," Mosovich replied. "We're going to need to start work-ups as soon as the mentats are ready. I'm not sure they're up to keeping up with us."

"That's going to be fun," Mueller said, grinning.

"Y'all don't do a whole bunch of physical training, do you?" Mosovich said, frowning, as the junior mentat bent over and threw up.

They had started, he thought, with the easy stuff. There was a route in the *Des Moines* that was pretty close to the route they were going to have to take to get to the place they *thought* the Imeg *might* be. So with all the blast doors open they had hoofed it from the notional entry point to the target compartment, working on coverage and general movement.

The SRS team was loaded for bear with leopard-suit space gear, heavy body armor, cloaks and full load-out. The mentats, after Chan's assurance that they could prevent injury from random shrapnel and bullets, were just wearing cloaked leopard-suits.

About halfway to the compartment, Mosovich had had to slow down to let the mentats catch their wind. By the time they got there, two of the junior mentats were pretty much useless. And even Chan wasn't looking all that hot.

"We do, yes," Chan said, breathing heavily. "But it is . . . spiritual based and . . . very low impact." He paused and took a deep breath. "Not very aerobic come to . . . think of it."

"Reality is we're probably going to have to be stopping to burn doors," Mosovich said, not even breathing hard despite wearing better than a hundred pounds of armor, ammo and battle-rattle. He figured that, all things considered, they were more or less going to have to think in terms of clearing the whole ship. He was not going to run out of ammo. "So you'll get a chance to catch your breath, then. But I bet you're not much use Sohon wise at the moment."

"No, we are not," Chan admitted. "And, yes, we must get in better shape. Fortunately, there are excercises we can perform to enhance our advancement in that regard. By the time we reach the target we will be prepared. You have my word."

"Uh, huh," Mosovich said. "Hope you're right. 'Cause it's gonna be all our asses if you're not."

"Cutting paste."

The hangar bay was the only place large enough to hold the training facility. Even with VR gear it helped to have a mock-up of an assault area. A series of light walls had been installed indicating the bulkheads of the area they believed the Imeg to be quartering. Heavier doors had been carried along to simulate the hatches they'd have to breach. In some cases they were planning on burning through the bulkheads but most of the time the hatches were a better bet.

Payback, the Alpha Demo specialist, pulled out a length of what looked like silver rope and put a man-sized oval of it on the hatch. The cutting paste was self sticking so he just laid in a detonator and rolled to the side of the door, holding up the activator.

"It may be possible, depending upon many factors, that we will be able to override the hatch controls," Chan noted on the command frequency. His left hand was gripping the back of the harness of Master Sergeant Field, the Charlie second stick NCOIC who was called, for reasons that even a mentat could not comprehend, Lieutenant Penis. Each of the mentats had a designated SRS lead. It was anticipated that they were going to have to concentrate on controlling the Imeg and couldn't be expected to also figure out where to go. So they just held on and went.

Sergeant First Class Arden Dugmore and Sergeant Charles Basmanoff, Dumbo and Friday respectively, were covering his back. Behind them two more sticks managed the lower level mentats.

"Better to train as if you can't," Mosovich said as Payback fired the charge. The high-energy paste cut through the plasteel as if it were so much paper and as the door began to sag a breaching charge went off, blasting it into the compartment. The Alpha first stick, Recto, Mangler and Sugar Plum, burst through the smoke and cleared the compartment in a buzz of flechettes.

"Clear," Master Sergeant "Recto" Owen said in a laconic voice. "Unknown alien entity, tentatively identified as an Imeg, in the room. Entity is active."

"Take-down team," Mustache whispered.

The two and three stick charged through the door and there was a buzz of static on the radio.

"Imeg immobilized. Bagging and tagging."

The take-down team came through the door with a large Tigger dummy wrapped up in rigger-tape. The stuffing of the dummy had been replaced with sand and it was clear that they were struggling.

"This was fucking Mongo's idea, wasn't it?" SFC Sullivan said.

"Yes," Mueller replied. "And your point, Altar Boy?"

"Exercise terminated," Mosovich said, looking at his buckley. "Fifteen minutes twenty-three seconds from entry to take-down. No way it's actually going to go this smooth, but that's not bad. Break it down for institutional scab-picking."

"We don't have any idea how big these guys are?" Recto asked.

"No clue," Colonel Mosovich replied. "They could be heavier than the Tigger dummy. They could look like Yoda. No fucking clue."

"What if they're, like, beings of pure energy?" Sergeant Alton "Sugar Plum" Sutton asked. The electronics and communications specialist shrugged at the looks. "Dudes, we're working with wizards. It's not a stupid question."

"It is unlikely that they are quantum state entities," Adept Elijah Hoover said. The sixth level Sohon adept was part of the Sohon assault trio and, thus, included in the entry team debrief. "Not impossible but the attainment of such an evolved state is one of the goals of the Way. You speak of a species as advanced as the Aldenata. If they have attained such advancement, it is unlikely that even fourteen adepts can contain one of them. In which case, we will find ourselves in a difficult condition."

"I've got a team nick for Hoover," SFC Cribbs said. His team name was Meister but Chan had already learned that it stood for "Drunk-Meister." The mentat had been studying the SRS in fascination since the voyage began and was pleased to finally have an opportunity to examine the assignment of such team names. "I say we just call him Understatement."

"Whirlwind," Mangler said.

"Why Whirlwind?" Recto asked.

"The Book of Kings," Adept Hoover said. "The Prophet Elijah was said to have been taken to heaven on a whirlwind, a dust-devil."

"Dust-Devil," Recto said to nods all around.

"Are you going to need to be physically present to control the Imeg?" Mosovich asked, looking at the results of the training so far.

"It is unlikely but possible," Chan said. "I think that we should be able to control them from practically anywhere on the ship. It is possible, however, that a closer presence may have enhanced effect."

"Then we're going to need to work on methods of inserting you into the room," Mosovich said, nodding but not looking up. "Doors are always crowded places in one of these things. And dangerous places too. Are you going in first or one of your juniors?"

"I think Hoo—Dust-Devil is the better choice," Chan said. "He has shown the most promise in Sohon . . . control techniques. He seems, in fact, to have much more of a flair for them than construction."

"Yeah," Snake said, nodding again. "For all he's like 'Me Monk' he's got the warrior look. Don't know if you consider that good or bad."

"For these conditions and necessities, it is alas good," Chan said. "I am fascinated by the assignment process of team names. It would be considered the height of insult for a junior to call a senior Lieutenant Penis among the Indowy or those raised by them. I was interested to see the process for assigning one to Adept Hoover."

"Team names are a sign of acceptance," Mosovich said, finally looking up. "More than that, really. They're very complicated. The official reason for them is that they reduce confusion in communication. Everyone has a unique name with no ambiguity. Pilots really started it. But there's more to it than that. Although everyone recognizes that there are higher and lower ranks on the teams, the necessity is for a sort of fluidity that recognizes that while ignoring it. Master Sergeant Owen, Recto, may give an order to Mangler and it will be obeyed. But in more formal units, Mangler might pass information to a higher authority and then be questioned about it. By eliminating the base thought about who is the higher from a certain portion of the consciousness, by eliminating the 'Dad' aspect of 'Master Sergeant' from that bit of brain, when Mangler makes a motion for six Glandri, Master Sergeant Owen accepts that data as Recto, a near equal to Mangler, instead of Master Sergeant Owen having to consider the *validity* of the information Sergeant First Class Dale has passed to him."

"Interesting psychology," Chan said, frowning. "One thing that it has been hard to explain to the Indowy, and that even we humans raised by them often forget, is that being superior in position is not always the same as being superior in concepts or current knowledge."

"Mentat Chan, Adept Hoover, master, student, yada,

yada, yada," Mosovich said, nodding. "There's a time and a place for hierarchy. In the middle of an entry is not necessarily one of them."

"We do not normally do . . . entries," Chan said.

"It's going to be a long war," Mosovich replied. "Better get used to them."

"I notice that there is no suggestion that I be given a team name," the mentat said, smiling slightly.

"You're heap big mojo," Mosovich said. "Way too big mojo to think about insulting you. I didn't, by a stretch, get into the full psychology of team names. But that's part of it. They don't want to offend. Another part of it is that while Hoover is also heap big mojo, he just has the . . . feel of wanting to be part of the team. And since they know they're going to be depending on him, they're willing to accept him even though he's not really 'one' of us. He's a respected associated specialist. They work with them from time to time. Bane Sidhe specialists in one thing or another. Commo, hacking, whatever. So there's a mental slot for him. Now, Pawle, he's got less interest in being one of the boys. So they haven't suggested making a team name for him. Oh, they've got one, they just don't use it around him."

"Are they aware he may know it anyway?" Chan said, frowning. "Even for a fifth level your communications are not terribly hard to intercept."

"Wasn't aware of that," Mosovich said, shaking his head. "It's always something. I don't know if he knows or not."

"What is his team name?" Chan asked.

"Skank," Mosovich said.

"Hardly a *pleasant* name," the mentat said, his brow furrowing.

"Pawle's got a real holier-than-thou attitude," Mosovich said. "If I thought it was going to interfere I would have brought it up. But he does his job, presumably. We won't really know until we get to the intercept."

"I hesitate to discuss the issues of junior adepts with you," Chan said. "They are...complex."

"And you haven't noticed that teams are?" Mosovich said, raising an eyebrow. "Just because you guys have got bulging foreheads, doesn't mean you're not human with human foibles. Small teams have been working the psychology of that for forever. Want my read on Pawle?"

"I will accept your input," Chan said gravely.

"Fine," Mosovich said. "All you mentats are bright. It's a necessity. Everybody's figured out that you've got to juggle quantum mechanics in your head while doing whatever it is you do. That takes big bulging foreheads. Pawle was, however, brighter than the average growing up. Which meant that, due to very basic human nature going back to the way that primates in the wild act, others tried to pull him down. Knowing the fact that he grew up in an Indowy environment, my guess would be passive aggressive techniques and occasional mildly aggressive. He probably just got shunned and ignored a lot. He ended up knowing he was smarter than everyone around him but with a massive inferiority complex. He's apparently arrogant because he's lacking self esteem. Or am I wrong?"

"You are a student of human nature," Chan said.

"I've been commanding small units of very elite troops for a very long time," Mosovich said. "I had a lot of classes once upon a time and I think I've surpassed most of them."

"And what would your recipe be for improving Adept Pawle?" Chan asked, honestly interested.

"Pressure him," Mosovich said. "He's bright but lazy which, believe it or not, is good. But he's also very unsure. Put him under pressure so high it either kills him or cures him. If he fails all you have is a guy stuck on stupid at fifth level. If he passes, he'll gain confidence from it. There are guys I've commanded who had esteem problems, but they generally get over them after whatever entry program is used by the group. The problem is that with his attitude he's a weak link. But Sohon's your side of this op."

"The problem is the nature of the mission," Chan said, frowning. "The essentially violent nature of the operation is . . . very much anathema to most of the Indowy-raised. The positions are voluntary. Of my students, only Pawle and Hoover volunteered to enter the enemy vessel. I am, I admit, unsure of the concept of pressuring Sohon adepts to exceed their level of comfort."

"How's your comfort?" Mosovich asked.

Chan looked at the table between them for a long moment.

"Perhaps too high," the mentat said. "My father was Admiral Chan Kushao, the senior Chinese officer in Fleet. Unlike the . . . latter officers, including those of the Race of Han, he was a man of honor."

"Indra?" Mosovich asked.

"Oh, far earlier," Chan said, snorting. "He was in command of CruRon Fourteen at Second Diess."

"That's where about the only thing we recovered was the *Yamato*, right?" Jake said. "The rest of the fleet, and all the cruisers, were if I recall clearly, scrap."

"I was...ten? Yes, ten." Chan sighed and shrugged. "The younger members were...younger when they were taken in by the Indowy. Many of them barely remember their parents. I can remember my mother crying when father's shuttle was gone. And I can remember my sisters."

"They...stayed in China?" Jake asked.

"They did indeed," Chan said. "One of the reasons I generally work for the Darhel at arm's length. I have gotten over the rage, but I will admit that I am perhaps less...tamed than the Indowy would wish. So," he said, looking up. "No, I have no issues with this mission. I am the son of a Chinese admiral, who was the son of a naval captain. Our family was one of the few of the Manchu to survive the Communists, mostly because my great-grandfather saw the writing on the wall and went over to them very early. My grandmother had a list of every Chan who had served under the Emperors going back several centuries. I may be a mentat instead of a ship's commander or a colonel. But."

"But," Jake said, grinning. "What are you gonna do about Pawle?"

"I think he chose to take the active role in his own attempt to get over his self esteem issues," Chan said. "To prove himself if you will. I also see the issues with that."

"One way that goes bad is they don't," Jake said, nodding. "That is, they crack under the pressure. The other way it goes bad is they overreact and end up a dead hero."

"Answer?"

"Training," Jake said. "And selection. You can sort of do both at the same time. Hmmm..."

"What are you thinking?"

"We haven't really been training you guys for resistance," Jake said. "Once we get up to full run, in about a week, I was going to be throwing wrenches in the ops to test my guys. I think we need to do that to yours."

"Glandri," Toucher said, pulling back. "Corridor's packed with them!"

"Alternate four," Moustache said, automatically. "Payback, seal this corridor."

"On it," the demo man said. The door closed and he laid a sealer on it, igniting it as the team retreated.

They turned a corner and hurried down it but before they reached the end there was a rave of sound that filled the corridor.

"Autogun," Daisy Mae announced. "Lieutenant Penis and Glasshoppah are graded as terminated."

"Glasshoppah?" Chan snapped.

"Thanks, Daisy," Mosovich said, grinning. "See you, Glasshoppah."

"*Glasshoppah?*" Chan repeated as the team continued down the corridor.

• "How can Master Chan be terminated?" Pawle asked as he hurried to keep up.

"Is it possible?" Master Sergeant Jesse asked. The third stick NCOIC was not a fan of his "principal." "It's possible. This is designed as a hard run. You and Dust-Devil are on your own."

"There is . . ." Dust-Devil said, then paused. "Oh . . . that is not fair."

"Master Chan is . . . playing the . . . Imeg," Pawle

said, panting. "He is attempting to shut down your weapons and prevent our movement."

"Well, you two had better fucking keep him from doing it," Hooter said. The second stick NCOIC looked back at Dust-Devil. "How's it going?"

"He's a *seventh-level Sohon*," Dust-Devil snarled. "It is not going well. Now let us concentrate!"

Payback laid a strip of cutting paste on the hatch and hit the igniter. It didn't flare.

"What the fuck?" he snarled.

"Master . . . Chan," Dust-Devil said from across the compartment. "Wait . . ."

The paste suddenly ignited, flaming even hotter than normal.

"Sk . . . Pawle," Dust-Devil said through clenched teeth. "Hold . . . reality."

"I am holding," the fifth level said, gritting his teeth. "I think I . . ."

Suddenly the heavy duty fire-fighting sprinklers cut on, dousing the team in a spray of water like a firehose.

"What the . . ." Moustache snarled as they cleared the far compartment.

"My visor just went down!" Mangler snarled, ripping the VR goggles off.

"Fuck," Buster shouted as his weapon was ripped from his hand.

The walls of the compartment deformed, closing in on the assault team.

"Hold . . . reality," Dust-Devil said. "Damnit, I can't fight him *and* the walls at the same time!"

"I . . . have it," Pawle said. The walls had stopped closing in and the water shut off. "Holding. Go, Moustache!"

"Payback," the team commander said, pointing at the next hatch. Which slid aside.

"We don't have time," Pawle said. "MOVE!"

As the team entered the final compartment they found Master Chan seated in a lotus, eyes closed and a faint smile on his face.

"Securing team," Moustache said.

Alphas One and Two darted forward and bounced off a field that was clearly invisible.

"That is not reality," Pawle said, his eyes closed. "Dust—"

The sixth-level mentat was suddenly lifted off his feet and slammed into the bulkhead.

"Dust-Devil is graded as injured," Daisy Mae said. "Up to you, Skank."

"I cannot..." Pawle ground out.

"You'd better do *something* fast," Cheeto shouted. The shooter from Charlie was covering the door of the compartment. "We got Glandri moving in."

This is not a fair test, Pawle thought. *The Imeg would be dealing with the other Sohon at the same time. In this case it is only you.*

I have factored for that, Chan thought. *Don't think this is the all of my ability, young one. But it is what I would have left if I was also attempting to destroy the attacking ship. And, think, there may be more than one. The reality is that there is no shield about me. Establishing reality is easier than changing it. Establish reality. And if you are talking you are not fighting.*

Fine, Pawle thought savagely.

❖   ❖   ❖

"Field's down," Spice said. He was ignoring the blood running down his nose from impacting the field. "So, do we get to taser Master Chan? Please?"

"Terminate exercise," Daisy Mae said. "And, no, don't taser Glasshoppah."

"Grasshopper?" Master Chan said. "That wasn't even the name of Caine's master. It was Caine's *apprentice* name!"

"And your point?" Mosovich asked.

"It's just . . . wrong," Chan said. "And, I might add, mildly insulting."

"That's the *other* point of team names . . ." Mosovich said.

"So when do I get a better team name?" Pawle asked. "I mean I *did* defeat Master Chan."

"You don't," Hooter said, shrugging. "Look, once you get a handle, well, getting it changed, like, takes an act of Congress."

The team, less the bosses, was having a bit of down-time. A bottle of high-grade moonshine had appeared from somewhere. The adepts refrained but they were still hanging with the SRS team. Which was a change. Normally they would have been back in their quarters doing whatever it was adepts did to blow off stress. Fucking meditating or making up koans.

"That doesn't seem . . . fair," Pawle said. "I mean, Adept Hoover gets Dust-Devil and I get . . . Skank?"

"Adept Pawle, my team name is *Lieutenant Penis*," Master Sergeant Field pointed out. "I knew a colonel one time whose team name was Buckbreath. Which, trust me, was worse than Skank. And practically nobody used it to his face."

"See, the thing is, you got to make it your own," Redman said, shrugging. "You go complaining about a team name, well..."

"...it shows you're not confident in yourself," Mosovich said. "Special operations, submariners, firefighters, they all have team names, they all play practical jokes and they all *push* all the time. If you can't handle the pressure, you're a pussy and don't belong in the unit. It seems stupid but it's a constant method of testing to ensure mental readiness to sustain the pressure of high-intensity combat. If you can't handle a little abuse from friends, you're not going to be able to handle the abuse from an enemy. The enemy is not going to care about your feelings, they're not going to let you hold up a stress card. They're going to try to kill you as hard as they possibly can so that you don't kill them. Horrible team names, practical jokes, psychological and verbal abuse, they're all methods that small high-intensity groups use to constantly test for the weak link. Most of them don't realize it, not intellectually, but they do it. The harder the job, at least ones that require team-work, the more you find people constantly testing. This completes your lesson for today, Glasshoppah..."

"Skank, toss me a water," Adept Hoover said, not looking up from the schematic he was studying.

The captain's cabin, not particularly generous in space, now had eight bunks arrayed in it. There was very little room to raise so much as one's head. To study the paper schematic, Dust-Devil had it plastered to the underside of the bunk above him and was moving it around using Sohon disciplines. He had the schematic for the ship already stored in his nannites but looking at the paper, for him, made it more real.

Pawle, without looking at him any more than he'd looked up, pulled a bottle of distilled water from the compartment behind his head and shot it across the room at very nearly the speed of sound.

Dust-Devil just held out his hand and caught it.

Doesn't it matter to you that he calls you that... name? Adept Sissy Harris asked. The sixth-level Sohon adept was the lead for the Sohon support team that was going to be staying on the ship. Their primary job was to be making sure the Hedren ship didn't escape the trap rather than engaging the Imeg directly.

No, Pawle thought back. *You either live up to it or you're not good enough to be on the team. Even if you live up to it, you might not be good enough. But if you can't take a little pressure like an embarassing team name you shouldn't even bother.*

She was as aware as Mentat Chan of Pawle's problems. He had always been brilliant at the theory of Sohon, but unconfident of his ability to execute it. She had seen vast improvement in the last week and considered his answer carefully.

Do you feel ready to face the Imeg? she asked.

I don't know, Pawle replied. *We don't know their power. If they are no more powerful than Master Chan, then yes. Especially if you guys give us cover fire.*

She could feel the doubt in his answer but it was not the usual self-doubt she had come to expect. It was simply rational unsurety based on their lack of knowledge of the enemy. It also lacked his usual arrogant tone.

The Indowy trained on the basis of interest. They used the open hand, from it you could take what you wished or were able. They encouraged, they praised but they never pressed or stressed. Pressure was anathema to their methods of training.

She was forced to wonder if that was the best way to train *humans*.

Or at least human *males*, come to think of it.

CHAPTER TWENTY-ONE

"Is the force going to make the schedule?" Mike asked, looking up at his daughter.

"Yes," Michelle said, looking at him carefully. "The actions should be in close time proximity."

"Then we'd better start shifting," Mike said. "You said four days, right?"

"Yes," Michelle said. "But, really, we won't know what the true capacity of the Imeg is until the attack on the transport."

"Never take counsel of your fears," Mike said, picking up his AID. "AID, I need General Tam, Tir Dol Ron and Rigas."

"I'm going to go join the assault force," Mike said as soon as the threesome had joined them.

"Even using a destroyer..." Tam said, his brow furrowing.

"Michelle's taking me," Mike said. "And on the

basis that even if it slips out, the Hedren can't get the information in time, the target of the assault force is *not* Gratoola."

"What do you mean," Tir Dol Ron asked angrily. "Gratoola is the—"

"Capital of the Federation," Mike said, sighing. "I know that, Clerk. And that it's strategically vital. I didn't say I'm not going to stop the attack on it. I'm just not going to defend from there."

"Daga Nine," Tam said, his face paling. "I was trying to figure out why you had the damned SS load all those pallets and field projectors. Are you *nuts*?"

"Crazy like a fox, Tam," Mike said. "You've got the reins while I'm gone. Don't let the Clerk screw you over. I *will* be watching."

He winked at Rigas and then they were gone.

"The condemned ate a hearty last meal," Harz said, taking three more slices of succulent pork.

The troops had been brought out of Hiberzine practically on top of the objective. They'd been told that after the meal and a brief preparation period, mostly to let the food settle, they were going to be loading up. The major portion of the prep involved reconfiguring their gear. Normally, personal gear was primarily hung on the outside of the vehicles. In combat it might be destroyed, but with so little room inside the vehicles it was practically a necessity. The order, though, was firm. *No* personal gear on the outside of the tanks and AFVs.

They were assured that, if possible, additional gear would be brought to them on-planet. But they were only to take what would fit.

Frederick was picking at his first plate of food. He

knew that as a soldier he should eat when there was food and sleep when there was security. But soon the Hedren would come. When he couldn't know and that bothered him.

"I think the yellow-shit does not have the stomach for good food," Joachim said, taking a bite of curry wurst.

"He will not be a yellow-shit much longer," Harz said, cutting into the pork. "That is, if we don't send his fiancée an urn of his ashes."

"I have asked to be given a decent burial," Frederick pointed out.

"When one of the modern tanks burns there is rarely much left to bury," Harz said. "The ashes are going to be mixed with those from your seat and personal gear."

The rejuv was no longer looking at his food but off into the distance as muscle-memory that was burned deep shoveled food into his mouth without the slightest slip or any need for thought.

"Actually, sometimes the drivers were almost intact. It depended on what hit. An HVM would sometimes kill them from pure overpressure. A plasma blast? Well, if it hit the turret often they survived. Direct hits and it was find any bits of bone that hadn't been turned to gas and scrape some of the char up. The ones that were really write-offs were the inhabitants of the turret. The blow-out panels worked more often than you'd think. But when they did not it was not worth looking for the bodies. I recall . . . damn, can see his face but I can't think of his name. Berlin was what we called him. Anyway, they took a plasma hit directly in the ammunition compartment and the blast penetrated into the turret. At least that was what we figured out later probably happened. The turret didn't jump. You saw that often. This time it stayed on but the ammunition just . . . burned. Very very fast. The cupola blew off, but not the turret. It was a pillar of white flame. Nighttime . . . cold. Just this thing like returning lightning to Thor. It seemed to go on and on but it couldn't have been more than a few seconds. It heated up the tank so much we couldn't touch it. When we came back through a few days later, retreating as we generally were, it was still warm but we could look inside. And there was *nothing*. At least nothing that wasn't heavy metal. Even the springs for the seats were gone; the fire had been so hot they'd been turned into iron gas. All the electronics, the sights . . . Just gone. Crew? Heh. The driver, though, he was still there. Sort of. We got him out in pieces. It must have been hell for him . . ."

He stopped and blinked his eyes, looking at his two crewmen.

"What, Joachim? Lost your appetite?" Harz said, taking another bite of pork. "Damn, am I done already? I must get more. This pig was raised with care just to feed me . . ."

"Yellow-shit," *Uberfeldwebel* Ginsberg said, sitting down with a filled plate. "Nothing kosher?"

Hagai had a plate of fruit and salad with a small beef steak. That was it.

"No, *Uberfeldwebel*," Hagai replied, shrugging. "It will be fine. I don't have much appetite, anyway."

"Of course you don't, yellow-shit," Frederick said, grinning as juices ran down his face. "My, this pork is good . . ."

"And of course if it is not kosher, you must not enjoy

it," Ginsberg said. "You can eat it as a last resort, but it must be eaten only to push off starvation."

"Yes, *Uberfeldwebel*," Hagai said, looking at him quizzically.

"I had a friend in school who was a Maccabean," Ginsberg said, shrugging.

"Is he in the Maccabaeus, *Uberfeldwebel*?" Hagai asked.

"No." Ginsberg took a bite of weiner schnitzel. "He was killed by a Posleen when we were on a training patrol. He used to try to jokingly convert me. He told me all I had to do was cut off the end of my dick and I was in with God. And I'd point out that that was the God who got so pissed at you guys for bitching about being out of water in the desert that he made you wander for forty years in same. Adding cutting off my dick was a bit much." He reached into his cargo pocket and pulled out a package.

"It's not much," the *Uberfeldwebel* said. "Just some rugelach. But you should have a good last meal before an operation. If you can't eat it, though, hold onto it. You'll find soon enough that you'll eat snails if they'll slow down enough. And be too tired to chase them."

"Thank you, *Uberfeldwebel*," Hagai said, looking at the small twists of dough wrapped around a filling. "I think I will just hold onto it. Now . . . is not the right time."

"Whatever," Ginsberg said. "Don't go crying on me. I can't stand men who cry. The next thing you know they're listening to emo music and then they might as well get an earring and move in with their best friend from school."

"Yes, *Uberfeldwebel*," Hagai said, grinning. "I will attempt to refrain from crying."

✧   ✧   ✧

"What the hell is that?" Frederick said as he clambered over Three Track to get to his.

Additional equipment had been moved into the bay since they were loaded and, in fact, where there had once been an open area was now a continuation of the platform also filled with equipment. The driver was unsure how in the hell they were going to get the tank out of the bay. Certainly they were going to have to wait for the entire rest of the brigade to get out of their way.

But the oddest part was that, somehow, someone had gotten a big platform installed under their tank. It looked like an aluminum loading pallet, but large enough to take the entire vehicle.

"That, my fine yellow-shit, is a P-5297 loading platform," Harz said, climbing up onto the turret and squeezing into the hatch. He had to duck and crawl because the overhead was just barely enough for the cupola to raise to full extent. "And on the rear of the platform, if you had time to look, you would find an M-3698 field generator."

"Thank you for the information, *Uberfeldwebel*," Frederick said. He recalled the conversation with Hagai about the devices—since he'd been in hibernation it was more or less yesterday—but hadn't had time since to think about it.

"Get in, get your shit secured and dog your hatch," Harz said. "There's a pressure check coming up. They're going to evacuate the whole ship to unload us this time."

"Very good, *Uberfeldwebel*," Frederick said, scrambling in quickly and setting his gear in place. There was no room in the driver's compartment, but he managed to slip in the few items he'd chosen to take with him for the initial landing. There was an issue sleeping bag, which fortunately was very small, a small amount of "comfort food," a spare pair of socks and a picture of Marta. Even those few items squeezed the space uncomfortably. He might have to ditch the socks.

He dogged his hatch and did a pressure check. His ears popped as the pressure in the compartment climbed and he worked his jaw to clear them.

"Seals are nominal, *Uberfeldwebel*," Frederick said.

"God help anyone's whose aren't," was all the tank commander said.

"Track Three, Seal Check."

"Nominal," Harz replied.

"Track Three Seal Check·Nominal, acknowledged."

"Ten vehicles with bad seals," 1A reported. "The Indowy are on it. They report ten minutes, maximum."

"Very good," Mühlenkampf said. "The Kobolds have saved this operation. Tell the commodore we will be prepared in ten minutes maximum. Order all vehicles to remain closed up."

"We're to stay closed up," Harz said.

"What is this bullshit?" Adler said. "We only have so much air."

"The scrubbers are good for a full day," the *Uberfeldwebel* replied. "There is plenty of time. And it is an order so that is enough."

"Seals are all repaired," 1A reported. "Visuals confirm that all vehicles have remained buttoned up."

"Commodore Winston," Mühlenkampf said, keying his microphone. "This is Vaterland Commander."

"Go Vaterland Commander."

"Vehicles are ready for EVA. Give me five minutes."

"Roger. Emergence in five."

"Stand by for retrans from *Generalmajor* Mühlenkampf."

"Here goes," Harz said, a grin in his voice.

"What goes?" Adler asked.

"My Brethren. Due to enemy spies it was necessary to keep all of you uninformed of the true nature of our mission. In less than five minutes this task group will emerge in the orbit of the Hedren-held world of Daga Nine. These assault transports will then open up and spill out the finest soldiers in the known universe. Following a bombardment we shall drop upon the enemy from orbit and take their transmission system, preventing them from striking deeper into Federation territory and in this way protecting the Fatherland. It is possible, even likely, that our forces shall be scattered in reentry. As your fathers and grandfathers before you did, move to the sound of the guns. Close with the enemy in your panzers and combat vehicles. Give them no mercy. Teach to those who would endanger the Fatherland that there is no force more fearsome in the universe than the Panzer leaders on the move.

"Today we strike like lightning from the hammer of Thor. For the Fatherland."

"Oh, he has got to be joking," Adler whispered.

"He's not," Harz said, a grin in his voice. "But I

bet there are very many people peeing themselves right now."

"You knew about this," Frederick said. "That was why you asked me about the platforms and the field generator."

"The platforms have repulsion systems on them," Harz said. "They have also been modified with a ribbon chute. We will drop very fast but the repulsion system will stop us instantaneously with contact with the ground. It has been tested. The ACS used them for resupply from orbit during the war. It will work."

"And the field generator?" Frederick asked.

"It is going to get very hot on the way down," Harz said. "The field generator will only prevent us from being burned up from reentry. It's *still* going to be hot."

The Marro sensor technician knew his duty. His duty was to curl in place and carefully watch his sensor readings. And he did his duty. Day in and boring day out. There was no real possibility of attack. A task force of battleships covered the approaches and he would have long warning of any attackers. But duty was duty and any disregard of duty might come to the attention of the Imeg.

It was, however, very boring. He didn't know how many times he'd wished that something, anything would happen to relieve the bore—

His eyes were fixed open with thin membranes shielding them from dehydration. Despite that, he would have blinked if he could have. Because what just a moment before was a *very* empty screen was now *filled* with icons. One, two, three, four... Nine ships!

It took him a moment to process any of the information. And then his first reaction was to run a diagnostic. By the time the short diagnostic was finished there were more symbols popping up. Thousands of them. There were more than a dozen ships in orbit and now it showed thousands of ground strike fighters being disgorged. And now there were icons of incoming kinetic weapons. *Big* ones. But the diagnostic said that the system wasn't suffering some sort of malfunction. That meant—

He couldn't move his tentacle *fast* enough to hit the alarm button.

The bombardment ship GFS *Mound* had rarely been used in the war. Even the task force that relieved Earth hadn't needed its services. One of the first Posleen planets that had been retaken had received its attention. The Posleen had not enjoyed the experience and the Hedren were about to find out why.

The *Mound* was, in reality, nothing but a highly modified bulk freighter such as had originally been used to move forces between planets. Nearly a kilometer long and with cavernous holds, the ship's modifications involved ways to move stuff out of its holds and onto certain courses, very fast, as well as binary, tunnel and ley-line, FTL engines. Its ship-to-ship weapons were pop-guns but it could toss out a *bunch* of kinetic energy weapons. They didn't go out very fast, but when you're firing in a gravity well, it doesn't really matter. Especially since it was punching out fifteen KEWs the size of a train engine every *second*. Secondary guns were, in the meantime, firing smaller KEWs at the rate of several *thousand* per second.

The KEWs really weren't much more than chunks of iron. Oh, they had tungsten fins and an internal gyroscope. But other than that they were just great big pieces of steel shaped vaguely like a dart. The rain of steel was aimed in various directions, but most of it was aimed more or less straight down at the just completed, and nearly charged, Hedren wormhole generator.

The Hedren fire was slow to start but brutal when it finally got into motion. Hundreds of lasers flashed upwards along with dozens of heavy meson guns. However, they were having a hard time hitting the *Mound* and her consorts. The air was almost literally *filled* with chunks of metal. Meson bolts capable of tearing apart a cruiser burst into pointless fireworks when they hit a KEW the size of a crowbar. Lasers had trouble with just the plasma and gases that were filling the sky.

Targeting the KEWs was automatic, but there were simply too many. Lasers flashed and flashed, but all it did was cut the darts in half. They were small enough they would burn up from reentry heat but most of them were large enough it took quite a bit of chunking to get to that point. Missiles flashed up as well, intercepting the larger KEWs and blasting them apart. But, again, there were a lot of KEWs and only so many missiles. Well before the *Mound* was out of chunks of steel the Hedren antiship missile inventory was exhausted.

And behind fell the tanks, AFVs, *panzerjaegers* and artillery carriers of the Vaterland in their very first *Augenhöhlentropfensturm*, an orbital drop storm.

> *"Vater unser, der Du bist im Himmel,*
> *Geheiligt werde Dein Name…"*

Frederick was praying as fast as he could but could not tear his eyes from the vision blocks. The world of Daga Nine was spread out below him and the panzer was dropping into a cloud of fire. The kinetic energy weapons, coherent and those that had been broken up by fire, were dropping beneath him to the surface of the world and they were burning. The effect filled the sky with orange fire, a volcano of torrential energy, into which the panzer was falling, the volcano falling away just as fast. At times they seemed to catch up to it then the distance would open, close . . . open. It was like one of those dreams where you fell and fell, the ground always only inches away but about to kill you at any moment. Energy screen or no, he did not think that there was any way that they could survive. And it was, yes, getting *very* hot. Sweat was pouring down his face for more than one reason.

He could see some of the fire coming up, but it was insignificant to the power of the dropping weapons.

"I saw an Eye of Baal from the ground one time," Harz mused. "That was what we called the Posleen drops. They would light the sky with fire in a great circle like a glowing red eye. Now I know what it was like from the top-side. I rather prefer this. And if you're going to pray, *Schutze*, might I ask that you at least not babble the words."

"Your pardon, *Feldwebel*," Frederick said, continuing to whisper the Lord's Prayer under his breath.

"Here, this will help," Harz said as a bass male voice started to recite the Lord's Prayer in Deutsch. Then a booming electronica synthesizer started up followed by a soaring chorus. "This is how to pray to the *Lord*, *Schutze*!" the track commander shouted.

"For the Lord did say unto his people, *make a joyful noise and rejoice* for I am *the Lord Thy GOD!*"

Vater Unser (E Nomine)	**Our Father**
Vater unser,	Our Father,
der Du bist im Himmel,	which art in Heaven,
Geheiligt werde Dein Name,	Hallowed be thy name,
Dein Reich Komme,	Thy Kingdom come,
Dein Wille geschehe,	Thy will be done,
Wie im Himmel	On Earth
als auch auf Erden,	as it is in Heaven,
Unser taeglich Brot	And give us this day
gib uns heute,	our daily bread,
Und vergib uns unsere	And forgive us our
Schuld,	trespasses
Wie auch wir vergeben	As we forgive those who
unseren Schuldigern…	trespass against us…
…In nomine patris	…In the name of the
et filii spiritu sancti	Father, the Son, and
	the Holy Spirit
Vater unser,	Our Father,
der Du bist im Himmel,	which art in Heaven,
Geheiligt werde Dein Name,	Hallowed be thy name,
Dein Reich komme,	Thy kingdom come,
Dein Wille geschehe,	Thy will be done,
Wie im Himmel	On Earth
als auch auf Erden,	as it is in Heaven,

Unser taeglich Brot	And give us this day
gib uns heute,	our daily bread,
Und vergib uns unsere	And forgive us our
Schuld,	trespasses,
Wie auch wir vergeben	As we forgive those who
unseren Schuldigern,	trepass against us,
Und fuehre uns nicht	And lead us not
in Versuchung,	into temptation,
Sondern erloese uns	But deliver us
von dem Uebel,	from evil,
Denn Dein ist das Reich,	For thine is the kingdom,
Und die Kraft und	The power and
die Herrlichkeit,	Glory,
In Ewigkeit…	For ever and ever…
…Amen.	…Amen
In nomine patris	In the name of the
et filii spiritu sancti	Father, the son, and
	the Holy Spirit
Amen	Amen
In nomine patris	In the name of the
et filii spiritu sancti	Father, the son, and
	the Holy Spirit
Amen	Amen
Vater unser,	Our Father,
der Du bist im Himmel,	which art in Heaven,
Geheiligt werde Dein Name,	Hallowed be thy name,

Dein Reich komme,	Thy Kingdom come,
Dein Wille geschehe,	Thy will be done,
Wie im Himmel	On Earth
als auch auf Erden,	as it is in Heaven,
Unser taeglich Brot	And give us this day
gib uns heute,	our daily bread,
Und verbig uns unsere	And forgive us our
Schuld,	trespasses
Wie auch wir vergeben	As we forgive those who
unseren Schuldigern.	trespass against us.
Vater hoere meine Stimme.	Father, hear my prayer!
Herr hoere meine Stimme!	Lord, hear my prayer!
Lasser uns beten.	Let us pray.
In nomine patris	In the name of the
et filii spiritu sancti	Father, and the son,
	and the Holy Spirit
Der Herr...	The Lord...
ist ein Schatten ueber	is my shepherd.
Deiner Rechten Hand...	I shall not want!
Amen	Amen
Vater unser,	Our Father,
Dein ist das Reich,	Thine is the Kingdom,
Und die Kraft,	And the Power,
Und die Herrlichkeit,	And the glory,
In Ewigkeit,	for ever and ever...
...Amen	...Amen

CHAPTER TWENTY-TWO

"Emergence."

The Posleen tunnel drive was extremely useful, tactically, but enormously expensive energetically. The only really functional fuel for it was antimatter, which was both costly to make and extremely unstable. But there was no way that any ship could have enough fuel space, bunkerage, for fusion bottles to produce the same power with any reasonable range.

Converting ships to use both ley-line transport, which was much cheaper energetically, *and* tunnel drive meant that something had to go.

In the case of the superdreadnought *Lexington IV* it had been Ronnie's pride and joy: the primary mass-driver. However, the Hedren in the Daga Nine system didn't have any ships really suitable for the main gun to engage. Would have been cute, mind you. Even their battleships would have come apart like tinker-toys. But they just needed the space.

What filled the space where the enormous mass driver had once been, its fusion bottles and capacitors, its grav drivers and magazines, was *nine* tunnel drives from Posleen Command Dodecahedrons, C-Decs, and one of the largest containment vessels of antimatter ever made. Even *with* that much antimatter, the ship only had the range to go from the nearest star to the Daga system. Going *out* they'd have to find a ley-line.

And they would be going out. They did not intend to stay. The mission of the *Lady Lex* was simple: Trash *everything* in the system then get the fuck out. They'd be back. But they'd have to refuel to do it.

And Ronnie didn't get to do the fun stuff like run the guns. Indowy crewed most of the ship, doing everything they could that a human wasn't absolutely critical for. The rest of the crew, mostly gunnery, tactical and sensors, was a mash of Indi crewmen and officers and some Northern European and Japanese "old guard."

But, in truth, they were just filling. The only thing Ronnie needed to run the *Lex* was floating beside her.

Unlike many of the being's fellows, the group that was coming to be known as the *Daisies*, Lex did not choose to have a real body. Each of the Command Cyborg Entities took for his or her personality that most closely associated with the ship they inhabited.

The *Lexington* had *never* had a girlie name. No former movie star or pin-up girl for her.

The *Lex* was called "The Blue Ghost."

"Hedren battle squadron designate BatRon One at one hundred thousand kilometers 135 mark 4," the entity whispered. She was barely visible, a cloaked and hooded cerulean apparition. "Recommend come to 134 mark 2 to close for engagement."

"Maneuvering, make it so," Ronnie said, her arms crossed. "Launch fighters, tell them to go for the heavies."

Battle Commodore Ularn watched the visual playback in wonder. Six ships had flashed into substance in mid-space. Well inside the normal dimensional warp point so they were using some other means of faster-than-light travel. But he ignored all but one.

"*What* is *that?*"

The single ship, alone, outmassed his entire task force. It was clear it was not terribly maneuverable. But if it got into engagement range they were all toast.

"The ship is one that was classed as salvage," the Marro intelligence officer replied. "One of their superdreadnoughts. The humans used them in a previous war but some were boarded in secret and determined to be unrecoverable."

"In that case, someone made a very *deadly* mistake," Ularn said. "Maneuvering, get us around that thing. Stay out of its range and close with the invasion fleet."

"Battle Master, that may be impossible," the Kotha Fleet Maneuvering Officer replied. "The human task force is in a geometry such that we cannot do both."

Ularn considered that information for a moment then ground his beak.

"Close the invasion fleet."

"BatRon One maneuvering to close the invasion fleet," the task force tactical officer said. "If they maintain current trajectory and acceleration, we're going to cross their T."

"And all the way back to the surface warfare days,

that's the killer app," Ronnie said, nodding. The six ships were all that they had had time to refurbish. To the extent they were refurbished. The *Lex*, two cruisers and three destroyers were all that stood between the Hedren task force and the invasion ships, none of which were capable of duking it out with warships.

On the other hand, of those six one *was* the *Lex*.

"Signal task force, close in line ahead, *Lex* leads the way. Order fighters to close from the rear. We got some destruction to deal out."

"They are going to cross our front," the Kotha maneuvering officer said.

"Engage with meson cannons at maximum range," Ularn replied. It was probably useless, but it was the only choice he had. That or avoiding confrontation which would have equal or worse consequences. At least dying in a space battle was relatively clean compared to what the Imeg would mete out.

The Hedren had the range. Their heavy forward meson cannons had a range of almost five light seconds. Each of the four Hedren battleships in the squadron, long cylinders bristling with secondary weapons, had two of the massive cannons forward. Capable of punching through six *meters* of homogenous steel, they were brutal devices of war. The ten cruisers and four destroyers each had lesser versions with the same range if not the same power.

And they used it, concentrating the fire of all thirty-six meson cannons on the *Lex*.

❖   ❖   ❖

"We're taking a pounding on the port side," the executive officer said. "Three plasma guns and two mass drivers off-line. Crews are on it."

Commander Burenda Kidwai knew his head should have been on a spike. Many of the officers he had come to know over the years, including *all* of his former commanders, were either under arrest or "permanently retired." Some had been killed in various incidents as the "Old Guard" reestablished control over Fleet.

Recognizing in his new commander, female that she was, a degree of frankness he had summoned the courage to ask why he had not joined them.

"You're competent," the bitch had answered. *"If you manage to keep your hands out of the till and remain competent, you'll go far. If you don't, I'm going to space your ass. End story."*

He had, thus far, carefully "kept his hand out of the till" and worked very hard to get this massive old warhorse into action. Yes, there were problems. Large sections of the old ship were still without environmental controls or even lights. Many of the drive bottles were still inactive, reducing the ship's already slow acceleration to a crawl. But he had done everything he could in a most "competent" manner to rectify those problems. And *all* of her guns were working, which was the important part. He did not want to breathe vacuum.

The ship shuddered, ever so slightly, at another barrage from the enemy guns.

"We can engage with mass drivers," he noted. Breathing vacuum because your ship gets pounded into scrap was no fun either.

"Let 'em shoot," Ronnie said. "Sorry, *Lex*."

"Portions of the metal of the aircraft carrier *Lexington*, sunk by the Japanese at the battle of the Coral Sea, were infused into this dreadnought in its construction," the ghost whispered. "More were added from the *Lexington II*, an aircraft carrier that withstood kamikaze strikes and fought on. In this iteration of my being, I am the survivor of virtual destruction three more times in the Posleen War. I have fought on sea and in space in every worthy battle to be found in this arm of the galaxy. This is the price of being a warship. I agree that we should close."

"Fuck yeah," Ronnie said.

"They are surely in range by now," the Kotha tactical officer said.

"Yes, they are," Ularn replied, grinding his beak. "They are waiting until they are in range to utterly *destroy* us. They are willing to take damage to do so. We must send a message to the communications relays. Tell the High Command that we have seriously underestimated the human willingness to fight. And tell them that's probably the last thing they'll hear from us."

The Hedren fleet was arrayed in a stellate pattern, the battleships at the center and the cruisers and destroyers arranged outwards.

The human fleet was in line astern. Which meant the Hedren could get angled shots on the human ships. But they could only hit one side and they were concentrating all their fire on the superdreadnought, trying to take it out.

Then it rolled.

❖   ❖   ❖

"Starboard batteries coming in range of Hedren targets," the tactical officer said.

"Shift control to automatic," Ronnie said. "Concentrate on the heavies. Bring fighters in from the rear. Tell everybody to hold on. *Lex*, open fire."

The enormous globe-breaking mass driver had been removed. But the *Lexington* had been designed to not only break globes, but to destroy the huge swarms of lesser Posleen ships. B-Decs, a C-Dec surrounded by twelve Lampreys, equated nicely to one of the Hedren cruisers. A C-Dec to one of the destroyers.

And the *Lex* was designed to take on *thousands* of such, not a mere handful.

Arrayed along her sides were literally hundreds of lasers, each capable of destroying a Lamprey. Nearly as many heavy plasma cannons capable of gutting a C-Dec. But the pride and joy were over two dozen grav-guns per side. Each of the GalTech 200mm mass-drivers accelerated a one hundred and fifty kilogram chunk of refractory heavy metal to ten percent of light-speed. The kinetic impact was equivalent to a sixteen megaton nuclear weapon.

The impacts from the Hedren meson cannons had barely caused the ship to shudder.

The Blue Ghost's first broadside nearly threw everyone off their feet.

"Report!" Ularn shouted, sealing his suit. The fact that he had to seal his suit in the deeply buried tactical room told him everything he really had to know. He was surprised he was *alive* to ask the question. "What do we have left?"

"*Ondun, Othelululi, Avakog, Baglitua, Rinarint, Savatulaulalo* and *Elondeg,* are all damaged and out of the battle," the maneuvering officer said. "*Bango, Ingona, Lirulimoru, Mirornc* and *Otha* are still in the fight. The rest are ... gone."

"We may be 'in the fight,'" the *Ingona's* commander said. "But our meson cannons and a good bit of our secondary weapons are out. We've not much to fight *with.*"

"All remaining ships, skew turn, engage with secondaries," UlARN said.

"Fighters incoming at kang tai delta eight," the fleet combat officer said.

"Ships maneuver for fighter engage—"

The Kotha didn't manage to get the word "engagement" out before the second barrage hit the task force.

"Their last two battleships just went up, sir," the *Lex's* tactical officer said. "One cruiser's still limping along and a couple of the others are sort of alive but drifting. One battleship drifting."

"Away boarding forces," McNair said. "Grab whatever intel and prisoners they can. Tell them to be careful; those ships are right on the edge of being bright flashes in the night sky. Task force break up and move to designated targets. Rendezvous at Karum ley point in no more than twenty hours. Send a message on the Himmit frequency and ask them to report that initial space forces in the Daga system have been reduced. Maneuvering, move us over to cover the retreat of the invasion fleet. And we might need to give the SS a little cover fire."

❖　　❖　　❖

"Do we have an ID on those vehicles?"

Group General Gweldund knew to his shame that this planet was lost. He had been left on the planet with little but construction and consolidation forces, so given the scale of the attack it was going to be hard to blame him. However, it was his duty to complete the transmitter and then *hold* it. There was no avoiding that truth.

But there were other forces on the surface as well as those in space. From the size of this task force that had appeared out of nowhere they were not enough ships to hold the system. Which meant that, eventually, the remaining forces would be reinforced both by the transmitter and from space. So, the more damage he did to the incoming forces the better.

"Sensors do not recognize most of them," Commander Savanass, the Marro chief of intelligence and sensors said. "Some of them are shuttles. The rest... Ah, I have a visual from Ingia Station." The Marro considered the image and then shook his head slowly back and forth. "These appear to be ground combat vehicles. But... they are not designed for orbital insertion. They are just... ground combat vehicles on platforms."

"Some sort of feint?" General Gweldund asked. "We do not have enough power to stop both the bombardment and the vehicles. I'm not sure we have the power to stop *either*. But if we concentrate on one, we cannot interdict the other."

"They appear to have some sort of shielding that prevents the worst effects of reentry," the Marro said, examining the sensor readings closely. "If they also have some way of slowing... they could be a ground threat."

"Shift fire to the vehicles," General Gweldund ordered. "There is no way to fully stop the bombardment. The transmitter *will* be destroyed. But we must make it possible to retake the surface."

"We will do our best," the Glandri officer in charge of defenses said. "But with all the metal that thing is throwing out in the way, there is no way we will get most of them."

"I must contact the Imeg for support," General Gweldund said, his tentacles wrippling. "They will not be pleased."

"Mein Gott," Frederick shouted as a Marder in front of him exploded in fire. He couldn't even tell what had hit it, just that it was destroyed.

"They're starting to get through the kinetics," Harz said blandly. "This should get interesting."

Frederick could only see it because the Leopard had, for some reason, turned over on its side and half upside down. There was no way to control the tank. All they could do was fall on the preselected routes. Two vehicles, a Leopard and an armored support vehicle, bumped, tangled, exploded into fire and pieces. Their Leopard dropped through the debris, a chunk of armor plating flashed out of the fire, slammed the vehicle and suddenly one of Frederick's vision blocks blanked. The system quickly spread the load but the view was slightly grainier. He wished he could just turn them off. The tank was now spinning and it was getting very disorienting. They also were starting to build up G forces and he was being pulled forward in his combat harness. He grabbed a sickness bag and was noisy with it.

"Ribbon chute coming out," Harz said. "Let's hope it doesn't tangle."

There was a thump, and the tank swung back and forth for a moment then ended up in a nose-down configuration. The KEWs were beginning to slam into the ground below them, bursts like nuclear weapons in a ripple across the ground, growing and swelling, thousands of them.

"We can't survive *that*!" Adler shouted.

"Most of it will be gone by the time we land," Harz said, yawning. "Most of it."

Sun-bright flashes, roiling mushroom clouds, and the panzer dropped straight into the heart of them. Frederick was momentarily glad. The view was, at least, cut off. All he could see was blackness shot with lightning as the clouds rearranged the massive energy released by the orbital kinetic weapons.

"How long until we hit?" Adler shouted.

"Coming up in four . . . three . . . two . . ."

The sensation of falling abruptly stopped with barely a bump. The Leopard seemed to pause for a moment, then dropped downwards, hard, slamming to the ground.

"Blowing bolts," Harz said to an almost unnoticed additional thump. "Forward, *Schutze*! Follow the icon on your blocks."

A karat had appeared, off-center to the right, and Frederick revved the engine of the Leopard then started towards it. He was still driving in utter blackness lit only by occasional flashes of lightning. And the ground was beyond rough, the panzer repeatedly dropping into craters that were, fortunately, easy enough to drive out of.

"Slow, here, *Schutze*," Harz said as additional icons started popping up. "We're reaching the assembly point."

The karat began to shift to the left and Frederick followed it slavishly. He realized after a moment that it was taking him down some sort of path. The path seemed to have nothing to do with the ground but as the other icons moved it occurred to him that the unit was being arrayed.

He considered the icons for a moment then then shook his head. Several panzers were missing, including that of the company commander.

"Stop," Harz said. "And now, we wait."

"For what?" Adler asked.

"To see who else made it."

CHAPTER TWENTY-THREE

"We made it," Daisy said.

From the outside there was little to see. Space was immense and even the best visual tracking systems had a hard time noting the brief flicker of starlight.

And just in case, the *Des Moines* had emerged in the visual shadow of a Jovian.

"Range to normal warp insertion for the Imeg ship is at nine light-seconds," the navigational officer said. "Recommend seven grav acceleration at 218 mark neg 12. That will put us in a swing around the subpolar region of the jovian and on line to intercept. If they're on time. If not, we can park in a Lagrange orbit and wait."

"Do it," Captain McNair said. He'd been studying his ass off on this space shit but it still didn't come naturally. And he didn't like that. He knew, as a captain, he had to understand every nuance of the environment. Unfortunately, he was still at heart a wet sailor. Three dimensions still sort of screwed with him. Fortunately, it didn't screw with Daisy. "I'm moving to the Battle Room. Inform me if there's any change."

"Coming with you," Daisy said.

"Absolutely," Jeff replied, grinning.

Technically, the compartment two decks below the bridge was called CIC, Combat Information Center. But Jeff had grown up in the days when it was simply called "The Battle Room." It was where the guns were controlled from and the radar and lookout information was received. He supposed "Combat Information Center" made sense but just as he damned well had called the crew to "Battle Stations," not "Condition One," he called it "The Battle Room." His new crew was just going to have to adjust.

"Any indications of cloaked ships?" he asked as he entered the compartment.

At the center of the compartment was a large holographic display of the immediate area. It could be zoomed in and out but generally was held as a bubble ranging out from the ship's location to ten light-seconds in every direction.

"Negative, sir," the tactical officer replied.

"And our friend?" Jeff asked, taking his seat and strapping in. The flex helmet for his suit was compressed into a small ball at the back of his neck. In the event of loss of air it would automatically deploy.

"Right on time," the TACO replied, using a light-wand to indicate the approaching ship.

"You know, I had a buddy back in the war," Jeff said. "That would be World War Two for you youngsters. He somehow got shanghaied into the commandoes that went over to mess with the Jerries. He said that one reason the Jerry sentries were so easy to kill was that they were just so damned regular. You could time their sentry beat to the second. Take that as a lesson, Lieutenant. Being absolutely regular in your actions is not a good thing in war."

"Yes, sir," the TACO said, trying not to shake his head.

"Daisy, connect me to the mentats, please."

"On line," Daisy said.

"Mentat Kang," Jeff said. "Imeg ship is on course and we're about to enter detection range. One hour to intercept. Time for you to work your magic."

Can you sense the ship? Mentat Shaina asked.

There are several, Sissy replied. *But that must be the one.*

Powerful, Kang thought. Very *powerful Sohon.*

Note the particles, Shaina thought. *Note the build-up of energy associated with their acceleration, the flex of the universe at their increase in mass. Even with our cloak, we give off traces. We must eliminate every trace. And we must do it invisibly. We do not want the Imeg sensing us as we sense it.*

I must go ready my team, Kang thought. *Ensure no trace.*

We will do our very best, Shaina replied.

"You up for this, Skank?" Redman asked as he strapped into his seat.

The three Banshee shuttles were lined up and prepared for launch. As the teams approached they spread out, distributing themselves so that if one of the shuttles was destroyed on approach, at least some of the teams would make it to the ship. The mission was still a go if they lost one shuttle. Two was an abort.

The interior of the shuttles was tight. Four ranks of seats ran down its interior, two outboard and two inboard. The boarders faced each other, knees interlocked. What with body armor, suits, battle-rattle and weapons, there wasn't enough room to swing a mouse much less a cat.

"I'm beginning to wonder," Adept Pawle replied calmly. "I can sense the power of the Imeg even here. It is powerful. Very powerful. And that is not the only problem..."

"There are *two* Imeg on the ship," Kang said, his eyes closed and apparently meditating. "One is a mentat in truth. Very powerful. The other...barely an adept. But he will still be a problem."

"We've got, what? Fourteen Sohon adepts and mentats?" Jake replied, his eyes closed as well. "Surely you guys can keep two under control."

"Colonel Mosovich," Kang replied. "Were I using Sohon, and I assuredly am not, I'm not sure that the Imeg would notice me from this distance. However, it is impossible to miss them. I do not want to reduce your confidence, but the relative disparity of force is that of, say, a battlecruiser to a battleship. We have two battlecruisers, a couple of cruisers and ten destroyers."

"Well, you guys better think about what it takes to become battleships, then," Jake replied. "It'll work out. And if it don't, we'll hardly know it."

Mentat Shaina and two of the lower level Indowy had taken up positions in the Battle Room.

Jeff was keeping one eye on the battle holo and one on the Indowy. But there wasn't much to see in the latter case. The Indowy didn't do a lotus when they were meditating; they knelt with their hands crossed, palms upwards and eyes closed. They'd been that way for the last forty-five minutes with no real change.

"We are detected," Shaina said. "Mentat Harris is closing down their communications. I shall be busy. Tuthiri will communicate."

"Close the target," Jeff snapped. "Prepare to launch shuttles. Open fire all secondary weapons."

"What class of ship is that?" Cruiser Master Goglugot said. "And where did it come from?"

Goglugot was a Kotha, as were most ship masters, the commander of the *Gorongur.* He had made this same run a dozen times so far and was less than pleased. He knew well the axiom of war that one should never develop a pattern. But the Imeg were less than interested in input from a lowly cruiser master. The Imeg loved order. Order was the way of the Hedren. So over and over again he had left on the identical schedule and entered warp at the identical point and now he was about to be fucked for it.

And would the *Imeg* take the blame? Unlikely. Not that he was probably going to face an Inquisition. Given the power of the ship he was up against, he was unlikely to face anything but death.

"A similar vessel was reported by scouts," the Marro combat officer replied. "It appears to be a new class. Capabilities are unknown. It was under cloak and apparently was enhancing with kratki. Thus we only detected it at less than a li. Neither the cloak capability nor the kratki enhancements were known to our intelligence. But the prominences forward are believed to be aesthetic."

"The prominences forward bother me less than the heavy weapons on its *side*!"

"Colonel," the shuttle pilot said. "We've been made. Launching in three . . . two . . . one."

There was a slight sideways acceleration and then gravity dropped away. The shuttles had anti-grav systems but most of their power was being devoted to maneuvering and inertial dampening.

Trained human pilots, given the right sort of seats and G suits, could sustain upwards of sixteen gravities of acceleration for brief periods. Maneuvers in Banshees in space could generate up to a hundred gravities. A hundred gravs would turn any human body into red mush.

To avoid being turned into red mush, all space combat vessels as well as ACS used inertial dampeners. The dampeners could reduce the acceleration gradient to nearly Earth normal. But they used a lot of power doing it. Using more power to create a notional "down" meant less maneuverability. And the pilots of the shuttles wanted all the maneuverablity they could get.

The space between the two ships was a cauldron of fire. Mass-drivers, grasers and plasma cannons filled the intervening space to the point the pilot wasn't sure that *any* of the shuttles would survive.

The Hedren ship used primarily grasers, gamma ray frequency lasers, while the human ship mounted mass-drivers and plasma cannons. The latter two were visible while the grasers were, unfortunately, invisible. They did, however, show up on sensors. And her sensors were showing *no* way through the fire.

"I thought the mentats were going to shut down the enemy fire!" her co-pilot snapped.

"Guess *that* plan is out the window," the pilot replied as the shields shuddered from a direct graser hit.

"The ship has launched small-craft," the combat officer said as the *Gorongur* shuddered under the power of the *Des Moines'* secondaries. "Shuttles or space fighters."

"Then engage and destroy them," Goglugot snapped, then grabbed his head.

The enemy is attempting to board.

The Imeg's thoughts lashed the Cruiser Master's brain with fire. And it wasn't like he needed the distraction.

"Only one thing on this ship worth boarding for, my lord," Goglugot replied, tightly. "I suggest you prepare to defend yourself. The Glandri are yours to command."

I will order them to deploy. If I or my apprentice is lost, it will go hard upon you, Cruiser Master.

"I doubt any of us will survive to face the Inquisition, my lord," Goglugot said. "For that reason, if no other, we will fight hard."

As the Imeg released him, Goglugot rubbed his cranium with a hand-tentacle.

"You know," he said, looking at the combat officer. "There are times I wish I was a lowly Marro."

"Too many arms, Cruiser Master," the Marro replied. "We're attempting to engage the shuttles but much of our fire is being diverted. I assume by kratki. Grasers are bending in space and splashing off their shields."

"I think I'll leave that for our Lord Imeg to deal with."

"Adept Tuthiri?" Jeff said, calmly. "The shuttles are taking fire."

"The human team is attempting to shut down the enemy's guns," Tuthiri replied, calmly. His fur, though, was rippling in distress. "The Imeg is preventing that. Also attempting to shut down our systems as well as trying to get the fusion drives to explode. *We* are preventing that. It is the best we can do at the moment. The Imeg is . . . powerful."

"Do we abort?" Jeff asked.

There was no reply.

Shaina, Sissy thought. *We could use some help here.*

We are strengthening the shuttle's shields, Shaina replied. *As well as protecting the ship. We cannot engage the Imeg nor its ship directly.*

Well, I'm not sure there's enough of us to stop this bastard, Sissy thought. *Kang, watch your ass.*

"Kang?" Jake said. "Mentat Kang? *Glasshoppah*?"

"Not . . . *now* . . ." Kang replied, his jaw tight. "This bastard is . . ."

"Do we need to *abort*?"

"Can your forces fight through the defenders without help?" Kang asked.

"Yes."

"Then, no, we do *not* need to abort."

❖   ❖   ❖

"Failure in mass driver controls," the gunnery officer snapped. "Mass drivers nonresponsive."

"Track it down," Jeff replied.

"Back up," Guns said, looking puzzled. "Continuing engagment."

"The Imeg is breaking through," Tuthiri said. "The lower level Imeg is holding reality on his ship while the higher level is attacking the *Des Moines* and the shuttles."

"I *felt* that," Daisy said, working her shoulder. "He'd better watch it or he's going to piss me off. And he doesn't *want* to piss me off."

"Maneuvering to dock," the shuttle pilot said.

The Banshee went through one of those maneuvers that was only possible in space, spinning through three dimensions and slamming its rear into the hull of the Hedren ship. Tractor clamps locked it in place as flexible seals slapped onto the armor of the warship.

"On and locked," she snapped. "Go, Colonel!"

As the lock dilated outward Payback slapped a heavy-duty burn patch onto the hull.

"Clear!"

The patch began to flare with eye-searing brilliance then got even hotter and stronger than normal.

"What the . . . ?"

"Kang's reinforcing," Mosovich said. "All teams, lock and load!"

The patch burned through the refractory hull in mere seconds, then the cut section of hull slammed outwards, bouncing off of the interior bulkhead. The seals were not perfect and the gaseous metal from the cutting patch was sucked out to the side in a torrent of wind from the interior of the ship.

The DAG teams ignored the wind, hopped over the low and very hot coaming, then spread out on the interior of the Hedren ship.

"Clear," Mangler said as he took a knee in the corridor. The light on the ship was low and a weird violet. But his combat goggles quickly adjusted it to human normal. They could do less about the gravity, which was a touch high.

A Marro whipped around the corner, a sealing kit in his hand, and hissed to a stop at the sight of the boarders. He barely had time to do more before being cut in half by a blast of razor-sharp flechettes.

"Clear," Mangler repeated.

"Tell the shuttles to blow clear," Jeff said as the ship shuddered under the fire from the Hedren cruiser.

"Shuttles, blow clear and retreat," the boats officer said. "Follow assigned vector."

"Clearing vector of friendly fire," the gunnery officer said. "They should be able to run right down the side of the ship."

"Tuthiri, get word to Colonel Mosovich that we're clearing the shuttles. Don't bother holding that area. Bridge, maneuver nose forward to the Hedren ship. Guns, warm up the QT. I'm tired of taking fire from this bastard."

"The shuttles are *leaving*," Mueller said as Payback slapped another charge on a door. "Maybe we should open this up—"

The blast door slid to either side, revealing an empty corridor.

"Like that. Thanks, Kang."

"Actually, that was Skank," Kang said, his face sweating. "I'm trying to keep the Imeg from *killing* us."

As he said that the shuttles blasted clear and there was a moment of wind again, quickly cut off.

"I hate vacuum," Mueller said as he trotted forward. "It really sucks."

"*Don't* make me laugh," Skank said. "I'm having a hard enough time concentrating." .

"Tuthiri, tell your people to make sure the QT guns are not interfered with," Jeff said as the ship maneuvered. It took a moment to pivot it to face the Imeg ship and it was taking fire the whole time.

"QT in target basket in five seconds," the gunnery officer said. "We're getting pounded. Twenty percent drop in fire on the port side."

"That is about to change," Jeff said. "Honey, I think you're the gunner on this."

"QT guns charged," Daisy said.

"Fire on bearing."

"I have lock," Guns said.

"Firing," Daisy replied.

"What the hell?" Mangler shouted as the corridor bucked and the air began to howl with depressurization again. Between the shuddering deck and the wind he slid into a sprawl, which was a good thing since a beam of green fire flashed over his head. "Glandri!"

The porcupinelike beings were spilling into a cross-corridor, laying down a withering fire with their neural whips. Mangler grabbed a stanchion and slid backwards, angling his railgun around the corner and firing. He wasn't blind, though. The scope on the rifle fed to his goggles and he could lay down some pretty accurate fire that way.

Glandri blood was blue. That became apparent as it splashed all over the corridor.

Recto and Stalker stacked up on him, firing from a kneeling position and standing respectively. Stalker, though, leaned a little too far out getting his shots and Mangler suddenly had a thrashing body on top of him.

"Stalker's down!" Recto snapped.

"Got 'im," Fudge replied, grabbing the ankles of the clearing specialist and dragging him backwards. As he did Stalker quit convulsing, shuddered once and then was still. "Fuck."

"Fuck this," Mangler said, reaching behind his back and pulling out what looked like a flare gun with a thick grip. "Suicide-bars! Clear!"

The antimatter grenade launcher did not have the same connection to his goggles but he didn't care. He just aligned it with the corridor, fired all five rounds in the magazine and ducked around the corner.

A moment later the cross-corridor flashed with fire. A Glandri, most of it anyway, hit the starboard bulkhead and flopped to the floor.

He slid his rifle back around the corner, got a good look, then stood up.

"Clear. But I don't think we're going to be using this route."

"Enemy fire had dropped to minimal," the tactical officer said. "Only two grasers firing... Make that none," he finished as the ship shuddered from mass-driver fire.

The enemy cruiser's surface had been stripped. It was open in multiple places and all of its gun emplacments were toast.

"That's an *ugly* weapon," Jeff said. "I like it."

"Fire again, sir?" Guns asked.

"We want the ship to keep functioning until we get the teams back," McNair replied. "So, no. Maybe later."

"*What* just *hit* us?" Goglugot asked.

"Unknown weapon," the combat officer replied. "Apparently generated by the 'aesthetic' forward prominences. All starboard weapons inoperative. Four port-side weapons operative. Multiple hull breaches. Weapon caused a positive reading on the kratki detector. A *large* positive reading."

"Can we still warp?"

"Negative," the maneuvering officer replied. The Hotha raised four tentacles in the race's equivalent of a shrug. "Engines are functional but all external warp nacelles are down. We have normal space drive capability and that is all."

"Begin maneuvers to attempt to return to Caracool," Goglugot said. "Continue to try to call for support. Surely *someone* must have noticed that there is a *space battle* going on around here!"

"Fuck," Jake muttered.

Where the Himmit thought the Imeg might be hiding was a bulkhead. They could cut through it, but that would take time. Time they didn't have.

They'd lost seven guys so far to the Glandri

defenders and the Marro were starting to weapon up. They had to find the Imeg, grab him and get the hell *out*.

Worse, their Sohon supports were starting to look rocky.

"Kang, can you figure out how to get to the Imeg?"

"Right, I think," Kang said, his face sweating. "Right, left, down two crossings then left again."

Jake sketched that out on the plans they had and sent it out.

"Let's *move*, people."

"The target is attempting to slingshot around the jovian," the tactical officer said. "Probably trying to run for home. Or maybe for support. Other ships in the system are attempting to close this position. Thirty minutes, minimum, before the first one comes into range. And that's a destroyer. Easy enough to take out."

"Cloaked ships?" Jeff asked.

"None apparent," the TACO replied. "But we can't detect them at more than five light-seconds."

"Stay alert," Captain McNair said. "And get word to the colonel that he needs to either get the Imeg and get out or abort."

"Clear," Payback said as he fired the cutting charge. He opened his eyes and looked at the charge that was just sitting there. The initiator had gone off, but not the charge. "Dust Devil!"

"Trying," Adept Hoover said, his teeth gritted. The charge flared, died, flared, died.

"Ain't gonna do it," Payback replied.

❖   ❖   ❖

Gerrard, Pawle thought, calling to one of the support adepts on the *Des Moines*. *Take over for me.*

It is . . . hard, Highlands replied. *The Imeg is immensely powerful.*

Fuck hard, Pawle thought, savagely. *Take over for me. I have more important things to do!*

The charge suddenly flared white-hot and the door flew into the far corridor.

"Go!" Skank shouted.

"Easy for you to say," Mangler muttered as green fire filled the corridor. He was laying down railgun rounds like he had unlimited ammo and he didn't. He was down two thirds of his initial load.

He pulled his railgun back to reload and was just seating another mag, both hands occupied, when what looked like a green-glowing crystal ball bounced down the corridor.

"Uh-oh."

He dropped his rifle and magazine, reaching down to scoop the thing up when there was a white flash.

Pawle held his hand up, deflecting the plasma explosion away from himself and Redman. But that was *all* he could deflect.

Mosovich winced as most of Alpha team was wiped out in one blast. The Hedren grenades were as bad as suicide bars.

"Bravo, bound forward and clear the corridor," he said, looking around. Most of Charlie had been out of the area of effect. The only portion that wasn't was Pawle and his team. Pawle and Redman were still there, and apparently unharmed, but Gombo and Leaf were both burned to a crisp.

"On it," Ugly said as Bubbles trotted down the corridor. "What the hell was that, Snake?"

"Bad stuff," Mosovich replied.

Bubbles extended his hand around the turn and fired two suicide bars down the corridor.

"Go!" he shouted as the explosions rent the air.

Chicklet and GE rounded the corner and laid down fire into the smoke of the explosion. There probably wasn't anything there, but it never hurt to be sure.

They trotted to the holes left by the suicide bars and maneuvered past them then down to the third door.

"This the room?" GE asked.

"Supposed to be," Chicklet said, then gasped, grabbing at his head.

GE turned his head to the side just too late to avoid having blood and brains splash all over him. He circled in place, looking for a threat. Then his head began to throb.

"What the fuck is *happening*?"

Concentrate on the Imeg, Kang thought. *Place all your power on the Imeg.*

We are, Sissy replied. *It is all we can do to keep it from destroying your team.*

Get the Indowy to protect us, Kang replied. *Keep the ship from communicating and attack the Imeg. That is your sole job now.*

❖   ❖   ❖

"Dust-Devil?" Hooter said, looking at the door. Two charges had gone out so far.

"Busy," the adept gasped, grabbing at his head. "Very busy."

"Got it," Pawle said. "Redman, get me up to the door."

Redman maneuvered the adept up to the blast door and set him in front of it. Like the other two, Pawle had his eyes closed. But he seemed to be seeing anyway.

The adept laid his hand on the door and leaned forward.

"The bonds of this material are a poor reality," Pawle muttered. "A bare *semblance* of reality..."

"Stack up and cover Skank," Jake said. "Entry team, get ready."

"You. Are. Not. *Real*," Pawle gasped as the door disintegrated into dust.

And Redman blew back in a welter of crimson.

"Oh, holy *fuck*," Dumbo muttered.

They'd found the Imeg.

"What the hell *are* those?" Hannibal screamed. He was pumping railgun rounds into the compartment and all he was getting was bouncers. The rounds wouldn't scratch the nightmares in the room.

"Imeg," Wind shouted, then blasted backwards to thump into the far bulkhead.

The two creatures in the room were nightmare, a mass of rippling black tentacles and armored bodies. The tentacles were coated in blades but that was not what was killing the team. It was the half dozen weapons each of them wielded. Expertly.

Suicide bars wouldn't detonate. Railgun rounds bounced off a hard-held shield. And still they continued to fire and slice, destroying anything that came near them.

"Back up," Kang said. "Get out of the doorway. Skank, Devil, on me. Mule, behind us. Target the one on the left."

"On it," Mueller said, managing to get a firing angle over the smaller adepts.

The three adepts managed to establish a shield that stopped the fire from the Imeg. Then they pushed back.

Keep them from reinforcing each other, Kang thought.

Trying, Dust-Devil replied.

Sissy, support here.

We . . . have them separated, Sissy replied.

Drive down the shield of the lesser, Kang thought. *It is not reality.*

Mueller could *see* the effect of the battle between the two groups. The air in the compartment was heating up as irresistible force met immovable object. He could even see the shields of the Imeg, now, glowing white-hot under the power of the human adepts.

And he could see when the one on the left finally collapsed.

Railgun rounds, though, bounced off the armor of the body. He searched for weaknesses and finally found one at the juncture of the tentacles and the body. The knuckle there was tough, but it finally surrendered and the Imeg was blasted back in a green spray of ichor.

Suddenly, the railgun was ripped from his hands, turned, and slammed forward, barrel-first, into his brain.

✧　　✧　　✧

As the redoubtable NCO dropped, Pawle shuddered and mentally stepped back.

Skank, what are you doing? Kang thought.

Wait, Master.

You can't hold up a stress card, Dust-Devil thought. *WAIT.*

Pawle, in fact, did not know what he was doing. But what they had been doing so far wasn't working. So he reached.

He reached, in fact, into the nearby engine room. Found the fusion bottles of the ship. Found the plasma power runs. Felt for the connections, felt for the *power*. And he *reached*.

The Imeg's shield began to glow white-hot and then went down and down and down and down…

"Mother *fucker!*" Mosovich shouted, sliding past the adepts holding the door. "I'm going to motherfucking *kill* your ass!"

A tentacle lashed across the room, its bladed edge flashing towards his throat.

Mosovich merely whipped out the Posleen monomolecular boma blade he'd held for nigh on sixty years, a boma blade he'd picked up on Barwhon seemingly ages ago, and held it up.

The armored tentacle hit the monomolecule edge and separated in half, the severed end clanging against a bulkhead as the remaining tentacle began to spray green ichor across the compartment.

Nearly a hundred years of combat experience, and nine adepts worth of protection, took Mosovich across the compartment. He didn't need protection from the tentacles of the nightmare in the room, he had all he needed in the razor-edged blade of his former foes. That and lots of experience.

He waded straight into the Imeg, which quickly realized that going tentacle to blade was a losing proposition. Its shield reduced by the combined force of the adepts, it retreated until it was backed into the bulkhead. It tried to open a hole in the bulkhead but the Indowy adepts prevented that change in reality.

Jake knew the objective was capturing the creature that had destroyed his friend. So he didn't, in fact, kill it. He just kept chopping and chopping, severing tentacle after tentacle, shortening them and shortening them, until the thing lay in a puddle of ichor, its tentacles mere pumping stumps.

He knew it was still deadly but he got down in that green blood on one knee and looked into one of its multifaceted black eyes.

"We're going to take you apart like a jigsaw puzzle," he whispered. "And we're not going to bother putting you back together. Kang, put this thing out."

CHAPTER TWENTY-FOUR

"Hey, Commodore," Mike said as he and Michelle appeared in the CIC of the *Lex*.

"General O'Neal?" Ronnie said, looking around. "Where...?"

"Long story," Mike replied. "Just be here a moment."

He looked over at Michelle who was looking very pale.

"You okay, Shelly?"

"You haven't called me that since I was a kid," Michelle answered. "And, no, the answer is, I'm not okay. *We're* not okay. Kang has the Imeg back on the *Des Moines*."

"Good news," Mike said.

"No, *bad* news," Michelle said, rubbing her forehead. "DAG was nearly wiped out doing it. Many of them *by* the Imeg. They're much stronger than we thought. Stronger than we could have believed. He's transferring the information across the mentats. But

565

the force we have here... If we can keep them from destroying the ships, the SS, we'll be lucky."

"Commodore, discontinue support missions and get your ships out of the system," Mike said instantly. "Contact Admiral Chun and add that order for *his* ships. Use remaining antimatter, all of it, to make max jumps towards the warp entry point then get the hell out."

"The Hedren are bound to send reinforcements..." Ronnie replied.

"Understood," Mike said. "You'll be back. But you need to come back fueled and with Sohon supports. Michelle, get all available mentats to base Delta X-Ray. And *we* need to go join the SS."

"Yes, Father," Michelle said, nodding. Then she winced. "The Imeg are up. This is not going to be good."

"Honey, being on the wrong side of a Posleen tenaral charge ain't good," Mike said, placing his hand on her shoulder. "This here's a walk in the park. Let's roll."

Gamalsarad, Emperor (Elect) of the Tular Po'oslena-kar, considered the message. It had been sent across nearly a thousand light-years, through dead star systems and the ley-lines of black holes, following the sinuous Hidden Path.

But it was a message the Tular had awaited for a very long time.

"Prepare the Fleet," he growled, his crest lifting as combat hormones flooded his body. "The time has come to Return."

"Destination, Emperor?" his aide asked.

"Earth."

Where the silent voices whisper
Find the course that is your own
And however great the obstacle
You will never be alone
For I have watched the path of angels
And I have heard the heavens roar
There is strife within the tempest
But calm in the eye of the storm...

The following is an excerpt from:

MISSION OF HONOR

DAVID WEBER

Available from Baen Books
July 2010
hardcover

Chapter One

ANY DICTIONARY EDITOR STYMIED for an illustration of the word "paralyzed" would have pounced on him in an instant.

In fact, a disinterested observer might have wondered if Innokentiy Arsenovich Kolokoltsov, the Solarian League's Permanent Senior Undersecretary for Foreign Affairs, was even breathing as he stared at the images on his display. Shock was part of that paralysis, but only part. And so was disbelief, except that *disbelief* was far too pale a word for what he was feeling at that moment.

He sat that way for over twenty seconds by Astrid Wang's personal chrono. Then he inhaled explosively, shook himself, and looked up at her.

"This is *confirmed?*"

"It's the original message from the Manticorans, Sir," Wang replied. "The Foreign Minister had the chip couriered straight over, along with the formal note, as soon as he'd viewed it."

"No, I mean is there any independent confirmation of what they're *saying?*"

Despite two decades' experience in the ways of the Solarian League's bureaucracy, which included as the

Eleventh Commandment "Thou shalt *never* embarrass thy boss by word, deed, or expression," Wang actually blinked in surprise.

"Sir," she began a bit cautiously, "according to the Manties, this all happened at New Tuscany, and we still don't have independent confirmation of the *first* incident they say took place there. So—"

Kolokoltsov grimaced and cut her off with a wave of his hand. Of course it hadn't. In fact, independent confirmation of the first New Tuscany Incident—he could already hear the newsies capitalizing *this* one—would take almost another entire T-month, if Josef Byng had followed procedure. The damned Manties sat squarely inside the League's communications loop with the Talbott Sector. They could get word of events there to the Sol System in little more than three T-weeks, thanks to their never-to-be-sufficiently-damned wormhole junction, whereas any direct report from New Tuscany to Old Terra would take almost two months to make the journey by dispatch boat. And if it went through the Meyers System headquarters of the Office of Frontier Security, as regulations required, it would take over eleven T-weeks.

And assuming the Manties aren't lying and manufacturing all this evidence for some godforsaken reason, any report from Byng has to've been routed by way of Meyers, he thought. *If he'd shortcut the regulations and sent it directly by way of Mesa and Visigoth—like any admiral with a* functional *brain would have!—it would've been here eight days ago.*

He felt an uncharacteristic urge to rip the display unit from his desk and hurl it across the room. To watch it shatter and bounce back in broken bits and pieces. To curse at the top of his lungs in pure, unprocessed rage. But despite the fact that someone from pre-Diaspora Old Terra would have estimated his age at no more than forty, he was actually eighty-five T-years old. He'd spent almost seventy of those years working his way up to his present position, and now those decades of discipline, of learning how the game was played, came to his rescue. He remembered the *Twelfth* Commandment—"Thou shalt never admit the loss of thy composure before thine underlings"—and actually managed to smile at his chief of staff.

"That *was* a silly question, wasn't it, Astrid? I guess I'm not as immune to the effects of surprise as I'd always thought I was."

"No, Sir." Wang smiled back, but her own surprise—at the strength of his reaction, as much as at the news itself—still showed in her blue eyes. "I don't think anyone would be, under these circumstances."

"Maybe not, but there's going to be hell to pay over this one," he told her, completely unnecessarily. He wondered if he'd said it because he still hadn't recovered his mental balance.

"Get hold of Wodoslawski, Abruzzi, MacArtney, Quartermain, and Rajampet," he went on. "I want them here in Conference One in one hour."

"Sir, Admiral Rajampet is meeting with that delegation from the AG's office and—"

"I don't care who he's meeting with," Kolokoltsov said flatly. "Just tell him to be here."

"Yes, sir. Ah, may I tell him why the meeting is so urgent?"

"No." Kolokoltsov smiled thinly. "If the Manties are telling the truth, I don't want him turning up with any prepared comments. This one's too important for that kind of nonsense."

❖   ❖   ❖

"So what's this all about, anyway?" Fleet Admiral Rajampet Kaushal Rajani demanded as he strode into the conference room. He was the last to arrive—a circumstance Kolokoltsov had taken some care to arrange.

Rajampet was a small, wiry man, with a dyspeptic personality, well suited to his almost painfully white hair and deeply wrinkled face. Although he remained physically spry and mentally alert, he was a hundred and twenty-three years old, which made him one of the oldest human beings alive. Indeed, when the original first-generation prolong therapy was initially developed, he'd missed being too old for it by less than five months.

He'd also been an officer in the Solarian League Navy since he was nineteen, although he hadn't held a space-going command in over half a T-century, and he was rather proud of the fact that he did not suffer fools gladly. (Of course, most of the rest of the human race was composed almost exclusively of fools, in his considered opinion, but Kolokoltsov could hardly quibble with him on that particular point.) Rajampet was also a formidable force within the Solarian League's all-powerful bureaucratic hierarchy, although he fell just short of the very uppermost niche. He knew all of the Navy's ins and outs, all of its senior admirals, the complex web of its family alliances and patronage, where all the bodies were buried . . . and precisely whose pockets were filled at the trough of the Navy's graft and corruption. After all, his own were prominent among them, and he personally controlled the spigots through which all the rest of it flowed.

Now if only the idiot knew what the hell his precious Navy was up to, Kolokoltsov thought coldly.

"It seems we have a small problem, Rajani," he said out loud, beckoning the gorgeously bemedaled admiral towards a chair at the table.

"It bloody well *better* not be a 'small' problem," Rajampet muttered, only half under his breath, as he stalked across to the indicated chair.

"I beg your pardon?" Kolokoltsov said with the air of a man who hadn't quite heard what someone had said.

"I was in the middle of a meeting with the Attorney General's people," Rajampet replied, without apologizing for his earlier comment. "They still aren't done with all the indictments for those damned trials, which means we're only just now getting that whole business with Technodyne sorted out. I promised Omosupe and Agatá"—he twitched his head at Omosupe Quartermain, Permanent Senior Undersecretary of Commerce, and Permanent Senior Undersecretary of the Treasury Agatá Wodoslawski—"a recommendation on the restructuring by the end of the week. It's taken forever just to get everyone assembled so we could sit down and talk about it, and I don't appreciate being yanked away from something that important."

"I can understand why you'd resent being interrupted, Rajani," Kolokoltsov said coolly. "Unfortunately, this small matter's come up and it needs to be dealt with . . . immediately. And"—his dark eyes bored suddenly into Rajampet's across the table—"unless I'm seriously mistaken, it's rather closely related to what got Technodyne into trouble in the first place."

"What?" Rajampet settled the last couple of centimeters into his chair, and his expression was as perplexed as his voice. "What are you talking about?"

Despite his own irritation, Kolokoltsov could almost understand the admiral's confusion. The repercussions of the Battle of Monica were still wending their way through the Navy's labyrinthine bowels—and the gladiatorial circus of the courts was only just beginning, really—but the battle itself had been fought over ten T-months ago.

Although the SLN hadn't been directly involved in the Royal Manticoran Navy's destruction of the Monican Navy, the consequences for Technodyne Industries had been profound. And Technodyne had been one of the Navy's major contractors for four hundred years. It was perfectly reasonable for Rajampet, as the chief of naval operations, to be deeply involved in trying to salvage something from the shipwreck of investigations, indictments, and show trials, and Kolokoltsov never doubted that the admiral's attention had been tightly focused on that task for the past several T-weeks.

Even if it would have been helpful if he'd been able to give a modicum of his attention to dealing with this other *little problem*, the diplomat thought grimly.

"I'm talking about the Talbott Cluster, Rajani," he said out loud, letting just a trace of over-tried patience into his voice. "I'm talking about that incident between your Admiral Byng and the Manties."

"What about it?" Rajampet's tone was suddenly a bit cautious, his eyes wary, as instincts honed by a T-century of bureaucratic infighting reared their heads.

"It would appear the Manties were just as pissed off as their original note indicated they were," Kolokoltsov told him.

"And?" Rajampet's eyes turned warier than ever and he seemed to settle back into his chair.

"And they weren't joking about sending their Admiral Gold Peak to inquire into matters on the ground in New Tuscany."

"They weren't?" The question came from Wodoslawski, not Rajampet, and Kolokoltsov glanced at her.

She was twenty-five T-years younger than he was—a third-gerneration prolong recipient with dark red hair, gray eyes, and quite an attractive figure. She was also fairly new to her position as the real head of the Treasury Department, and she'd received it, following her predecesor's demise, only as a compromise between the other permanent senior undersecretaries. She knew perfectly well that she'd been everyone else's second choice—that all her current colleagues had allies they would really have preferred to see in that slot. But she'd been there for over a decade, now, and she'd solidified her powerbase quite nicely.

She was no longer the junior probationary member of the quintet of permanent undersecretaries who truly ran the League from their personal fiefdoms in the Foreign Ministry, Commerce Department, Interior Department, Department of Education and Information, and Treasury Department. She was, however, the only one of them who'd been out-system and unavailable when the first Manticoran diplomatic note arrived. As such, she could make an excellent claim to bearing no responsibility for how that note had been handled, and from her expression, Kolokoltsov thought sourly, she was thoroughly aware of that minor fact.

"No, Agatá," he said, moving his gaze to her. "No, they weren't. And just over a T-month ago—on November the seventeenth, to be precise—Admiral Gold Peak arrived at New Tuscany...to find Admiral Byng still there."

"Oh, shit," Permanent Senior Undersecretary of the Interior Nathan MacArtney muttered. "Don't tell us Byng opened fire on *her*, too!"

"If he did, I'm sure it was only because she provoked it!" Rajampet said sharply.

"With all due respect, Rajani," Permanent Senior Undersecretary of Education and Information Malachai Abruzzi said tartly, "I wouldn't bet my life on that." Rajampet glared at him angrily, and Abruzzi shrugged. "As far as

I can tell from the Manties' first note, none of their ships did a damned thing to provoke him the *first* time he killed several hundred of their spacers. That being so, is there any reason we ought to assume he wouldn't just as cheerfully kill a few thousand more for no particular reason?"

"I'll remind you," Rajampet said even more sharply, "that none of us were there, and the only 'evidence' we have of what truly happened was delivered to us, oh so generously, by the *Manties*. I see no reason to believe they'd be above tampering with the sensor data they provided to us. In fact, one of my people over at Operational Analysis commented at the time that the data seemed suspiciously good and detailed."

Abruzzi only snorted, although Kolokoltsov suspected he was tempted to do something considerably more forceful. The vast majority of the Solarian League's member star systems looked after their own educational systems, which meant, despite its name, that Education and Information was primarily concerned with the *information* half of its theoretical responsibilities. Abruzzi's position thus made him, in effect, the Solarian League's chief propagandist. In that role, it had been his job to find a positive spin to put on Josef Byng's actions, and he'd been working on it ever since the Manties' first diplomatic note reached Old Chicago.

So far, he hadn't had a lot of success. Which wasn't too surprising, Kolokoltsov thought sourly. When a Solarian admiral commanding seventeen *battlecruisers* opened fire without warning on three *destroyers* who didn't even have their wedges and sidewalls up, it was going to be just a trifle difficult to convince even the Solarian public he'd been justified. Nor was there much chance that any reports or sensor data the Navy finally got around to providing were going to make things any better—not without an awful lot of "tweaking" first, at least! Rajampet could say whatever he liked about the data the Manties had provided, but Kolokoltsov agreed with Abruzzi's original analysis. The Manties would never have sent them falsified data. Not when they knew that eventually the League would be receiving accurate tactical data from its own people.

"All I'll say, Rajani," Abruzzi said after a moment, "is that I'm just glad the Manties haven't leaked this to the newsies . . . yet, at least. Because as hard as we've been trying, we haven't been able to find a way to make *them* look like the aggressors. And that means that when this *does* hit the 'faxes, we're going to find ourselves in a very difficult position. One where we'll probably have to *apologize* and actually offer to pay reparations."

"No, damn it!" Rajampet snapped, betrayed by anger into forgetting, at least briefly, his former wariness. "We can't establish that kind of precedent! If any pissant little neobarb navy decides the SLN can't tell *it* what to do, we're going to have a *hell* of a problem out in the Verge! And if Byng's been forced into another exchange of fire with them, we have to be even more careful about what sort of precedents we set!"

"I'm afraid you're entirely correct about *that* one, Rajani," Kolokoltsov said, and his frigid tone snapped everyone's eyes back to him. "And, unfortunately, I'm equally afraid Nathan's mistaken about the Manties' degree of discretion where the newsies are concerned."

"What the hell do you mean?" Rajampet demanded. "Go ahead—spit it out!"

"All right, Rajani. Approximately ninety minutes ago, we received a second note from the Manticorans. Under the circumstances, the fact that we decided to opt for a 'reasoned and deliberate' response to their original complaint—and refused to let anyone think we were allowing ourselves to be rushed by any Manticoran demands—may have been less optimal than we'd thought. I don't imagine getting our response to their *first* note a couple of days after they banged off their *second* note to us is going to amuse Queen Elizabeth and her prime minister very much.

"And the reason they've sent us this second note is that when Admiral Gold Peak arrived in New Tuscany she issued exactly the demands the Manties had warned us about in their first note. She demanded that Byng stand down his ships and permit Manticoran boarding parties to sequester and examine their sensor data relative to the destruction of three of her destroyers. She also informed him that the Star Empire of Manticore intended to insist upon an open examination of the facts and intended to hold the guilty parties responsible under the appropriate provisions of interstellar law for the unprovoked destruction of their ships and the deaths of their personnel. And"—Kolokoltsov allowed his eyes to flip sideways to Abruzzi for a moment—"it would appear it wasn't all part of some sort of propaganda maneuver on their part, after all."

"I don't—" Rajampet's wrinkled face was darken and his eyes glittered with fury. "I can't believe anyone— even *Manties!*—would be stupid enough to really issue *demands* to the Solarian Navy! They'd have to be out of—I mean, surely this Gold Peak couldn't possibly have thought she'd get *away* with that? If Byng blew her damned ships into orbital debris, the only person she's got to blame for it is—"

"Oh, he didn't blow up any of her ships, Rajani," Kolokoltsov said coldly. "Despite the fact that she had only six battlecruisers and he had seventeen, *she* blew *his* flagship into...what was it you called it? Ah, yes! Into *'orbital debris.'*"

Rajampet froze in mid-tirade, staring at Kolokoltsov in disbelief.

"Oh, my God," Omosupe Quartermain said quietly.

Of everyone present, she and Rajampet probably personally disliked Manticorans the most. In Rajampet's case, that was because the Royal Manticoran Navy declined to kowtow satisfactorily to the Solarian League Navy's supremacy. In Quartermain's case, it was because of how deeply she resented Manticore's wormhole junction and its merchant marine's dominance of the League's carrying trade. Which meant, among other things, that she had a very clear idea of how much damage the Star Empire of Manticore could do the League's economy if it decided to retaliate economically for Solarian aggression.

"How many ships did the Manties lose *this* time?" she continued in a resigned tone, clearly already beginning to reckon up the restitution the Star Empire might find itself in a position to extort out of the League.

"Oh, they didn't lose *any* ships," Kolokoltsov replied.

"What?!" Rajampet exploded. "That's goddammed *nonsense!* No Solarian flag officer's going to roll over and take something like that without—!"

"In that case, Rajani, I recommend you read Admiral Sigbee's report yourself. She found herself in command after Admiral Byng's...demise, and the Manties were kind enough to forward her dispatches to us along with their note. According to our own security people, they didn't even open the file and read it, first. Apparently they saw no reason to."

This time, Rajampet was clearly bereft of speech. He just sat there, staring at Kolokoltsov, and the diplomat shrugged.

"According to the synopsis of Admiral Sigbee's report, the Manties destroyed Admiral Byng's flagship, the *Jean Bart*, with a single missile salvo launched from far beyond our own ships' effective range. His flagship was *completely* destroyed, Rajani. There were no survivors at all. Under the circumstances, and since Admiral Gold Peak—who, I suppose I might also mention, turns out to be none other than Queen Elizabeth's first cousin and fifth in line for the Manticoran throne—had made it crystal clear that she'd destroy all of Byng's ships if her demands were not met, Admiral Sigbee—under protest, I need hardly add—complied with them."

"She—?" Rajampet couldn't get the complete sentence out, but Kolokoltsov nodded anyway.

"She *surrendered*, Rajani," he said in a marginally gentler voice, and the admiral closed his mouth with a snap.

He wasn't the only one staring at Kolokoltsov in horrified disbelief now. All the others seemed struck equally dumb, and Kolokoltsov took a certain satisfaction from seeing the reflection of his own stunned reaction in their expressions. Which, he admitted, was the *only* satisfaction he was likely to be feeling today.

On the face of it, the loss of a single ship and the surrender of twenty or so others, counting Byng's screening destroyers, could hardly be considered a catastrophe for the Solarian League Navy. The SLN was the biggest fleet in the galaxy. Counting active duty and reserve squadrons, it boasted almost eleven thousand superdreadnoughts, and that didn't even count the thousands upon thousands of battlecruisers, cruisers, and destroyers of Battle Fleet and Frontier Fleet . . . or the thousands of ships in the various system-defense forces maintained for local security by several of the League's wealthier member systems. Against that kind of firepower, against such a massive preponderance of tonnage, the destruction of a single battlecruiser and the two thousand or so people aboard it, was less than a flea bite. It was certainly a far, far smaller relative loss, in terms of both tonnage and personnel, than the Manticorans had suffered when Byng blew three of their newest destroyers out of space with absolutely no warning.

But it was the *first* Solarian warship destroyed by hostile action in centuries, and no Solarian League admiral *had* ever surrendered his command. Until now.

And that was what truly had the others worried, Kolokoltsov thought coldly. Just as it had *him* worried. The omnipotence of the Solarian League Navy was the fundamental bedrock upon which the entire League stood. The whole purpose of the League was to maintain interstellar order, protect and nurture the interactions, prosperity, and sovereignty of its member systems. There'd been times—more times than Kolokoltsov could count, really—when Rajampet and his predecessors had found themselves fighting tooth and nail for funding, given the fact that it was so obvious that no one conceivable hostile star nation, or combination of them, could truly threaten the League's security. Yet while they might have had to fight for the funding they *wanted*, they'd never come close to not getting the funding they actually *needed*. In fact, their fellow bureaucrats had never seriously considered cutting off or even drastically curtailing expenditures on the Navy.

Partly, that was because no matter how big Frontier Fleet was, it would never have enough ships to be everywhere it needed to be to carry out its mandate as the League's neighborhood cop and enforcer. Battle Fleet would have been a much more reasonable area for cost reductions, except that it had more prestige and was even more deeply entrenched in the League's bureaucratic structure than Frontier Fleet, not to mention having so many more allies in the industrial sector, given how lucrative superdreadnought building contracts were. But even the most fanatical expenditure-cutting reformer (assuming that any such mythical being existed anywhere in the Solarian League) would have found very few allies if he'd set his sights on the *Navy's* budget. Supporting the fleet was too important to the economy as a whole, and all the patronage that went with the disbursement of such enormous amounts was far too valuable to be surrendered. And, after all, making certain *everyone else* was as well aware as they were of the Navy's invincibility was an essential element of the clout wielded by the League in general and by the Office of Frontier Security, in particular.

But now that invincibility had been challenged. Worse, although Kolokoltsov was no expert on naval matters, even the synopsis of Sigbee's dispatches had made her shock at the effective range—and deadliness—of the Manticoran missiles abundantly clear even to him.

"She *surrendered*," Permanent Senior Undersecretary of the Interior Nathan MacArtney repeated very carefully after a moment, clearly making certain he hadn't misunderstood.

Kolokoltsov was actually surprised anyone had recovered that quickly, especially MacArtney. The Office of Frontier Security came under the control of the Department of the Interior, and after Rajampet himself, it was MacArtney whose responsibilities and . . . arrangements were most likely to suffer if the rest of the galaxy began to question just how invincible the Solarian Navy truly was.

"She did," Kolokoltsov confirmed. "And the Manties did board her ships, and they did take possession of their computers—their fully *operable* computers, with intact databases. At the time she was 'permitted' to include her dispatches along with Admiral Gold Peak's so we could receive her report as promptly as possible, she had no idea what ultimate disposition the Manties intend to make where her ships are concerned."

"My God," Quartermain said again, shaking her head.

"Sigbee didn't even dump her *data* cores?" MacArtney demanded incredulously.

"Given that Gold Peak had just finished blowing one of her ships into tiny pieces, I think the Admiral was justified in concluding the Manties might really go ahead and pull the trigger if they discovered she'd dumped her data cores," Kolokoltsov replied.

"But if they got all their data, including the secure sections . . . ."

MacArtney's voice trailed off, and Kolokoltsov smiled thinly.

"Than they've got an enormous amount of our secure technical data," he agreed. "Even worse, these were *Frontier Fleet* ships."

MacArtney looked physically ill. He was even better aware than Kolokoltsov of how the rest of the galaxy might react if some of the official, highly secret contingency plans stored in the computers of Frontier Fleet flagships were to be leaked.

There was another moment of sickly silence, then Wodoslawski cleared her throat.

"What did they say in their note, Innokentiy?" she asked.

"They say the data they've recovered from Byng's computers completely supports the data they already sent to us. They say they've recovered Sigbee's copy of Byng's order to open fire on the Manticoran destroyers. They've appended her copy of the message traffic between Gold Peak and Byng, as well, and pointed out that Gold Peak repeatedly warned Byng not only that she *would* fire if he failed to comply with her instructions but that she had the capability to destroy his ships from beyond his effective range. And, by the way, Sigbee's attested the accuracy of the copies from her communications section.

"In other words, they've told us their original interpretation of what happened to their destroyers has been confirmed, and that the admiral responsible for that incident has now been killed, along with the destruction of his flagship and its entire crew, because he rejected their demands. And they've pointed out, in case any of us might miss it, that Byng's original actions at New Tuscany constitute an act of war under interstellar law and that under that same interstellar law, Admiral Gold Peak was completely justified in the actions she took. Indeed," he showed his teeth in something no one would ever mistake for a smile, "they've pointed out how restrained Gold Peak was, under the circumstances, since Byng's entire task force was entirely at her mercy and she gave him at least three separate opportunities to comply with their demands without bloodshed."

"They've *declared war* on the Solarian League?" Abruzzi seemed unable to wrap his mind around the thought. Which was particularly ironic, Kolokoltsov thought, given his original breezy assurance that the Manticorans were only posturing, seeking an entirely cosmetic confrontation with the League in an effort to rally their battered domestic morale....

—end excerpt—

from *Mission of Honor*
available in hardcover,
July 2010, from Baen Books